DO THEY KNOW IT'S CHRISTMAS... YET?

By
James Crookes

For Nikki.

None of the following happened. Yet.

ONE

It probably was illegal, but so was letting your dog shag one of the Queen's corgis. Which wasn't part of the day's plan, merely a fact that Jamie had shared on the way there.

Of the five of them, George was unquestionably the worst candidate for the task – even including five-month-old Lucan, who slept throughout the whole thing. But then George was head of the household. And it was his idea.

Further along the socially distanced railway carriage, an irate lady beneath a reindeer face mask was gesturing towards the Summers family and muttering at the flustered train conductor.

"Jamie, you're blinking on every one," said George as he grimaced through reading glasses at the group selfies on his iPhone.

"Do we need his eyes? He's blinked in every photo since he was born," said Andrea, before turning to her son. "Close your mouth, Jamie."

"Can't," replied Jamie. "Dad said, 'open your eyes wide,' and this happens when I open my eyes wide."

"I didn't say 'open your eyes wide'. I said, 'don't blink'," replied his father.

"You look like someone's rammed a Twix up your arse," observed Tash, unhelpfully.

"We'll have no chocolate up arses on Christmas Eve, thank you very much, Tash," said Andrea, before adding, "Remember to breathe, Jamie."

Jamie exhaled loudly, visibly relieved.

"Can e'eryone shut the huck uck and snile klease?" instructed George through his toothsome smile, attempting another round of selfies. His family lowered their face masks and smiled.

"Excuse me, those seats are reserved," the conductor shouted.

"Yes, that's right," replied George, still taking photos.

"Can I see your ticket, please?"

"Extremely busy here," said George, his thumb clicking the whole time.

"Typical, I'm going to lose my virginity in a prison shower," said Jamie, squirming at the prospect of being arrested for failing to display a valid ticket. "To a man," he added needlessly.

"Those seats are reserved," repeated the conductor.

George glanced up at the digital displays above the seats. 'Reserved: London, St Pancras International to Derby'.

"Yes, yes. It says it, look," he acknowledged dismissively. He replaced his mask and started squinting through the latest selfies. "That one might do, I suppose," he conceded.

The others repositioned their masks, and Andrea started to gather their belongings. "You heard the lady, family. We're not welcome. Christmas is cancelled. Off we get."

George joined in with his wife. "Yes, we'll have to spend it in London. Great Grandma will understand. She's been isolating since March, but she'll have to get used to Christmas alone sooner or later."

The family squeezed into the aisle.

"If you show me your tickets, I can direct you to your seats?" said the hapless conductor.

"No, it's fine. Great Grandma can meet the baby another time," replied George. "If she lives that long."

"But the train's about to set off," said the conductor.

"Don't you worry about us," piped up Andrea as they approached the end of the carriage. "We got off the London Eye at the top."

With that, the automatic doors to the entry and exit vestibule slid closed, and the family were gone. Immediately the doors opened again, and Tash marched back down the carriage.

"Baby," she muttered by way of explanation for her sudden reappearance.

"It's every time, George," said Andrea as she watched her daughter pick up the baby carrier from the table. Tash couldn't help but notice the conductor and other passengers staring in disbelief.

"There was a lot to think about. Don't blink. Lean in. Smile."

They watched in silence as she walked back to the sliding doors.

"Tash loses points for abandoning Lucan again," said George.

"Can we stop calling him that!" Tash was getting flustered.

The train started to move slowly.

"Quick, quick, quick!" said Jamie. "The doors lock at five miles an hour."

"Wow! That's incredible," replied Tash. "I thought I'd heard all your dull facts."

Jamie successfully opened the carriage door to the platform, and they all stumbled off the train.

A brass band playing 'Last Christmas' reverberated around the iconic atrium of St Pancras International, sadly from a digital playlist connected to a Covid-secure PA system.

"To the car, before we get a parking ticket," said George marching ahead like an enthusiastic scout leader dragging his exhausted pack through a stagnant bog. He confused the barrier guard by flashing a fistful of used train tickets, and the disabled gate was held open for the family to reach the escalators without breaking their stride.

"This is my least favourite family tradition," muttered Andrea, struggling to keep up.

"Really?" replied Tash. "You have just one? I have a list."

TWO

"Sake! Fuck snow, and fuck Christmas!" Tash was being loud again.

"Tash! Not in front of Lucan!" Jamie covered the ears of his baby nephew, who was swinging gently on his chest in time with his awkward trudging through the ebbs and flows of drifting snow.

His sister inched on ahead, clumps of ice and snow filling the inside of her boots. Each step was a mammoth effort. "They remember nothing before they're five. And don't call him that."

"Grandma's gonna want to know his name," muttered Jamie.

"I'm not scared of Grandma," snorted Tash. "Don't tell her I said that."

They walked a few more steps before Tash broke the silence, a little too assertively.

"I'll know his name when I know his name."

"You are scared of Grandma," said Jamie. "We're all scared of Grandma."

"Well, of course. We're all trudging two miles through a blizzard with a five-month-old baby 'cos we're scared of Grandma." She fell over again, and this time she was in no hurry to get up. "Fuck snow! Fuck Christmas! And fuck Grandma!"

"Tash!" Jamie covered Lucan's ears.

Tash lay still for a moment and then reached out her arms, expecting her brother to pull her to her feet. But Jamie was lost in thought.

"You're just in a bad mood 'cos it's nearly the end of another year," he explained kindly before continuing.

"And all you did was miss out on a big promotion at work and became a single mum… And let's face it, your next milestone birthday has a four in front of it."

"Thanks for the year in review, Jamie. None of that had occurred to me," replied Tash.

Jamie's plain-spoken approach to life never suppressed his sister's sarcasm. Some had called his Asperger's an affliction, his family called it a blessing. Jamie's humour, honesty and positivity were an enviable personality cocktail.

"Oh yeah," continued Jamie, buoyed up by Tash's response. "Moving back in with your mum and dad is a real backwards step."

"And never moving out in the first place is….?"

"Inspired. I kept the biggest room." Jamie meant every word. "Although now might be a good time to tell you that we're sharing at Grandma's."

"Sharing bedrooms?" Tash was struggling to get back to her feet. She brushed a bead of snot from the tip of her nose for the millionth time. Jamie nodded.

"What? She said she was clearing Grandad's study for you! She literally texted me this morning. 'I am clearing Grandad's study later for Jamie'. Those were her words…"

"I don't like the plan either, Tash. What if I'd wanted to bring a girl back?"

Tash laughed. Then saw his face. "Oh, I'm sorry, you meant it?"

"Well, you never know. It could happen."

"Your time will come. Relationships are over-rated anyway. I'd love to be single."

"You are single."

"I mean legally single. I have to pay lots of money to be single again. Whereas you, you get to be single for free. Who's the winner here?"

Jamie was the perfect gentleman, he just wasn't great at first impressions and so could count his romantic relationships on no hands. But that didn't mean he hadn't been in love; it was just the unrequited type. He took some getting used to. Like couscous. Or a colonoscopy.

"Your time will come, Jamie. Remember what Grandma always says..." said Tash.

Jamie nodded for a while, then asked, "What does Grandma always say?"

"I can't remember actually I was hoping you might. Something about gloves or mittens."

"There's a hand for every glove!"

"Yes! That's it!"

They both walked in silence, delighted to have remembered.

"It's not actually that clever, is it? Cos there probably isn't, if we're honest," said Jamie.

"She does talk a lot of shit, I'll give you that."

Jamie giggled, then remembered, "She's had another fall."

Tash turned to face him. "Another one? When? Is she OK?"

"She's fine. She slipped, putting Grandad's bauble on the tree this lunchtime. She messaged Dad. He didn't want to worry you. Or Mum."

There are some Christmas traditions that everybody hates. Well, almost everybody. And that's the problem. It's fair to say that at least one person still receives joy from the same festive routine, year on year on year. And because Christmas is about love, most people continue to go through the motions – however tedious – for the benefit of the minority. In this instance, the minority was just one person: Grandma.

And Grandma scared the shit out of them all.

So it came to pass that for over twenty years George and Andrea Summers had left the family car outside their London home and travelled 131 miles north to the city of Sheffield by train. Then they walked the remaining two miles to George's childhood home to spend Christmas with his widowed mother. Dot was happy with this arrangement, after all, it was her suggestion, and it was deeply rooted in superstition and grief. Her husband had died on Christmas Eve after a tragic car crash just yards from their front door. Dot's subsequent Christmas ban on travel in any kind of motor vehicle had been respected by her son, his wife and their children, Jamie and Tash. Essentially this had been a family of four embarking on a near 300-mile round trip every December 24th without using roads.

Or at least that's what they told Grandma.

In truth, every year they would drive up the M1, exiting at Chesterfield to drive past the famous crooked spire of St Mary's Church, and on through the A61 to the southern side of Sheffield. Here they would park on the same side-street, roughly a hundred yards out of sight of Grandma's house. They would wearily walk the final steps on foot, turning into view of her lounge bay window laden with suitcases and bags of festive gifts, content that their exhausted acting would arise no suspicion in the 81-year-old matriarch of the family.

But now there were five of them. A son had been born to Tash in the middle of the hottest July in living history. Five months on, this beautiful baby boy remained un-named. Tash's lifelong indecisiveness and procrastination had really come to the fore on this matter – possibly fuelled by the ribbing and coaxing from her parents and brother. She would not be rushed. Not with this. Her indecisiveness was only bettered by her absentmindedness. In those five months she'd accidentally left her son on a bus. And also a tube train.

And a supermarket.

And a GP surgery.

And a park.

And a cafe.

Her father George had arrived at the conclusion that his grandson was choosing these moments for a bit of time to himself, so nicknamed him Lucan after the infamous British peer who disappeared into the ether never to be seen again. The comparisons ended there, with no insinuations that the baby was guilty of murder, unlike his namesake. Understandably Tash hated the name, so naturally it stuck.

This morning had started pretty much the same as most previous Christmas Eves. After their St Pancras train selfie to send to Grandma, a delayed tube back home to load the car, and an interminable queue onto the North Circular Road, they were perfectly timed to hit the back end of roadworks on the M1 northbound around about 2pm. Just three hours later than planned. By 3pm, the roadworks were well behind them. Unlike the snow, which was very much in front of them. Visibility was poor, and traffic was crawling. So it was no surprise that George had decreed that Michael Bublé could stick his jolly fucking holly up his jolly fucking arse before they'd reached Watford Gap services. To emphasise the point, he'd also tossed Bublé's CD out of his window, something he instantly regretted after being reminded it was a gift from Tash two Christmases before. An apology fell on deafened ears. Lucan had seen to that, he was in full festive voice because of his full festive nappy.

This was the first December since his father's death that George finally conceded defeat by snow. The family car had crawled, slipped and slid sideways across the surprisingly quiet streets of Sheffield at a slowing pace until eventually one of the city's seven hills claimed victory over his silver Skoda estate. The family abandoned the vehicle just under one mile from Dot's home. Luckily they were suitably dressed for the inclement weather, as their pretence of a train journey and two-mile hike meant they were suited and booted in Aldi's most elegant ski attire from their seasonal middle aisle. Andrea had also purchased two pairs of Aldi ski goggles in case anyone ever wanted to go on a skiing holiday because the price was so very reasonable. And two Bluetooth enabled ski helmets because you never know, do you? She'd only gone in for gin and an inflatable lap tray.

Andrea was a very fit and active 59 years of age. She enjoyed the few perks of being senior receptionist at a GP practice. The biggest was easily gaining access to doctor and nurse appointments before the general public, especially during the Covid pandemic, and her hypochondria meant these were always with unfounded cause. But this year she had been mortified to learn that she was 'a typical weight' for a lady in her age group. Typical weight. How embarrassing. As someone who had been proudly (and effortlessly) 'slightly underweight' her whole life, Andrea immediately became a slave to a newly acquired Fitbit. This small wristwatch would bleep when she became too sedentary and suggest she move about, and it had been most unhappy during her motionless hours on the M1 today. So abandoning the Skoda in a snowstorm was the perfect opportunity to 'get her steps up'. Andrea had yomped assertively ahead, insisting George keep up as she didn't want to face his bloody mother alone. Jamie and Tash watched as their parents disappeared ahead into the blizzard. Tash had tenderly slid her son into a papoose inside Jamie's coat, pulled a waterproof hat gently over the baby's hood, and then methodically loaded her brother and herself with backpacks and gift bags. Ten minutes later, their legs were heavy, the snow was twelve inches deep, and the drifts that smothered the pavements and abandoned cars made the mission ahead seem monstrous. Tash had lost count of the number of times she'd fallen over.

But suddenly Jamie's spirits were lifted by a magical Christmas apparition. "Look!" Jamie euphorically pointed up the road to an impressive oak tree that sprouted from the blanket of white on the ground. "Grandad's tree!"

A solitary Christmas bauble twinkled under the harsh light of the hideous bright white LED street lamps that had recently invaded the city. Beneath the weathered bauble, a wet and tired yellow ribbon hung limply tied around the trunk of the tree. This tree was visible from Grandma's living room, so their finishing line was beckoning.

Tash paused briefly to squint through the confetti snow before a multi-coloured LED Rudolph stole her attention. Attached to a stone-fronted house, it was competing with an out of scale blue and white Santa fixed to the neighbour's porch. It won the contest by suddenly starting to flicker quite madly before fizzing to black. Tash set off with renewed vigour. Then she fell over again.

****

Despite her harsh words to Jamie just ten minutes before, Tash was strangely affected by seeing her Grandma open the door to the three of them. A homemade brace adorned Dot's neck, and her left hand was heavily strapped with a bandage. Suddenly she appeared vulnerable and frail, and Tash felt a twinge in her chest. It didn't last long – in fact, only about as long as it took for Grandma to speak.

"That colour does nothing for you, Natasha."

"Happy Christmas, Grandma," replied Tash, choosing to ignore the fashion tip. "What's happened here, then?" Tash pointed at Dot's many bandages.

Ignoring her, Dot pushed her granddaughter to the side with her good hand and squinted at the precious parcel strapped to her grandson's chest.

"Oh, look at him… Look at him! Bring him in from the cold so I can see him."

Jamie was hauled past his sister into the brightly lit hallway so that Dot could get a good look at her great-grandson. The smell of boiled cabbage filled his nose, with delicate notes of bleach, burning logs and more than a hint of Yves Saint Laurent *Opium* perfume. Probably a quarter of a bottle. Yes, Jamie was in nostalgic territory now.

Tash struggled in with her bags, Jamie's bags and then the family gifts. She let out a long sigh after dropping the final parcels onto the doormat.

"Not there, Natasha, how are we going to close the door?" said Dot. "Shut the door, Jamie, there's a good boy. Keep the heat in. Mind your fingers."

Dot lifted the sleeping baby from Jamie's chest and held him towards the big light. She did nothing to hide her disappointment. "Oh. He's no looker, is he? Maybe he'll have a hidden talent."

"Well, we can always hope, can't we?" replied Tash, as she struggled to remove her many layers of scarves and coats.

Dot glanced at her granddaughter. "You're getting fat." She meant no malice. She simply spoke plainly, with no internal filter. "There's no such thing as baby weight, you know. Just laziness."

"Good to know," said Tash with a patient smile.

"Go on through to the living room."

Jamie peered his head around the door and then back to his Grandma. "Where are Mum and Dad?"

"They're getting out of their wet things. I've left them my bathwater. You can have it once they're done."

"That's alright, Grandma, I bathed on my birthday." Tash smiled at her Grandma, then added, "Which is in October, by the way. It's every October."

She followed Jamie into the warm living room.

It was a beautiful Victorian property. Grandad Ernest had provided well for the family, and they'd wanted for nothing – within reason. He had been, like so many other men in the city in those days, a steelworker, but his career had taken an unexpected turn. Constantly inventing solutions for practical problems at home, he'd started to do the same at work and taken upon himself to design an industrial-scale nozzle that revolutionised the manufacturing process of alloy steels. It effectively created capacity for doubling output. It was a stroke of genius, and Ernest knew it. A humble and modest man he surprised his employer by presenting his revolutionary plans along with a letter from the Patent Office, clearly stating he was the inventor. Knowing this technology would change processes on a global scale, his bosses were happy to negotiate a mutually beneficial financial arrangement. In truth, they shafted him. Ernest handed over his idea in exchange for £10,000 plus instant progression to the highest pay scale on the shop floor, and a full final salary pension. Happily, he never learned that he'd cost himself somewhere in the region of a million pounds over the rest of his career. Still, his decision had meant his bank balance was always in the black, he could afford a secondhand car every three or four years, and he could take his family on holiday every summer. Ernest was a hero in the factory. He was David, and he'd taken on Goliath.

Sadly this biblical status soon faded amongst his workmates as envy took over. Eventually, he retired early with work-related stress. It was one thing to champion a brother who beat the capitalist bully boss, it was another to tolerate his sartorial supremacy at the social club, let alone his nearly-new Austin Maestro.

He made the best of a bad situation by becoming a full-time inventor. Happily, his pension continued to put food on the table and petrol in the car, as he soon learned an inventor's income can be unpredictably sporadic. For every cheese slicer design he sold to Tupperware, he'd abandon a dozen other prototypes from corner microwaves to battery-warmed wellies.

Jamie was immediately unsettled by the living room. "Where's the Christmas tree, Grandma?" He spun around to make sure he hadn't missed it in one of the many alcoves or cupboard tops.

"I couldn't face it this year love, not after my fall," Grandma gestured her neck and arm. "Have a Quality Street. I've picked out the shit blue ones and given them to the kids next door."

"You were on the mend! What happened today?" asked Tash.

"Don't fret. I slipped coming back from Grandad's tree."

"Oh no! What did the doctor say?" asked Jamie.

Grandma was dismissive. "I don't need to call the doctor. These bandages are doing the trick."

Tash looked concerned and reached out to straighten her Grandma's blouse collar but was brushed aside.

"Don't put your cold hands on me, Natasha. You'll send me to an early grave. Have you washed them, yet? I haven't come this far to get that bloody virus from a super–spreader like you."

Tash didn't take the bait. They all sat down in silence, firmly put in their place. Then Jamie spoke through a hazelnut in caramel.

"Great news about Grandad's tree, Grandma!"

"They've picked on the wrong person with me," said Grandma. "Cutting down trees, my eye. Build some bloody classrooms or re-open the Hallamshire Casualty, that's a council's job! Not making squirrels homeless."

Jamie and Tash smiled kindly.

"They sent me to prison, you know."

Tash cast Jamie a concerned glance, then gently spoke. "That was Virginia, Grandma. It was Virginia that got arrested."

Dot was busily sorting through her newspaper rack by the green draylon settee. She handed Jamie a copy of *The Sheffield Star* newspaper that she'd saved from her infamous victory over the summer. The year before Sheffield City Council had authorised a purge by felling hundreds of the city's most magnificent trees from the cracking pavements. They explained the cull was necessary because of the ailing condition of the majority of them. They were a danger to pedestrians and motorists. Experts and locals begged to differ and soon started holding 24-hour vigils around the trees identified for removal. Large yellow ribbons adorned those on death row. The national press picked up the story when one of Dot's friends (Virginia) was arrested by police on public nuisance offences. She'd simply used a bicycle lock to attach herself to a silver birch at the foot of her path. The whole cull was all a very sorry state of affairs. It caused immense stress for Dot, as one of the trees identified for removal was where she'd said her final goodbye to her husband.

Christmas Eve, 1999, on a mission for Oxo, Ernest had driven cautiously out of their cul-de-sac onto the side road. He was immediately struck by a stolen vehicle speeding in the opposite direction. It was a crime that shook the neighbourhood. Dot had heard the collision and hurried out to find Ernest climbing out of their crumpled car. The other vehicle was nowhere to be seen. She'd helped him to the roadside where he sat on the frozen ground and leant against a tree while she attempted to stem the flow of blood from a single cut above his eye. She knew something was wrong when her husband, a man of few words, started to proclaim his eternal love for her. He'd told her that her skin was as beautiful as the day they were married 41 years before. He'd told her that her eyes were the same perfect green as their granddaughter, Natasha. He'd told her they might have to make do without gravy for their Christmas dinner tomorrow. In between deepening breaths, he'd told her that he wasn't feeling right. Not right at all. Seconds later, he closed his eyes for the last time. The adrenaline from the shock of the collision had caused a massive cardiac arrest. He died in his wife's arms.

Every Christmas since his death, Dot had hung a golden bauble from the lowest branch of the oak tree where she'd spoken to her husband for the final time. And she was first to tie a yellow ribbon around its trunk when she learned in horror that it was threatened with destruction. So it was with immense relief that she finally hung a 'Tree Saved' sign around its middle when the council backed down in the face of ongoing national uproar about the needless annihilation of oaks, sycamores and birch trees. And now an independent report had vindicated her pressure group's claims.

"So what are we calling this little funny-face then, Natasha?" Dot asked, smiling as she gazed into the baby's eyes.

"Well, not that to start with," said Tash.

"Still no sign of the father?" Dot was licking a handkerchief and wiping Lucan's chin.

"It's not like that Grandma, you know it's not like that," replied a weary Tash, brushing the handkerchief away. "Nathan and me decided it was for the best."

"I'm with you. He made a mutual decision, did he?"

"Where is the Christmas tree, Grandma? I can put it up," said Jamie, keen to change the subject. "It's not Christmas without a tree. What about him – he needs a tree!" He gestured at his nephew. "His first Christmas!"

"Yeah, he's right Grandma. Let's brighten things up a bit, shall we?" said Tash, standing up, happy to do anything to avoid further interrogation.

"Oh come on, I don't want all that mess now. You've only just arrived."

Dot looked at her grandchildren and a wave of emotion swept over her. Their faces had changed so little since that first Christmas without their Grandad. Some laughter lines had appeared, some facial hair too – mostly Jamie's, and all the last traces of freckles had gone, but these were still the same kind, beautiful children who had written a last-minute letter to Father Christmas asking him to bring back Grandad, whilst Grandma stoically held back tears on that horrific day. Despite her loss, Dot had been the driving force behind a Christmas-As-Usual just two hours after her life fell brutally apart.

"The tree and decorations are in the garage loft." Dot allowed herself a smile.

Jamie and Tash both whooped like children and Jamie leapt up from the settee.

"But don't touch anything, don't break anything, don't leave the light on and don't fall down the steps … cos you're a clumsy little sod, Jamie. I've always said that," added Dot.

"Merry Christmas to you too, Grandma," said Jamie. Then under his breath for his sister's amusement, "Let's hope you don't die peacefully in my sleep tonight."

As they walked from the room, Tash corrected him. "People die peacefully in *their* sleep, Jamie. That's the expression."

"I know that's what people say. But face facts, it's only the one left behind who slept peacefully. The person dying is silently wailing and choking and flapping around trying to wake the other one up."

"You make a good point."

THREE

Jamie forced his whole body weight against the heavy wooden garage door, and after what seemed like an ice age, it slowly slid along its ancient rusty steel tracks. With just enough space to slide through, Jamie squeezed himself out of the snowstorm and into the garage. He flicked the Bakelite switch on the wall to reveal a forgotten pile of boxes and old garden tools that had taken the place of Grandad's car. The smell was a comforting blend of dried out ageing timber and damp brickwork. To one side, an open-backed staircase rose to a 3/4 height painted door. Jamie carefully climbed the creaky steps and tried the worn brass doorknob. The shabby yellowing glossed door opened, and he ducked as he walked through into a wonderland of shelves, cupboards, boxes and work-surfaces. The area was smaller than he remembered, and he soon found the old pine cupboard that Grandma had described and pulled the dusty doors open. Inside, the sight of the boxed tinsel Christmas tree made his heart skip with nostalgia. He tenderly removed a Woolworths 4ft Winter Wonderland Pine from its home and paused to marvel at the price sticker – still in place. £2 1s 4d. Clearly a typo, he thought. S? D? WTAF?

Removing the box from the cupboard had revealed a web of carefully stored fairy lights. A rainbow of colours was just the flick of a switch away. Jamie could feel his pulse giddily thump as he carefully lifted the collection of miniature Victorian lanterns and Cinderella carriages bound together by twisted green cable. Finally, he turned his attention to a large cardboard box with a white sticker covering its original contents of Golden Wonder Cheese & Onion Crisps. There, in Grandad's unmistakable draughtsman's handwriting were the words *Christmas Tree Decorations and Tinsel.* Jamie carefully dragged the tree, the lights and the box back towards the stairhead. He stopped as he passed an impressive selection of multi-socket extension cables hanging on another door that provided access to the remainder of the attic. Knowing that Grandma's house averaged one plug socket per room, Jamie decided to bring one of these too. Frustratingly, as he unhooked one, it unravelled until he held the plug in his hand and the straightened cable stretched taut against the door. A simple tug wouldn't free it. On inspection, Jamie observed that the other end of this long cable – the part with the actual extension sockets attached – was on the other side of the locked door. The cable disappeared into a drilled hole in the wood. He gave up and coiled it loosely back onto its hook. He tried the next one, which came loose freely but revealed another of Grandad's immaculately written notices, stuck with yellowing sellotape to the door.

"Keep Out."

Jamie should probably have done just as Grandad had requested.

But he didn't.

The key turned first time.

****

Three generations of the Summers family sat around a festive looking table in Dot's large dining kitchen. An Aga kept them all toasty, and some vintage nativity decorations adorned the table. Most of them the work of a childhood Jamie. Tash's efforts had somehow got lost along the way.

Tash had once – rather charitably – described Grandma's Christmas Eve dinners as a party on the tongue. She never expanded on that, but her brother and parents knew she meant the kind of party where someone trudges dog shit into the house and then pukes on your curtains having necked all your Baileys. The menu was the same each year: a selection of every single frozen meat available at Sainsbury's ("All your meats," as Grandma called them) garnished with buttered slices of bread, cucumber slices, quiche slices and a jar of pickled onions. Last year Dot had experimented with an Iceland dish she introduced as "A bird what's up a bird, what's up another bird," but she had reverted to form this December, as the three bird roast had provided insufficient variety for her.

As Freddie Mercury was 'thanking God it's Christmas' on Dot's Echo Dot speaker (an early Christmas present from her son), her family were growing increasingly anxious about her mental wellbeing. Tash had recited the earlier Virginia anecdote to her worried parents, and they'd conceded it wasn't the first time Grandma had become befuddled. Andrea had read a plethora of different blood test results over the phone to most of Finchley's inhabitants over the years, so her medical know-how was nearing doctor-calibre. Subsequently she was leaning towards some kind of short-term amnesia from Dot's first fall, probably made worse by banging her head earlier in the day when she hung her memorial bauble on the big oak tree. Dot's accomplishment this morning was actually quite impressive. The lowest branch was at least a metre over her head, yet she'd successfully hooked the golden decoration in place using a small stool and an extendable clothes prop. It was during her dismount from the stool that she'd slipped and fallen face-first onto the gritted pavement.

Watching his mother chase a chicken drumstick from one side of her plate to the other, George couldn't help but feel sad suddenly. His mum was a shadow of her usual self. Her lip was grazed, her eyes look sunken, and her homemade neck brace held her tiny face in an unnatural position. Her bandaged hand rested next to her half-filled glass of Harveys Bristol Cream – her only seasonal weakness. She was onto her second glass, and this had reassured George in a small way as it indicated that finally she was relaxing. He knew that was because she was surrounded by family. Shakin' Stevens started to sing.

"Ah, Shaky! I always loved a bit of Shaky," said Dot, smiling. She then shouted loudly – as she had just been taught by her son. "JAMIE. TURN UP SHAKY!"

"No. It's Alexa. You ask Alexa, Mum. You need to say 'Alexa'," said George.

"We can't keep asking her," replied Dot. "She must be busy. Let someone else use her. Jamie's closest."

Her rationale made the family smile, and Jamie dutifully leant over and tapped the volume button so that no-one could be mistaken that snow was definitely falling, all around us. And children were certainly playing, having fun.

"Let's all raise a glass to Dad, and Grandad," said George, raising his in the air.

"You don't celebrate death days," replied Dot.

"Well, no, I wasn't celebrating…"

"What about Hitler?" asked Jamie. "I'd celebrate his."

"Can't argue with that," agreed Tash.

"This meal's lovely, Dorothy. You've gone to such trouble, thank you," said Andrea dutifully as she poured herself a top-up of the rioja they'd brought with them.

Dot smiled. "Thank you for bringing the wine, Andrea. Although I didn't think you'd be drinking it all in one go."

Andrea placed the bottle back on the table.

"You made a good job of the tree, Jamie," said George. "It looks very festive!"

"It's like an actual Christmas fairy got involved…" started Tash.

"Ahh, I love it when you're nice to one another." Andrea looked close to tears.

"…by eating a tinsel burrito and then puking on it."

"I like it. Very festive. Ten out of ten." George liked to rate things numerically.

"Oh, my God!" said Jamie, suddenly struck by a thought. "Guess what I found in the …" Jamie was interrupted by his Grandma.

"Don't say God, Jamie – it's sacrilegious!"

"Sorry. Guess what I found in the garage loft, though?"

"Grandad?" asked Tash. Her joke was met with much tutting and disapproval from the family.

"Oh my God – I'm only kidding!"

"Don't you start using His name either, Natasha! And on Christmas Eve of all days. How offensive to baby Jesus," said Dot. "I want no more Gods or Jesuses or Christs tonight, thank you very much…Fucksake."

This was unusual language for Dot, and the family's shared looks of surprise were missed by her. Knives continued cutting, Shaky continued exchanging kisses, and belts continued stretching before Jamie tried again.

"Seriously though. Guess what I found in the garage loft?"

Andrea was eyeing the rioja again, George was struggling with the lid on the gherkin jar, and Grandma was just plain uninterested.

"I hope you turned the light off," she mumbled as she inadvertently flicked a pickled onion clean off her plate with her blunt knife. She followed it underneath the table.

"Leave that, Mum," said George, lifting the festive table cloth. His mother ignored him.

"Grandad's Christmas sleigh!" Jamie wasn't giving up.

Tash looked delighted. "No way? His actual one?"

"He'd added some stuff to it, but it's all there. The walls, the lights. Everything!"

"Mum," protested George again.

"Added stuff to it? What do you mean?" Tash asked her brother.

"My old computer and stuff. Wires. Looks wicked!"

"He used to spend ages up in that loft," came Dot's voice from under the table.

Andrea seized the moment to top up her glass.

"Called it his time machine," muttered Dot as she appeared back from under the table, pickled onion in her good hand.

"Ah! I wonder why he called it that?" said Tash with a glow of nostalgia. "Bless him."

"Because he spent so much time up there?" said Dot with the sort of patience you might give to an irritating child when it hasn't quite grasped the bleeding obvious. "Although he wouldn't these days. Not with all that porn on the internet."

Dot blew some fluff from the pickled onion and placed it on her son's plate.

"Be more careful next time, Georgie."

George caught Andrea's eye again. Tash spotted this, then she did the same with Jamie. George spoke gently.

"Why don't you turn in, Mum? It's been a long one. Get some rest for the big day?"

"I can't go to bed yet. I've got to put the tray out for your Dad's cocktails," said Dot pointing at a red bow tie on the kitchen side. "I've got his tie out, too."

It was then that the rest of the room realised Dot was unwell. Her husband's great festive tradition had been Christmas morning cocktails, served in his trusty red dicky bow. He'd invented an ingenious contraption to squeeze a whole netted bag of satsumas and crush ice at the same time. If that wasn't enough, he'd added a tap at the bottom to decant the chilled mix into their most elegant glasses. The adults' drinks were topped up with champagne as he called it (it was cava) and the kids with homemade lemonade. This tradition had sadly died with Ernest. It wasn't out of respect as far as George was concerned, simply that he couldn't work his father's machine. He'd tried and tried the day after his father passed, but the result only contributed to the sadness of the last twenty-four hours. On the first anniversary of his father's death, Christmas morning was toasted with hot chocolate and marshmallows. A tradition that stuck until this year, when his mother had just announced that her dead husband was back in charge of tomorrow morning's drinks.

George let his Mum's remark hang in the air for a moment, and when she didn't spot her faux pas, he kindly reassured her that he would sort out the tray for Dad. She should get some rest.

And it's a good thing she did because what her family embarked on next would have infuriated her.

FOUR

"It's just a bit of concussion, George. Please try not to worry," said Andrea reassuringly as she stood by the hearth and examined the underside of an ornamental china rabbit.

Andrea had seen instances like these in her patients over the years, and they soon passed with no cause for concern. George nodded thoughtfully as he placed another log into the wood burner. He closed the door and moved out of his wife's way.

"There are handwritten labels under all her Crown Derby. Look." Andrea squinted to read the underside of a hand-painted koala bear and then held it towards her husband. "D.S. Look! She's leaving this to your brother."

"What? That won't mean David," protested George feebly. "It's probably something from the factory."

In defiance, Andrea picked up a similarly painted robin, examined the underside and held it up before announcing, "G.S. That's you. She is quite literally flipping you the bird. This is worth half of that koala."

"Why's she done that?" asked Jamie.

"Old people do strange things, look at Noel Edmond's beard," replied Andrea as she lifted up a Waterford crystal vase. "She's allocated all her belongings to the family with little stickers. Cheaper than a will," she read from the underside. "Another D.S."

Jamie lifted up the blue glass bowl on the table next to him and squinted at the underside.

"Probably better to empty that first, Jamie," said his mum, pointing at the collection of mixed nuts that now covered his Christmas slippers.

"D.S." read Jamie.

"What?" George was shocked.

His mum joined in. "We bought her that from Italy!"

Jamie stared into the technicolour glow of the Pifco fairy lights that hung on the Woolworths Christmas tree. Tash tiptoed into the room, examining her iPhone. An app showed a sleeping Lucan and the muffled sound of a clock ticking alongside him.

"You were a while. He's not got too cold on the way up, has he?" asked Andrea, as she casually swapped some stickers over, improving her husband's inheritance in a moment.

"Or maybe you misplaced him again?" said George, smiling to himself. "Can you think when you last had him?"

"Very funny" replied Tash. "You should think of another joke, then you'd have almost two."

"He perhaps felt a bit strange in a different room. Is it warm enough in there?" asked Andrea.

"He's fine. He's sleeping. I've just been sorting the formula for his night feed in the kitchen."

"I wish it was a time machine," said Jamie, still gazing into the tree.

"Well, this is it," said Andrea, not listening. "Have you picked those nuts up?"

George flicked through the *Christmas Radio Times* TV pages. “Same old rubbish, year after year.”

“People like tradition at Christmas, Dad. Look at Uncle David. Christmas Eve – church. Christmas Day – church,” Tash observed.

“He's a vicar, Tash.”

“Yeah, but he could change it up a bit.”

“He's a vicar, Tash.”

“No. But I'm just saying. Every Christmas the same!”

”He's a vicar, Tash.”

Jamie walked over to the tree, straightened a satin bauble, and took a step back to admire his handiwork. The tree looked as authentic as you could wish for with 1960s aluminium foliage and sixty years of accumulated baubles.

“Imagine it. An actual time machine.” He was hypnotised by the twinkling fuchsia, teal and amber lights.

“What do you mean, love?” muttered Andrea, now trying to avoid burning her hand on a light bulb as she examined the inside of an opulent lamp shade.

“Grandad's Christmas ride in the garage. She said it was a time machine.”

“She was confused,” said George. He felt incredibly protective of his mother and her sudden quirky behaviour.

“Who's A.J.S.?” asked Andrea, now fiddling with something on the side table.

“That would be you,” answered Tash.

“Ooh! She's leaving me this!” Andrea held up a huge black remote control and started clicking it around the room. “What's it for. What would I want this for?”

"You two loved that Christmas ride as kids," said George. "You used to sit in it together and visit the North Pole."

Jamie sat back on the settee. "Imagine if it was an actual real time machine."

"Oh, like one of the real ones?" said Tash, pouring a glass of wine for herself. She plonked down next to her brother.

"I'd go back to this morning, and I'd call Grandma and tell her not to go out in the snow. I'd say to wait for us to arrive so I could put Grandad's bauble on the tree," said Jamie. Everyone looked at him. "If it was a time machine."

"Lame," replied Tash.

"Why lame?"

"You have the whole of all time ever, and you want to go back twelve hours?"

"I could have stopped Grandma falling over," replied Jamie. It was a simple decision as far as he was concerned.

"Twelve hours, Jamie! What about all the amazing moments in history? Live Aid? The birth of Jesus?"

"Wow. Two really similar things right there, Tash," said Jamie.

"That's going to bother me that is," muttered Andrea as she sat down, defeated by the remote control.

"It wasn't all that, anyway," said George.

"The birth of Jesus?" asked Tash. "Our Lord and Saviour?"

"Live Aid. Everyone forgets that Status Quo opened the show. It wasn't all Freddie Mercury and David Bowie. It went on for bloody hours. It was only on BBC2," explained George, as if the channel was conclusive proof of his argument.

"What's that got to do with anything?" said Tash.

"I'm saying – at the time, it wasn't all that. They still put Grandstand on BBC1. Business as usual. It's just the passage of time that makes it seem such a big deal," said George as best he could through a mouthful of pretzels.

"The millions of lives it saved were a bit of a big deal though, Dad. No?" said Jamie.

"What are we talking about?" asked Andrea as she found her glass of sauvignon blanc. She'd ditched the rioja in favour of a clearer head in the morning,

"Time machines," answered her daughter. "Jamie could have gone anywhere in the whole of time ever – and he chose 9 o'clock this morning."

"Really? Isn't that when Piers Morgan's on?" replied Andrea.

"Where would you go then?" Jamie challenged Tash, who soon thought of her answer.

"The first Glasto."

Andrea looked lost. "The first what?"

"Glastonbury."

"Why did you call it Glasto?"

"Everyone calls it that."

"I don't call it that. Why do people call it that? Is it quicker to say? How much time are you saving? Say it again, and I'll time you."

"That's where I'd go," concluded Tash, refusing to argue any more.

Her mother still wasn't accepting her daughter's destination. "It was just a muddy field with a few folk bands. What is it with your generation? Thinking there's something so worthy about music? So profoundly important?"

"I just said that about Live Aid," agreed George.

"Where would you go then, Mum?" asked Tash, visibly irked.

Andrea sipped her wine and gazed into the fire as she pondered her answer.

"Christmas truce in the first World War. When the English and them other ones had a ceasefire to play that game of football."

"Them German ones?" said George, helpfully.

"Whoever they were. When the human spirit showed us all the futility of war and the love of fellow man."

"Deep," agreed Tash.

"Or my first root perm," pondered Andrea. "Could have been so bad, but I totally smashed it. Jilly Bedford was so jealous."

"Didn't Mrs Bedford have alopecia?" asked Jamie.

"She did, Jamie, and I'm regretting saying that now, but on balance I'm sticking with it cos she was a cow, and it was a pretty spectacular perm."

"What about you, Dad? Where would you go in a time machine?" asked Jamie.

"That day you met Nick Knowles?" asked Tash.

"A lot of people cry when they meet their heroes, Tash," defended Andrea.

His loving family gazed in his direction as he stared at the homemade tinsel star on top of the Christmas tree, the schoolwork of his then five–year–old daughter, the single piece of her handiwork carefully treasured through the years by her Grandma.

"I'd go back to your birthday, Tash," said George, suddenly looking quite emotional.

"Which one?" replied his daughter. "Eighteenth? When you did that thirty-minute speech?"

"It was forty," said Andrea. "Although it was good, I'll give him that. He even made the dog cry."

"No. Your actual birthday," said George, his gaze fixed on the threadbare tinsel that clung for life to the coat hanger star. The room absorbed this awkward skew of affection to just the one of his two children. Jamie was first to speak through a self-conscious smile.

"Not mine? What was so good about hers?"

"There was nothing good about it," said George. Were his eyes watering?

"I am still in the room actually," said Tash.

"I wasn't there," replied her father.

"You were working," explained Jamie. He understood why he'd missed it.

"Should have been there though," concluded his dad.

Andrea squeezed her husband's hand.

"You were working!" replied Tash. "Lots of Dads miss their kids' birth."

She interrupted the awkward silence she had created. "I'm not talking about Nathan. This isn't about me."

"Where were you working?" asked Jamie, now struggling with the lid on the Quality Street tin.

"That's the thing," replied George. "I was only a mile or so away. I was doing a pitch."

"We were going to be rich!" said Andrea, smiling at the memory.

"Pitch for what?" asked Jamie, just as the Quality Street lid flipped off and exploded one kg of assorted chocolates in coloured wrappers - minus the blue ones - over his Christmas jumper. Grandma never bought the small tins.

"You've heard of Alan Sugar?" asked George.

"Lord Sugar," corrected Tash.

"Well. You know how everyone streams music these days?" continued George.

"Might need to speed this along a bit, honey. It's Christmas Day in three hours," interjected Andrea.

"Back in the eighties, people could do two things if they wanted to listen to music. They could buy it. Or they could steal it. That means you'd (A) go down to HMV or Woolworths and buy your favourite song on a single – or L.P. if you were flush. Or (B)," George leaned in to add some gravitas to his next point, "you'd tape the charts on a Sunday."

"I don't even know what that means, but please don't waste too long explaining," said Tash.

"On one of THEM!" said George, pointing to Dot's Sony music centre. It was almost antique now, and she had draped a velvet table cloth over the top so it could hold a vase of plastic flowers, or plastic holly as currently on display. Dot loved a flower you could dust. George wandered over and lifted up the fabric cover to reveal the black plastic front HiFi tower that once filled his father with such joy. It was still in working order, but Dot only listened to the battered radio in her kitchen these days. Hence the Echo Dot gift.

George pointed out the turntable at the top under the smoked grey plastic lid, the radio dial below, the graphic equaliser beneath that, and then the twin cassette decks at the bottom. Having successfully explained the purposes of all the components without sending his children to sleep, he focused on the second cassette deck. Maybe the second bottle of wine was helping.

He continued his lesson and pointed to the deck on the right. "This one could record stuff. See the Record button that you pressed at the same time as the Play button? You'd do it to record LPs or cassettes for your mates. It was illegal, but everyone did it. But what a lot of teenagers did, was use this to record the Top 40 on a Sunday. The charts."

All stared back.

"Off the radio," he explained.

"And you invented that?" asked Tash, slightly missing the point George was making.

"Wait," said Andrea. "He's nearly finished."

"No. I didn't invent that. But here was the problem. Half of the Top 40 were crap, so you only wanted to record the songs you liked."

"Pause button. I'm ahead of you," said Jamie, pointing at the cassette deck. "You'd pause the recording when a duff song came on, and then continue when it ended."

"Correct," said George. Jamie was delighted to be proven right. This sort of thing hadn't happened much in school.

"But here's the thing," continued George. "When you were taping a song you liked, you'd have to guess when the DJ was gonna start talking over the end bit, and you didn't want his voice in the middle of your mixtape. So you'd be hovering over the pause button, trying to predict when to pause the recording."

Tash interrupted her Dad. "Nightmare. What with that and just three TV channels, it's amazing you guys made it to the nineties."

"I invented something pretty amazing," said George proudly.

"Your Dad invented something pretty amazing," corrected Andrea, implicating Ernest in all this.

"We invented something pretty amazing," conceded George.

"Is it to do with what you've been talking about so far? Cos I can't lie, it's not really giving me the feels," said Tash.

"When you heard the DJ start talking at the end of your favourite song, you pressed my SMART–PAUSE button. It paused the recording AND rewound the tape by two seconds at the same time. So when you wanted to carry on recording your next favourite song, the gobshite DJ's voice had gone!" George opened his arms to his audience. "Any questions from the dragons?"

"Actually, that is clever." Tash looked disappointed to be so pleasantly surprised.

"That's brilliant, Dad!" said Jamie. "Did you sell it?"

"Here's the thing. Alan Sugar was king of the HiFis back then. He'd wiped the floor with everyone else with his Amstrads. If anyone was gonna buy this technology, it was gonna be him," said George.

"And did he?" asked Jamie.

"No."

"Night everyone," said Tash, climbing off the sofa. "Next time throw in a spoiler alert, Dad."

"So what's that got to do with Tash's birthday?" asked Jamie. Tash didn't want to miss this, so sat back down on the edge of the sofa.

"I found out where he was going to be and went along to pitch the idea. An industry show. The PLASA Light and Sound exhibition," George gazed into nowhere as he lost himself in the memory. "Bloomsbury Crest Hotel, Tuesday the 23rd of October, 1984. I had to buy a suit."

"You went out on my due date?" asked Tash.

"It wasn't your due date, you were early," explained her mum.

"OK. But I was born at like ten o'clock that night, or something wasn't I?" asked Tash. "Night do was it?"

"It was a very long meeting, wasn't it, George? These things often go on into the early hours," explained Andrea, and George nodded.

"So you met Alan Sugar, then?" asked Tash, a little impressed by this new claim to fame.

"He told me I was too late for him," said George. "He said personal computers were going to be the next big thing. I told him he was wrong."

"And was he?" asked Jamie.

"No."

"So you didn't sell the idea?" asked Jamie.

"I think that's a given," said Tash. She circled the floor. "This isn't the Bahamas."

"Your Dad stayed over at the hotel. He didn't want to drink and drive," interjected Andrea.

"So you missed my birth cos you were pissed?" asked Tash, quite astonished at the thought.

"I wasn't drunk, Tash," replied George. "Just over the limit. Besides, you weren't due for another couple of weeks."

"I called the hotel, but they couldn't find him because they'd messed up the rooms. He only got my message when he checked out," added Andrea. "It was all a bit of a mess."

"You gave birth alone?" asked Tash, astonished at the prospect given the army of people who offered to be her birthing partner when Lucan was born. Albeit none were the father.

"Different times, Tash. Your dad was with me the following morning," explained Andrea, smiling strangely at her daughter. Her eyes glistened a reflection of the fairy lights.

"So if you went back in time, you'd ditch your meeting with Lord Sugar and head straight to Mum?" asked Jamie, delighted at the show of love and regret.

"No, I'd still meet Alan Sugar," replied George. "I'd just pitch him the iPhone or something. Then I'd go to your mum."

His family laughed.

"But I would have been there for your mum." He squeezed Andrea's hand even tighter.

"Why have you never told us this before?" asked Tash.

"I don't know. Maybe cos we've never had a time machine before!"

"That's really lovely, Dad," said Jamie, who was easily overcome with emotion at times like this. "Thank you." Even though the story wasn't about him, he wanted to acknowledge his father's kindness to his mum. Albeit theoretical.

They sat and listened to the crackling of the fire. From the kitchen, they could hear Sia's warning that 'Puppies Are Forever, Not Just For Christmas' on Dot's smart speaker. Tash glanced over at the photograph of Pepper, her grandparents beloved Airedale Terrier and wished Sia was correct. Pepper mourned along with the rest of the family when her master Ernest died, and her companionship had helped Dot tremendously. She was still missed by them all.

"Or I'd watch Elvis filming his '68 Comeback Special," said George.

FIVE

When Tash awoke, her immediate impulse was to reach over and snuggle Nathan. They had been apart for more than a year. Still after an incredibly deep sleep – something she rarely managed – she would awaken in the bubble of her brief marriage. It was a sharp intake of breath and huge fart from the other side of the room that dragged her back to her reality. Typically this exertion of wind would be followed by the stirring of her son waking, but Lucan was silent, clearly sleeping through his own antisocial behaviour. Tash's eyes followed the brilliant white stripe down the flock wallpaper, across the candlewick cover of her single bed across to the window and the bright moon in the night sky. But for the snoring of her son, Tash might be a child again. This was the bedroom she had shared with Jamie every Christmastime. Lucan's little outburst had not woken Jamie sleeping deeply on the other side of the chimney breast. Tash had left the curtains open so that Lucan could fall asleep looking at the relentless snow falling from the almost white night sky. Now the gap served to do two things. The first was to explain to Tash why this room was absolutely freezing. Grandma's curtains were heavily lined for a reason and leaving them open allowed the heat to escape through the single glazed sash window. The second was to place a question mark in her brain. She could see the snow was still swirling like a collection of mini cyclones, so how could the moon be casting any kind of light into the room? She sat up and pulled a chunky knit sweater over her pyjamas and slipped out of bed to check on her son. Lucan was swathed in sheets and blankets, and his forehead felt warm enough to reassure Tash that he wasn't about to succumb to frostbite. Intrigued by the light bisecting the room she tiptoed to the window and immediately felt her heart rate almost double.

Someone had broken into the garage.

The door was ajar, the light within shining brighter than the star of Bethlehem. (Grandma bought all of B&Q's 200-watt lightbulbs just before the EU banned them, and this one was doing its finest work from the single pendant hanging from the brightly painted ceiling). Tash instinctively turned to her brother to wake him. His bed was empty. She picked up her iPhone and saw that she was two hours into Christmas Day. She tiptoed from their bedroom, habitually clicking on the baby monitor app in a single movement.

Tash was able to literally walk in Jamie's footsteps to the garage. She'd slid a pair of Grandma's wellies on to keep the snow from soaking her pyjama trousers. Once inside, she shook herself down and stomped her feet on the cold concrete floor.

"Jamie?" she whispered in the direction of the staircase.

Nothing.

As she inched towards the foot of the garage staircase, she was suddenly struck with a chilling thought. *What if it isn't Jamie? What if it is burglars?* Yes, robbing a household on Christmas morning was a pretty heinous crime, but she'd be naive to think criminals take December 25th off. She looked around for something to arm herself. Her choices were limited, so she opted for a tin of Dulux paint. If the weight of the canister was anything to go by, it was only half full. Still, it would do as a cosh, with the added benefit of tagging the suspect with pure brilliant white gloss. Perfect for any police officer in pursuit. She continued up the stairs, holding her breath the whole time, but as she neared the 3/4 height door, she froze. A voice emanated from the other side. A voice that did not belong to Jamie. This voice was American. Or Canadian. Which is the same voice unless you are American or Canadian. She slid her phone into the rear pocket on her pyjama trousers, lifted her weapon over her head and silently counted herself down from five to one. On the count of one, she took a deep breath and kicked the door with all her might and also with her foot. A millisecond later she hurled the tin of paint into the attic room, surely neutralising the threat that waited within. That was the plan.

How was she to know that the door would be locked from the inside? So Tash's actual outcome was a little different to her projected one. Her foot went clean through the rotten wood of the door, and the paint tin deflected back onto her. The tin superbly coated her jumper with sticky white oil-based paint on its noisy way down the wooden staircase onto the garage floor. This was a biblical fail of terrifically loud proportions. Immediately the American voice stopped.

And now Tash was stuck. Her leg was jammed through the hole of a locked door, and she could hear footsteps coming towards her from the other side.

The sound of a key slowly turning filled her with dread. Should she scream? Use her phone to call 999? But, it was over too quickly. There was nothing she could do.

"Hi Tash. You couldn't sleep either?" asked Jamie as he opened the door, causing Tash to hurl herself towards him because of her attached leg.

"What you doing?!" reacted Jamie, covering his face with his hands, convinced he was under attack.

"My fucking foot went through the fucking door so when you opened the fucking door my fucking foot and fucking me went fucking with it!" replied Tash as she slowly tugged her leg free. She rubbed away at her shin as she picked up Grandma's welly from behind the door.

"Have you been painting something?" asked Jamie, glaring suspiciously at the smelly paint that adorned her top.

"Yes, I've been painting the garage door, Jamie. I thought I'd paint the garage door at 2am on Christmas morning," replied Tash, as loudly as she thought the hour would allow.

Jamie let this sink in.

"You're kidding, right?"

"Yes, I'm kidding. I thought you were a murderer or something. Who was talking to you?"

Jamie looked baffled. "No–one."

"I could hear an American voice."

Jamie held up his phone. "I was watching a YouTube video about batteries."

Tash shrieked like a child.

"Oh my God! Grandad's actual Christmas actual ride!"

Grandad's Christmas ride was a legendary Summers' family tradition when Jamie and Tash were young. His £10,000 windfall from work was used in part to indulge himself back in the mid–1980s when he'd convinced Dot to let him buy a Sinclair C5 for £399. The C5 was invented by British entrepreneur Clive Sinclair in his glory days of computing. The doomed C5 was launched in January 1985, and essentially it was a polypropylene bodied three-wheeler battery-powered go-kart. Despite a media buzz on its launch, there were insufficient customers prepared to compete with buses and cars for road space while sitting out of sight in a pedal-assisted tricycle wearing no helmet. It didn't stop Ernest from buying one in the following months, and treating his firstborn grandchild to trips around the garden to shrieks of delight from giddy Natasha, and later – after some pretty significant engineering alterations to its length and seat – with Jamie too. The three of them sitting in a row riding in circles around the cobbles made Ernest's life complete. The toddlers adored it, and soon Ernest opted to improve it further. To make it the ultimate Christmas sleigh. Not the sort most Grandads would make. This was the kind of sleigh you might find in a department store during the weeks before Christmas. This was even better than the sleigh in Santa's grotto at the S&E Co-Op on Ecclesall Road. Queuing families would snake through the brightly lit toy department past racks of Scalextric, Girl's

World, Monopoly and Sindy dolls, all competing for their place on your letter to Father Christmas.

When your moment finally came, a modest door would open into a magical waiting room. Cotton wool was irrefutably snow, and cardboard shapes were unquestionably wooden chalets housing elves and reindeer.

Then it was time.

Actually time.

To walk through to the flight deck on the roof of the Co-Op where you were seated in a wooden sleigh, with maybe four or five other families. The stars in the night sky only served to light the suggestion of Rudolph upfront, and the fan of the snowstorm merged with festive music as the euphoria of a night flight took over your every single nerve ending. The suited and booted elf would ring her sleigh bells and announce the start of your trip. And then it happened. You flew. There can be no doubt of that fact. The sleigh started to rock gently up, then down and side to side. The silhouette of Rudolph's antlers shook too as he pulled you aloft with all his might, his red nose lighting the way. Doubters were silenced when the Co-Op flight deck and views of Sheffield rooftops were left behind to be replaced by moving street tops of snow-covered villages and towns, then forests and then seas. After a smooth descent and gentle landing at the North Pole you would exit and a snow-laden path to the big man himself completed the deceit. Not to mention the generic boxed toys wrapped in red (girls) or green (boys) crepe paper. Different times.

A cynic, or maybe an engineer, might beg to suggest that the walls were painted rolls of canvas that moved in synchronisation from vertical rollers at the front of the sleigh to vertical rollers at the back. But the artwork was so superbly creative that even the landing convinced you that you had reached the North Pole. And yet the most vociferous doubter would be silenced after disembarking onto the opposite side of the sleigh – now miraculously with snow underfoot. Surely proof that through the door of the log cabin ahead lay the big guy himself. And sure enough, there he was. He even knew your name. What more proof did deniers need? For every child, a miracle had just occurred. For Ernest, a challenge had been set. A challenge that he smashed on his first attempt.

Tash let her cold fingers gently smooth over the back of her grandad's sleigh. It was so much smaller than she remembered. To make his Christmas ride, Ernest had amended the rear of the C5 with a double 'Raleigh Chopper' style seat. A Motorola car cassette stereo was suspended with Meccano straps under the front moulding of the chassis. A cassette tape sat in the ejected position. Tash spotted something new.

"He's added something, this is new right?"

Jamie nodded. Clearly distracted by his frustration to get the thing working, but he too glanced over at a Sinclair ZX Spectrum computer which has been bonded onto the front. Above it stood a Pye Tube-Cube black and white 7-inch TV connected with a curly telephone wire. Beneath them was an alloy steel casting with a hazard sticker attached. It looked like a mysterious overgrown snail's shell with wires soldered to entry points. And it may have been a trick of the light, but it seemed to have the letters MAS or NAS cast into the side.

"Where are the walls?" asked Tash.

Jamie leapt to work and extracted what appeared to be two rolls of carpet, but thinner. Like rolls of cotton fabric. He stood each on its end over some upright poles positioned either side of the front of the C5. Identical poles stood at the rear, each holding vertical cardboard tubes, with bulldog clips placed top and bottom. Jamie gently started to unfurl the first roll of fabric which spun smoothly on its poll, not unlike a kitchen roll dispenser, albeit five feet tall. This allowed Jamie to walk with the extracted material and attach it with bulldog clips to the rear vertical tube. He repeated this on the other side of the C5. Now, the sleigh was sandwiched between two beautifully painted Christmas scenes of snowy villages and fat snowmen.

"Those back rollers are still connected to the motor, look," said Jamie, indicating cables running from each to the underside of the C5 and into a heavily adapted battery pack. He also eyed a wire connecting this to the computer console at the front. "I wanted to get it working for Lucan, so he could have a ride in the morning."

Tash was genuinely touched. "But it's broken, right?"

"Well, it's not that it's broken. It just doesn't work like it used to. He used to flick the key at the front, didn't he?"

"I suppose it could have been smoke and mirrors," said Tash, leaning in to look at the cable ties holding wires along the side of the chassis.

Jamie flicked the ignition switch on and off a few times in frustration.

"What's this?" asked Tash, lifting a cluster of three-pin plugs cable tied together.

"Ah! We need power!" exclaimed Jamie. "The extension cable!"

He leapt up and paced over to the door, reaching for the curious adaptor he'd seen wired through the drilled hole. He unfurled it towards the plugs and inserted them all one by one. Happy that they were all securely in place he walked through to the stairhead and found the plug at the other end of the cable and plugged it into a solitary dusty socket screwed to the door frame. He excitedly flicked the switch.

"Anything?" asked Jamie as he made his way back through to Tash.

"Nothing."

Jamie ruffled his thinning hair as he tried to make sense of the challenge he faced. How come this wasn't working?

"Let's get a selfie, for old times," said Tash as she giddily lowered herself onto the front half of the long seat. Jamie reluctantly flopped down behind his sister; clearly not yet satisfied he'd tried everything to make this feeble machine live one last time.

"Pass me my phone," said Jamie, pointing to his battered Samsung on the countertop.

"No need," replied Tash as she delved into her rear pocket and extracted hers and postured herself in the screen. She adjusted it slightly to frame Jamie and some of the beautiful scenery that Grandad had painted onto the fabric sides of the ride.

"Smile, Jamie."

Jamie was distracted by something in front of Tash. "Look, Tash, look at that."

Tash recoiled. "Don't say spider. Please, don't say spider!"

Jamie was pointing at the ignition key that Grandad had retro-fitted to the sleigh. Above it, a single red light was now glowing.

"Turn the key! Turn the key!" Jamie was getting giddy.

Tash took a deep breath, leaned forward and turned the key. Nothing.

"Sake," muttered Jamie.

But then a low buzzing sound came from the front of the C5. It was followed by a long single beep. The Pye TV screen turned from black to grey. Then fuzzy. The brother and sister sat in silence for a moment. Then the screen flickered again. This time it went white. At the bottom of the tiny screen, text slowly appeared.

© 1982 Sinclair Research Ltd.

"My old Spectrum! It still works! Crazy!" said Jamie.

"He turned this thing into an office!" replied Tash, laughing. "Bless him!"

Jamie smiled, not quite reconciling all the different variables on the adapted C5.

"He kept the Christmas music, though!" said Tash, pushing the cassette into the car stereo, remembering how to make it play. Although it didn't play. It merely turned around and around with no music. The TV screen was now intermittently flashing.

"It's a program. He's connected the cassette to the computer. It's loading a program," said Jamie.

But nothing happened. They waited. Still nothing.

Tash yawned. "Oh well. Never mind. I'm gonna head back in. I'm cold," she checked her iPhone app for signs of Lucan waking, but he was sleeping soundly.

An electronic tune started playing, and both glanced up at the screen. It was lit up, and text typed out in front of their tired eyes.

Destination Date :

A cursor blinked invitingly. Tash read this out loud to her brother.

"What does that even mean?" she added.

Jamie smiled. "Time machine. I bet he made a virtual time machine! You put in a date and then the screen takes you there. Let's see what he made!"

"What do you mean, see what he made?"

"See what this does? Type in a date and see what sort of things he programmed it to do! Maybe it plays a song or shows you some facts about the year," said Jamie.

"I can't think what to put."

"You could earlier," said Jamie, remembering her amusement at his lame attempts to go back to breakfast time. "What about Dad's thing, do Dad's thing, and I'll film you. We can show him tomorrow on your phone that we went back in time for him, to your birthday!"

"Don't get too close and use a filter," objected Tash.

"Pass me your phone." Jamie was buzzing.

Tash begrudgingly handed it over with a threat. "Keep it short."

Jamie opened the camera and started to film "Hi Mum, hi Dad, we found Grandad's time machine, so we're going back in time to Tash's birthday, we'll come and find you, Dad, and tell you to get to the hospital!" He laughed to himself.

"What do I type?" asked Tash as she leant over to the Spectrum rubber keyboard.

"Twenty-three," said Jamie

"Yeah," said Tash as she typed, she noted the cursor displayed her numbers and moved along the screen a little. "Ten for October," said Tash, still typing, "eighty-four," she looked up.

The screen read:

23 10 84

"Brilliant! You ready?" asked Tash.

"Ready!" said Jamie.

Tash hit the ENTER button and the screen went blank. Then nothing happened.

"Balls," said Tash.

"Sorry for the swear," apologized Jamie to the camera.

The screen flickered, and text typed in front of them again:

Time :

"Time," read Tash. "I dunno. What time shall we go to?"

Jamie – still filming – suggested 4pm. Tash typed it in using the twenty-four-hour clock.

She looked at the screen and read the display aloud. "Sixteen, Oh, Oh… and enter."

The screen went blank, and then text appeared again.

Location :

"Location. Oh, bloody hell. This is taking ages. I'm freezing."

"It was that hotel. Dad was at that hotel. Bloom something. It was Blooming hotel or something." Jamie didn't want this to end.

Tash dutifully started typing and was delighted to see something she hadn't observed on antique PCs. The screen was offering autocomplete on her typing. She read the options as they appeared as her fingers hit the keyboard.

"Bloomberg, Bloomingdale, Bloomsbury."

"That's it, Bloomsbury!" said Jamie.

She carried on reading "Bloomsbury, London or Bloomsbury Holiday Inn, London? They're the only two options in London… That will be the hotel, right?"

"Try it."

Tash selected the latter until her screen went blank again. Then the typing appeared one final time. She read the text as it appeared.

Destination Date: 23 10 84

Time: 16 00

Location: Bloomsbury Holiday Inn, formerly Bloomsbury Crest

ENTER TO TRAVEL

"How does it know it used to be called the Bloomsbury Crest?"

"Clever Grandad," said Jamie. "Hit ENTER, then." He too was growing cold. He blew on his hands, still filming on his sister's iPhone.

Tash reached forward and pressed the rubber button one final time.

They were both shaken by the sudden familiar jolt of their shared seat. And just as all those years before, they surrendered completely to the moment. Pure joy filled their hearts as the C5 defied all logic and slowly rose up and down, and gently rocked from side to side as it soared effortlessly through the winter night sky. The painted walls moved on either side, and unmistakable music played through a single speaker behind Jamie. It was an incredibly kitsch 60s version of 'Sleigh Ride'. Yet, at that very moment in time, it was unquestionably the best song that had ever been recorded. Tash looked back over her shoulder at Jamie, and through her sudden warm tears, she saw a trail of his. He stopped filming his sister and instead gave her a squeeze. The lighting in the room seemed to have dipped too, and lights flickered impossibly from all around. Just for a moment the two of them forgot all about adulthood. All about bosses. All about bills. All about exes. All about expectation and failure. They were children again. And everything was perfect. Father Christmas would soon be drinking the modest glass of sherry they had left for him, before delivering some magic into their carefree home. Time stood still.

For a moment.

Maybe she was getting older, but Tash had never realised just how much the ride jolted its passengers about. Jamie had the same thought at the same moment. He also realised that the walls were moving far quicker than he'd remembered. It was when her knee struck her chin that Tash lost some of her festive cheer. She struggled to grab her phone from Jamie and place it in her pocket.

"Jamie, this isn't right, I'm going to stop it."

"OK," replied Jamie, holding onto the seat with whitening knuckles.

But Tash couldn't keep her arms or hands straight over the keyboard. She dropped them back onto the handlebars that were nestled underneath her legs, a quirk of the Sinclair design. She gripped tightly like their lives depended on it. The curious cast iron snail was scorching hot on her shins.

The attic was now in complete darkness, but for the muted glow of the Pye screen. White noise was winning an audible battle with 'Sleigh Ride'. Electrical clicks and fizzes were adding a strange rhythmic percussion. The artwork to their sides was now a blur, and both could feel their heads forced uncomfortably backwards like the downward fall on a rollercoaster. All logic told Tash they couldn't come to any serious harm as Grandad had suspended the whole axis on a hydraulic set of tubes to allow the motion of the ride. Yes, she could hear the wheels spinning like crazy, but she knew they were suspended in the air. They were going nowhere. That logic was perfectly sound and entirely reassuring until the hydraulic mechanisms holding them aloft suddenly snapped and the C5 dropped with a mighty slam onto the garage loft floor. Three wheels screeched along timber boards and projected the vehicle and its passengers at almighty speed toward the oak–clad wall in front of them.

So this was how I will die, thought Jamie. How shit. He hadn't even been to Disneyland.

Tash thought only of her son. *Why the hell had I come outside in the first place? Death? Really? Now?* Followed by, *How did your Mum die? Oh, she was playing go-karts with my uncle one Christmas.* This was not good.

When the polypropylene front of the C5 inevitably struck the wooden garage wall, the timbers offered little resistance. The oak was rotten just like the door that trapped Tash's leg only a few precious minutes earlier. Both were horrifically convinced they were about to meet their mutual demise. They would smash through the wall and drop to their inevitable deaths on the concrete path in the garden behind the garage.

Except they didn't. They didn't drop, and they didn't die. They just carried on going.

SIX

The timber floor gave way to tarmac. The December blizzard dissolved into drizzle. And there was light. Two lights to be precise, and they were coming towards them. Tash couldn't compute what had happened, but her innate response was to pull the handlebars to one side to avoid the oncoming threat. The C5 immediately veered left, and the bright lights swung the opposite way. Jamie looked down at the ground to see they had left a roadway of some sort and had now mounted a kerb, expertly steered by his sister upfront. He looked over his shoulder to see the two lights belonged to a black taxi cab which came to an abrupt stop thanks to some railings around a sunken garden. A horn sounded over the crumpling impact of metal and smashing glass. And then there was a moment of silence, but for Frankie Goes To Hollywood's manic bass and synth rhythms of 'Two Tribes' thumping on medium wave radio through the half-open taxi window. It was too much to take in. Jamie looked at his sister, who was now applying the brakes as speedily as she could.

They were on a built-up street with traffic all around. The ground, the buildings and the sky were all grey. Tash noticed her hair was getting wet from the drizzling rain.

"Are you OK?" asked Jamie as the C5 finally stopped on the littered pavement.

"No! Are you? What the fuck, Jamie?" Tash couldn't take this in.

Traffic had now stopped, and they could hear car doors slam. People were rushing towards the taxi. Jamie struggled to see past the good Samaritans, but when he succeeded he was relieved to see the taxi driver seemed to be talking to them. He was fine.

Until he caught Jamie's eye.

"Them! It was them!" shouted the cabbie, pointing along the road to Jamie and Tash.

"Tash, drive on. Drive on!" shouted Jamie.

"What?"

"They're coming for us, just drive!"

Jamie looked back and spotted a police officer talking to the taxi driver, who was still pointing at him. The PC set off towards the C5.

"Christ, the police!" he squealed.

"We haven't done anything! What do you mean?" Tash flicked away at the ignition. It was dead.

"Drive Tash! Drive!"

"There's no power, Jamie! It's dead!"

"Pedal! Pedal!"

Tash did precisely that. The C5 was equipped with pedals like a child's ride-on car. It was slow and Jamie used his feet on the ground too to try to propel them faster, but there was no mistaking that they were in the shittest getaway car in history. The end of the pavement gave way to a ramp leading to an underground NCP. Tash turned the handlebars and they gathered pace as they descended below ground only to come face to face with a classic Range Rover exiting the car park. Both swerved, just as before, and this time their opponent avoided any scrapes but skidded sideways to a halt blocking the entrance where the ramp met the road, preventing the police officer's pursuit. At the bottom of the ramp was a sharp turn left into the car park, and now the only thing between the C5 and a potential hiding place was a striped high-vis barrier at head height.

"Duck!" shouted Tash to her brother. Both did, opting for the same safe space for their heads, resulting in a mighty crack as their skulls struck one another. The C5 skidded under the barrier and along the concrete floor of the dimly lit basement car park bouncing past vintage parked vehicles on either side. Tash was busily scanning for a parking space so wasn't expecting a Golf GTI to pull out into their path. She let out an almighty scream, and in full support Jamie joined in too, unaware of the reason. The driver of the VW heard their cries and superbly selected reverse to rejoin her parking space with seconds to spare. Tash and Jamie sailed safely past her windscreen and out of sight, with the shrieks of Jamie echoing around the concrete bunker.

"Brake Tash! Brake Tash!"

"I don't want this – I don't want any of this!"

She finally managed to gain control over the C5 just before they reached the staircase doors, and capably performed a ninety-degree turn to spin the tiny vehicle into a gloomy motorcycle parking spot at the end of all the parking bays.

Then there was silence. No cars. No horns. No voices. No police.

"I don't think you can park here, Tash. It says motorbikes, look." Jamie pointed to a painted motorbike on the wall.

"Are you fucking kidding me?" Tash spun around to glare at her brother whipping him with her wet hair.

"No, I'm not look," Jamie was still pointing.

"So we're looking for a space for a … a… what would you call this, Jamie? What would you call this actual fucking devil's business thing?"

Jamie was silenced. Just for a moment.

"Well, it's a three-wheeled vehicle, isn't it?" He felt the tip of his nose before examining the wet blood on his fingertips.

Tash stared at him again, took a deep breath and tried to compose herself. But her trembling voice betrayed her.

"Jamie. What just happened?"

Jamie thought about it for a moment, before answering his sister with disarming confidence.

"It's a dream, isn't it? I'm dreaming, and you're in it." He sniffled his nose a little to stop the bleeding.

"Right. Cos it feels real. That's all," replied Tash fumbling in her pocket for her iPhone. She pulled it out and squinted at the screen, clicking it a few times, before escalating panic set in.

"No signal. There's no signal. The app won't load. I can't see my son." She made dramatic statements at significant life moments. That was her thing.

"We're underground. Don't panic. There's no signal, that's all. What else could it be?"

Tash looked over at the stair doors.

"Let's get above ground."

****

The single door at the top of the staircase opened onto another anonymous-looking street. If her bearings were right, Tash concluded they were on the opposite side of the building where they'd shaken off the police. She stepped out onto the wet pavement with Jamie close behind. Facing them were concrete grey flats with large empty balconies. The first thing that struck Jamie was the number of vintage cars on the road, just like the ones they'd left behind in the basement. Tash was distracted by her phone screen, occasionally holding it up to the sky hoping to get some bars, 5G, 4G, 3G, she'd take any G right now.

"These cars are tiny," observed Jamie as he examined the black plastic bumper on the front of a red VW Polo. Parked behind was an extraordinary looking thing. Jamie sauntered alongside it and then around to the boot so he could read the badge. "Montego," he said aloud. He took a step back to take it all in. "That is one shit car." He leaned in to read a sticker in the back window. *Support the miners*. Then another, *Radio One. 1053 and 1089-*

An unusual sounding siren interrupted him before he reached *VHF*. It sounded like the toy horn his grandad had fitted to his BMX bike one Christmas that had three settings – police, fire and ambulance. All of them sounded like variations of a slowed-down smoke alarm. The one punishing his ears right now reminded him of the *fire* one, and he turned to see a white car with orange stripe turning into the road. 'Police,' was painted along the side in a crappy Arial font. Jamie and Tash froze to the spot but the car sped past them and took the next left, presumably heading to the scene of the smashed taxi.

"That's a Renault, gotta be. Or Citroën," summed up Jamie incorrectly as the Rover SD1 drove out of view. "Really, really shit." Another siren squalled around the corner, and a tiny ambulance followed the route of the police car. That too had a strange orange stripe painted around the middle.

"Jamie, there's no signal," said Tash, panic rising in her voice. "It's the buildings. They're too tall," she muttered as she walked along the road towards what looked like an open square.

"Steady Tash, that policewoman could be there," said Jamie.

Tash's wellied feet splashed through puddles; her paint-splattered jumper was covering most of her PJs. Jamie struggled to keep up, his sleepwear was just as gaudy as his sister's but happily covered in some part by the opened puffa jacket he'd worn to warm his visit to the garage loft. He too was wearing boots, thankfully his own. As they reached the corner of the building, Jamie stopped his sister going further by grabbing her jumper collar, simultaneously cutting off her air supply with one swift motion.

"Jamie!" Tash didn't take well to the instant choking.

But Jamie was distracted. In fact, he looked suddenly pale. His mouth was hanging open.

"What? What is it?"

Jamie pointed to the sign mounted on the corner of the building. Tash looked up and read it.

Bloomsbury Crest Hotel.

They both looked at one another and then perused the street. Yes, the cars were all old. And so much smaller than the cars they travelled in every day. They slowly peered around the corner to the front entrance of the hotel. It wasn't really standing in a square, more a wider section of road with a central area. The ambulance staff were tending to the passenger of the crashed taxi, and the police car was parked in front of it, blocking the road from additional traffic. Dark-suited men and women were walking past the commotion into the hotel, obliviously clutching briefcases and flight cases. An A-frame sign stood outside the main glass doors of the hotel foyer displaying a garish neon-coloured poster with black writing. It read,

PLASA Exhibition '84
Registration Floor 1

Tash started making gasping noises as she fought for breath. Whooshes danced around her ears. She could hear the blood pumping around the veins in her head. Her peripheral vision started to become grey and speckled. Jamie intervened, he could see his big sister was spinning out so stepped in to avert a crisis.

"Breathe slow, sis. Breathe slow, look at me. Look at me. Stop looking over there, breathe slow, sis. Yes?"

Tash struggled to avert her eyes from the poster but eventually did as Jamie told her. Slowly she managed to calm her racing pulse.

"Nice and slow… You OK?"

Tash nodded. "I'm OK. I'm OK."

"You sure?"

Tash nodded again. "I'm OK."

"Nice and slow," reiterated her brother, gently rubbing her shoulder.

"Nice and slow."

Tash breathed deeply again. "I'm OK."

She slowly breathed out through gritted teeth.

Jamie nodded, glanced over at the sign, then fainted.

SEVEN

Jamie came around, propped up against the wall where he fell. The first thing he saw was his sister tapping frantically into her iPhone.

He heard himself speak. "Just breathe, sis. You're doing great."

Tash barely glanced down at him.

"What are you doing?" he asked.

She waited for a moment. Then leant in to squint at the screen. "Sake! Still no signal."

"There won't be, will there?"

"For what reason?"

"For the perfectly logical reason that there is no mobile phone signal cos mobile phones haven't been invented cos it's 1984," Jamie replied like she was an idiot.

"There's nothing logical about any of those words, Jamie."

"Well, there is."

"It's not 1984. It's not 1984. It's NOT 1984!" shouted Tash.

Jamie clocked that his sister's raised voice was causing attention to bystanders. "Tash, calm down, people are staring."

"That's cos they can see us!" she replied, shouting at an elderly shopper, "YOU CAN SEE US, RIGHT?"

The elderly lady clutched her handbag closer to her chest and crossed the road to avoid confrontation. Tash turned back to Jamie. "And she can see us because we're here. And – because we're here – it means 1984 and 1987 have already happened, Jamie. In full. We've both been born, learned to walk, gone to school, learned to drive…"

"Well, I learned to drive," interrupted Jamie.

"I learned to drive!"

"I thought you meant passed the test."

"You're going to bring that up now?" Tash was astonished. "Mr Seven Tests."

"I have dyspraxia, Natasha. And I was just correcting you."

"Staaaaand'd!" came the cry of a man across the road.

Jamie looked over to see a newspaper vendor with a bag of *Evening Standards* across his chest; he was folding one for a suited middle-aged lady in exchange for some coins. By his side was an *Evening Standard* poster board displaying the headline: 'London France Bomb'. Jamie sprinted across the street, beeped by a Ford Granada that skidded to a stop just inches from him.

"Sorry, sorry," appealed Jamie with both hands on the car bonnet before continuing across the road. The vendor was already folding a crease into another paper and handing it towards Jamie as he reached him.

"Thanks," said Jamie, taking the paper. He let the folded tabloid drop open, displaying the full front page.

'Explosives Found Ahead Of Mitterrand's London Visit' claimed the bulk of the ink. Alongside that headline, an advert for Dixon's boasted stock of the Amstrad CPC464 computer with colour screen for only £349.90.

Jamie's eyes frantically scanned this wall of information, finally settling on the text under the header.

Tuesday, 23rd October 1984. Price 20p.

"Twenty pee, mate," said the vendor, his face crumpled under a flat tweed cap, soggy from soaking up the rain. He opened his palm for payment. Jamie looked up for a moment, clearly not listening.

"Say again?" asked Jamie.

"Say what?" replied the confused vendor.

"What did you say?"

"I said, punk boy, twenty pence."

"Why you calling me a punk boy?"

The vendor made a half-hearted gesture at Jamie's attire beneath his coat. "Punk boy, new romantic, tramp, whatever, mate. But that's not yours until you pay," replied the man, snatching the newspaper back.

"Right. Yes," said Jamie, suddenly fumbling in his puffa jacket pocket. Nothing. He tried another pocket. Nothing. The vendor had seen it all before. But then a smile spread across Jamie's face as he withdrew a coin from a rip in the lining. He examined it and handed it over.

The man held the coin to his eye to examine it too. "The fuck's this?"

"Two-pound coin," replied Jamie.

"I'm too busy mate, earning a living," responded the seller, tossing the coin in the air and turning to walk away with his newspaper back under his arm, shouting "Staaaaand'd!" as he went.

Jamie picked up the coin from a puddle and turned to cross back to his sister, again causing a car to slam on its brakes and beep. Jamie signalled his apologies as he raced over to Tash.

"The cars are so bloody small! How you supposed to see them?"

Tash was attempting another reset on her iPhone when Jamie reached her.

"Good news and bad news," said Jamie.

"I'll just take the good, please." Tash didn't look up from her screen.

"The good news is Grandad was a genius," said Jamie, his eyes perusing every single detail of the street he now found himself. The parking meters, the amber street lamps glowing at the start of their shift, the rows of red phone boxes, and of course, the tiny, tiny cars.

"Nah," replied Tash. "That's not really floating my boat."

Jamie continued. "The bad news..."

Tash again refused to look up, so Jamie reached out and placed his hand over her screen. He gently lifted her chin with his other hand and gazed into her eyes. "The bad news is the two-pound coin hasn't been invented yet."

Tash absorbed Jamie's claims before protesting again.

"Jamie, either we are dreaming, or I am dreaming, or you're dreaming, or someone's dreaming, but what I do know is – this is not real. I just need to get this app working so I can check on my son. Because – what I do know is – it's the middle of the night on Christmas Eve."

Tash stared into her brother's eyes. A tear started to roll down her cheek.

Jamie wiped it away and continued in a slow, calm, methodical tone, "Tash. Grandad built a time machine. Grandma isn't going mad. We are in 1984. On your actual birthday."

"How the hell can you say that?"

"It was the date on the newspaper," said Jamie, moving to one side of the pavement to let a handful of suited men and women past them.

"I'm going to need more than that, Jamie!" shouted Tash, before being jostled by another suited man.

"Sorry love! Sorry," apologised the man, briefly casting a glance back at Tash as he followed the group of colleagues ahead of him.

Tash was about to unleash a lesson in manners but stopped when her eyes settled on the man's face. Silently she reached out to Jamie's sleeve. He followed her gaze. Both stood perfectly still as they watched their 26-year-old father turn to catch up with his colleagues before they all disappeared into the hotel reception.

"How was that for you?" whispered Jamie, completely aghast.

Tash stared as the revolving doors continued to spin.

"He didn't recognise me…" she whispered.

"He's got so much hair," said Jamie, rubbing his scalp. "Did we know he had that much hair?"

****

Inside the hotel, Jamie and Tash stood in the foyer and immediately realised how cold they'd become. Tash attempted to make some kind of style from her soaking wet hair in one of the many mirrored walls and pillars, but the oil-based white paint wasn't helping. The reception carpet and the walls were fifty shades of grey. Any surface that wasn't grey was either mirrored or pink. The chairs were black leather with chrome tubular arms and legs. Sade purred 'Your Love Is King' from speakers cleverly disguised as suspended ceiling tiles. Jamie couldn't help but think the aesthetics of the ceiling would be vastly improved if the ceiling tiles looked more like speakers. Tash stared at the formal welcome board that listed the day's events and where they could be found within the hotel. Sure enough, underneath *Chartered Surveyors Luncheon in the St George Suite*, the second line down read: *PLASA, registration floor 1, Exhibition Hall.*

Behind the main reception desk, a bouffant-haired young lady was pointing a big black clicker remote control at a wall-mounted colour television, one of those massive ones with a big box attached to the back. Jamie guessed she was probably sixteen or seventeen years old, eighteen at most. Her blue eye shadow seemed to glisten beneath a quiff of unmovable wet-look gelled blonde hair. Jamie wandered over, intrigued as to what passed for TV entertainment three years before his birth. The TV wasn't broadcasting footage though. Instead, it displayed lots of text over garish coloured boxes that reminded him of his ZX Spectrum. The top of the screen read: Ceefax. This was the BBC Teletext service, and much as it had continued into Jamie's childhood it never held any appeal for him, so today he was witnessing its lo-fi capabilities for the very first time. Helen, as her name badge read (along with her job – Trainee Receptionist) typed in the numbers

1-7-6 whilst pointing the remote control high up at the screen. Nothing happened for a while, and then the screen changed. More neon-coloured boxes and words appeared, but the title was now *UK Top 40 Singles*. The words seemed to please Helen, who mouthed "Yes!" and punched the air.

"Good news?" asked Jamie.

Helen was immediately flustered and dropped the remote control.

"Sorry, sir, can I help you?" she asked, instantly questioning whether she should call for security given the sorry state of the wet homeless man struggling to make eye contact with her.

"I was just wondering what the good news is?" asked Jamie, genuinely interested.

His kind demeanour and warm voice reassured Helen, who answered honestly.

"They release the new charts on a Tuesday. I just wondered who was number one." She smiled at him hoping to avoid a bollocking from a secret shopper. The reception manager arrived behind the desk and glanced up disapprovingly at the TV. Her gold embossed name tag read: Susan, Reception Manager.

"Is that you again?" barked Susan at her YTS assistant. "Leave it on the news headlines."

Helen looked mortified. Jamie intervened.

"No, it was me. I wanted to know who was number one."

"I'm sorry, sir," replied Susan. "Wham! Freedom. Again," she said, reading from the screen. She glanced

Jamie up and down and then looked over at his sister. "Are you in the business?"

"The business?"

"The music business. You're wearing pyjamas?"

"Yes!" replied Jamie. "Yes. We're in the business."

"Excellent. How interesting," replied Susan, with a voice and face that indicated the complete opposite.

"Excuse me, madam, we'd like your help, please," came an approaching voice. "Did any of your guests witness the accident outside?"

A police constable was walking purposefully over to the reception desk. Behind him in the street the ambulance drove away, and the taxi turned slowly back into the road.

Jamie and Tash took this prompt to call for the lift, which arrived almost immediately. Helen waved a meek thank you to Jamie as he dashed inside.

The Thomson Twins' 'You Take Me Up' played through a speaker in the lift ceiling, which delighted Jamie as they were in a lift, and they were about to be taken up.

"Floor one," said Jamie to himself as the lift doors closed. His finger reached out to the buttons.

"Hang on," said Tash, knocking his hand away. "Why are we going to floor one?"

"The exhibition," explained Jamie. "That's why we came into the hotel, isn't it?"

"Yes, it probably was what you were thinking. But here's a better idea. Fuck the exhibition. I need to get home to my son, Jamie! I don't like any part of this," replied Tash. "We need to get back to the C5." She pressed B for the basement car park.

The lift started to descend.

"Tash, what's the hurry? I know you're spooked. But take a moment. Dad's up there!"

Within moments the lift bell sounded, and the doors opened onto the bleak, dark basement car park. Directly ahead – maybe twenty cars away – the PC was talking into her radio handset. She slowly turned her gaze in the direction of the lift. Jamie frantically smacked the button for floor one over and over but not before they were spotted. The PC blew a whistle and sprinted towards them. Time stood still for the brother and sister as they each held their breath willing the lift to spring into action. Jamie's finger was now tapping the '1' button like he was playing Space Invaders and the galactic mother ship was millimetres away from annihilating his spacecraft. She was ten cars away now. Now nine. Now eight. Jamie tried to casually avoid eye contact with their assailant, but Tash was captivated by the PC's electric blue eyeliner. With seconds to spare the doors closed and the lifted hummed upwards, taking them to their next destination.

"Why did you do that?" asked Tash.

"Do you want to get arrested?" asked Jamie.

"For what? Maybe we should just explain everything to her!"

"Terrible idea, Tash. Terrible. Right up there with getting pregnant by your ex."

"What? Really? Now? You go there now?"

"Sorry, but I don't think it's our best idea to tell the police we arrived here in a time machine," explained Jamie. Tash couldn't argue. They listened to the Thomson Twins for a few moments.

"He wasn't my ex when I got pregnant," said Tash.

"He was. You'd separated. He was your ex."

"But we got back together!"

"For one night," protested Jamie. "Then you split again."

"Are we listing one another's faults? Cos I have a spreadsheet at home."

The altercation ended with the opening of the lift doors.

The decor of the corridor on floor one suggested: 'We refurbed the reception last year, but welcome to the rest of the hotel which last saw a paintbrush in 1973'. The carpets were brown, and the wallpaper cream with swirly brown flecks. An oak sign with golden hand-painted writing displayed their options. To the left were the stairs and a cocktail bar, to the right, the exhibition hall. The sound of hundreds of delegates filled the walkway. As they turned across the carpet, they took a moment to stare into a full-length mirror that hung between them and the next lift. They didn't look good. They didn't look good at all. Jamie's black puffa jacket hung limply over his striped Christmas pjs which in turn snagged on his CAT boots. Tash had rat tails of damp hair stuck to her face, and her paint splashed jumper clung to her reindeer trouser bottoms. But it was Grandma's boots that genuinely let the ensemble down.

The sound of squeaking wheels announced the arrival of a friendly-looking housekeeper pushing a laundry trolley. Piles of dirty towels filled the top shelf, and two laundry bags full of residents' clothes hung from each end.

"Are you Ruby?" asked Jamie, moments after fleetingly scanning the housekeeper's name badge.

"Yes?" responded the lady, slightly taken aback that anyone could even see her. She'd long since assumed her duties deemed her invisible.

"This is Ruby!" introduced Jamie to Tash, who forced a smile that just about disguised her bewilderment.

"Hello… Ruby," said Tash.

Jamie was thinking fast. "Did you not hear the announcement?" he asked, gesturing at the ceiling as if there were some public address system secreted away.

"Announcement?" asked Ruby.

"Yes. Yes," replied Jamie, "Announcement. They need you in the …" his eyes darted around the corridor, settling on the oak sign "They need you in the cocktail bar."

"The cocktail bar?" repeated the housekeeper.

"You can leave this with us," said Jamie, placing a hand on the trolley, "It was quite urgent apparently."

Ruby glanced at the wet couple in strange clothes.

"I've never been in the cocktail bar. Why would they want me in the cocktail bar?"

Jamie leaned into Ruby, and calmly explained just inches from her face. "I don't want to spoil things, but I think it's something to do with…" He was slowing now as his brain tried to catch up, "Something to do with overtime."

Ruby flipped. "I don't want overtime. I work enough hours as it is. What do they mean overtime? Why do they want to talk about overtime in the cocktail bar?"

"We were just saying the same thing, weren't we?" Jamie said to Tash.

He placed both hands on the trolley. "We'll mind your trolley. Off you go."

Ruby set off at a pace muttering her contempt for compulsory overtime, and immediately Jamie summoned the lift.

"And don't take any shit from them!" shouted Jamie.

"What are we doing?" asked Tash.

"Come on," muttered Jamie, impatiently thumping the lift button again.

Ruby had disappeared into the room at the end of the corridor, and it wouldn't be long before she returned. "Come ON!" said Jamie at the closed lift doors.

"What are we doing?" tried Tash again.

"There's a load of clothes." Jamie gestured at the bags on the trolley.

Tash still looked confused. "So?"

"We can get out of these wet pyjamas!" explained Jamie, still glaring at the doors, his attention flipping towards the cocktail bar from time to time.

"Steal laundry?"

"Borrow it, yes."

"We don't need clothes. We're going home."

"Yes. Of course. But it's not been too straightforward so far, has it? We have police looking for us on two floors so far. We'll find things far easier if we blend in."

Tash started reluctantly delving deep into the washing and dry cleaning bags.

"Hey?!" came a cry from down the corridor. "Nobody wants me in there!" shouted Ruby, now racing back towards them.

The lift pinged, and the doors opened. Tash pushed the trolley and her brother inside, squeezing herself in last. She turned to press the top floor button.

"Stop!" Ruby shouted. Tash spotted the 'Close Doors' button and thumped it like crazy. The doors slowly closed just as Ruby came into view, but she was too late.

Inside the lift, Jamie spoke first. "Thanks."

Tash managed a smile despite her despair.

"Let's just buy a bit of time," continued Jamie. "We'll change clothes, head to the exhibition – really quickly – just in case we can see Dad, and then go straight back to the basement. We'll just need to find a different way there. Come on. What do you say?"

Tash took a moment to absorb this. "No. We get changed then we go home."

"Or that," replied Jamie. "Let's put that idea on the table too. Yes."

Tash reached out and started to pull clothing from the bags, discarding pieces onto the floor in the hope of finding something, anything, that was dry and would fit. Jamie did the same with a bag near him. Tash spotted a suit bag on the bottom shelf and unzipped it.

"Ooh, this is very you," she muttered to her brother.

EIGHT

The Exhibition Hall lay before them. A more stylish poster than the one in reception proudly announced: PLASA Light & Sound Show! 1984

The letters were drawn in three-dimensional style and seemed to leap from a backdrop of amps, speakers, microphones, coloured lights, cassette decks and digital displays.

"I'm throwing two minutes at this, Jamie. Two minutes, no more," insisted Tash.

"Might not even need that!" Jamie was delighted that he'd twisted her arm.

The floor thumped with the bass of Nik Kershaw's biggest hit of the year. It was playing behind the doors ahead as Tash and Jamie approached them in perfect time with the music, it was impossible not to. But this was OK with both of them, something about it felt good. They swerved past a handful of delegates at the registration desk, and each pushed a door open to enter the room.

The delegates inside witnessed a perfect vision of sartorial 1984 Britain strut into the room. The brother and sister continued to walk in sync with the rhythm of 'I Won't Let The Sun Go Down On Me'. No-one could have suspected that this power couple had come from the future. Jamie was dressed in a grey polyester suit, with coloured flecks throughout the material. The lapels were pencil-thin, and the sleeves rolled up to show off the paisley print lining. His trousers were baggy at the top and tight at the ankle. A peach-coloured shirt was just visible behind a black leather tie. Yes, the shirt had gravy stains on it, but that's why it was in the laundry, wasn't it? That and the fact that the suit was three sizes too large and the trousers snagged on his CAT boots was merely an unfortunate detail. Beside him, his sister Tash had replaced her paint-splashed jumper with something almost identical. A black sweatshirt with a printed white paint splatter design, the ruffled collar of a white blouse standing up around her neck. A white rah-rah skirt completed her look, red wine stain imprinted down one side. The wellies weren't visible in a crowd, so she was relatively happy. Besides, she'd accessorised them with funky-coloured socks tied like wristbands around her legs.

The Exhibition Hall was quite a grand name for what was in essence a large room. Tash noted depressingly that most of the delegates were men as she scanned the sea of faces and displays of the latest tech equipment through the smoke that filled the air. It had been almost a year since they had seen so many people in the same room as one another, especially without face masks.

"Everyone's so thin," said Jamie.

"Everyone's so male," said Tash.

"Look at all the fags!"

Sure enough, sales reps and buyers rubbed shoulders while cradling a wine glass in one hand, and a cigarette in the other. It seemed impossible to see anyone that wasn't smoking. They stopped walking to peruse the room. Strobe lights lit up banks of swirling, coloured bulbs. Human-sized speakers shone under spotlights and banks of graphic equalisers flashed in time with the amps that drove them.

"What's the plan?" asked Jamie.

"Find Dad, tell him to get to hospital, get back in the C5, get home to my son," came Tash's matter-of-fact reply. "We have ninety seconds."

"Right," agreed Jamie, before unhelpfully adding his most pressing thoughts, "Assuming it starts up and assuming we can make it work again, and assuming it takes us back to where we came from, and assuming we don't get arrested for stealing these clothes or for making that taxi crash."

Tash listened to her brother's voice over the loud music, and suddenly the bizarre reality of the situation hit her again. "Oh my God, Jamie. This has to be a nightmare. I blame Grandma's meal. How long had she had that quiche?"

"Look at that!" Jamie delightedly set off in the direction of a HiFi system with a vertical turntable, spinning a 12-inch picture disk magically above twin cassette decks. The sound waves from the brass intro to Howard Jones's 'Pearl In The Shell' hit Jamie's face like a hurricane. Tash followed him. Jamie glared at the revolving vinyl that seemed to defy gravity. A stylus mounted on a vertical arm rested perfectly in the grooves of the disk.

"How does that even work?" he whispered to nobody in particular.

"Sam, Bush Electronics," replied the rep standing alongside the HiFi, holding out his hand to Jamie.

"We are NOT here to check out the equipment, Jamie." Tash was adamant. "Look for Dad. Or Alan Sugar."

"He's not here this year, love," shouted Sam over the sound from his speakers.

"What? Love?" replied Tash, heavy on her sexist retort.

"Sugar. Not here this year," replied the twenty-something man, oblivious to Tash's irritation.

Tash expertly reached out and turned down the volume on the Bush HiFi.

"Amstrad ARE here this year, my father is going to speak with Alan Sugar," replied Tash.

"Amstrad are. He's not. It's all about home computers now for him," continued the rep. Then he laughed. "He's wrong, of course. Who wants a computer at home? It'll be the end of him."

"Where are they?" replied Tash.

The rep pointed to the far end of the room. Tash and Jamie looked over and saw the familiar Amstrad logo above a crowd of excited people.

"Come on," said Tash, setting off immediately, with Jamie struggling to keep up.

The Amstrad stand had many tower stereo systems on display, but sure enough an even bigger row of computers and colour monitors were creating a buzz of interest from the crowd. Jamie reached forward to stop Tash just short of the stand.

"Tash!" Jamie gestured at the back of a suited man.

There, barely six feet away from them, was their younger father. He stood clutching some hand-drawn plans on a sheet of foolscap paper, in discussion with another man, both preoccupied with his ideas. The other man wore a name badge: S. Samuel. Beneath his name was the Amstrad logo.

It was clear to Tash and Jamie that this was not a meeting with Alan Sugar as their family folklore had it. It was also clear that S. Samuel was ending the discussion. All the time shaking his head at their Dad.

Young George disappointedly shook S. Samuel's hand and turned to walk away, shoving his get rich scheme plan into his new Top Man suit pocket.

"Why would he lie about that?" asked Jamie.

"George!" shouted Tash at her dad.

Jamie looked mortified. "Tash! What are you doing?"

"What we came here for!" Task took one step towards her father, who had now turned to face his children. Not that he was a parent. Yet.

"Yes?" replied George, a little confused to hear his name from a stranger.

Then Tash's brain melted. "We… We, er…"

Tash was fascinated by her father's face. His skin looked so young. His lips looked so full. His eyes were bright. He had hair. He really was quite a handsome young man. A wolf whistle interrupted the moment. They all glanced over to a stunning brunette lady in her early twenties. She was power dressed without a doubt, but from one woman to another Tash noticed a lot of leg and even more chest was on display. She held up a room key and winked at George. She raised a stolen bottle of wine from the drinks table.

"Two oh nine!" she shouted and then turned to leave doing a little dance to Elton John who was singing an anti-apartheid song from a Toshiba cassette deck underneath a huge cardboard ad: *Hello Tosh, Gotta Toshiba?*

"Deny the passenger, who wanna get on…" sang Elton.

It was a lot to take in.

George's expression was a mixture of embarrassment and euphoria.

"Who the fuck's that?" demanded Tash.

"I beg your pardon?" replied her father.

"You heard. Who. The fuck. Is that?"

"Leave it, Tash." Jamie hated confrontation of any kind.

"Do I know you?" replied George.

"Not yet," replied Tash.

"Tash don't say too much," said Jamie.

"Georgie!" shouted the young lady, she was at the double doors now. "Two. Oh. Nine!"

"Did you want something?" asked George.

Tash's eyes were filling with tears. She could only shake her head at the man before her. With that, George followed the mystery lady towards the exit.

"What's going on?" asked Jamie. "What just happened?"

"Well his late-night meeting with Alan Sugar never happened, did it, Jamie? He just pitched his crappy plans to some random and then had it off with some slapper."

Jamie stared in amazement as his father left the exhibition with someone who most certainly wasn't his pregnant mum.

****

"I just think we need to tread carefully, Tash. Remember what happened in *Back To The Future*, when Marty nearly stopped his parents from meeting," said Jamie as he struggled to keep up with his sister's marching along the second-floor corridor. The hidden ceiling speakers were doing no justice to 'Hot Water by Level 42, but Mark King's bass was pumping even more adrenaline around Tash's veins.

"Two things Jamie. One, that was a film. And two, that was a fucking film."

"That's one thing," replied Jamie's logic.

"Maybe. Felt like two."

She was clearly distracted. "OK – here's another second thing. Mum and Dad have already met, that's why she's about to give birth to me. On her own," Tash stopped at this. "I can't believe I just said those words. It's like I believe I'm truly here. Which I don't. Cos I'm not."

At that, she fumbled for her phone inside her jumper and flicked the screen one more time. "Nope. Still no signal. This is actually happening."

"What are you going to say?"

"I don't care Jamie. Anything. Everything. I'm fucking livid at him. And I could do without this, cos every minute we're here is a minute I'm away from my son!"

"Well it's not really, is it? Every minute we're here is another minute in 1984. The future hasn't happened yet. So you're not actually spending ANY time away from Lucan."

"Oh my God, don't turn into Doctor fucking Who! Do you see my son? No. So I am away from my son. And I never spend time away from my son!"

"Well, you left him on the train yesterday. And before that you..." but he was interrupted.

"Can we not please? And anyway, yesterday hasn't happened yet, has it? Apparently."

"Yesterday has happened. Just not our yesterday."

"I'm not doing this, Jamie. You're not a time traveller, and I don't want any of your Star Trek bollocks. Not now. Yawn off."

"The Doctor is a time lord. Not a time traveller."

"How's the girlfriend situation coming along?"

"Just be careful, Tash. Don't say who we are," said Jamie, again hot on his sister's tail.

"Two oh seven, two oh eight..." read Tash on the bedroom doors. "Two oh nine." She knocked on the plywood door like the whole of London was under attack.

"That's it, Tash, nice and calm like we planned," whispered Jamie.

Other bedroom doors opened first, and the protruding faces each met with reassurance from Tash.

"Fuck off. I'm not knocking on your door. Yours neither, fuck off. Have a nice evening. Fuck off. Thank you."

Jamie hated it when Tash lost it. He was extremely nervous about his father opening the door.

Tash knocked again, quite madly. "Open up, George, come on, let's have you."

A key turned in the door and it slowly opened. Sure enough, standing before Tash was her impossibly young father. Happily, observed Tash, only his jacket and tie were missing. His shirt and trousers remained on.

"Sorry to piss on the party George, but your wife has gone into labour, and she's in the St. Thomas Hospital," announced Tash. She said the word 'wife' with extra venom and considerable amplitude to ensure she reached the depths of the dimly lit bedroom behind her father. George looked stunned.

"Who is it, George?" came a female voice from the bedroom.

"It's… my wife."

"Your wife?!" shrieked the lady.

"No. No. Not here. She's in hospital…" explained George to his lady friend. He turned to his daughter. "Is she OK? How do you know her? Who are you? Is she OK?"

"She'd like you with her please," replied Tash.

George looked at his daughter, then his son. An observer might say his face registered some recognition of the pair before him. Or maybe his conscience was getting the better of him.

"Please, can you go to her? Now," pleaded Tash, suddenly quite emotional. No part of this moment was how she would have ever wanted to meet her younger father.

George reached back into the room, picked up his tie and jacket and brushed past his children into the corridor. He stopped and suddenly felt the need to explain:

"I've never done anything like this before." Then he turned and was on his way.

"George?" appealed the voice in the bedroom. "George?"

"You lose marks for this George," said Tash.

George pressed the lift button, but when no doors opened, he opted for the stairs.

Tash looked down to see her father's handwriting on a scrunched-up sheet of paper. She picked it up.

"He's dropped his plans," she said, and after a cursory glance, she pocketed the paper.

"He did say this was a day he wanted to change, sis," said Jamie.

Jamie always arrived at the right conclusion, thought Tash. Annoying prick that he was. She fell into her brother's arms and squeezed him tight, tears falling from her cheeks. This was all too familiar. Her own marriage had been an extensive catalogue of errors, and the parallels of a cheating husband and delivering a baby solo were too much for her.

A familiar voice broke the silence. "That's them!" said Ruby, from along the corridor. A security guard was suddenly approaching Jamie and Tash at a breakneck pace.

"Come on!" shouted Jamie. They set off down the stairs faster than they thought possible.

In the hotel lobby, they caught up with their father, but at the doors, George took a right into the evening street, and Jamie and Tash took a left and followed the road to the same ramp that they descended on the C5 earlier on in this mad hour. They took the corner a matter of seconds before the security guard leapt out into the evening rain.

"We've done it, Tash" said Jamie, short of breath. "We've done it! We told Dad about Mum, AND we're going home! What a day!"

Euphoria swept across Jamie's face. Tash was thinking of one thing only, and the sooner she held her son again, the better. They both sprinted the full length of the underground car park, keeping in the shadows in case the PC was still loitering. She wasn't. Jamie spotted the dark corner where they abandoned the C5 and led his sister over the final few metres. Running in boots and wellies was difficult, and their calf muscles were burning as they reached their destination. Both peered into the dark space at the same time. Both inhaled deeply at the same time. Both said "Shit" at the same time.

The small parking space was empty.

Empty.

Utterly full of nothing.

They stood in silence. Silence only broken by the sound of two steel Transit van doors clunking open, and a massive suited giant leaping out onto the ground. In less than two seconds Jamie and Tash were being restrained by this brutal machine. He was unreal. Three seconds later they were bundled into the back of the transit van. Five seconds more and the van was screeching out of the car park.

NINE

"Are you kidnapping us? Cos we've had a very long day, and I'm never sure how it works with wees?" asked Tash. Her refusal to accept her reality had instilled her with some kind of intrepid self-confidence, and Jamie was unsettled by it.

They sat in the moving Transit van on an uncomfortable bench seat. In front of them was a vast tarpaulin sheet covering a mysterious object, and behind that, the giant was staring back at them, gently rubbing the scratches on his face. Tash had been pretty brutal in her attempts to avoid abduction. But then who wouldn't?

"I mean, I don't need one now, but you should have a contingency. Bit of a sitch with my pelvic floor."

The giant ignored her. He was easily six feet four or five and even seated he had to duck his head to fit in the van.

The Transit continued shaking along the streets of London. Tash tried to start a conversation one final time.

"Let me know when we're halfway. We can switch seats, shake things up a bit? New memories?"

Jamie peered under the tarpaulin, and his suspicions were confirmed. The C5 had been carefully lifted into the van and abducted with them.

"You know this is ours?" said Jamie.

The giant pushed the tarpaulin back down, then produced a screwdriver from a box.

"Quattro?" he asked intimidatingly.

Jamie and Tash squared up in their seats. He'd not uttered a word since he'd bundled them into the back, and now he was holding a screwdriver. He repeated his threat.

"Quattro?"

Jamie glanced at Tash, who shrugged back at him. Jamie looked back at the giant and finally found his voice, not that he recognised it. It was quiet, dry, and he sounded about nine.

"Quattro." Jamie nodded, as if to say he understood.

The giant turned his attention to Tash. "Quattro?"

Tash nodded frantically and copied Jamie. "Quattro."

The giant looked exasperated now.

"Do you want a can of Quattro?"

The giant leant to his side and jammed the screwdriver into the lid of a cool box. It popped off. He reached in and held up a can of Quattro.

Jamie sighed audibly before suffering a bout of verbal diarrhoea.

"Oh! Yes, please." He took the can. "It's a drink, Tash. Look. He got it from the cool box thing. It's a drink. He used the screwdriver to open the lock. On the cool box! He was offering a drink. It's called Quattro. From the cool box."

"Yes, thanks, Jamie. I saw that. Do let me know if he stabs one of us," replied Tash, accepting a can for herself.

"Turn this up, Raymond," instructed the giant through the glass. He clearly had one ear on the radio.

Raymond complied, and Hazel Dean was soon singing how she's got to find a man, and the giant was joining in.

"Searchin' looking for love..." he sang.

"Do you know why we're here? Or are you just paid to kidnap and sing?" asked Tash.

He stared back at her.

"Sorry, I assume you're paid. Maybe you do this for free?"

"Strong words from a thief," replied the giant.

"I've never stolen a thing in my whole life."

"Well, that's not true, is it?" said Jamie, raising his fizzy drink to his lips and pouring some into his mouth and some down his stolen suit.

"Shut the fuck, Jamie!"

"I'm just saying. You did have that phase."

"Everyone has a phase. I was a teenager."

Jamie turned to the giant to defend his sister. "She returned most of it."

"Fuck sake, Jamie. Stop talking."

"And it's not easy breaking back into a zoo."

"Jamie!"

****

There was no other way of describing their current situation than 'locked in a cage in a warehouse', but that doesn't adequately portray the warmth of it all. The warehouse was immaculately painted and maintained. Racks of large brown boxes and crates filled the space, and the cage was more of a secure central office area. Essentially, Jamie noted, the cage was to keep people out rather than to keep people in. For inside the vast fenced-in area were desks, sofas, cupboards, rugs and lamps. Tash sat alongside Jamie on an oxblood leather Chesterfield sofa. Each clutched a china cup of piping hot Earl Grey tea. The rotund driver turned out to be a late 50-something softy called Raymond. And embarrassingly for him, the central office phone had rung twice, and on both occasions, it was clear that his wife was on the other end demanding his immediate attendance. He was fighting his conscience, should he be a model employee or be a model husband? The former was winning but it wasn't without its challenges. His perspiration levels visibly doubled during a call with his wife.

Half an hour or so ago, the giant had left the siblings and the C5 in the solitary care of Raymond, who spent longer apologising for the inconvenience than explaining the purpose of it. The silence was broken by the distant hum of an engine which soon grew louder and Raymond stood up delightedly. "Here he is! Here he is." He rubbed his hands like all his problems would now be over. A long black Mercedes limo drove alongside their cage. The rear door opened, and a twenty-something gentlemen climbed out. He was dressed in a dark overcoat and wore black gloves. Raymond unlocked the cage office door and welcomed him in.

"Good evening, Mr Hobson."

"Evening, Raymond. How's Margaret?"

"She's very well, sir, thank you. It's Maureen."

"Excellent. Excellent," replied Mr Hobson, clearly now distracted by the sight of the pimped C5 vehicle parked before him.

"This is Tash, and this is Jamie," explained Raymond.

"Dudley Hobson," said the businessman, offering his hand to the sister and brother simultaneously, without averting his gaze from the C5.

"This is just a misunderstanding actually," said Jamie.

"Good. Good!" replied Dudley. "So, who do you work for?"

"Erm. Decathlon." Jamie was happy to comply with all negotiations.

Dudley glanced at Raymond. "Who are they?"

Raymond shrugged.

"They sell bikes and outdoor stuff," explained Jamie. "Brent Cross branch?"

Dudley was non-plussed.

"Tents?" said Jamie, like this would break the impasse.

Dudley turned to Tash.

"London School of Economics, I'm a lecturer," she answered.

"The LSE?" snorted Dudley. "Are you telling me the LSE are involved in industrial espionage?"

"No. I don't think so," replied Tash innocently. "I teach Financial Risk Management."

Dudley waited for a smile from Tash that didn't arrive.

"Are you taking the piss?" he asked.

"No. No. They seem to be a bit, erm.." interjected Raymond. "A bit confused." He didn't want the convivial atmosphere turning sour.

Dudley listened to Raymond and then turned to the sister and brother and tapped the C5. "What can you tell me about this?"

"Grandad made it," said Jamie.

Dudley turned to Raymond. "Is this true? Who is their Grandad?"

"He's dead apparently. It's all bit tricky," said Raymond.

"Dead?" replied Dudley, suddenly alarmed. "No-one's died in the facility, have they? Who's died?"

Raymond simply shook a "No" and then shrugged.

Dudley took a deep breath then pointed at the C5 again.

"This is the Sinclair C5. And by 'Sinclair', I mean Clive Sinclair. He developed this. Well, he developed this before you butchered it. It's highly sensitive, and it's top secret. Nobody outside Sinclair has seen this or has access to this. The public launch is scheduled for January. I've already said too much. So, it begs the question, what are you doing with it?" Dudley was extremely friendly. He was simply confused by his circumstances. Just over an hour ago he was attending a trade exhibition for entertainment technology, and then suddenly his pager went crazy. A member of his trusted staff had seen an adapted C5 in the basement of the hotel. It was the most bizarre evening of his career.

"Have you checked inventory?" Dudley asked Raymond.

"Nothing is missing," replied the flustered little man. "They're all still there."

"Are we under arrest?" asked Jamie.

"What?" came Dudley's reply, mortified at the thought.

"I wondered if we were under arrest in any kind of way? Cos I'm on a probationary period at work, and I'd need to declare this," Jamie was looking anxious. "I took a couple of tyres home by mistake, without paying."

Dudley stared at Jamie.

"They were on an electric bike at the time," explained Jamie. "Like I say. Just a mix-up."

"An electric bike?" muttered Raymond. What will this fool imagine next?

"You can leave any time you like," said Dudley gesturing at the open gate.

"Oh. Great!" Jamie looked visibly relieved and starting to walk to the C5.

"But you can't take that," said the troubleshooter, pointing at the C5.

"But it's ours," said Tash.

"It can't be yours, for the simple reason that none have been sold yet," he replied.

"That is an excellent reply, Tash," said Jamie, impressed by Dudley's summary of facts.

"But before you skedaddle, could someone tell me what's going on?" asked Dudley.

Tash and Jamie looked at one another, then Jamie turned to Dudley.

"It's a time machine. We came here so my dad could watch my sister being born."

Dudley listened as Jamie pointed at Tash, then nodded slowly, trying to hide his irritation.

"You don't want to tell me. OK… Who do you work for at the LSE?" he asked Tash.

"Francine Dexter."

"Never heard of her. But I do know Alex McGaskill down there…" Dudley let this name hang in the air, but if Tash was concerned by his revelation, she was hiding it well. Dudley extracted a small pad and pen and wrote on it.

"So let's see what Alex can tell me about Francine Baxter."

"Dexter," corrected Tash.

Dudley scratched out his writing and corrected his mistake. "Dexter."

He replaced his pad threateningly into his overcoat pocket, but this lost some of its impact as he was trying to place it in the side with no inner pocket. His eye contact with Tash was broken by him opening his coat to find a home for the pad, not to mention the pen which fell onto the floor not once but twice.

"So it's decided. I shall have to speak with Alex and then Francine. Maybe she'll give me some answers. Just make sure they don't take that anywhere, Raymond."

Raymond nodded.

Dudley thought for a moment and then reached over to the largest desk which was overloaded with paperwork, boxes of stationery and a multitude of electronic gadgets. He lifted a Polaroid Instamatic camera.

"Just in case you're thinking of disappearing…" he smiled and took a photo of Tash and Jamie staring blankly back at him. Raymond was standing behind them by the C5.

"I know people that can find… people," threatened Dudley. It wasn't his best line. He really needed to plan the end of sentences before he started them. He waited for the photo to spit out of the base of the camera and then wafted it dry as he walked back to his car. He failed to open the rear door and had to knock on the driver's window for the giant to lean into the back and pop up the lock to allow him to climb into the car.

"You don't need to lock it all the time, Jermaine," was the final thing they heard before the car pulled away. Dudley made a point of gesturing at both his eyes and then pointing at Tash with the same fingers as the car disappeared. He'd clearly seen both Godfather films.

This might have left Tash with some constant fear of any repercussions, but the car was soon in view again as it reversed back out of the warehouse.

"Only one way out, sir," helped Raymond "The other door is blocked."

The car slowly retraced its route in, the whole time with Dudley repeating his 'my eyes are on you' gesture at Tash, whilst waving the photo at her. And then the car was gone.

"I'm sure we'll get to the bottom of this," stammered Raymond.

"I'm sure we will. You kidnapped us," replied Tash.

Raymond looked mortified. "No-one's been kidnapped!"

And then the phone rang again. Raymond jerked to pick it up and listened for a second.

"I'm doing my very best darling, I really am."

Sensing he had eavesdroppers, Raymond turned his back on Jamie and Tash and attempted to appease his wife as discreetly as possible by whispering directly into the receiver.

Tash gestured to Jamie and at the C5. Together they moved in on it, safely out of Raymond's gaze. It was Jamie who first spotted obstacle number one: The cable-tied power cables were protruding from behind the seat, all still plugged into the main socket bank, but it looked severely scratched from being dragged over the tarmac roads and pavements. Despite that, it appeared workable other than the primary wire that extended from it was missing the three-pin plug at the end. It most probably ripped off during their ejection from Grandma's garage attic. In its place were three sorry wires, brown, blue and green, each with copper tips fraying from the end.

"How would you feel about holding them into a socket for me?" whispered Tash.

Even Jamie realised this was a joke. He scanned the cage to identify something – anything – from where he could steal a plug. Raymond was shuffling from one foot to another as he appealed again down the phone "I can't leave until I hear from Mr Hobson.... No, it's not that simple, I..." Raymond leant in towards the phone "I have to detain a couple of individuals in the office… I've no idea, they're a bit confused, so…" Raymond listened again. "Well no, I think they'd rather be somewhere else too." Then he baulked. "I'm not a kidnapper!… No-one's going to prison… I just need to keep them here until Mr Hobson … Hello? Hello?"

Raymond realised his call had come to an abrupt end. He reluctantly placed the receiver back on the base. Bolstered by his worsening domestic situation, he decided he should try to help move things along a little at work, so turned to his prisoners.

"I don't suppose you want to try again and explain where you got this? My wife needs me to pick her up from work, and the traffic's always a nightmare. I really should have set off by now."

Tash glanced over at Jamie and then back at her captor.

"We can show you," replied Tash.

"Show me?"

"We need a plug," said Jamie, holding up the bare wires.

Raymond thought for a moment. What's the worst that could happen? He took a step over to examine the wires, then glanced at Jamie and Tash.

TEN

Raymond had removed a 13-amp plug from a broken fan heater that sat amongst other superfluous office equipment in the bottom drawer of a tall filing cabinet. He tightened the plug cover expertly, having speedily wired the inside. Next, he walked to the only solid wall of the office and dragged some heavy brown boxes to one side, revealing a cluster of power outlets beneath a large fuse box. He placed the plug into a socket and flicked on the switch.

Immediately the TV powered on, and the screen glowed grey.

Raymond walked over to look at it. "That needs tuning." He leant in to scroll the tuning dial on the side of the case.

"No – we need to tune it back to the computer signal," said Jamie, but he couldn't stop Raymond climbing into the front seat. Jamie leant over Raymond and tuned it back, just as the white Sinclair Research screen gave way to the Destination Date request. He immediately started typing.

"Get in, Tash!" said Jamie, as his fingers typed 25 12 20.

He hit the ENTER button to get the next prompt.

As Tash climbed in behind Raymond he suddenly looked concerned. "Hang on, tell me what you're doing?"

The screen went blank, flickered, and then refreshed just as it had in the garage attic.

Time :

"Two a.m," said Tash. "It was two a.m., Jamie."

"What was two a.m?" asked Raymond.

"When we set off," replied Tash.

"One of you is going to have to explain what's happening or I'm going to turn this off."

As Jamie expertly typed, he did his best to set the record straight.

"It's perfectly simple. Grandad bought this C5 when he retired, and we used to play on it, and then he decided to pimp it up to be a Christmas ride."

"Decided to what it up?" asked Raymond.

"Pimp," explained Jamie.

"Then he died and then twenty years later we found it again," said Tash.

The screen went blank, and then text appeared again.

Location :

As Jamie strained to lean over Raymond, he started to type the word: Sheffield. The scroll down boxes appeared again and immediately he was delighted to see the option of Sheffield, Home. He selected it.

"What are you trying to do – exactly?" asked Raymond. "I just need to know how you got this? What's all the typing about?"

ENTER TO TRAVEL appeared on the screen. Tash stifled a giddy squeal. The past couple of hours had felt like an eternity. Her son would awaken from his sleep oblivious to the fact that his mum had been on a horrific diversion through the 20th century.

Jamie lifted his finger over the ENTER button and paused. "Would you mind if I sat there, Raymond?"

Raymond considered this. "Why?"

"Just, you know, so I can demonstrate how we got this," reasoned Jamie.

Raymond absorbed this for a moment.

"Why do you need to sit here?"

"It can sometimes give an electric shock," lied Jamie. And thinking quickly, he pointed to his boots, and Tash's. "That's why we have rubber soles."

Raymond's 58-year-old knees were about to seize up for the night, so the prospect of getting out of this dodgem car was incredibly appealing. Naturally, it was far more difficult to clamber out than in, so it wasn't an incredibly elegant dismount. His left leg was now successfully on the warehouse floor, but his right was trapped beneath the foot pedal of the C5, and he had to yank at this a couple of times to free it. When it finally loosened, his whole body hurled towards the floor so he reached out his arm to catch his fall. His hand knocked the dial on the TV, and the screen display turned to the snowstorm. Electric static buzzed through the TV speakers as a flustered Raymond found his feet and apologised to Jamie.

"Get in, Jamie," whispered Tash "The computer knows where we want to go."

The sound of the interference was incredibly loud – sensory overload for Jamie, who was looking for the volume dial.

"Sorry, sorry," said Raymond. "Just retune it."

Raymond played with the tuning dial, and the screen started to change. The static noises and snowstorm went up and down and up and down. Jamie froze to the spot as he waited for Raymond to make this noise go away. All eyes stared at the screen, as Raymond spun the dial.

"Here we are…" said Raymond, leaning with one hand on the C5 seat, preventing Jamie from sitting on it. Finally, the interference dipped as a shadow appeared on the screen. Raymond fine-tuned it once more, and a voice replaced the noise. Raymond peered behind the TV and pulled out a telescopic aerial which made the screen image beautifully crisp. Despite themselves, Jamie and Tash were both intrigued to see a TV broadcast from long, long ago. Except it was live.

The lady on the screen was dressed smartly and sitting behind a desk. She was reading the Six O'Clock News. The whole set looked very sparse, but for an image behind the anchor of a mother cradling a distressed baby.

"… Our correspondent Michael Buerk has been back to Korem after four months, and he found the situation far worse," said Sue Lawley.

The screen changed to an African wasteland, and hundreds of faces gazed lifelessly at the camera lens.

A reporter's voice calmly narrated the distressing footage.

"*Dawn, and as the sun breaks through the piercing chill of night on the plain outside Korem, it lights up a biblical famine… Now, in the 20th century. This place, say workers here, is the closest thing to Hell on Earth.*"

Confused and suffering children's wails spilt from the tiny portable TV and filled the cage. The three viewers stared wide-eyed at mourning parents, bereft as sons and daughters faded in their arms. Brothers watched helplessly as sisters took their final breaths. Infants stared in confusion at their mothers lying motionless on dusty ground, unaware they were being orphaned as TV cameras filmed their horror unfurling.

Jamie leant into his sister. "This is history. This. This is famous. We did this in GCSE."

Tash ignored her brother, transfixed as a mother watched her daughter die in front of her. Families stood in line at a makeshift morgue to grieve the loss of starved relatives, as more corpses were added to the dead, one after another after another after another.

Jamie saw Raymond reach to wipe a tear from his eye. Tash let hers flow freely and drip onto her hunched-up skirt.

"This report," began Jamie, realising that his voice was faltering, "this is the report that Bob Geldof saw. This is what made him angry. This is what made him put Band Aid together."

Jamie was conflicted. His eyes were hot with tears, but his chest was tight with excitement to be witnessing the exact moment that would change the world forever. In the coming weeks, an unprecedented collective of British pop-stars would abandon all their tabloid rivalry and chart aspirations to assemble as one to record the very first charity record. With it, they arguably changed the approach to fundraising on a global scale forever.

Jamie smiled at his sister, a thought filling his head. "He's watching this right now! We're watching it, and he's watching it! We did this in GCSE!" he repeated.

Raymond heard the whisper. "Who's watching?"

"It's nothing." Jamie realised his euphoria was a little out of tone with the room.

"Terrible," said Raymond. "This shouldn't be happening in 1984. It's terrible."

The report ended. All three were transfixed by the tiny portable TV screen. The newsreader changed the subject. Bizarrely, a photograph of Bob Geldof was now on screen where the mother and daughter had been before the VT.

"We are just receiving reports that the founding member and lead singer of the punk group The Boomtown Rats, Bob Geldof, has been involved in a serious motor collision in central London this evening."

"They're never still going, are they?" said Raymond, walking away to answer the phone one more time. If a band weren't on the telly anymore, he assumed they'd split up. The newsreader continued:

"A taxi and an unknown vehicle were involved in a head-on collision in Bloomsbury just after five pm. The taxi driver escaped uninjured. A spokesman from Mr Geldof's record label, Phonogram, say he sustained head injuries and is currently in a serious but stable condition in St Thomas' Hospital. Police are appealing for witnesses after a three-wheel silver or white go-kart was seen escaping the scene. It is unclear where the vehicle is being hidden, but the public are being told not to approach the driver or drivers. It is not known if Mr Geldof was wearing a seat belt. Campaigners for seat belts safety are keen to see the government extend last year's seat belt laws to cover the compulsory wearing of rear seatbelts in vehicles where they are fitted."

Tash was looking at her brother.

"Jamie. The computer knows where we want to go. Hit ENTER."

But Jamie was dumbstruck by what he'd just seen.

"Jamie. I can't reach it. Hit it."

"Tash. Did you not hear what she just said?"

"Jamie. I need to see my baby. NOW!"

"Tash. He hasn't seen the report. Bob Geldof hasn't seen the report."

"What? You don't know that. Hit ENTER."

Jamie stared at the TV News. It was now covering the afternoon's visit of President Mitterrand to London, but Jamie could only hear the ringing in his ears.

"Tash. We changed history."

Raymond was oblivious to the exchange, he was receiving another ticking off from his wife.

"Jamie. We've just found out that the police and now the whole of London are looking for us. We're one click away from my son. He needs his mum. Click ENTER Jamie, please click ENTER!"

"Tash! Bob Geldof is in hospital because of us! Probably unconscious! Christ! Because of this thing. He hasn't seen that news report. The news report that made him contact all his famous mates to record a song that raised millions and millions of pounds for all those babies we just watched on the news. You can't seriously be picking one baby over thousands of others?"

Tash glared at her brother as she absorbed his response.

"So, what are you saying? We form a band and record a Christmas song? What the fuck are you going on about? Shall I call up Sting and see if he can get some mates together? Oh no, wait – I haven't got a fucking signal on my fucking phone cos fucking mobile phones haven't been fucking invented cos it's nineteen fucking eighty-four!"

Tash took a breath to let Jamie think. Then she started again, with a more placatory tone. "We need to cut our losses and get the fuck out of here, Jamie. Stop being a prick about things. Besides – they'll still do Live Aid!"

"Are you kidding? Live Aid got its name from Band Aid. You're not thinking straight, Tash. We're involved in an international catastrophe of internationally catastrophic proportions!"

"Jamie, you are so dramatic. Every little thing is not a catastrophe. Hit ENTER and do it now!" Tash strained to lean past her brother to the Spectrum keyboard. Her finger was just three or four inches away from the ENTER key. Jamie was leaning back in his chair to block her like he used to as a child when she wanted to swap seats and ride up front. With one final push, Tash lurched forward and thumped the ENTER key. The TV screen went black.

Tash glared at the screen. It was a long stare. In fact, she suddenly realised, this might be the longest stare she'd ever done. She was yet to blink.

"What's happened?"

"Sorry!" said Raymond, holding up a plug from the other side of the cage. "I think I kicked the plug out!" He was laughing in an oblivious way that made Tash want to smash his face in. And she hated violence.

"Put it back in," demanded Tash. "Now!"

"No can do, I'm afraid, love," answered Raymond as he pulled on his overcoat. "There's been a bit of a change of plan, actually."

"What plan?" replied Tash, turning to her brother. "What plan? What was the plan and what's the new plan? The plan's the plug. Tell him, Jamie. The plug is the only plan."

"My wife needs a lift," explained Raymond.

"There's not much room in here, dickhead!" replied Tash.

Raymond laughed. "No. In my car. I just called Dudley's car phone, but he's not picking up. So it looks like I'm going to have to take you with me."

"Where are we going?" asked Jamie. "Can we come back? Cos we need to come back."

"Of course you can come back. But I can't leave you here, you see. Especially with her being a bit weird and everything."

"I can hear you," said Tash.

"We're heading to Woolies in Lambeth," said Raymond like this helped. He extracted a large dust sheet from a drawer to cover the C5. "Out you get."

"And how will you explain us to your wife?" asked Jamie, climbing out as Raymond continued hiding the stolen go-kart.

"Well, that's the tricky bit actually. I'm glad you brought that up," said Raymond, helping a reluctant Tash out of her seat and dropping the sheet over the rear of the C5.

"So?" asked Tash.

"You're, er, you're going to have to go in the boot." Raymond looking genuinely pained by this. More so than them.

ELEVEN

"He's not your normal kidnapper, is he?" remarked Jamie as he pulled open a packet of bacon flavour Piglets. Tash slurped Um Bongo through a straw. Both were hideously squashed in the boot of Raymond's car. For years Raymond had dreamed of owning an automatic Ford Granada in racing green with black vinyl roof, but Holburn Motors car lot hadn't been selling one the day he settled for a four-speed manual Austin Princess in red. He'd left two Duracell pop up torches in there, a tartan rug, some snacks, and had secured the boot slightly open with rope, so they didn't "accidentally suffocate like that tortoise did on Blue Peter."

Radio One was playing loudly and 'I Want To Break Free' by Queen was accompanying their uncomfortable journey to Woolies. The irony wasn't lost on Tash.

"This is like a sleepover or something," said Jamie as he plopped a handful of the pig–shaped crisps into his mouth. He stopped chewing and squinted at the bag with the help of his torch.

"These crisps hurt. Should crisps hurt?"

"Right. OK. Here's the latest plan," said Tash. "As soon as we get back to the C5 we do NOT deviate from this. Plug it in. Switch on the computer, and the moment the startup screen pops up, it's "25, 12, 20, 0200 hours, Home, ENTER." Even if the telly screen doesn't work, those are the things we need to type in. Just wait a minute after the computer beeps and then we go for it."

"Tash, there are two reasons we can't do that," replied Jamie, persevering with another mouth full of bacon crisps.

"Two?" asked Tash. "I thought it was just one. I thought we just had to write a song, book a studio and assemble a supergroup of singers? I thought we were classing our charity record as one sort of overall project thing?"

"The song's written, Tash. We don't need to write the song!" This was one of the few times Jamie had missed his sister's sarcasm. He started to sing to help the penny drop, "It's Christmas time, we've no need to be afraid…?"

"Beautiful that, Jamie. Do you have Bono's address?" There was silence, but Tash couldn't leave it at that. "And it's 'there's' no need to be afraid, not 'we've'. Sake, you don't even know the fucking words."

"Although, unless we sort things out with Bob Geldof, the song won't get written if you know what I mean. Now, this is where it gets confusing." Jamie looked lost in thought. "If the song were never written, maybe we'd just forget it when we got home? Weird."

"What's the other reason stopping my exit strategy? What's reason two?"

"Well. You'll laugh at this," said Jamie. His manner implied that his sister would not find his latest problem even remotely funny.

"Try me," said Tash, flicking her eye with Um Bongo as she released the plastic straw from her mouth too soon.

"Well. It's actually a very good thing that I didn't hit ENTER when you told me to earlier on in the warehouse."

Silence. Then Tash pointed her torch at her face and said as intimidatingly as possible.

"How so?"

Jamie was completely unaware of the full impact of his revelation, so embarked on it with vigour and a fresh mouthful of Piglets.

"Remember when we set off? From Grandma's garage loft?"

"It's funny you should say that. Of. Fucking. Course. I. Fucking. Do… Next?"

Jamie choked on a Piglet.

"These are delicious, and they hurt." He squinted at the packet one more time.

"What's-the-actual-funny-other-actual-reason-that-we-can't-actually-go-back-to-my-actual-baby-boy?"

"The millennium bug," said Jamie.

Tash waited.

Then, losing her patience, she opted to ask again whilst simultaneously squirting her juice box through the straw into her brother's face. "Speak – More – Words!"

Jamie dried his face on his sleeve and continued.

"The millennium bug was supposed to kick in when 1999 turned to the year 2000. Basically, all the computers invented before like 1989 or 1990 had basic calendars on their motherboard."

Tash stared again. She held up her Um Bongo juice box as if to threaten, "I have more."

Jamie continued. "So, when they invented computers, dates were six figures. Right? Day day, month month, year year. Like today would be 23, 10, 84."

"With you. Happy birthday me. Woo!"

"Nobody thought about the changing century. So nearly every eighties computer had a fault built-in. It wouldn't shift to the 1st of January 2000. It would go back to the 1st of January 1900. It only had one hundred years programmed into it. Which meant all the programs were messed up, cos like a Tuesday wouldn't turn into a Wednesday over New Year's Eve. It would turn into like a Sunday or whatever the 1st of January was in 1900. Which meant all the systems needed updating. People thought bank cash machines would stop working. Planes would fall from the sky."

"Nice recap. Why am I having it now?" asked Tash.

"The Sinclair computer Grandad used to make his time machine… It was made in the early eighties. It had no future-proof technology. So, when we typed in 1984, it would only take two numbers. 19 or 84. We chose 84, and here we are."

"Joy," said Tash as patiently as she could. "What's your point?"

"Earlier on, when we typed in 20 for our destination year… The computer would assume we meant 1920," explained Jamie.

Jamie was now rifling through a paper bag for more sustenance. He removed a Texan bar.

"Nougat?" he read. "Worth a punt." He ripped the bar open and took a big bite. It was chewier than he predicted, and his teeth were stuck.

"Well, that's a good thing, right? We dodged a bullet," responded Tash.

Jamie's face did a squinty expression that demonstrated, "Well, kind of, but I have good news/bad news," while his teeth wrestled with the glue that was a Texan.

He chewed for what felt like ten or eleven years. 'I Want To Break Free' turned into Wham!'s 'Freedom'. It was a bump in the road causing Tash's head to hit the boot lid that prompted her next explosion.

"For fuck's sake, Jamie, talk to me! That's a good thing, right? We just need to fix it, right?"

"Well, as I see it there is no fix. We are stuck on the dates that the Sinclair computer recognises," said Jamie.

Tash thought for a moment. "Hang on. If what you're saying is right… when we typed in 84, how come we didn't go forward to 2084?"

"It's a good question. An excellent question. But what I'd say to that question… is…"

Jamie took another mouthful of Texan.

"Oh my actual shitting hell, speak Jamie. Speak. Stop eating crap sweets."

Through a mouth full of 'chocolate flavoured candy' and nougat, Jamie was able to make himself heard.

"I don't know why. But we didn't did we? We went back to 1984. Maybe the computer only recognises the century it was programmed in," he shrugged. "Funny really."

"No, Jamie. No. It's anything but funny. So, you're saying we can't go back to my baby ever?" Tash's voice was becoming more and more shrill as the realisation sunk in. "We are stuck here? In the shittest decade with the shittest sweets and the shittest cars – forever?"

'Freedom' fought with Jamie's munching noises.

"Great music though," he replied, mainly because he meant it.

The car slammed to a halt, and both their heads struck the back of the rear seat.

The engine stopped, then the radio. The driver's door slammed and they heard Raymond's Hush Puppy shoes walk to the rear of the car. He stage whispered to them through the opening of the boot.

"I'm going to ask you both for your continued understanding of the situation. I won't be long. I'll be as quick as possible."

Tash was fiddling with something, and Jamie tried to pick a ball of nougat out of his wisdom tooth. Raymond waited for another second or two, then spoke:

"Knock once if you can hear me." He leant into the boot and strained to hear one more time.

The sound of the boot hitting Raymond's face was strangely spongey with an undertone of snapping cartilage. It took him and Jamie by surprise, Tash less so. She had been undoing the knot in the rope that held the boot ajar. As Tash sat up into the evening air, she saw Raymond clutching his bloody nose with a stream of scarlet running down onto his C&A suit.

"Oh my God, Raymond, I'm so sorry!" said Tash with genuine concern. "I didn't know you were there."

"We knew he was there. He was talking to us," replied Jamie.

"Yes, I knew he was there, but not there there!"

"I think I need to sit down…" mumbled Raymond before falling and hitting the ground face first.

"That's it. You have a sit down," said Tash leaning out of the boot to get a better look of Raymond with her flip torch.

TWELVE

Tash and Jamie sat in the front of the Princess, Tash fumbling around the ignition for the keys.

"No keys. NO KEYS!" she shouted.

"Do you think I should drive? You don't have a licence."

"You don't have a fucking licence. You haven't been born yet! Where are the fucking keys?"

It was a swift manoeuvre for Jamie to climb out, open the boot lid, fumble in Raymond's pockets, remove the keys, check Raymond's pulse one last time, slam the boot and return to the passenger seat. Tash took the keys and started the engine. As she engaged first gear with a grinding crunch of the gearbox, they were both jolted by tapping on Jamie's window.

"Who are you? Where's Raymond?" said a middle-aged lady wearing a brown anorak. She knocked again, this time much harder. "Stop! Stop! I'm his wife. Who are you?"

"It's his wife," said Jamie.

"Yes. Yes. Thank you, Jamie. Yes. I did put two and two together," replied Tash as she revved the balls off the engine.

"Thiefs!" shouted Maureen, who immediately thought better to herself and started to mutter, "Thieves? It's thieves, isn't it? Not thiefs." Then she screamed again. "THIEVES!"

The Princess sped off down the amber lit street.

"Tash! She needed a lift! This is HER car! You just left her!"

"Do you mean we should have offered her a ride? With her unconscious husband in the boot?"

A police siren whirred to life, and a blue flashing strobe illuminated the inside of the Austin.

"Stop, Tash. Stop," said Jamie, glancing over his shoulder to see Maureen climbing into the back of a panda car just before it set off behind them.

"Two unconscious men, a stolen C5 and stolen a car, Jamie. How would someone explain that sort of thing? Asking for a friend."

"Tell them we're taking him to the hospital?"

"It's good, Jamie, but it's not the one. They might want to know why he's in the boot, you see? Seems a bit sort of harsh, taking someone to hospital in a locked boot."

At this, Tash performed a handbrake turn that saw the Princess change direction by 180 degrees as the police car continued past them. Tash watched the police car attempt a three-point turn in mad traffic, but not before a lorry and a bus placed themselves between the panda car and the Princess. Tash took a sharp left to shake the police off their tail. Or her tail. She wasn't sure if it meant your own single tail when you shake someone off it, or if two of you shared the one. She could figure this out later.

"Hospital!" shouted Jamie, pointing at a road sign along the road.

"What?"

"A sign. For the hospital!"

"We're not actually taking him to hospital Jamie, that was a line for the police wasn't it?"

"Well – where are you going? I don't understand."

Tash slammed on the brakes. Both lurched forward as the car stopped.

"You're right. We don't know where Raymond works. And that's where the C5 is. This is terrible."

"We can ask him when he comes around?" said Jamie.

"Yes. That's one idea. And no idea is a bad idea. Even though that one is. I don't think we should open the boot at all, to be honest. Seems a bit kidnappery."

They sat for a moment then Tash suddenly rammed the car in reverse and retraced their route to the previous junction at high speed. The police car sailed past the end of the road, and Tash was able to reverse into oncoming traffic then continue a few cars behind the police. She stopped at the Woolworths where Raymond had driven them and peered around.

"Come on," snapped Tash as she opened the car door.

****

Inside Woolworths were the stragglers of an after-hours training session. Tash and Jamie marched over to the team.

"Excuse me, has anyone seen Maureen?" asked Tash.

"We're closed," explained the manager, a stern look on her face.

"I don't want to buy anything," replied Tash.

"Look at these TVs!" Jamie was genuinely beguiled by the retro-looking machines encased in greys and blacks and veneered wood. Sab, a trainee shop assistant, shared Jamie's enthusiasm. She followed Jamie's gaze to the colour TV and video display.

"Lovely, isn't it? Check this out…" Sab picked up a remote control with a wire connecting it to the TV and pressed '0'. The screen flickered to show William Shatner and Leonard Nimoy discussing something quite pressing while leaning on a wobbly wall of the Starship Enterprise.

"See those colours?" said Sab.

"A remote control with a wire!" replied Jamie.

"The VCR has infrared remote," Sab sniffed a sale. "Ferguson Videostar. Front loader. Fourteen-day timer!"

"Fourteen-day timer?" asked Jamie.

"We had product training after work." Sab pointed the remote at the TV and paused the channel.

"I didn't think you could pause TV in the 80s?"

"In the what?"

"I thought it was a Sky plus or TiVo thing?" Jamie was a little bemused. "Mum used to tell us in her day, you couldn't pause live TV?"

Sab looked for a smile on this joker's face that didn't appear.

"This is a recording," Sab smiled as she flicked the slow-motion button and Captain Kirk slowly raised his hand to his chin. "Check it out – completely clear screen. No lines. Same with forwarding too."

She pressed a button, and the Star Trek credits rolled in double speed.

"It's got four heads," she explained. "We just did it in training."

"Four?!"

"I know, right!?"

"What does that mean?"

"The thing inside normally uses two heads that the tape passes through. They read or record the video and audio. This has four," replied Sab. "Which is double. Twice the quality."

"That's lovely, but we're looking for Maureen," said Tash. "Is she still here?"

"Maureen left. Who wants to know?" asked the manager.

"Oh no, she left?" Tash acted as disappointed as she could manage, secretly hoping Maureen wouldn't re-appear with the police at any moment.

"We need to get a message to her husband," said Tash. "You don't know where he works, do you? It's a warehouse somewhere?"

"I can tell her you were looking for her. Write the message down, and I'll make sure she gets it tomorrow morning," said the manager handing a pen and paper to Tash.

"No, that's too late."

The TV was now showing the weather forecast at double speed.

"Turn that off now, Sabnam," said the manager. "It's not a toy."

Sab turned to her manager and nodded "Sorry. Yes."

In the seconds it took Sab to ask Jamie to stand out of her way so she could point the remote at the VCR,

Jamie saw the BBC One clock counting down to six pm in double speed. The News intro started at the same pace.

"When did you record this?" asked Jamie.

"We just did it in training," answered Sab.

"Today? This is today's news?" Jamie watched the end of the opening titles and Sue Lawley talking to camera. Sab nodded as she stopped the video playing and switched off the TV.

Jamie stared intently at the silver fronted VCR. He remembered Grandma had one like this, but hers had a DVD player in it too.

Then he spotted it. EJECT. He pressed it. At this, a whirring noise was followed by the video-cassette ejecting in part from the front of the device. It rested temptingly half in and half out.

"Tash?" said Jamie.

"What?"

"After three…"

"After three, what?"

"After three, run," whispered Jamie.

Now everyone was confused.

"Three!" shouted Jamie as he reached out to swipe the video-cassette, then sprinted to the front doors, his sister in tow.

"What are we running for?" asked Tash as they jostled their way through the double doors onto the main road. They both leapt into the Princess. "We don't know where he works."

"I've got a copy of the news on video!" Jamie wafted the black plastic cassette in the air. "Things are looking up!"

"What do we do with that?" asked Tash as she started up the car and sped off.

"I don't know yet. But we probably need to go and find Bob Geldof or something."

"Run the 'or something' option by me…"

Jamie thought. "We take this video to Bob in hospital and let them check out Raymond while we're there. Bob can write Band Aid. Raymond can get some stitches."

"Perfect. We just need a rock-solid back story, a video player and a miracle. Oh, and the name of the hospital?"

"St Thomas' Hospital. They said on the news."

"Your capacity for insignificant detail is amazing sometimes, Jamie."

"Thanks"

"It was a criticism."

They drove for a few moments. "She liked the look of you."

"Who did?" replied Jamie.

"The girl in the shop. Shame really, cos when we get home she'll be about retirement age. Unless that floats your boat."

"Next left," said Jamie, pointing to a road sign.

"How do you know that?"

"We've done three sides of a rectangle, and this will rejoin the first road. And that had a sign for St Thomas' Hospital."

Tash took the turn.

"Your capacity for insignificant detail is amazing sometimes, Jamie."

THIRTEEN

Raymond's head felt numb, but he was distracted by how cold he'd become in the darkness of the boot. Able to suss the mechanism of just about any mechanical component, it was not difficult for him to release the boot catch, but the cold and the darkness impeded his ability to do this. And the movement of the car was making things even more difficult. He could hear the bickering of Jamie and Tash from up front. He was pretty sure from their tone and from the sporadic movement of the Princess that they were parking up. Jamie was trying to help.

"You're fine on my side, keep it coming."

"Don't talk to me when I'm reversing," replied Tash harshly.

"You've got loads of space, keep going!"

"This is fine!" Tash argued as the car slammed to a halt. Raymond's face again bore the brunt of the impact inside the boot. He shook his head clear and released the lid. It was dark outside, and he was able to clamber out slowly and catch his breath in a squatting position behind the bumper of the car. It was wonderful to be on solid land, he'd found himself feeling queasy in the boot, so he drew some deep delicious lungfuls of the cold night air. Suddenly he heard the car door slam and footsteps approach him. It was too late to run, not that he had the energy; he simply tried to hide in the shadow of the car, after all they'd tried to kill him. These were clearly ruthless people.

The footsteps returned to the front of the car, the door slammed, and in a moment the engine had started again. Inside the car, Jamie smiled at his sister. "I told you there was room!"

"Don't talk to me when I'm reversing," repeated Tash as she ground the gearbox one final time and then reversed utterly and entirely over Raymond.

The car shook, and Tash looked at Jamie. Both exited the vehicle to see the cause of the problem.

"Oh, my God! Raymond! He fell through the boot!" screamed Tash.

Jamie offered his hand and dragged the short man from under the car.

"You ran over me!"

"No. Well, maybe. In a way. But we brought you to hospital," said Tash brushing grit and oil off Raymond as he straightened up.

"Don't touch me!" Raymond recoiled, convinced he was under attack again. "You're trying to kill me!"

"It was an accident," said Jamie. "We wouldn't kill anyone."

"What's the name of the warehouse you took us to, Raymond?" demanded Tash. She just needed to cut to the chase.

"What?" he answered. Dried blood under his nose continued in a trail over his teeth and onto his newly ripped suit.

"You've ripped your suit, Raymond," said Jamie.

Raymond was mortified. "Christ, Maureen will go mental." Then the penny dropped, and he glared at his watch in the hope of reading it in the darkness. "Maureen! I was supposed to collect Maureen!"

"She's fine," lied Tash. "She got an Uber."

"She got a Noober??" echoed a baffled Raymond. Jamie was shaking his head at his sister, who styled things out beautifully. "What's a Noober?" repeated Raymond.

"I've no idea Raymond, I said taxi." She turned to her brother, "He's delirious."

"You tried to kill me. Twice. With my own car!" Raymond tried to straighten his ripped suit.

"Well, that's not true to start with," replied Tash in a Mary Poppins style. "Silly sausage." She straightened Raymond's tie, ruffled his thinning hair and looked over at the Casualty entrance. "We're here by mistake, and we need to get home, we told you that earlier."

"Why would I believe anything you tell me? Nothing you say makes any sense!"

"Nonsense," replied Tash. "Right, what's the plan, Jamie?"

Jamie held up the VHS and smiled at Raymond. "We need to find a video player to show this to Bob Geldof so he can write Band Aid and stop a famine in Ethiopia."

"And if we have time, we could use some help with millennium bug, too," added Tash.

Raymond glared at both of them for a moment.

"What?"

"Other than the nose-bleed and the car thing, haven't we been upfront with you, Raymond?" asked Tash.

"Well, you haven't really told me anything."

"We have told you everything. You've just chosen to ignore us," explained Tash.

"Oh, God! Dudley will be back at Butler's by now!" Raymond strained his eyes at his watch.

"Butler's, write that down, Jamie."

Jamie checked his pockets for a pencil that he didn't have. "I can't," he protested. "Put it in your phone." Tash extracted her phone and typed into her Notes.

"What's Butler's?" asked Tash.

"Butler's Wharf. The warehouse. What's that?" asked Raymond, suddenly distracted by the glow from Tash's iPhone screen.

"Are you OK, sir?" asked a warm voice.

They all looked up to see a middle-aged nurse at the end of her shift. She was fumbling in her handbag for the keys to the Mini City alongside them.

"We're fine thanks," replied Tash then added, "aren't we Dad?" looping arms with Raymond and setting off to the hospital.

"I'm not your dad," protested Raymond.

Jamie offered a mumbled, "He's had a bit of a tumble," in the general direction of the nurse who observed Raymond's painful limp as Tash coerced him out of sight.

Outside the Casualty entrance, another nurse positioned a wheelchair at the rear of an ambulance. Attached to it, a suspended drip swayed from side to side, and a folded grey blanket covered the back of the seat. The nurse applied the brake and stepped into the rear of the ambulance to fetch her patient. Without breaking a stride, Tash took the hand break off the wheelchair and wheeled it away. She had seated Raymond in it and entered the hospital before anyone noticed it was missing.

Once inside the Casualty department Tash covered Raymond's legs with the blanket, tucking the end of the drip tube underneath to complete this masquerade. Jamie followed behind, a little overwhelmed by the noise of the crowds waiting to be seen, and the melee of staff scurrying back and forth. He clutched the precious VHS tape close to his chest.

"We'll get you checked out, then get back to the warehouse," muttered Tash. "How's your leg?"

"I think it's just bruised," replied Raymond. "But this doesn't look right, does it?"

He held up his right hand. His middle finger was sticking upwards at ninety degrees from the back of his hand. Altogether in the wrong direction. Tash swallowed in an attempt to stop herself from puking then managed to shout, "NURSE!"

Then she fainted.

****

Tash tiptoed over to the crib to lift her stirring son into her arms. It was still dark outside, but the snow had stopped falling, and her phone read 07:35. It was so good to be back in the cramped spare room.

"Happy Christmas, precious," whispered Tash as she planted a long kiss on the soft, warm fuzzy-haired scalp of her baby.

She lifted him to the window and held him cheek to cheek. They gazed out onto the snow that smothered the garden and reflected the amber glow of the street light over the wall. Tash wondered why this one hadn't been replaced by the ugly LED ones that had slowly destroyed the romance of all winter nights for future generations. The rest of Sheffield had.

She glanced over and saw Jamie deep in slumber in the single bed that nestled beneath the warmth of the airing cupboard.

"Tash," came a gentle whisper. It was warm and affectionate, but it wasn't the voice of her mum.

"Tash," repeated the voice. It wasn't Grandma either.

"Tash."

Tash turned and tiptoed over to the bedroom door. She recognised the voice, but she couldn't put a face to it. Had someone come to visit on Christmas morning? Maybe one of Grandma's friends? Why so early? Tash turned the doorknob and peered into the face of Mrs McAllister from Home Alone.

"You left Kevin. You need to go back for Kevin," Tash found herself muttering.

"Tash, can you hear me?" replied Mrs McAllister.

"Yes. You left Kevin. He's on his own. In the house."

Tash blinked a few times, and when she opened her eyes, Mrs McAllister looked different. For a start, she was Jamaican and dressed as a nurse. Behind her was a brightly lit hospital curtain.

"Hello, Tash, you had quite a fall," explained the nurse. "I'm Shanice. Can you hear me?"

Tash nodded, which made her headache even more apparent.

"My head kills."

Shanice peered closely into Tash's eyes, then reached to a trolley behind her.

"Take these," replied Shanice, handing her a small plastic pot containing two round tablets and a cup of water. Tash glared at the round tablets. She hated taking the old-fashioned round ones.

"What are they?"

"Paracetamol."

"Have you got any caplets?"

"Any what?"

"I can't take these fuckers. I hate them. Can you snap them in half?"

"Really?" asked the nurse, reluctantly complying with the request. "Your father's in the next bay. He's having a cast set."

"My father?" Tash's brain was struggling to play catch up.

"Broken wrist. His legs seem fine. The x-ray was clear. Just bruised and swollen."

"X-ray? How long have I been out?"

"About an hour, on and off. You kept muttering Kevin. Is he your husband?"

The events of the last few hours came flooding back as Tash leapt to her feet.

"Where's Jamie?"

"Sit down," insisted Shanice. "Who's Jamie?"

"The man I came in with!"

"You mean your father?"

"No, the other man," replied Tash, frantically pulling back the curtain next to her bed to see an elderly man's naked arse as he bent over the bed. A nurse was applying some kind of creme to a dog bite. Well, she hoped it was a dog bite.

"Sorry!" Tash pulled the curtain closed again and tugged open the curtain on the other side of her bed revealing Raymond sitting up on a trolley bed. For some reason he was wearing a hospital gown, his clothes piled up by his feet. He had a black eye, a neck brace, and a nearly finished cast around his right hand. The blood trails under his nose had dried almost black. A nurse was applying more material to his new white boxing glove.

"Where's Jamie?" asked Tash.

"Yes, hello, Tash. I'm very well, thank you. How are you?" replied Raymond.

"Where is he?"

"No idea. I helped you up when you fainted. He disappeared."

"You shouldn't have let him out of sight! He hates these places."

"Sorry, I was kind of distracted by the lady who head-butted the floor. Which was you by the way."

"I've got to find him!"

"You can't go anywhere until you see a doctor," said Shanice. "Please sit down."

"I'll take over from here," came Jamie's voice. "Thank you, nurse."

Tash looked up to see Jamie dressed in a long white NHS coat with pale blue epaulettes. The VHS was still clutched tightly in his hand.

"I'm a male nurse," over-delivered Jamie.

"Thanks for the information. I'm a female one," replied Shanice. "Have we met?"

"I'm normally on the shift that you're not on," said Jamie. "But you two," he glanced at the nurse tending to Raymond, "are needed in triage."

The two nurses glanced at one another and turned to leave. Shanice spoke up on her way out.

"This lady has a mild concussion. Her vitals are normal. She's a little confused."

Jamie reached to the clipboard at the foot of his sister's bed and started to read.

"Yes, I'll take it from here, thank you."

"That's how you work the bed," explained Shanice.

"Yes. Very interesting." Jamie replaced the electric bed manual to its home as the nurses disappeared from view.

"Where did you get the uniform?" asked Tash.

"They've got a laundry!" replied Jamie.

"Stop wearing other people's clothes! You just walked in and helped yourself?"

"I said I was a male nurse and had forgotten to bring my outfit."

"It's just a nurse, Jamie. You're just a nurse. Just say, nurse. And it's a uniform. They just gave it to you?"

Jamie nodded.

"Right. Let's get back to Butler's," announced Raymond as he climbed up off his bed.

"Excellent!" replied a surprised Tash.

"Wait! I still need to show this video to Bob," protested Jamie.

"We've been here ages, Jamie. What have you been up to?" asked Tash.

"Are you kidding? I've been getting changed and trying to find out where he is!"

"So, where is he?"

"Intensive Care."

"No shit. Where is that?"

"Sixth floor. East Wing."

"And where are we now?"

"1984." He really thought this was a good answer.

"Geographically," replied Tash.

"Ground floor. St Thomas' Hospital."

"He's very literal, isn't he?" remarked Raymond. "Bit quirky."

"He has Asperger's. I quite like it actually," responded Tash somewhat aggressively.

"I didn't mean anything by it," apologised Raymond. "I've never heard of it."

Tash turned to her brother. "How are you planning on showing it to him?"

"I'm dressed as a male nurse. It allows me to move around unquestioned."

"I got that part. Assuming we find him, and assuming he isn't dead, how do you show him the video?"

"Gynaecology ward has a TV and video for training. They tell you anything in this outfit! It's brilliant."

"And where is the Gynaecology ward?"

"Floor eight!"

"East wing?"

"North."

"Sake," snapped Tash. She took a deep breath, checked her phone for signal again then made to leave. "Come on then. Go, go, go, go."

Suddenly a newly assertive Raymond blocked her path.

"We're going to Butler's. Nowhere else. I'm sorry I've tried to be as fair as possible. But that's just the way it is. You've convinced me you're harmless, but I can't just let you run around London. We need to get back to my boss."

Maybe his arse sticking out of the rear of the back-fastening gown undermined his attempt to intimidate his captives. Or his neck brace. Or his bloodied nose.

Jamie and Tash looked at one another and then walked around Raymond and exited the cubicles.

"I mean it!" shouted Raymond after them.

"Yep," shouted Tash.

Raymond had no choice but to follow his captives. "Stop. Stop right now."

"Yep," muttered Tash, as she and Jamie marched to the East Wing lifts, Raymond just a few steps behind.

FOURTEEN

Stairs wouldn't have been Raymond's preferred method of reaching the eighth floor of any building. He wasn't in the best of shape and running in a hospital gown was a real test of that little bow you tie around the back. Luckily, he was at the rear of this convoy, so his brilliant white arse was only mooning at the stairs they left behind. In front of him, Tash was barking at Jamie up front, who leapt two steps at a time. They had summoned the lift and waited patiently to remain as inconspicuous as possible, but the sudden appearance of two police officers in the lift lobby prompted their decision to take the stairs. They overheard the officers approach a group of student nurses just metres away and ask if they'd seen a couple in their thirties behaving suspiciously around the hospital.

"They're wanted in connection with a suspected kidnapping and stolen vehicle. We believe they've just left the Casualty department after treatment."

As the students shook their heads, Tash, Jamie and Raymond had snuck through the door to the stairs.

"Slow down Jamie, slow down," begged Tash.

"Nearly there," said Jamie.

"How do you know we're nearly there? There are no bloody signs anywhere," snorted Raymond, trying to pull the flaps of material together to cover his arse.

He was right. The concrete steps just kept on going up, and unless you were counting the flights, you would have to exit onto each floor to establish your whereabouts.

"Top floor. I'm sure of it," explained Jamie.

"No! We've done eight, surely? This is like the sixteenth or seventeenth flight!" Tash stopped to catch her breath.

"Oi!" came a shout that reverberated up the stairs.

All three froze and looked at one another. Then, each slowly peered over the bannister into the stairwell and down to the ground floor. Looking back up was one of the police officers. "Wait. Wait there. Police!"

Jamie, Tash and Raymond set off again at a very impressive pace. Well, Jamie and Tash did. Raymond did his usual pace, which was set to maximum.

At the next turn Jamie's toe didn't make the step up, and his knees slammed down onto the sharp edge of the cold concrete slab. An innate attempt to stop his fall saw both hands lurch forward, causing the VHS cassette to drop from his grasp. He watched helplessly as the tape bounced, flipped and spun into the void that was the gaping centre of the stairwell. Tash and Raymond glanced over as the cassette bounced impossibly onto the handrail alongside them and landed half an inch from the edge of a step one flight behind Raymond.

"Keep coming. Keep moving!" shouted Jamie as he dashed back down the stairs. "I'll fetch it!" He sailed past Tash and Raymond who continued up to the top floor as instructed. Jamie took one final turn, and the video was in his sight. He could also see the police were now just three floors beneath him. He took one giant leap to the next half landing and scooped up the black plastic VHS box, spun around and made after the others. As Tash reached the top, she opened the door and stepped onto the landing. In front of her was a massive number '8' sign. Still holding the door open, she slumped to relieve a very painful stitch, before managing to shout behind her.

"Eight. This is eight!"

"Stop! Police!" came the shout again.

The echo of the police officers' footsteps was getting louder in Jamie's ears. At the top, Raymond followed Tash through the door onto the eighth floor. Jamie was only one level below them. He didn't realise he was this fit, and it pleasantly surprised him. He wasn't sure of a route once he caught up with Tash and Raymond, but he was confident they could lose themselves amongst the inevitable corridors and then establish a path to the training room where they –

SMASH

Everything stopped.

Jamie was literally stunned.

All he knew was that he was now standing perfectly upright with a grey snowstorm in his eyes, and the sound of plastic bouncing on metal. As his vision cleared, he watched the video cassette drop and then bounce and then drop and then crash all the way to the ground floor. In front of him was an open wooden fire door. The same door that had brutally interrupted his ascent. And peering around the door was a familiar face.

"Oh, thank God! This way! Quickly!"

And with that, he was dragged onto the landing of the 7th floor.

His brain could not formulate any kind of defence or alibi that might satisfy an arresting officer. Still, something told his befuddled mind that this wasn't a police officer clutching his arm so tightly. No. This was the tight grip of his father. His younger, thinner, stronger father.

"Nurse! Thank God! There's no-one here. There's no-one on the ward!" said George.

He looked very anxious. Almost delirious. "My wife. My wife is giving birth now. She wasn't dilated, and now she must be dilated. The contractions are so close together, and she's giving birth. She's giving birth now!"

All Jamie could do was nod at his father. Stupidly nod. Silently nod. Manically nod.

"Yes," he heard himself saying.

Then he heard himself say, "Well, let's get to her then." He also thought he heard himself say, "I'm a male nurse," but chose to ignore this as it made his toes curl. Jamie didn't want to abandon his sister, but he also knew he had to get away from the stairs as quickly as possible. As he glanced back over his shoulder, it was clear the police officers in pursuit had not seen his exit. Through the slotted window in the door, he saw a police officer continue upstairs to floor eight.

Jamie scurried past the signs for 'Birthing Centre' and a busy receptionist on the phone. All he could hear through the thumping pulse in his ears was the ringing of telephones and the muttering of his father. Where was everybody? He could hear some explanation from an anxious George that staff levels were low, there had been some kind of sickness bug and the ward was waiting for more staff to cope with the sudden demand from patients.

They stopped outside the double doors of the labour ward. On either side were four other single doors each with the same sign screwed to them, 'Delivery room', and beneath that a number. The one that George opened had the sign, 'Bed 32'.

"Here, in here," muttered George, his fingers awkwardly ruffling through his thick hair. He ushered Jamie in and there, sitting in the classic textbook birthing position was Jamie's beautiful young mum. Jamie was struck by what he saw. Her complexion looked so youthful. Her cheekbones so pronounced. Her lips were so full. Her hair was darker than he'd ever seen. Her eyes were so bright. But more than that, Jamie couldn't help but observe she had her legs wide apart and a shining pink scalp was protruding from inside her.

"Fanny! Oh, my God! I can see your fanny!" Jamie was surprised to hear himself say that out loud. Maybe almost as surprised as his parents were to hear a nurse describe it that way. Although not as surprised as his parents were to see the nurse avert his gaze to the ceiling like he'd walked in on a stranger in an aeroplane toilet. He was actively looking anywhere other than at his patient.

"What?" asked George.

Jamie waited for about two or three years before speaking.

"No, I was just saying it's funny," stammered Jamie. "Funny that she wasn't diluted and now, she is. Diluted. Funny, funny, funny."

"Dilated," corrected George.

"Yes," added Jamie. "I think she's having a baby."

"How are we doing?" came a fourth voice. Jamie turned to see a midwife standing in the door smiling at the expectant parents.

"Oh! We are coming along quickly," observed the kind-faced woman. Her name badge read Midwife, Nurse N Conde. George tiptoed to Andrea's side and placed a nervous arm around her shoulder. Jamie breathed a sigh of relief that an actual medic was now in attendance.

"Excellent, Nurse Conde. Excellent. I'm a male nurse and just came to see how things were going, but you're back, so that's made things a lot less hairy for all of us!" Jamie immediately regretted his choice of words. "I didn't mean to say hairy!" He gestured in the general region of his mum's personal area. "Which is fine because it's 1984 and that's the trend. It's trendy. On-trend. Lovely. I meant lovely as in summing up, not that's it's lovely. Not that it isn't lovely. Have a good day," Jamie was walking to the door, still with his eyes fixed on the ceiling tiles.

"Not so soon, if you wouldn't mind. We're a little stretched on the ward, a lot of staff are unable to work. We could use as many spare hands as we can," smiled Nurse Conde, gesturing to the small wall-mounted basin. "If you could wash your hands, then we can help Mummy on her way."

****

Tash regretted asking Raymond if the police had gone. The two of them had found shelter behind an unattended desk in the antenatal waiting reception. But now

Raymond was standing to get a good view of the main landing outside the lifts, which unfortunately meant his arse was protruding from his hospital gown approximately seven or eight inches from her face.

"He's waiting for the lift," whispered Raymond.

A police officer was indeed waiting outside the lift doors. Suddenly the doors opened and inside was a second officer, she was holding up the retrieved VHS cassette

"He's getting in now. I reckon they're going down."

"On account of this being the top floor?" said Tash. "Maybe they're going sideways?"

Tash leant away from the dimpled arse and tugged at Raymond's gown.

Raymond looked over his shoulder at Tash who gestured at his gaping nakedness.

"Sorry."

"Jamie never came through the door. He must be on another floor. This is the worst news ever. How the fuck do I find him in here? This place is massive." Tash's voice faltered as she pressed the glass on her phone and gently rubbed the image of her son on the home screen.

"He's going to find the TV thing on this floor, isn't he? The video TV thing? Let's head there. That's our best chance," suggested Raymond. He needed Jamie as much as Tash did now. He'd left his place of work against his boss's instructions, he'd abandoned his wife at her workplace, the police were hunting the people who stole his car – both of whom he'd kidnapped although he'd subsequently lost one – and now he'd lost all of his clothes. Not his best day. His only chance to reprieve himself was to get the brother and sister back to Butler's

Wharf and hope that he managed to do so before his boss returned. As for his wife, he had no idea. Maybe he would have to move into the shed again. Or go and live in Guatemala under an assumed name. He'd heard the weather was excellent, and actually, maybe he'd just do that anyway.

"I should be in bed," whispered Tash. "It's Christmas."

"Riddles. You talk in riddles," sighed Raymond as they set off looking for the Gynaecology training room.

FIFTEEN

Dudley Hobson looked long and hard into the non-plussed eyes of Maurice, a security guard with very little time for toffee-nosed twats.

"I am extremely busy, and I have been passed from pillar to post. I must speak to Alex McGaskill immediately."

"She won't see you today," repeated Maurice, leaning on the polished oak desk that separated them. Maurice had worked in the Old Building on Houghton Street for almost ten years now, and he was consistently unimpressed by entitled or arrogant visitors to the LSE.

"The lady in Connaught House said this was the main reception," said Dudley.

"The lady in Connaught House was correct," answered Maurice.

"Well then please tell Alex McGaskill that Dudley Hobson is here. On behalf of Sinclare Securities." He was delighted that the business name he'd picked sounded exactly the same as Sinclair. Surely this would do the trick.

"No."

"What?"

"She won't see you today."

"She knows me. We went to university together," replied Dudley offering his business card.

"You're gonna have to go now, mate," explained Maurice.

"Why are you not calling her?" asked Dudley, prodding the reception phone that sat on the desk between them.

Maurice prodded the phone in the same way and replied, "Because she's left for the day."

He smiled. Dudley didn't. Then Dudley had a thought and extracted his small pad from his inside pocket. Behind him, a middle-aged man appeared in an office doorway with a young girl, most probably his daughter. She giddily helped him to turn the key in the lock of his office door for the day. A doll in her hand flopped lifelessly as she skipped on the spot.

"In which case, I'd like to see … Francine Dexter," read Dudley from his handwritten note.

Maurice let this land for a moment, then looked up to the man now fastening his overcoat as his daughter skipped on the spot.

"Professor Dexter?" said Maurice.

The man looked over. "Evening Maurice, everything OK?"

"Yes, sir. This gentleman wants a word … with your daughter."

The professor glanced over at the two men, then back at his daughter.

Dudley looked confused as he squinted at his own handwriting and the young girl that stood before him.

SIXTEEN

"One more, just one more, my precious. You are making me so proud," encouraged Nurse Conde. She had a warmth that couldn't be taught. Her vocation in life was nursing thought Jamie, that was indisputable. For a moment he wondered if she was still working now, in the future. She had patiently instructed Jamie how to dispense gas and air at intervals to reassure Andrea and ensure she didn't push until the right time. She did it all effortlessly, and with such a warm conversational tone to keep the expectant mum as calm as possible.

And now Jamie was looking at nearly all of his sister's squishy face. This experience was unlike anything Jamie had seen on TV. This was life-affirming and wonderful, thought Jamie. Only ruined by the fact he'd spent ten minutes staring at his mum's fanny. One thing was clear, though, his dad was pretty useless. George had felt a bit squeamish at the outset so opted to remain 'head-end' sitting on a chair and sipping water in between his own controlled diaphragm breathing.

"Breathe in seven and out eleven," reminded Nurse Conde, to the grey-looking father-to-be.

So that's where the family got that, thought Jamie.

And then the baby was out, just like that. And for one millisecond, she was the newest person in the world. And that was pretty amazing. The newborn baby slid onto the damp white bed sheet and was scooped up and wrapped effortlessly by this saintly mid-wife before being handed to her mother – all in a matter of seconds.

"A baby girl," said Nurse Conde, her face beaming. She clearly never tired of the joy childbirth brings.

Andrea allowed herself a massive smile as tears filled her eyes. The adrenaline that flooded her body momentarily numbed the pain, and all she could do was stare at this perfectly wrinkled face.

"You are amazing, Andrea, you are amazing, I love you," said George, planting a kiss on her wet forehead, and another on the squidgy cheek of his daughter.

"Hello, baby girl," whispered Andrea.

"Baby girl?" repeated Nurse Conde. "You haven't thought of a name yet?"

"We only thought of boys names!" answered Andrea, unable to take her eyes away from this miracle. She recoiled briefly as if her body had refused to stop the contractions.

George looked up at the midwife. "But we clearly need one! What's your name?"

The midwife smiled at George. "My name is Nkechinyere-Ayotunde," she replied.

There was silence.

George attempted it back, a little too slowly to convince anyone he's heard.

"Nick-?" He was interrupted before he got any further.

"Nkechinyere-Ayotunde," repeated the midwife, superbly stifling a smile.

More silence.

"That's nice," said George.

"It's a nice name," nodded Andrea, wondering why the hell had George started this bloody conversation?

"Lovely name," agreed George.

George caught Andrea's eye, then they both asked, "Do you have a middle name?"

Miss Conde shook her head.

George had a thought. "What was your mum's name?"

"Nastasia."

"Natasha?" He liked this.

"Nastasia," corrected the midwife.

"Woaahhhh," moaned Andrea.

"OK, darling. It's OK," Nurse Conde nodded to Jamie. "Some more gas and air,"

"My father called her Nasty!" she continued in a bedside manner. "Or Tasha."

Jamie helped his mum hold the mask to her tired young face.

"It looks like her brother or sister is ready now!" said the midwife.

Andrea nodded and squared herself for round two. Jamie's ears started ringing again. Brother or sister? What? Another baby? Like a twin?

WHAT?

The machine next to his mother started to beep and Nurse Conde glanced over at the screen.

Andrea looked over at the midwife. The concern was visible on her face.

"Baby is perhaps a little uncomfortable," assured the midwife as she reached to press a green button by the bed head. "We shall have some help from the obstetrician to see things go well."

Until now Jamie hadn't even registered the wire from his mum's bump to this piece of equipment. "Can you fetch Dr Calver or Dr Wong please, nurse?" Nurse Conde was looking at Jamie. Her voice tone had changed a little. "Now."

Jamie ran to the door and into the landing. He was met head-on with Dr Wong coming in the opposite direction, already responding to the call from Bed 32. He turned back to open the door for her, and she marched straight past him to his young mum. Jamie didn't follow. Instead he watched through the small glass panel in the door as the green button was pressed again. Another doctor in scrubs was soon standing alongside Dr Wong and Nurse Conde. Andrea was now lying flat on the bed. George was clutching her palm tightly. The crease that was so familiar to Jamie had now appeared in his young father's forehead. Jamie was nudged out of the way as another medic entered the room. Within seconds the scene was one of constant movement. A solitary nurse standing over a wheeled crib was attending to newborn Natasha. Andrea was now hidden by a wall of staff all calmly going about their work. But Jamie could see a pace. A kind of urgency. Everything had changed.

Minutes or hours passed, Jamie couldn't tell. But now things had changed again. The pace had dropped. The movement ceased. Heads slumped. Dr Wong was very slowly but very definitely shaking her head at Andrea. Andrea was crying. George was crying.

Something warm dropped onto Jamie's hand.

He looked down and through suddenly blurred eyes, he could see his tears rolling down his wrist.

So, this was why his father wanted to go back to October 23rd, 1984.

SEVENTEEN

Dudley leaned his head into the domed top of the public payphone that hung on the wall of the main corridor off reception in the Houghton Building. He looked seriously pissed off as he finished twisting the final number of the dial and waited for the line to connect. With the phone handset clamped between his ear and shoulder, he flicked through the loose change he'd extracted from his pocket. He squinted at a metal sign screwed to the payment box informing that the minimum call charge had increased since August from 2p to 10p. As he inspected the copper and silver in his upturned palm, the call connected and soon, the pulse of the ringing tone in his ear became hypnotic. Finding a 10p piece, he placed it in the opening of the payment slot, his finger poised above waiting to hear the pips of the call being answered. At the other end of the phone, Butler's Wharf to be exact, a phone rang in the empty office cage. And rang. And rang. He would have a long wait. But he must be patient. His future depended on not fucking up the Sinclair deal. His career – not to mention his financial status – depended on it. His decisions through the years had not been good ones, and he stood at a precipice now. Deliver this contract or face certain bankruptcy and most probably prison too. He wasn't about to let two cocky upstarts destroy his life.

EIGHTEEN

A phone rang at the reception of the Gynaecology reception desk. The department seemed very quiet by comparison to the rest of the hospital, in fact most of the rooms that spilt off the corridor were in darkness. A solitary porter reached over to answer the call and was soon wishing he hadn't.

"You need to speak up," said the porter. He listened intently.

"Where?"

He listened again.

"I'm the only one here. You'll have to ask someone else."

He listened more intently.

"OK! OK! Calm down! I'm coming now – where are you?"

He struggled to hear again.

"The main lifts? … OK. On my way, sir."

With that, he hung up the phone, stepped around the desk and walked down the corridor towards the lifts. As he turned the corner, Tash appeared from a cleaning store door and ran past the unmanned reception into the empty Gynaecology department. Raymond was soon behind her, having hung up the phone marked "Staff only" in the waiting room behind the Antenatal Education Clinic. He'd not enjoyed impersonating a demanding surgeon, in fact, he was sure he'd panicked and called it the Jynaecology department on the call but was clearly so assertive his mistake had gone unquestioned. Tash stopped at a bank of light switches and flicked them all. The corridor lit up ahead of them, and she continued on her way, reading the signs projecting from doors as she ran.

"This goes against all my principles," muttered Raymond trying to keep up.

"Awful. Terrible. Sorry. Whatever," replied Tash, then her eyes lit up as she read Training Suite.

Typically, it was the final door, but her legs reached it in seconds. She twisted the aluminium door handle and then smashed her face trying to continue through the locked door.

"Fuuuuuuuuuck!" she cried as she rubbed her forehead. "A double headache! Sake!"

"Is it locked?"

"No. I was wondering if you could cancel one headache with another one."

Tash leaned against the glass door panel and by placing her hands either side of her eyes she was able to peer into the room. Rows of sterile red plastic seats faced a wooden countertop that displayed various flip charts, pamphlets and to one side a full-colour wooden and plastic model of a uterus. To the other side, sitting beautifully in the near darkness, was a wooden-sided TV built into a black-framed trolley, and underneath was something that surely must be a video player. The silhouette offered so much promise that it reminded her of the shape of her mountain bike that waited in the dark next to the unlit Christmas tree when she was 12. An inanimate object, completely unaware of the euphoria it commanded in merely being.

"I see it!" squealed Tash. "I see it!" Then she stopped. "Christ, it's massive. How the hell do we shift that?"

Raymond struggled to look around Tash into the dark room, his neck brace didn't help.

"It's on wheels, isn't it?"

"It's still massive. I look like Bananarama's mother, and you've got your bollocks out, we're hardly gonna go unnoticed are we?"

"Excuse me. Can I help you please?" The porter was back and was walking towards them at an incredible pace.

"Shit," muttered Tash.

"You shouldn't be in here," remonstrated the porter.

As he upped his pace and started to protest again, it looked like Tash and Raymond would be back at square one again. Or so Tash thought.

One moment the porter's red face was expounding the sanctity of locked training rooms and unmanned departments at night time, and the next he was gone. Replaced by one of the hospital's sturdy wooden fire doors, this time kicked open by an overzealous Jamie who leapt into the corridor out of breath.

"Sorry, I got a bit lost," he appealed to his sister and Raymond. "I'm still looking for the training room. This floor is massive," lied Jamie.

As the door swung closed, it revealed an unconscious porter lying on the ground. Jamie was oblivious as something else had caught his eye.

"Training suite!" Jamie had spotted the sign above his sister's head.

"It's locked," replied Tash, one eye on the comatose man.

"Oh my God, you killed him!" said Raymond rushing over to the porter. Jamie turned in horror and watched Raymond listen to his chest. In doing so, he displayed the fullest view of his arse that Tash had seen so far today.

"No. Calm down, everybody. He's alive, he's just been knocked out." Raymond smiled over his shoulder.

"I bet that was the door hitting him in the head," said Jamie, who turned to have another look at Raymond before adding, "I can see your balls."

"Are those keys?" asked Tash looking at the bunch of brass and chrome pieces hanging from the porter's belt.

"This man is unconscious!" protested Raymond. "You're an animal!"

"So he needs to see a medic. And when he does – cos we'll make sure he does – they will probably put him in one of those gowns," Tash gestured at Raymond's gown.

"So?" asked Raymond

"I'm just saying, we'd actually be saving them a job."

"What? You don't mean…?"

Tash nodded slowly. "Shall we look the other way?"

Two minutes later Tash was outside the lift. The porter was still out cold but now wearing Raymond's gown and seated in a wheelchair.

The lift bell rang, and the doors opened – happily displaying it was empty. Tash leant in and pressed G for the ground floor. She then thought better of it and pressed 1. She thought again and opted to push every button. Next, she stepped back out onto the landing and gave the porter's wheelchair an almighty shove. She was clearly enthusiastic as his chair continued to the back of the sizeable lift and his feet stopped him from going farther by hitting the back wall with a slam. He bounced back and slumped to one side, slowly falling from the chair as the lift doors started to close. Tash tilted her head to watch him slowly slide onto the lift floor just as the doors finally closed, allowing herself a slight grimace that this hadn't gone as well as she might have wished.

NINETEEN

Dudley had hoped his anxiety wouldn't trigger his facial tick, but his eye was definitely flickering as he listened to the 'beep beep' of the unanswered ring tone that looped endlessly from his massive car phone handset. His free hand fiddled with the coiled wire that connected the handset to the briefcase-sized box that made up the second part of the unit. The Mercedes was dark inside, but the rear light was illuminating his twitching face. He spotted Jermaine looking at him in the rearview mirror from the driving seat. Dudley switched off the overhead light and continued to listen to the unanswered phone line. 'Talking Loud & Clear' by OMD played quietly on the six-speaker stereo, as the black car moved smoothly through the evening London streets.

In Butler's Wharf, the same phone rang out in the same empty office cage, heard only by a spider that was scared of mice, and a mouse that was scared of spiders. So at least it wasn't just Dudley and Jamie and Tash and Raymond having a shit day.

TWENTY

Jamie was crouched at the lock in the door examining the inside of it. "Five levers. Looks to have a brass plate, so chances are it's a brass key too."

Raymond – now dressed as a porter in ridiculously oversized clothes – reluctantly lifted the keys up from his new belt. Amongst them all, there were only three brass ones, and only one looked to have more teeth than the others.

"This one then," he concluded.

"Aren't you in yet? Hurry up. I'm throwing five more minutes at this," said Tash as she ran back to meet them.

Raymond lifted the key into the lock. Sure enough, it turned. Tash leapt forward to open the door, the force of which pulled Raymond forcefully inside too as the key in the lock was still attached by a chain to his new trousers.

"We're in Jamie – we're in!"

Raymond struggled to remove the key from the door and then stood guard outside it.

Tash raced to the TV stand and soon unplugged the set and the VCR from the wall socket. Jamie was distracted by the massive model of a uterus, which incorporated twins suspended upside down inside. Jamie found himself reaching out to gently touch one of them.

"I wonder if you knew before Mum did?" He stopped, hoping he'd just said this to himself.

"Jamie, stop being a perv and help please!" said Tash

Jamie turned to his sister and realised his eyes were filling up again. Happily, the darkness didn't betray him. He stepped over to help glide the TV trolley towards the door.

"I don't have the tape anymore," whispered Jamie.

"What?" snapped Tash.

"That police officer got it."

"But you picked it up?"

"Then something happened."

Raymond peered his head in. "Can we try and move things along a bit, I'm really not very comfortable with all this."

"So what the fuck are we doing with this thing, then? Sake Jamie! Have you any idea what we've been through whilst you were fannying around this place? Where did you go? What happened?"

Jamie opened his mouth to talk, to explain what he'd been through in the past hour. To share some of his grief. But why would he burden his sister? His living sister. He changed his mind.

Raymond peered his head around the door. "Why didn't I just go back to Casualty for my clothes?" He waited for some kind of reaction from the siblings.

"We tried. We tried, Jamie. But right now, I have a son that needs his mum. A baby, Jamie. Can you imagine how I feel being so far apart from him? You don't know! How could you know? You're not a parent! Let's face it, you'll never be a parent. Tell him, Raymond."

Jamie looked hurt by his sister's cruel but probably accurate summary of his life map.

"Tell him what?" answered Raymond walking in from the door.

"Tell him how it's different for parents – we feel something others don't."

"I don't have kids. Maureen couldn't, erm, well we, we couldn't. We don't have kids."

Tash absorbed this for a period of time that felt respectful but also indicative of the limited time they had to hand. "Normally I'd do a stop down 'how awful' upbeat thing, then say some kind of understanding thing, erm, then something profound, then another upbeat thing, but I don't have time right now. Just imagine I've said all the right things and imagine that you really respected me because of how perfectly I'd gauged the room?" said Tash.

Raymond thought about this. "Thanks for your understanding."

"Exactly! Well done. What I'm saying is – being apart from your kid is the worst feeling. The absolute worst, Jamie."

"Maybe not worse than those mothers who couldn't feed their babies in Africa?" asked Raymond.

Tash considered this. "Hmm. Wasn't really hoping for your input at this stage, Raymond, what with you being childless. Maybe. Maybe not. I don't know. It's not knowing when I'll see him again that's the main thing. It's a horrible feeling."

"I can think of a worse feeling than that." Jamie couldn't help himself from speaking.

"Well, I'd like to hear it."

"I don't think you would."

Jamie started to cry. Tash's demeanour transformed.

"Jamie, what is it? What's the matter?" She leapt over to rub his back and sit him down on a plastic seat. "Raymond, do something. Jamie doesn't cry. He's crying."

"I want us all to go back to the warehouse. Now," said Raymond.

"You had a twin sister, Tash, she didn't make it. And there was nothing I could do."

"What?"

Tash re-processed what Jamie had said. He stared back at her, nodding. She didn't realise how much water her eyes could pour onto her face in such a short period of time.

"You were there? You've seen Mum?" Tash was astonished. Horrified and astonished.

"And her fanny." Jamie was sobbing now.

"You said steer clear of changing things, Jamie. You said the butterfly effect."

"What's the butterfly effect?" asked Raymond. "What's happening?"

"Like in *Back To The Future*," said Tash. Her nose was running now too.

Tash removed her phone and wiped her eyes so she could gaze again at her baby.

"It's not been released yet, Tash. It's next year, he won't have seen it," explained Jamie.

"You really do talk in riddles. The pair of you," said Raymond.

Jamie wiped his tears away and looked at Tash.

"We can do something about those other babies though, Tash. We can. You know it's the right thing to do." He walked to the window and looked out into the amber street lights of Lambeth.

"Jamie, you don't have the tape, we can't fix things without the tape."

"No. You're right," he conceded. "I totally messed up."

The room felt cold. It felt stark and heartless. Brutal. Like the world.

Jamie started fiddling with the window. He managed to loosen the locked handle by crazily forcing it back and forth, over and over, quite manically. In a moment, it was wide open.

"Jamie. Jamie! What are you doing?"

Tash watched in horror as Jamie stepped up onto the ledge of the window and threw himself through the opening, eight flights above the car park.

The scream she let out was unearthly.

TWENTY ONE

In the car park, two police officers were exchanging details with Maureen, as they examined Raymond's Princess for damage. An ambulance drove in behind them, hospital visitors walked across the car park, and a handful of discharged patients waved goodbye to staff. The streets of London offered all manner of evening sounds, ranging from cars crawling past to groups of city traders boasting about their day's haul – amplified no doubt by a few pints of Budweiser, the newly available American beer. If you didn't know about it, you weren't worth knowing about. It's no surprise amongst this distraction that the three of them didn't notice the window cleaning boom lowering itself at high speed from the eighth floor and down the outer side of the ugly building. Nor the male nurse inside it who was ignoring manic heckling from above.

"I thought you'd fucking jumped, you prick!" shouted Tash from the open window.

Jamie continued his descent, biting his tongue for concentration and not taking an eye off the police officers behind the Princess.

To say that Jamie's exit from the boom was undignified would be generous. He'd somehow managed to navigate a ninety-foot drop but then struggled to climb over the edge of the aluminium handrail designed to keep window cleaners in. Happily, no-one saw the male nurse hit the car park face first and then struggle to detach his nurse epaulettes from the handrail, but he did it with the commitment of a man on a mission. Without a second thought he marched straight over to the police officers, remembering to slide his surgical face mask over his mouth in case they or Maureen recognised him. He even ruffled his thinning hair like this made a difference.

"Sorry to interrupt you two policemen, but I'm a male nurse," he announced.

"And I'm a female policeman" replied one of the officers.

The sarcasm was lost on Jamie, he was too intent on his next line.

"An eyewitness claims a video cassette stolen from my ward has been retrieved by one of you."

"Eyewitness?" asked the PC.

"Yes. A videotape. For some training that I am doing in half an hour, for student nurses about erm, about intimate matters of the human body."

"And that would be this video, would it?" asked one of the police officers holding up the VHS cassette.

"Yes, that's the one. It's about very medical parts of the body, specifically the ones needing attention on my training course."

The PC looked at Maureen and held up the cassette. "Is this something you recognise?"

She shook her head.

"Not something that could have been in your husband's car?" she continued.

She shook her head again.

The PC looked back at Jamie. "Can we take your name and department, in case we need to get this back?"

The other PC withdrew a pen and pad, and Jamie did his utmost to see this through.

"Of course. I'm Doctor Dre. 4th floor. ENT."

"I thought you said you were a nurse?"

"That's right. I took exams for both 'cos I wasn't sure. So I'm Nurse Doctor Dre. 4th floor, ENT." He leant in to look at what the PC was writing as if to offer help. "That's Ear, Nose and er, Ear Nose and …"

As he suddenly found the word "Toes", his voice was pretty much silenced by the other three saying "Throat." Not that he heard them.

With that, he snatched the videotape and walked assertively back to the reception doors. He glanced back to establish he was no longer being watched and once happily in the clear he diverted his path towards his window cleaner's boom. Remembering how difficult it was to get out, he carefully stretched one leg over the barrier until he was half in and half out. It was at this stage that he realised he was straddling a small door which slowly opened giving him a gentle swing through 90 degrees. He struggled to dismount and then walked through the doorway into the central part of the boom, closed the door behind and looked up. He started to manipulate the pulley system and worked his way back up the side of the hospital. It took far longer to get up than it did down. Time for Jamie to revisit his last conversation in his head. He leant over the handrail and shouted to the police officers, "Throat. Yes." Happily, his voice was lost in the cold night air.

TWENTY TWO

The Tower Hotel had opened its doors just eleven years ago, but its bold concrete facade had subsequently divided public opinion countless times. Originally designed to breathe life into the faded and forsaken St Katherine Docks, it ultimately cast a vast foreboding shadow over the multi-million-pound apartments that came thirty years later, blocking their views of the iconic Tower Bridge. But for now, it was only loathed by half of the people who saw it, but certainly not those who were lucky enough to stay in one of its south-facing rooms. They had arguably the best view of the Thames from any hotel across the whole of London. In fact, anyone gazing from their boat-themed bedroom windows this dreary October evening would have been lucky enough to enjoy the spectacle of Tower Bridge raising its bascule lower decks to allow a masted ship to pass through. A majestic privilege for a tourist. An irritation to all the traffic on Tower Bridge Road that had to stand to attention until it slowly sailed through. Including Dudley Hobson. He waited impatiently in the back of the black Mercedes with the car phone still glued to his ear. Scritti Politti's 'Wood Beez' filled the car with Green Gartside's impossibly sweet voice, and after what seemed like an hour (it was eleven minutes), his car turned left off Tower Bridge Road and bounced over the cobbled street stones behind the huge Butler's Wharf building. Another sharp left swung him through a gateway underneath a cast iron archway with ornate swirls and loops circling the rusty lettering of 'Bay 3'. Dudley glanced out through the rear window – the phone still to his cheek. His face a combination of fury and complete horror.

TWENTY THREE

Jamie was right, the ICU was on the 6th floor of the East Wing. They had so far managed to avoid suspicion as they moved through the floors and wings of the hospital, Tash dressed in her contemporary clothes, Jamie dressed as a nurse, and Raymond a porter, pushing the TV and video cabinet. Jamie clutched the VHS tape so tightly that the small perforated pattern from the rear of the case was now imprinted perfectly on the palm of his sweaty hand.

As they approached the ICU reception area, things fell bizarrely into place.

"Right. This is when we need to think carefully," said Jamie as they approached the desk.

The solitary nurse on duty looked very flustered, and the sight of Jamie made her face light up.

"Thank God! Can you cover for me whilst I pee? This phone hasn't stopped ringing. *The Sun*, *The Mirror*, *The Mail*," listed the weary-looking nurse. "We've got some punk rocker in here, and they seem to think we're hiding something from them! I'll be back in two minutes, can you hold the fort? If anyone rings we've been told by the Ward Manager just to say 'no comment'."

"What if someone dies?" asked Jamie nodding in compliance as he absorbed his new job.

Tash glared at him.

"Pardon?" asked the nurse as she walked away.

"If someone dies and then someone calls to see how they are, what do I say?" asked Jamie. "In Casualty, they usually ask them to sit down."

"I'll be two minutes," said the nurse.

The moment she was out of sight, Tash leapt behind the desk to examine the handwritten names on the whiteboard muttering as she read.

"Geldof, Geldof, Geldof… there's no fucking Geldof…"

The phone rang.

"Oh my God, what will I say?" said Jamie.

"Don't say anything, don't answer it!" Tash's fingers now methodically pointing across the whiteboard as she read. "There are no Bobs."

"What about Robert?" asked Raymond helpfully

"I should answer, I said I'd help," said Jamie.

Tash read from the board, "Robert Zenon… NOK P. Yates." She turned to Raymond. "What's NOK?"

"Next of kin?"

"His girlfriend was Paula Yates. Is Paula Yates," said Jamie, deafened by the demanding ring of the phone.

"It has a line through it – what does that mean? They're not here at all? It's been crossed out."

"Hello?" said Jamie holding the phone to his ear. He listened before saying "No comment" and hanging up.

Tash glanced back at him. "Was that the press?"

"Someone asking if I wanted a cup of tea."

"Good answer, Jamie. Very good answer."

Raymond picked up a clipboard from the desk and flicked through handwritten notes. He read out loud: "R Zenon – Victoria HDU. What's that?"

"High Dependency Unit," answered Jamie.

"Is that here?" asked Tash.

"Floor 8 East Wing," recalled Jamie.

"It might not even be him? Shall we just cut our losses?" said Tash.

"We need to find out, Tash!"

"Fuck sake!" Tash was losing her patience. "Come on."

Jamie stopped her. "I'm covering the desk for the nurse."

"No. You said you would cover the desk for the nurse. Like Raymond told his boss he'd keep us in that warehouse."

Raymond looked particularly hurt by this.

"Come on," repeated Tash, and they all followed her to the lift, dragging the TV unit again.

TWENTY FOUR

Dudley leapt out of the rear door the very second the Mercedes came to a stop alongside the caged office. He ran through the wide-open office chain link door to get a better look. He didn't need to. The whole enclosure was visible from all three sides as the fencing hid little. A leather Chesterfield sofa sat alongside an antique walnut desk, and a swivel office chair was neatly tucked into the opening. There were no signs of any scuffle or foul play. He spun around a few times in case his eyes were playing tricks on him, but no he was alone in the cage. Beneath a dust sheet the adapted C5 remained untouched on the cold concrete floor. His brain was struggling to process what could possibly have become of his two guests, let alone his reliable office manager.

He removed the sheet and paced around the machine in an attempt to comprehend what was the hell was happening.

He followed the cable from the rear up to the switched-off plug socket. He flicked it on.

He turned to look at the Frankenstein machine. Nothing. Then he saw the screen start to glow and soon his many questions were fighting for room in his head with the continuity announcer on the small portable TV.

"*Whistle Test* with AC/DC and Van Halen is over on BBC Two right now, then Sue Baker reviews the brand-new Vauxhall car – the Astra – in *Top Gear*. That's at half-past eight. Right now, here on BBC One, a psychopathic gunman's on the loose in *Cagney And Lacey*."

As the saxophone theme tune started to play, Dudley fumbled with all the dials and buttons on the set before he was finally able to switch it off.

The Sinclair account had been a godsend to his storage and distribution business. He'd even renamed the firm from Hobson Holding & Securities to Sinclare Securities. Well, the letterhead anyway. In writing, it was clear that Sinclare had a unique spelling, so legally he couldn't be confused with Clive Sinclair or his booming enterprises. But verbally he felt it added sufficient clout to really increase his kudos. After all, Sinclair had entrusted him with the watertight storage of their confidential 1985 killer product, the Sinclair C5. It made perfect sense to him to align his own brand with theirs. Other than right now two rogue industrial thieves were running amok with a member of his team. How the hell had they got access to one of these machines, and why on earth had they bastardised one into some kind of fairground attraction? Was it a threat from an underworld competitor? Dudley was so out of his depth, but he'd seen enough episodes of *The Sweeney* and *The Professionals* to know that you fight fire with fire.

TWENTY FIVE

The HDU was far less eerie, maybe because it was a hive of activity with staff coming and going. It looked like an expansive area screened off into small compartments by those bleak NHS curtains that nobody designed, cos nobody wanted to look at them, so nobody bothered to make them even slightly pleasing to the eye.

"OK, you can do this, Raymond. Just like we practised. Do this, and we'll be back at the warehouse in fifteen minutes," whispered Tash as they neared the main desk at the opening of the ward.

"Practised?" asked Jamie, suddenly very alarmed. "We haven't practised anything."

"You were being a Spiderman window cleaner at the time," replied Tash. "You ready?"

Raymond took a deep breath and shook his head. "Absolutely not."

"Rhetorical question," said Tash "Get on with it."

They walked over to a staff nurse who was signing off a vast ream of paperwork with careful initials here, ticks there, and strikethroughs in other places.

"Hey!" exclaimed Raymond, at a volume even he didn't think he was capable of.

The ward manager looked up at the short plump porter standing before her. He had a black eye, dried blood under his nose, a neck brace, and a plaster cast on one of his hands. He stood with a nurse and a lady dragging a TV and video stand.

"Sorry, were you talking to me?"

What followed was an exquisite representation of how a South London security guard assumed an Irish father of a pop star would speak. In his defence, Raymond's grandfather was from Dublin, so he channeled as much of him as he could muster.

"I don't fecking care wha' the fecking boy says or wha' the fecking doctor says, or wha' you fecking say, he's ma boy, and he needs his Da, and I'm going to see him now. My name's Geldof, I bet he's said he's fecking Zenon or something, cos he's a fecker, but I know he's here cos Paula feckin' told me and she told me to bring this feckin' telly as well and the video wossaname too so he can watch all the feckin' pop videos and what have yer. And THAT'S a specialist brain nurse what wants to see him and THAT'S his sister also, so I'll take no feckin' shite from anyone, what bed's he in, sweetheart?"

In fairness, the Irish accent was pretty good, it even surprised Raymond, and the nurse had clearly been instructed that her special patient would be expecting some kind of special treatment, so maybe this was it? She looked at Raymond, then Jamie, then Tash, then back at Raymond again. He swallowed.

"Where's me boy?"

"It's nearly nine o'clock and visiting hours are strictly over by five-thirty p.m.," said the nurse.

"He might not make it to tomorrow if he doesn't see this feckin' brain nurse here. And that'll be your feckin' fault." He turned to Tash and nodded at the ward manager's name badge. "Take her name."

Tash paused and then devoid of other options she reached out to gently remove the pen from the ward manager's hand. She looked around for some paper. Failing, she leant over the desk and lifted the document the ward manager had been working on, ripped off the corner, and wrote the lady's name on the scrap of paper.

"So," Raymond continued, "will I see him now?"

The nurse looked at Jamie, compelling him to fill in the gaps. "I'm a nurse doctor, actually. Did both lots of the exams." He smiled. "It is quite important that we see him."

"Wait here, I'll see what the shift manager has to say," replied the nurse, and she scurried into the ward.

"Ah, good girl. We won't move an inch," answered Raymond, smiling at the nurse with as much blarney charm as he could muster.

"You're good," whispered Tash. "Not even slightly xenophobic."

Jamie was now reading more notes on the desk.

"Bay 3: Zenon. RTC. Observation for 12 hours."

They looked up and saw a suspended sign hanging from the mottled ceiling tiles. It read, 'Bay 1'.

"Come on," said Tash setting off.

Jamie was suddenly nervous. "Do we know how we're going to pitch this?"

Tash was not slowing down, in fact, she was already at the curtain positioned under the sign reading 'Bay 3'. She gently peered between the gap in the curtain and could see the vivid white hair of a young lady talking in a husky voice, soon followed by even deeper Irish tones and then laughter.

Tash turned to Jamie. "Do first – think later? Stick the video in."

She gestured at Jamie's sweaty hand and the machine that was suspended under the TV on the vast black trolley.

Jamie lifted up the precious cassette and presented it to the VCR opening. His hands were shaking, and his mouth was dry. This was surely not happening. Four hours ago he'd got out of bed for a wee, and his intrigue had sent him out into the snow and up into his Grandad's abandoned garage loft. And look at what was happening right now. He was about to show a world-changing news report to a reluctant hero. And he – Jamie Summers – would himself be part of history. Part of the solution. His brain was suddenly flooded with images of Bono going bright red as he sang his famous line in the video filmed in Sarm West studios '*Well tonight thank God it's them instead of you.*' He even allowed himself a wry smile. This is one to tell his grandkids. If his kids chose to have kids. If he had kids. If he ever got married. If he met someone that would date him. But he was brutally dragged from this euphoric vision by Raymond's voice, and he couldn't quite get the cassette into the machine.

"Betamax," said Raymond, looking at the machine. "The tape's VHS."

Tash looked at Raymond, at the cassette, at the video player, at Jamie. "What?"

"Betamax," repeated Raymond, now looking at Tash. "The tape's VHS."

"So how do we get it in?"

"We don't. We need a different video player."

"What do you mean?" asked Tash.

"You need a different video player – there are different sorts. You need one that'll play that tape."

"Like the one that recorded it?" asked Jamie.

Raymond nodded, his face turning to despair.

"That one in Woolworths?" asked Jamie.

Raymond stopped looking so helpful.

TWENTY SIX

The BT Trimphone was on its way out in 1984. British Telecom had launched the In-Phone TV commercials the year before in an attempt to get Britain using new plug-in phones. These could be switched between the new sockets that customers were also being encouraged to install in multiple rooms around the house. Raymond had convinced Maureen that once they bought shares in BT, they would probably get discounts, and they only had one more month to wait. So their 1970s Trim phone – which basically looked like a three-wheeler version of the typical home phone – was making its distinctive shrill and demanding tones from the wood chip walled hallway in Gaywood Close. Margaret Thatcher's Right To Buy scheme meant they – and all other council tenants – had been offered a 33% discount on their home's current market value. They had after all been paying handsomely in rent to the council for their 34 years of marriage together, but soon they would be lord and lady of their own manor. A modest cube of a house boasting two compact bedrooms and two cramped box bedrooms, or four bedrooms as Maureen liked to collectively call them.

Maureen was dressed in her tennis gear despite being resigned to the fact that her court booking slot at Brixton Recreation Centre had been forfeited. Her carpet slippers flattened the green shag pile carpet as she paced towards the telephone seat (still a hallway feature given their phone was hard-wired to the GPO box inside their obscure glazed front door). She always answered within three rings, she wasn't common.

"Hello?"

"Maureen, it's me," came the familiar nervous voice of her husband.

There was an audible sigh of relief. "Thank God for that, I thought it was the leisure centre about the tennis court."

"Yes. Yes. I forgot. You've missed tennis. Sorry about that."

"What on earth will I say? You'll have to go and explain it was all your fault."

There was a pause which Raymond opted to break. "I'm fine, by the way."

"Where the hell are you? Two yobbos stole your car, why did you let them do that? You knew about tennis!"

Raymond interrupted. "They need to get into your work. They need to get in now."

"What? Who? What do you mean? What's wrong?"

"They're prepared to let me go if we can get access to your store. I mean if they can."

"Let you go? What do you mean, let you go?"

"They don't want any police involved."

"Police?! What's happened? Where are you? What do you mean prepared to let you go?"

"Calm down. I know this is strange. They're being very nice to me. I've had an Eccles cake."

In the hospital corridor lined with payphones, Tash cast Raymond a strange look as he watched a half-eaten

Eccles cake on a trolley of finished dinner plates glide past. "They just need to borrow something from your work."

Maureen wasn't letting this go. "Who are *they*? What do they need to borrow? You're not making sense, Raymond. Are you in a pub?"

"They need to borrow a video recorder," explained Raymond.

"What for?" Maureen understandably thought this was absurd.

"I can't say – but they're serious."

"Well then lend them our video recorder!"

"They need a VHS."

"A what?"

"A VHS. Ours is a Betamax."

"I told you we should have bought the other type! I said it!"

"You didn't."

"I thought it. And now it's going to get you killed!"

"No-one's getting killed. I just need to get into Woolworths."

"My key is for opening up on Saturday mornings, no other time. I could get in trouble."

"I'm in trouble, Maureen. I'm in trouble. Please – meet me there as soon as you can."

"How am I supposed to get there? You lost the car, and the police have it now."

There was a pause, then Raymond took a very deep breath and suggested something he never thought he'd suggest to his wife.

"On the bus?"

The reaction to this was worse than her response to him being held hostage.

TWENTY SEVEN

Three figures loitered in the shadows on Lower Marsh in Lambeth. The red and white Woolworth's sign was maybe thirty yards down the street.

Raymond broke the silence. "She hates buses. She won't forget this in a hurry."

"Nightmare," offered Tash, not looking up from the home screen on her phone.

"What is that?" Raymond tried to catch another glimpse of this magical slender box.

"IPhone XR," explained Jamie.

"A phone," helped Tash.

"If that's a phone, how come we didn't use it to call Maureen?"

Jamie explained. "No signal. It's 4G, and you don't have 1G yet."

"It's all very *Blakes Seven* with you, isn't it?" replied Raymond, referencing a bewildering BBC sci-fi series that he was delighted had come to an end. "Codes and nonsense. That's why I struggle to believe a word you say."

"It's a camera too," said Tash, snapping a pic of a bewildered Raymond.

"Course it is. Plays tapes too does it?"

"No. Plays music, though," Tash pressed the screen a couple of times and held it up so Raymond could hear The 1975 performing 'If You're Too Shy (Let Me Know)'

He was blown away by the sound coming from this small handheld game or whatever it was but tried to conceal it.

"And that's from the future too, is it? That's from 2020?"

"2018. It's a 36-month contract."

"A what?"

"You pay for the phone over three years."

"Three years? To pay for a phone?"

"To answer your question, yes. The song is 2020," helped Jamie.

Raymond listened for a moment "Sounds like something off *Top Of The Pops* last week. So music hasn't evolved in thirty-six years? You must think I'm an idiot."

"Fair point," added Tash. "Big eighties influence."

Then Jamie had what he thought was a light bulb moment: "*Auf Wiedersehen, Pet*!"

"What?" Raymond was understandably confused.

"*Auf Wiedersehen, Pet* – it's a TV show!"

"What about it?"

"The guy from that – the Geordie one,"

"I didn't watch it," interrupted Raymond, before reluctantly adding: "They were all Geordies, weren't they?"

"You've heard of it, though. Well one of the guys from that – this is his son's band!"

Jamie smiled at Tash like he'd made a breakthrough.

Tash stared at Jamie. "How did that work out for you? In terms of sort of helping?"

Across the road, an old lady stopped walking and glanced over at the commotion.

"Can you turn it off, we're trying to be inconspicuous?" whispered Raymond, half smiling at the pensioner to reassure her. She continued on her way, and Tash turned off the music. Jamie was still thinking about the phone.

"It's also a video camera and TV and game player, and you can stream on it, and you can check your email and do your online banking too."

Raymond stared back. "I don't know what most of those words mean."

"You can pay for stuff with it," said Jamie.

"What? You hand that over, and you get your change back in smaller phones?"

"We're not lying to you, Raymond. Why would we? What do we have to gain by lying to you?" said Tash. It was a fair argument.

The road next to them was fleetingly illuminated by harsh light, not as intense as car headlights, but enough to get their attention. They looked up and spotted a tall lady, maybe mid-twenties, flicking a torch across the backs and fronts of parked cars. Soon she was less than ten feet away from them, clearly unaware they were in the shadows.

Jamie couldn't help but take on the role of good Samaritan. "Is everything OK?"

Clearly shocked, she jumped around to apologise.

"I'm sorry, I'm trying to…" she started to explain herself in an unmistakable American drawl.

A passing motorcycle illuminated her porcelain white skin. Her mop of pink hair did little to hide her sheer horror when her torchlight finally fell on the faces of the three people in the shadows. She was instantly mute. They all raised a hand to block the intense light coming from her hand. She stared at them for a second and then turned on her heels, sprinting past Woolworths and down the first side street.

"I'm guessing that's not Maureen?" asked Tash.

They all looked around as a double-decker bus noisily announced its entrance into the road. Raymond squared up in anticipation of the next stage of the plan. He now seemed twice as nervous as he had been just seconds before, which was quite an achievement.

"This is her," his mouth sounded dry as he squinted at the solitary figure waiting by the front doors of the bus as it pulled into the bus stop a couple of car lengths away from them.

"Right," said Tash, grabbing Raymond's elbow quite roughly.

"Steady on, you've got my skin."

"This has to look authentic Raymond, you're such a wuss."

They observed as Maureen was remonstrated by the conductor for standing at the wrong door. How was she to know you had get-in doors and get-off doors? There was one opening at the back the last time she rode a bus, and this new arrangement didn't suit her one bit. She walked to the exit doors and stepped cautiously down onto the dark pavement. The light from the Midland Bank griffin logo lit her anxious face as the bus drove away.

"Is that you, Raymond?" Her voice was faltering.

"It's me, Maureen," answered Raymond. "Raymond," like this would somehow help.

Maureen started to walk towards the three but was stopped by a very deep voice.

"Stop!" came Jamie's attempt at being macho. It even surprised Tash. "Cross the road so we can see you – wait outside Woolworths." They all noticed how challenging it was to sound aggressive and say Woolworths in the same sentence. But Jamie gave it his best shot.

Maureen did as she was told, followed by Raymond and his prisoners, although for now he was theirs. This all suddenly looked very authentic with Tash coercing him across the road and Jamie at the rear.

"You're not the IRA, are you?" asked Maureen as she tripped across the road looking over her shoulder. "We voted Liberal. We don't want to get involved. We don't support anyone. Raymond has asthma."

"We're not the IRA," explained Tash. Her words sounded bizarre in her own ears.

As they finally came into the light of Woolworths' front window, two things happened.

Jamie blurted, "My God, Paul McCartney hasn't changed one bit, has he?"

Give My Regards To Broadstreet, McCartney's new album poster filled one of the windows. *Includes the hit single: No More Lonely Nights. Out this week, record and cassette £4.79.*

Simultaneously Maureen shrieked at Jamie.

"You were in the hospital car park! You spoke with the police! You're a liar! You're not a nurse!" She interrupted herself after seeing her husband in the light. "Raymond, you're dressed as a doctor. What's going on?" Then she saw his black eye, bloodied nose and neck brace and hand in plaster. "Oh my God, what have they done to you?"

"I'm a porter, actually," protested Raymond like it mattered.

"Where's your suit? That was a Christmas present!"

"Which Christmas? 1968?" asked Tash.

"It's at the hospital," he replied.

"Could we have the keys?" interrupted Jamie.

Maureen fumbled in her purse, trying desperately not to take her eyes off these assailants.

"This is aggravated robbery, you know." She handed over a chunky brass key and a further Yale one.

Tash took them from Jamie and fumbled with them as she attempted to find the keyhole in the oak framed glass door. It turned out there were three, two for the brass Chubb key and one for the Yale. The moment the door opened a warning beep of the burglar alarm made itself known.

"Alarm," snapped Tash. Maureen dashed to a display of TDK cassettes and JVC blank video packs and the racks of goods magically swung open. Behind the hidden door she simply twisted a dial on the burglar alarm box to silence it. Then she flicked on the shop lights.

Tash immediately jumped. The strip lights had illuminated a beautiful pink or purple-haired lady standing less than two feet away from her. "Oh my God, I thought that was an actual woman," she shrieked as he stepped back to see a life-sized cut out of Boy George with magnificent purple hair and stunning contoured makeup. '*Waking Up With The House On Fire*, Culture Club's new album out October 25th on LP and cassette' was printed across his chest.

"We all did, actually didn't we, Maureen?" said Raymond.

"Let him go now, you've got what you wanted." Maureen stopped herself saying any more. Had she gone too far? She wasn't quite able to gauge the mood in the room. Oh God, why had she said that?

Tash looked at Maureen and then let go of Raymond's elbow. "Of course, sorry."

Jamie set off to the TV and video section, and Tash walked towards the packages of plugs, headphones and wires.

"We'll need a scart lead," muttered Tash glaring at the white and brown coils of pre-packed wire. "Maureen, scart lead. Where are they?"

"A what lead?"

"They do this a lot," sighed Raymond at his wife. "They have their own words for things."

"Scart. To connect the video player to the TV."

"You need a coaxial," explained Raymond.

Maureen turned to Tash. "In front of you."

"Scart not invented yet, Raymond?" asked Tash in a matter-of-fact way as she pulled a coiled cable from a display. She looked over for her brother. "Have you got a video, Jamie?"

"Nearly," he muttered from across the store.

"What does nearly mean?"

"The Ferguson has a 14 day timer, but the Panasonic has a smaller remote." He was genuinely perplexed. Too much choice was not good for him.

"We're not keeping the fucking thing!"

Maureen jumped at the profanity. "Are you making a bomb?"

"A what?" Tash was astonished.

"Is that what you need the timer for?"

"You can tell her the truth as far as I'm concerned, Raymond. We only needed to get in here. We've managed that. And thank you by the way," Tash addressed the thanks to Maureen, who she'd only just noticed was in tennis whites and trainers, her anorak had covered most of the kit outside. Maureen looked at her husband. She glanced at the front door again.

"They reckon they came here from Sheffield. They were celebrating Christmas," started Raymond.

"Gets earlier every year." Maureen wasn't surprised, just a little disgusted.

"Christmas 2020," Raymond explained.

"What does that mean? What does 2020 mean?"

"Listen to me, Maureen. They say they're time travellers from 36 years in the future and unless they borrow this video recorder…" Raymond was interrupted by Tash:

"Which we'll return…"

"Which they'll return," continued Raymond before Tash thought better of it.

"Well, which Raymond will return."

This was met by a non-plussed face from Raymond, so Tash held up her phone and flicked the screen to reveal her baby son by way of explanation. "We need to get home."

"Which I'll return…." conceded Raymond. "Basically, it's simple... And do tell me if I have misunderstood this?" He looked at Tash, then continued, "Unless they can play tonight's BBC News to a pop star, they reckon thousands of people will erm, well, thousands of people will erm. Well, thousands of people will die"

"Oh my God, you are terrorists!" Maureen's hands leapt to her cheeks.

Jamie was now heading towards them with the Ferguson video recorder Sab had demonstrated.

"I went for the Ferguson Videostar," said Jamie. "Soft-touch buttons!"

"My sister had nothing but trouble with soft-touch on her JVC," offered Raymond.

"I thought they weren't stealing it, Raymond?" said Maureen. "Stop helping terrorists!"

Raymond sighed. He was having a bad day. "I'm not sure I believe it Maureen, but they're not terrorists, they're brother and sister, and they seem very confused. They're lost, and they think they caused an accident and they need to make sure the person who got injured in the accident sees something off the news 'cos he missed it."

"Well, when you put it like that it makes no sense whatsoever."

"Stop right there!" came a shout from the front door.

They all turned to see the massive frame of Jermaine in the doorway, which was confusing as it wasn't his voice they'd heard.

"This ends here," continued Dudley, finally peering around his human safety screen, somewhere just above Jermaine's belt. Tash was more exasperated than horrified.

"Oh bollocks," she sighed. "How did the fucking Chuckle Brothers find us?"

"They were at the house when you called," explained Maureen to her husband, suddenly quite buoyed by Dudley's arrival. "They told me to keep quiet about it. They listened on the bedroom phone like in Magnum P.I."

"They knew you were coming here?" asked Raymond.

She nodded.

"But still made you take the bus?"

"They didn't want anything to seem suspicious. So I had to sit next to a glue sniffer and a chain smoker on a …. bus," she struggled with the word like a vicar might struggle with the word threesome.

Dudley stepped out from behind Jermaine, and channeling his best Roger Moore 007 impression instructed his staff, "Lock the doors, Jermaine."

Dudley slowly paced over to the others before perching sideways on a large metal display basket of Cadburys Fruit and Nut. It took a few moments to get comfortable as the basket edge was sharp and he was currently sharing his arse with a couple of haemorrhoids, but soon he was satisfied. He liked this persona he'd created for himself. This was very much like one of the cops he'd seen in that new ITV show that started last week, it was called *The Bill* and would be on again tonight, in fact, he wished he'd set the video cos it looked like he might miss it because of all this nonsense. Damn. Just like the detective in that show, he'd even remembered to put his leather gloves back on in the car, so he could ceremoniously remove them now. The first came off well, the second wouldn't tweak off his fingertips, so he ended up turning it inside out to get it off and was left holding a pretty sorry looking ball of a glove. He shook this with limited success so casually turned his head to one side so he could blow into the glove in an attempt to turn it the correct way around.

Maureen made her way over to stand alongside her husband's boss, making her team quite clear to anyone who still harboured any doubt. Dudley looked surprised.

"You can piss off over there!" instructed Dudley. "Stand with your faded little husband. Who – by the way – is sacked."

Maureen looked more mortified than Raymond as she walked over to him. Profanity and redundancy in one exchange. How brutal. Dudley turned to glare at his silent audience. He spoke menacingly.

"I am going to say something now, and…" Dudley was unceremoniously interrupted by Jermaine.

"There's no bolts," Jermaine gestured at the front door. "I'll need the key to lock it."

Dudley absorbed these developments.

"Block it – that will be fine," nodded Dudley. He slowly turned back to continue his speech.

"I am going to say something now, and…" Again he was interrupted by Jermaine.

"I can't lock it. It needs a key."

"I said, block it. Block it! I heard what you said, so then I said block it. With a B"

"With what?"

"B! B! BLOCK! Block the door!"

The penny dropped. Jermaine nodded and stood squarely before the entrance. Dudley turned again. "I am going to say something," started Dudley but again Jermaine interrupted.

"Sorry, you were mumbling a bit the first time."

"I don't mumble, Jermaine!" He took a breath. "We'll pick this up later."

"Say again?"

"We'll pick this up later!"

"Can we get on, please?" said Tash. "Just give us the top line."

Dudley glared at Tash for a moment. "You, young lady, have made a fool of me."

"You've done that yourself. Didn't need my help."

"And what do you mean by that?"

"You're sat on a fuck load of chocolate to start with."

Dudley stood up and felt his arse. Sure enough, when he examined his hand, it was coated in Fruit and Nut. He changed tact immediately in an attempt to maintain his control of the room.

"You don't work at the London School of Economics," he was pointing at Tash now.

"Yes, I do," she replied, "I just haven't started yet."

Dudley flipped. "I have worked my ruddy socks off for the past seven years building a company that commands respect from some of the biggest business names in the United Kingdom…" He then counted them on his fingers. The list was a little lacklustre to start. "Laker…" he began before interrupting himself. "That wasn't my fault," he muttered, before continuing his list. "Smart R's Jeans, Ipso Calypso."

Tash couldn't let that one go. "Excuso The Fuckso?"

Dudley explained like surely everyone knew the brand. "Tic-Tac rival? You know the one? Fruit version? Comes in Lego compatible boxes?"

"Finally! Sweets you can build with!" Jamie was genuinely impressed.

"It's an impressive list," said Tash. She didn't mean it of course.

"It is, and I haven't finished…" He paused for effect for this final one, it needed to land with the impact it deserved… "And last year – Sinclair Research."

There was a silence as Dudley continued to nod at them. Happily, Jermaine broke it.

"You've got chocolate on your arse."

Dudley didn't need to look back at Jermaine. The moment was too big for that. He held his gaze on the siblings and answered, "Thank you! Been told."

He glared again at Tash and Jamie.

"Sorry, is that it?" asked Tash.

"We really need to be off," explained Jamie.

"You know damn well that you are in possession of a highly confidential commercial product, not yet launched to the British public. Not only have you stolen it, you – or your people – have systematically dismantled it for research purposes, and then destroyed it with bizarre modifications. Do not deny it."

"Well, it's all true other than the stolen bit," said Tash. "Raymond told you, none of your stock is missing."

"Well let's start with how you explain that? I have all night." Dudley reached over for a packet of Opal Fruits.

Maureen looked mortified, and whispered to her husband, "Is he going to pay for those?"

Tash squared up to Dudley. "How would your client feel about you breaking and entering into a high street store? I'm guessing that wouldn't be good for his brand?"

"I didn't break into anywhere!" Dudley snorted at the thought as he pulled a bit of paper off a green sweet, confused by this line of questioning, and equally miffed that there was always a tiny bit of paper that remained whenever he tried to open one of these bloody sweets. There was an impasse. Dudley turned to Jermaine. "I think we've been nice enough, Jermaine."

"Pardon?" asked his giant.

Dudley was too busy playing the Bond villain. "I think we might need to be a bit more persuasive."

"Say again?" asked Jermaine, screwing up his massive face in an attempt to make his ears work better.

Dudley raised his voice. "I think we might need to be a bit more persuasive."

Jermaine nodded. But did nothing. Dudley glared at him. "When I say we, I mean you."

"Of course! Sorry."

There was a pause. Jermaine broke the silence. "Do you mean get the gun?"

The mood in the room changed in an instant.

Dudley clicked his fingers and nodded. Jermaine reached into his jacket and produced a handgun and set off slowly towards the prisoners.

Maureen screamed. Raymond stood in front of her. Tash's jaw dropped. Jamie said out loud, "Gun! Jermaine's got a gun, and he's walking towards us."

None had seen a gun in real life before, only on TV or in films. It was tiny and looked absurd in Jermaine's plate-sized hand. Tash wondered how many people had looked down the barrel of it in the final moments of their life. Jamie wondered why the handle was a pearl white colour, and how much it would fetch on eBay, and can you actually list firearms on eBay?

Tash was suddenly distracted by something in the doorway; it was fleeting but unmistakable. Someone had flashed towards the hidden cupboard Maureen had opened just moments before.

"Listen. There's no need to be silly. I was just saying that the police might disagree if they found you locked in here," said Tash. "Without us."

With that, the shop fell into darkness. The store was illuminated only by the amber glow of the street lights, and that barely reached beyond the front windows. Everyone momentarily froze. Then things changed.

All that Dudley knew was that people were moving. He could hear footsteps and shouting. A figure switched the burglar alarm on and closed the display door.

"Shoot one of them!" shouted Dudley at a bewildered Jermaine who was utterly useless in the dark. "You shoot one of them!" replied Jermaine. He sprinted down the board game aisle convinced he'd seen the silhouette of someone. He was right. He was struck by Dudley coming across his path at the junction with 7-inch singles. Both hit the floor hard. As Dudley climbed to his feet, he watched Sab help Raymond and Maureen step outside, before slamming the front door shut and locking it twice from the outside. Raymond was gesticulating that Jamie and Tash were still inside and frantically knocking to get out on the other side of the door. Dudley was on his feet now. Jermaine was up next.

"Raymond! Raymond! Let us out!" begged Tash.

"We're locked in, and he's got a gun!" shouted Jamie.

"Seven eleven breathing, Jamie. Don't lose it," replied Tash. "Breathe in seven, breathe out eleven."

Dudley pushed Jermaine ahead of him past the cutlery and crockery aisle. He needed to capture this evil pair, he couldn't fail, it simply wasn't an option. "Go! Go! Go!"

"RAYMOND! PLEASE!" screamed Tash as she thumped the door again. The beep-beep-beep of the setting alarm was deafening to Jamie. Raymond snatched the keys from Sab and frantically unlocked the door and pushed it open. Tash leapt outside, but Jamie was overwhelmed and frozen to the spot. Jermaine was now just one aisle length away from him.

"Stay there!" barked Dudley. "Don't move!"

At that moment, Tash leapt into the shop and physically dragged Jamie outside. Raymond slammed the door shut and managed to get the key into a lock just as Jermaine reached it.

"Lock it, Raymond!" shouted Tash. He did. Twice.

Then Maureen screamed. Louder than she'd ever screamed before. Dudley had snatched the gun from Jermaine and was pointing it through the glass at Tash. She froze. The moment would live in her head forever, but it lasted one second before Raymond stepped in front of her, blocking her entirely from the aim of Dudley's gun. My God, his boss looked different. His face was pure hatred. Evil. Possessed.

Raymond gazed at his employer and could see the child in his face. He'd not actually known Dudley as a boy, but he was unmistakably a human who hadn't grown up the way any parent would have wished. Wrong decisions here and there. Some bad breaks. But undeniably Raymond could picture the child in his face. And strangely he didn't hate his potential assassin, despite the gun pointing squarely at his head. He just felt sad. Sad that today he'd observed thousands of babies dying on a TV screen. Thousands of babies who would never get the chance at life. Never have the opportunity to make some wrong decisions like this bastard in front of him. Raymond's head filled with the horrific exchange in the hospital when Jamie explained to Tash that she was a surviving twin. What makes the lucky ones, the ones that live, turn to hate? Raymond was also astonished that so many thoughts could dance through his brain in such a short period of time. Including his own childhood. He'd not expected his life to end like this.

Dudley's hand trembled as his finger looped over the trigger. He couldn't let this selfish man destroy his dreams. He'd paid Raymond a salary for years now, what gave him the right to hold him hostage like this? All Dudley's plans of success had fallen through his fingers year on year on year. And now this one was over too. And it was the fault of this dishonest man – he'd stolen intellectual material and sold it to this brother and sister. If they were brother and sister. All of these thoughts flashed through both their minds before anyone could even mobilise their bodies. Then Dudley took one final aim at Raymond and squeezed tight.

TWENTY EIGHT

The bus shelter smelled of piss. At least that was the same as 2020, thought Jamie. And naturally, what he thought he said. "This smells of piss."

Tash was rubbing Maureen's back as she tried to control her breathing. She was clearly in shock.

"We should be playing tennis," mumbled Maureen. "This shouldn't have happened."

"Try to calm down," reassured Sab.

Maureen burst into tears. "I've never seen a gun before. I can't believe Raymond knew he was working for thugs," said Maureen.

Jamie looked at Tash. They both looked back at Maureen. They felt helpless.

"How many times? I had no idea he had a gun," protested Raymond, standing in the shadows using one arm to steady his shaking body against Freeman Hardy & Willis.

After the gunshot, Raymond had convinced himself he'd been shot. He'd read stories of people who'd been on the receiving end of a bullet and recalled their astonishment that they felt like they'd been punched, or winded, or sometimes nothing. Nothing at all.

The moment the tip of the gun flashed, he felt sure he was in the latter category. He simply couldn't feel the shot that would kill him. Then he realised that the glass remained undamaged in the door. There was no smash.

No bullet hole. The ringing in his ears wasn't enough to block the shrieks of Tash telling him to run. And that's what he had done.

"Was it a blank then? It must have been a blank," asked Tash.

"Dudley didn't know it was a blank," surmised Jamie. "It was Jermaine's gun. Why would Dudley fire a gun if he thought it was carrying blanks?" It was a rhetorical question, but Jamie soon spotted his audience were captivated by his conclusions.

"I'm just saying. Dudley did want to kill Raymond. We can be sure of that." Maureen shrieked again, and her tears continued to fall. This was one time where some kind of thought-filter might have improved the mood of Jamie's audience.

"Alright, Jamie," hushed Tash.

"It's a good thing you did what you did," said Jamie to Sab.

"What are you doing here?" asked Maureen. "You'd gone home."

"This is my route home from night school," answered Sab.

"Well, your English is excellent," replied Raymond kindly, still catching his breath.

"I'm studying accountancy."

Tash was shocked. "Fuck sake, Raymond! Didn't have you down as a Nazi!"

"She's British, Raymond!" said Maureen.

Raymond looked utterly ashamed. "I didn't mean to be rude, I genuinely thought that…"

He was interrupted by Jamie. "1984, isn't it? They're all still learning not to be pricks. I don't think he meant any harm, Tash."

"I'm really sorry," apologised Raymond, even in the darkness all could see his face was now the same shade as the post box outside Fine Fare supermarket.

"No offence taken," replied Sab. She'd experienced genuine racism. She knew this was the ignorant kind. Indefensible, but a legacy of Raymond's generation. Then she did a double-take at Jamie, suddenly realising she'd seen his face before.

"You stole that videotape!"

"They've stolen a video recorder now!" said Maureen "Terrorists! We're caught up in some gangland warfare, Sab!"

"We're borrowing it," said Jamie. Maureen didn't look convinced. Jamie tried to hand over the video player and the cassette. "You hold it. Take it! I mean it. We're borrowing it," explained Jamie. "You hold it."

Maureen directed the video towards her husband, who struggled to hold the chunky silver machine between his good arm and cast one. Jamie rested the cassette on top.

"See," said Jamie holding up empty hands "We've stolen nothing."

"We should call the police! We need to find a phone," said Maureen.

"He had a gun!" The impact of the past three minutes was finally coming clear to Raymond. "Jermaine had a gun." Clearly he'd spent his employed years in blissful ignorance of the depths his boss had sunken to stay afloat. The silence that followed was only brief.

"I can never go to the tennis club again," muttered Maureen, looking at her watch. "There's a fine if you don't use your slot." Raymond opted not to remind her it wasn't really a club. The municipal sports centre would take bookings from anyone. In her defence she'd been watching a lot of *Dallas* and *Dynasty*.

"Right," interrupted Tash. "This is the plan. We take the video player and the video cassette to the hospital. We play the news to Bob Geldof."

"Bob Geldof?" asked Sab.

"Long story," said Tash, then she turned to Maureen. "We return the video to you. Then we head back to the warehouse and go home. Leaving you all to carry on with your lives."

"Carry on? Aside from an assassination attempt, you've got him fired! We were going to buy our house. This is awful!" Maureen started to cry again.

"And you missed your tennis slot," said Jamie.

"I'm sorry about all this Raymond, this wasn't meant to happen," said Tash. "None of this was meant to happen."

"You were buying a house?" asked Jamie.

"Council," explained Raymond, playing things down. He hated boasting.

"We live in it! It's our home, and we were going to buy it!" said Maureen.

"They're doing this 'right to buy' scheme," explained Raymond. "You get a reduced price if you've been renting for some time."

Maureen was finding a tissue in her anorak. "He's saved his whole life, and we were going to use that as a deposit. What's the point of a deposit with no income? You've ruined everything,"

"I was hoping to get some of those British Telecom shares too. You know, when they float next month?"

"Oversubscribed. Ray. You'll struggle to get rich on that," said Tash.

"They're not on sale yet, what do you mean oversubscribed?"

"I know Economics history. It's my job. And all this is thirty-six years ago," said Tash. For the first time, she seemed to be accepting her reality. "How many did you want?"

"How many?"

"How many BT shares?"

"Well, I was hoping for a thousand pounds worth." Raymond stood up proudly. He suddenly felt like he was one of those suited traders on the Stock Exchange.

"Don't tell her our business, Raymond. She's a criminal!" said Maureen.

"If you sold at the right time, you might make a fifty per cent return next year," concluded Tash, "If you sold at the right time."

"Fifty per cent?" Raymond's eyes lit up. "On top of my investment?"

"Not gonna make you rich on your three hundred quid, is it?"

"No, I said a thousand, not three hundred."

"People got something like a third of what they asked for," explained Tash.

"Why is she talking like this?" asked Maureen. "Tell her to stop it. I don't like it."

"We're from 2020," explained Jamie. "This has all happened you see… But I get it. You don't believe us. I totally get it."

"You're from 2020? The year 2020?" asked Sab, waiting for the punchline.

Jamie nodded. "Totally understand why you don't believe us. We didn't believe we were here either."

"Who's king in 2020?" asked Sab, smiling at Jamie.

"What?"

"Is Charles King? Or is it William? I'm interested in your truth."

"Neither. We're still on the Queen."

"Really? She must be like ninety?"

"I can prove it!" Jamie fumbled in his pocket. "I've got a two-pound coin!"

"Two-pound coin!" Maureen was tutting with the same disbelief as if someone had said electric car.

Everyone watched Jamie fumble about his nurse's uniform before he realised it contained no trouser pockets.

"I had one." Jamie sounded suddenly dejected.

Tash produced her phone. She swiped open her photos and scrolled, then held up the screen.

"VE Day. 75th anniversary. May. This year. Street party. 2020."

Maureen and Raymond leaned in suspiciously and looked at this impossibly bright and detailed screen. Sab looked beguiled by it.

"That's not a street party," said Maureen after a few seconds. Raymond spoke up as kindly as he could. "Well,

I can see what she means. There aren't many people there, are there?"

"That's a long story," explained Tash.

"Of course it is," replied Maureen sarcastically. "You'll have time to tell it in prison."

"Okay, if you must know, there's a global pandemic – a killer flu. The government closed down every job and sent people home. They paid their salary for months – all to save the NHS. You can't even have your family come and visit most of the time. It's all been a bit much, to be honest. I didn't realise how upset I was, actually. It's been horrible. We have to stand two metres apart."

"Or one-plus, Tash. It's been one-plus for ages," interrupted Jamie.

"What's one-plus?" asked Sab.

"No-one really knows." Jamie shrugged to the faces staring at him.

"It's called social distancing," said Tash. "Still doing it. Still wearing masks to the shops and elbow bumping."

"We live in bubbles."

"Oh, we were doing so well, Jamie," Tash was clearly annoyed. "That's gonna take some explaining."

"I have to be honest, this does all sound a bit HG Wells now," said Raymond apologetically.

Tash tapped the iPhone screen. "Look at the bunting!"

Raymond squinted at the screen, so Tash pinched to expand it.

"VE Day, 75" he read on a union jack flag.

"What is that machine?" said Sab, glaring at the iPhone.

"IPhone XR," said Tash.

Jamie tried to help with a bit more detail. "It's like a phone and a camera. You can shop on it too. Calculator. Fitness trainer. Calendar... and pretty much everything else."

Sab looked very interested as she tentatively took this impressive tool from Tash.

"Can we call the police on this, then?"

"No. You haven't invented the network yet... No signal," Tash pointed at the corner of the screen. "No bars look."

"No what? Where are the buttons?"

She then swiped through a few screens.

"Touch screen," explained Tash. Sab took a beat to absorb this information.

"Donald Trump's been American president for the past four years," interjected Jamie.

"Never heard of him," said Maureen.

"Massive orange billionaire businessman," explained Jamie.

"Maybe he could give Raymond a job?"

"Well not really, cos he got voted out, you see," Jamie wasn't great at spotting sarcasm.

Tash looked at Maureen, then at Raymond. His battered face and plaster cast did little to alleviate her guilt. She decided to throw as many facts into the session as possible. "Two of the Beatles are still alive, ALL of the Rolling Stones are alive. They're still touring! So's Rod Stewart. Footballers are ALL millionaires."

"Not all of them, Tash," protested Jamie.

"Who won the last World Cup?" asked Raymond, suddenly buoyed by the subject.

"France," answered Jamie, "We came fourth."

"Who won Wimbledon?" asked Maureen, and then immediately regretted her collusion with criminals.

"It was cancelled. So were the Olympics," said Jamie.

"Cancelled?" asked Raymond, suddenly disappointed. Until now what they'd claimed had seemed feasible, but cancelling an Olympics was absurd.

"Pandemic," explained Tash. "People are dying from this brand-new virus."

Then a thought struck Raymond.

"Are you er…?" He took a step backwards.

"No. We're fine. We're fine!" reassured Tash.

There was a further awkward silence of disbelief whilst the class of '84 weighed up the visual signs of good health of their time travelling colleagues.

"We're fine!" repeated Jamie.

Tash realised Sab was still swiping away at her phone, so snatched it back and tucked it safely inside her jumper. She turned to Raymond and Maureen, with a new approach forming in her mind.

"You like your tennis, don't you?"

Raymond nodded. Maureen nodded.

"Do you have a pen and some paper?"

"No. Maybe you could magic them from the future?" suggested Maureen. "Or bring them over in a flying car?"

Sab pulled a pen from a zip pocket in her student bag and handed it to Tash.

"Thank you," said Tash, before turning to Raymond. "Your savings, are we talking thousands?" She felt around her borrowed skirt pockets as she spoke and found something of interest between her fingers.

"Erm, ten." Everyone could hear the trepidation in Raymond's voice.

"Don't tell her that!" said Maureen, flicking Raymond around the head.

Tash pulled out some scrunched papers and unfurled them. In amongst her father's SMART PAUSE plans was a solitary green one-pound note, clearly forgotten when the owner placed it in the laundry. She started to write on the back of it.

"Can I ask a question?" asked Maureen. "Why are we standing and talking? Why aren't we calling the police?"

"I can see why you might wonder that," replied Tash as she finished writing. "I really can. She placed her Dad's plans back in her pocket and started to fold the banknote in half, but suddenly the low hum of traffic was interrupted by the shrieking bells of a burglar alarm. Tash quickly shoved the note into Maureen's anorak pocket and zipped it closed. "Don't lose that," she muttered as they all looked along the street to see a flashing light on the alarm box outside Woolworths, but the door was still firmly closed.

"What's causing the alarm?" asked Jamie, staring at the storefront.

"The alarm has movement sensors inside the store," explained Sab.

They absorbed this information, and then Maureen had a thought. "Or they might have just opened the back door."

"Back door?" asked Tash.

"Well, it's around the side. By the railway sidings," replied Sab, gesturing down a dark street.

The roar of a car engine and the squeal of tyres ended the pleasantries. The Mercedes had mounted the kerb before most of them even saw it.

"Run!" shouted Jamie.

Jamie and Tash ran one way, with Sab following a few paces behind. Maureen and Raymond ran the other, still clutching the video recorder. It turned out that Dudley was at the wheel of the car, which may explain the kerb mount as his driving skills were dubious at the best of times. Jamie and Tash ran straight into the wall that was Jermaine. This time he was ready. He effortlessly locked the siblings in a neck hold and dragged them to the rear of the German car. Jermaine had no interest in Sab, who managed to run into the shadows. Jermaine used his massive foot to clip the car boot open, which popped up to reveal yet another gloomy black prison for his captives.

"Don't kick the bloody car, Jermaine. I'm leasing this! Back seat! Put them on the back seat. I want to talk to them," barked Dudley from the driver's window. "What is it with you and kicking things? This isn't the bloody *Professionals*. And take this."

Dudley dangled the familiar gun out of his car window. Jermaine dragged Tash and Jamie to the back door and managed to open it without releasing his glue-like grasp on the siblings' necks. The process caused Jamie's face to hit the door several times and Tash to trip over her own legs but after four almighty shoves the pair of them were forced into the back of the car, which seemed to bounce before they even landed side by side on the rear leather bench seat. Jermaine slammed the door shut on them, took the gun from Dudley and walked around the back of the car to throw the gun into the dark boot and then slam it shut. He walked up to the passenger door. It was locked. Dudley lowered the electric window with a pleasing hum and glared menacingly at his employee.

"Get Raymond. And don't come back without him."

Jamie leaned forward to the open passenger window and yelled into the shadows. "Raymond! You've got to show Bob that video! Raymond!"

Jamie was thrown back into his seat as Dudley sped off into the London evening traffic.

As she straightened her posture on the slippery leather seat, Tash looked over at Jamie who was struggling to make sense of the past five minutes. His eyes were filled with tears.

"I'm so sorry, Jamie," she whispered kindly. "I'm so sorry."

Jamie sat in silence, his brain a deafening overload of stimulus and frustrated thoughts.

Tash squeezed his hand. "We tried, you can't say we didn't try. Sometimes you can only do your best."

Jamie glanced through the window of the child-locked car door and watched as warm streetlights and stone buildings whooshed past. A knot suddenly formed hard in his chest. A matter of hours earlier, he'd stupidly tried to recapture his youth by pissing around with an abandoned toy from his childhood. He'd even got his sister involved. What was he thinking? She was a mother. She had responsibilities. How the hell had he managed to completely change the course of history and fail at all his attempts to correct his terrible decisions? He had been unable to put history back on track. The ghoulish images of the BBC News report filled his head one more time. The despair, the famine, the horror.

Tash, on the other hand, was not quite so conflicted.

Finally, she thought, I'm heading home. Just the small matter of the millennium bug to figure out. But how hard can that be?

TWENTY NINE

Raymond and Maureen had run in the opposite direction to the others. As they exited the Upper Marsh tunnel under the Waterloo rail station tracks, Raymond was surprised that they kept moving for so long. Maybe their weekly tennis sessions had helped their fitness levels after all? The darkness beneath the high-rise flats up ahead beckoned them as a safe space. They slowed down as they reached the first of the conical pillars that held up the impossible town in the sky and set themselves down onto the cold flagstone floor. The shadow of the block above provided all the cover they needed. Raymond peered around the stark concrete leg and spotted the silhouette of Jermaine doubled over with a stitch having made it through the tunnel. It was soon clear to see that he had lost sight of his prey. He turned to head back into the darkness towards Woolworths.

"He's gone the other way," whispered Raymond.

Maureen burst into tears. Raymond gently placed the video recorder and cassette down beside him and wrapped his good arm around his wife.

"Raymond," she started to speak, but it was a little too loud for Raymond's liking.

"Shh," he interrupted as gently as he could.

"Don't shush me!" She hated being shushed.

"He's only fifty yards away, Maureen." Raymond placed a palm over her face in despair.

Maureen slapped furiously at her husband, who removed his hand.

"Take me home, Raymond. Just take me home." She started to cry.

"Of course, sweetheart. Of course." He embraced her. "I'm really sorry."

The affection between them was unquestionable. Until now, a stranger might assume this was a stale, loveless marriage with its glory days firmly locked in the past. But there was no mistaking that the two sorry silhouettes under the council flats by Waterloo were very much a Romeo and Juliet for 1984. Raymond was even wondering if he might be pushing their beds together tonight, after he'd put them in the same room of course. But then he spoke again.

"We'll just play this video to Bob Geldof, and then I'll flag us a taxi. How about that, eh? No buses for my princess tonight."

It's probably better that he couldn't see his wife's eyes right now. Or her face. It wasn't a good look, even she would admit to that. And why not? She had clearly married an almighty prick.

"What?" growled Maureen.

"We can get a taxi home. I'm paying!"

Then Maureen's voice echoed proudly off the underside of the concrete monolith above, and deep into the Upper Marsh tunnel, not to mention the sheet glass windows of St Thomas' Hospital right across Lambeth Palace Road. It would have been impressive had it not filled Raymond with sheer dread.

"WHAT KIND OF A MAN ALLOWS HOOLIGANS INTO HIS LIFE TO DESTROY HIS LIVELIHOOD? HIS WIFE'S LIVELIHOOD? TO STEAL THEIR FUTURE? AND CONSIGN THEM TO A MISERLY PENSION IN A POKEY LITTLE SHIT-HOLE SHOEBOX OF A HOME?" Her voice got even louder as she finished with, "AND NO FUCKING TENNIS CLUB!"

With that, Maureen gave an almighty punch of her clenched fist right into the stomach of her seated husband. He gasped for air, fully winded like a schoolboy in his first rugby game.

After he caught his breath, Raymond spoke. "I've never heard you swear before, Maureen."

"Well, you've never pissed me off so much before, Raymond."

They were silent. Their eyes just starting to get used to the darkness.

"I'll find another job."

"There's almost a twelve per cent unemployment rate!"

"Well, yes. Might take a while."

There was more silence.

"Sorry," said Raymond.

After even more silence, he spoke again.

"I didn't know you thought our home was a shoebox."

"It's not a shoebox, Raymond, it's just no palace, is it?"

"We made it a palace, Maureen. We made it one. We wanted a home in a nice area. A decent size. Bit of a garden for some swings. Near good schools..." He stopped himself.

Maureen took a deep breath. "I know. I know."

"We didn't know we wouldn't need the schools, did we? We didn't know back then?"

Maureen could have been mistaken, but the headlights of a passing car seemed to reflect moisture under Raymond's eye.

"We didn't know," Maureen agreed, and embraced her husband.

They held one another as the traffic rumbled past. Above them fourteen storeys of households continued watching TV, running baths, listening to music, reading books, sipping cups of tea, and generally having a pretty unremarkable Tuesday. All of them completely unaware that beneath their feet, two lost souls were reuniting for the first time in years.

"It's not about me, Maureen," explained Raymond. "None of this has been about me. I saw the news tonight, and it's horrible. Children are dying. Babies are dying. Jamie and Tash said they'd made a mistake..."

"I don't want to hear their names again."

"No, you must. You must, Maureen. They're brother and sister, and they said they'd made a big mistake tonight that meant something terrible is going to happen on the other side of the world.

All they wanted to do was show tonight's news report to a man in that hospital. They said he would make a big difference. But he needs to see that video of the news, Maureen. Don't you see? It's not about me, or you. Or Dudley. It's about the kids in Africa."

"You make it sound biblical."

Raymond pulled himself to his feet, and offered his good hand to Maureen, still sitting on the floor. She took it and pulled herself up.

"The way I see it is, we can watch that famine roll out every night on TV and wonder – could we have changed anything? Or we can do what Jamie and Tash were trying to do? It's not illegal, it's not risky, it's not even difficult."

Maureen looked over to the bright lights of the hospital across the road.

"Are we going to do this?" asked Raymond. "Together?"

Maureen took a deep breath, nodded at her husband and took one step forward. They both heard the crisp sound of a plastic video cassette crunching underneath her foot.

THIRTY

Inside Butler's Wharf it was apparent to Jamie and Tash that Dudley's mood was not good. Not good at all.

"I am on a ninety-five per cent completion contract," he spat the words in Tash's direction. "You'd understand that, with your LSE connections?"

Tash glanced at her brother. He'd taken badly to being tied to a chair next to her. Far worse than she had.

Dudley continued. "Oh, no, wait! You don't work there!"

"You don't mean ninety-five per cent of your fee is payable at the end of the project?" asked Tash.

"Clever girl. You do understand business then?"

"Better than you. Why would you pay rent on a place like this for twenty-four months with no contingency from your client to cover your liabilities? That money's earning decent interest in their account when it could be paying your fixed costs!"

"What?"

"Interest rates in 2020 are one-tenth of one per cent, I could understand such a crap contract with our rates. But what are they right now? Nine per cent? Ten per cent?"

"You're still pretending to be Buck Rogers?"

"Who?" asked Jamie.

"My livelihood is on a knife-edge. If I mess this account up, there's one place for me. And I'm not going there. I've seen what it does to people. It can break a man," Dudley paused for dramatic effect. "You know where I mean, don't you?"

"Butlins?" asked Tash.

"Prison!"

"That was my second guess. That or Center Parcs."

"Where?"

"Although I think we just had a bad experience 'cos it was a pull-down sofa, but the food was average at best."

Jamie interrupted. "That was Mum's cooking though, Tash. Can't blame the venue."

"You find everything funny," said Dudley. "Everything isn't funny. Everything isn't funny."

"Can I say something please? Sir?" asked Jamie.

"Don't call him, sir, you fanny!"

"No, it's OK, he can call me sir. I like that actually. Go on. Question from the young man. You. What is it?"

"Why are you so cross? Raymond told you that none of your little buggies was missing. So how can this be one of yours?" Jamie gestured with his head at the pimped up C5 that sat lifelessly on the floor between them.

"Because you've broken in here, probably, at some point. And you've copied one of these machines, and you've gone away, and you've created your own version, in a way, and you're going to bring it to market before Sinclair!"

Tash stared at the C5 that her grandfather had 'improved'. It was pretty tricky even in this light so see it positively. "Would anyone buy that?"

"Don't know! Depends what you've done with it, doesn't it? I say you, I mean whoever you're working for."

"Do you have kids?" asked Tash.

"Not married. Too busy."

Dudley paced around the extended C5, occasionally pausing to lean in and squint at some of the modifications.

"Well, that's one way of explaining it," mused Tash.

Jamie tried to solve things with a deep breath and some clarity. "We borrowed this from our Grandad on Christmas Day, 2020, although he died in 1999, so technically we did steal it, and I'm not sure how – but we both sat on it, and it started up, and it used to be a Christmas ride, but now it's a way to travel in time, and we chose Tash's birthday which is today, but we accidentally knocked down Bob Geldof so he missed the news about the famine in Ethiopia and that means he won't write a Christmas song that raises millions of pounds and saves thousands of lives and also leads to Live Aid when Queen were brilliant, but it was only on BBC2. So the thing is, as it stands – unless Bob Geldof sees tonight's news, he won't save all those lives, and there'll be lots of death, and it's your fault, and by that I mean it would be our fault, but we have a plan, but you're stopping us from doing our plan cos you keep locking us up here, so the deaths are going to be your fault."

"Well, when you put it like that, it all makes perfect sense."

Dudley leant in and flicked on the TV and scrolled the tuner for a while, causing the snowstorm fuzz to light up the screen. He scrolled a little more until it changed to silent black.

"Ooh! Look! A stereo too!" said Dudley as he pushed the cassette into the player. "So, does this use normal magic, or is there a 21st-century type of magic that you need to conjure up?"

The computer attached to the C5 beeped. Dudley leaned over to read from the screen which had turned white.

"Destination date. How exciting! We just type in where we want to go, do we?" He squinted and started to type. "So we put, Christmas Day…" He typed as he spoke. "Twenty-fifth… of the twelfth… and the year was 2020, was it?" He continued typing, but his skills were rudimentary, using one finger and a tongue. The tongue was only used as something for his teeth to bite whilst he typed, but it was clear he couldn't use the keyboard without doing so. His eyes were seeking the keys, so he didn't notice the second twenty type over the first. "What time was it when you left the future, Princess Leia?"

"Oh, piss off," replied Tash, starting to feel her eyes fill with tears again.

"Ooh! Twenty-four-hour clock!" observed Dudley. "Very space age. I'll put twenty-three hundred hours, just enough time to hang out a stocking and wait for Father Christmas," He typed and read again: "Location? Erm… Let's say… Let's say…. Where's Christmassy? Where's the place in that Bing Crosby film? That had a lovely Christmas song, didn't it? White Christmas. Where was that, then?"

"Vermont," said Jamie.

"Jamie, what the fuck!" replied Tash.

"Vermont! Brilliant." Dudley spelt out the US state as he typed. "Then I guess if I were to sit in this time machine, then I would end up in the year you came from, but in Vermont? Feeling all Christmassy? Is that right?"

As he spoke, he was already making himself as comfortable as possible on the plastic seat. "Christ, these are uncomfortable."

He squinted again at the screen and read again "What's a ZIP code? It needs a ZIP code."

"It's like a postal code," said Jamie. "It won't go anywhere until it knows the exact place."

"Jamie, stop helping the prick man!"

"Ooh!" said Dudley as he touched the keyboard "I have options, look!" He turned and smiled at the siblings "You really did make this thing very thorough, didn't you? If I was like nine or ten years old, I'd completely buy this."

He squinted at the drop-down menu next to ZIP code, and selected the first one, happily reading it out loud, in his best American accent.

"Zero five, four zero one."

The machine seemed to accept this.

"Don't touch anything else. I'm warning you!" said Tash.

"I press ENTER now, do I? And then I meet Bing Crosby's great-great-great grandson?" He sneered as his finger clipped the keyboard.

"No!" shouted Tash! "Jamie, unplug the machine! Unplug it!"

Jamie stared at the cord wrapping him tightly to his chair. "How?"

At first, the siblings heard a low hum, but then the kitsch version of 'Sleigh Ride' started to play from the speaker at the rear. Dudley peered around to hear where the sound was coming from.

Jamie was frantically struggling to slide his plastic chair over to the power cable supplying electricity to the C5. With his hands tied on his lap and his legs tied to the chair, this was not stylish, or fast. Slow would be a better word. Futile even better.

"Jamie!" Tash was bereft now.

Then the sound of squealing tyres echoed around the warehouse.

"It's moving! It's moving, Jamie!"

Jamie hurled himself face-first onto the floor and started to shunt himself across the concrete. The dirty white power cable was now just inches away. He spun around on his back and frantically kicked his legs in an attempt to catch the cable and pull it from the socket. But he was half a second too late. The wire had become taut, and it removed itself from the plug socket as the C5 continued forward. There were six or maybe seven yards of ground before the vehicle would strike the office wall fencing that enclosed them. The C5 top speed was twelve miles per hour, but it covered that ground very quickly. Dudley attempted to shout " Fuuuuuuuuuuuu..." but his profanity was silenced by the vehicle's impact onto the fencing. Immediately the whole warehouse fell into darkness.

THIRTY ONE

“Tash, Tash, are you OK?” asked Jamie. His face still pressed against the concrete floor.

“I’m OK,” came Tash’s voice from the darkness. “What the fuck happened?”

“It went dark.”

“Thanks, Jamie. I wasn’t sure what had happened, but that makes sense now.”

The eerie black silence was interrupted by Tash venting at the top of her voice.

“I’m having a really bad day, actually!” Her shrill tone reverberated around the warehouse.

“I’ve found the fuse box,” muttered Jamie. “Well, it feels like a fuse box. It smells a bit burny.”

“For Christ sake, don’t kill yourself, Jamie, don’t touch it.”

There was a loud fizzle and bang, and the lights came on. Jamie rolled over and looked up at his sister. He had an instant headache, and his arm felt like he’d been kicked by a horse wearing ice skates.

“I think I just had an electric shock,” said Jamie, his hair clearly standing up like the time he touched the Van De Graaf generator in GCSE Science.

“I think I just had an electric shock,” said Jamie. Again.

Tash’s expression was pure horror.

“What? What? Do I look bad? Am I scarred?”

His body was still on its side and tied to his chair. Tash slowly tried to raise her hands to gesture at something, but they were restricted by the cord binding her to the chair.

"Speak sis, speak. Am I deformed? My head kills. I feel sick. Speak!"

Tash just shook her head, she was muted by the horror of what she saw. Then the penny dropped. She wasn't looking at Jamie, she was looking at something else. He rolled over and saw what was filling her with dread.

There was a burnt hole in the office fence panel where the C5 had struck.

But that was all – just a hole.

No Dudley.

No C5.

Nothing.

"We. Are. Fucked," whispered Tash. She started to rock as a deep hollow sound started to make its way through her chest. Tash and the act of crying were not good or attractive partners.

Jamie didn't like seeing his sister at rock bottom. She was the sensible one. She was the fixer. But now she had given in.

He rarely saw her this way, so when he did something tripped in his brain. He needed to fix this situation and fast. "Don't say that Tash. Don't say, that. We just need to get untied." Jamie shuffled towards the fuse box again. "I can use the fuse thing to burn through my rope."

"Don't be bloody stupid, what are you talking about?"

"It's a metal box. It's got a sharp edge, it's all rusty. I can scrape the rope up and down here."

Jamie started to rock backwards and forwards as his tied hands rubbed precariously near to the opened fuse board.

"See? It's not dangerous," Jamie sounded very reassuring. He was almost hysterically upbeat as he worked. "Okay? Just… one…. more…. Like this, Okay? Just stay calm."

He continued rubbing frantically up and down. "I think I just had an electric shock."

"I'm out of thoughts, Jamie! My brain hurts. I don't know what to think!" The pitch of Tash's voice was increasing at an alarming rate. She was hysterical. "I'm never going to see my son again. I've abandoned him! What's he going to do without me?"

She thought for another moment.

"The Prick will be back. He'll realise what's happened and he'll be back. We need to move out of the way, he might hit us when he arrives!"

There was a deafening bang from the fuse box, and the darkness returned.

"Jamie?"

"Jamie?"

Nothing. Just more black and more nothing. Tash suddenly felt more alone than at any time in her life.

****

Jamie opened his eyes and immediately realised two things. His headache was now inside and outside his head, and he was blind too. The blindness thing really pissed him off, cos one of his favourite things was looking at stuff. From TVs to mountain bikes to fluffy dogs and that kind of thing. Then he remembered he had been fiddling with the fuse socket so maybe he'd tripped the lights again and might not be blind after all. Next, he heard some whimpering before a dull thumping sound took over. At first, he thought he'd imagined it. But then it came again.

Thump. Thump.

"Is that you, Tash?"

"Jamie! Jamie!" Tash's voice came from somewhere nearby. "I thought you were fucking dead, you prick!"

"Are you thumping?" he asked.

Thump. Thump. Thump.

"No. It's not me. It's been happening for ages. I'm shitting my pants, to be honest. I'm stuck in the fucking past – IN THE DARK – I've orphaned my son and on top of all that I thought you were dead and that a fucking thumping psycho zombie might come and eat my face."

"Oh wow! My hands are freed!" Jamie fumbled in the darkness and was able to loosen the rope around his legs to remove himself from the chair. "My second electrocution must have burnt the string! Excellent!"

"Don't go for a third Jamie, step away from the fuses. Follow my voice and come and untie me," Tash let out a long sigh. "Oh my God, I really thought you were dead... Turns out I quite like you."

There was much shuffling in the dark and muttering and general smashing of lamps, knees being smacked on chairs and other wrong-direction type noises before Jamie eventually found his sister strapped to a chair. The final clue was the unworldly scream she let out after he trod his size tens on her wellington-booted feet.

The thump-thump-thump noise didn't relent. It was intermittent but now more of a thump-thump-thump-thump-thump. Sometimes less, but usually more. And it wasn't going away.

"Do my arms first, Jamie. Then I can do my feet."

"Good idea," acknowledged Jamie, who would actually never have arrived at this logical approach.

"Get off my tits, you freak! That's just weird!"

"I can't see anything! I don't know where your arms are! I'm not great at knots, to be honest. Knots or laces."

"You could have been Jamie. I tried to help, but you're a quitter."

"They get me stressed." The rising irritation was evident in his voice.

"You can't wear velcro shoes forever, Jamie, it's weird."

"The things is, I can, Tash, actually." She'd struck another of his dyspraxic Achilles' heels, and she was actually disappointed at herself because she knew it.

"Turn the car lights on!" shouted Tash, excited by her epiphany.

"What?"

"Turn the car lights on!"

"Where the fuck's the car?"

"It was the other side of the fence gate door thing. It was behind us."

Jamie set off slowly shuffling his feet with his hands out in front of him like he was playing blind man's buff in the darkness. Soon he felt the rusty chain-link of the office boundary fencing.

"I'm at the fence!" he shouted, really loudly.

"I'm closer than you think!" she shouted back just feet away from him.

"Sorry."

"Find the gate."

"I'm doing it, I'm doing it." Jamie's fingers slid over the surface area of the fencing until he suddenly felt the cold steel upright of the supporting post. And yes! Yes! It had an opened gate attached to it!

"I'm through the gate door thing! I'm walking to the – fuck!"

The fuck came the moment he walked straight into the bonnet of the Mercedes.

"Found it!" he managed to shout despite this new pain in his legs. He slid his hands along the smooth bonnet and found his way to the driver's door. The moment his thumb squeezed the handle, the interior light illuminated the inside of the car, casting life-affirming rays horizontally around the warehouse and into the office enclosure. Jamie could finally see Tash who was looking over her shoulder at him. Her eyes squinted at the sudden brightness, but Jamie could see they were red from crying.

THUMP! THUMP! THUMP! THUMP!

Wow. That was loud now. It actually made Jamie jump as it seemed to vibrate along the car door. He leant into the car and flicked a few switches, and sure enough, the car headlights came on making the warehouse brighter still.

"The noise is coming from the car, Tash!"

"What?" Tash seemed suddenly childlike to Jamie. Lost and scared.

"The boot! There's someone in the boot!" answered Jamie as he made his way to the back of the car. The rear lights illuminated Jamie's face a vivid crimson red.

"Don't open the boot! Untie me!" Desperation was taking the place of her usual caustic sarcasm. "Dudley will be back any minute – he'll plough right into me! Untie me!"

"There's no oxygen in a boot, Tash, we know that. At least Raymond left us some air gaps."

Jamie grappled for the release catch above the registration plate. He flexed his fingers until he found the steel button. An expensive German click accompanied the boot lid release. Jamie lifted it fully open and gasped at what he saw.

"Oh my God! Torch lady!"

Tash twisted to get a better look. Inside the boot, a pink-haired lady sat up and took a mightily deep breath. She looked almost suffocated, her face was swollen and sweat glued clumps of hair to her face. She took two or three more shaky breaths then slowly looked up at her saviour.

"Take two steps the fuck back," she shouted, in an American accent.

"What?" said a surprised and still smiling Jamie, raising both his hands to calm the situation.

She lifted a hand torch from her pocket so she could focus her attention and perused the office desk. The beam landed on the Polaroid camera. “Get that Instamatic,” she demanded.

“What?” queried Jamie.

“Just do what I fucking said,” replied the American as she raised a gun to Jamie’s face.

Well this is another unfortunate hurdle, thought Jamie as he headed over for the camera.

THIRTY TWO

The twenty-five-year-old lady had clearly made some kind of effort with her appearance, Harvey Eikenberry was in no doubt of that. It wasn't the kind of effort that would have secured her a second interview at a law firm, particularly his, but luckily for her she wasn't applying for a job at his law firm. Her hair had been sort of styled, she'd removed her double mint gum as she'd sat down, and her makeup had been applied with the benefit of a mirror, albeit maybe a cracked one. In a dimly lit room. He wasn't convinced by the multitude of beads and scarves around her porcelain white neck or her black-painted fingernails. Especially the amount that had been smeared around the edges of each nail onto her skin. But she looked better than he had seen her in years. Harvey was seated behind his antique mahogany desk laden with expensive-looking pens and books. His arthritic fingers were flicking formally through a three-page document that appeared to be on very expensive paper. He'd opened the letter in front of her, as was the term of his contract with his client. She'd never seen a waxed sealed document other than in old English movies, and Harvey's skills with his silver letter opener were second to none.

Once opened, he'd fallen silent for what felt about three years, but it was probably more like two minutes as he absorbed the content of the document. Then he raised his head and spoke to the lady sitting on the slightly cheaper chair on the other side of his desk.

"As you are aware, today marks your twenty-fifth birthday and the terms of my client's instructions are contained in a complex multi-faceted final Will and Testament." His voice was calm and reassuring, but not overly warm. "You are aware of his former Will implemented at the date of his passing, and this is the second and final version. The sequel Will, if you will."

He continued to address the lady who had blanked his witticism.

"Now, I acknowledge that I have received several satisfactory references from your sponsors and from your doctor, landlord and employer…." He said the word 'employer' like you or I might say chlamydia. Suffice to say, a Saturday job at Ben & Jerry's was employment but maybe not the kind of job anyone in their mid-twenties could argue was part of a strategic career plan.

He glanced again at the document and read an excerpt:

"Your monthly expenditure allowance will continue to be paid at the same rate, increasing annually in accordance with the Consumer Price Index under US law."

"Wow. I can finally put a deposit on a new skateboard," snorted the lady, unable to maintain eye contact with him.

Harvey paused to acknowledge her impertinence and continued.

"At the time of your 25th birthday, it is made clear in this document that you now have the opportunity to receive the full amount of the complete estate of the deceased – in its entirety – on a non-negotiable conditional basis. As of the close of trading yesterday, that estate amounts to eleven million, three hundred and sixty-nine thousand dollars in cash, plus two commercial properties and one residential property in Burlington, plus one residential property in Massachusetts."

She sat up. "The house in Martha's Vineyard? I was named after that place, did you know that?"

Harvey paused, nodded and then continued. "In addition to the aforementioned, there is a fleet of vehicles, antiquities and art as listed herein."

"That's one fucking party house," mused Martha, unable to move on from the mansion she'd spent many happy childhood summers.

Harvey winced at the language and handed over a very glossy multi-page booklet. She flicked through it in wonder.

"I have a question?" she said.

"Please?"

"So, I continue to get my twenty bucks a month, but I have an option to be the richest mother fucker on the East Coast?"

"It's more than twenty dollars a month young lady, my records indicate that you are receiving an allowance of – " he was interrupted.

"It pays the rent on my kennel and maybe puts a few meals on the table. You know he was jerking me around."

"If the accommodation is no longer agreeable to you, you are free to seek further income streams to better your eighteen dollars a week from Ben and Jerry's Scoop Shop?"

"Whatever. Tell me about this option thing? Am I missing something? Cos it sounded like you just offered me eleven million Christmases in one day?"

"I said it was an opportunity, not an option. It's a single task of action you must undertake as instructed by the deceased before his passing."

"I haven't done drugs in over a year, Harvey. What more does he want from me? He's still pulling my chains from behind the grave."

"It's beyond the grave," corrected Harvey.

"It's behind. He's got a nameplate on a fucking wall thing. Surrounded by his dead actor pals and media buddies. So he's behind the grave. Am I wrong, Harve?"

The lawyer chose to return to the matter in hand,

"If you fail to attempt the task or fail the task, you will forfeit the inheritance as aforementioned, and you will forfeit your monthly allowance with effect three calendar months from today."

"Excuse me?" she replied, suddenly sitting up straight. "Rewind that part?"

Harvey removed his glasses and removed two further envelopes from his expensive mahogany drawer. One was a rich brown foolscap type sealed with wax, and the other pure white one with Pan-Am printed across the top.

Harvey held up the brown envelope.

"You must do what is instructed inside this envelope. All that I know is that it does not contravene any US or international law, it is time-sensitive and that you must undertake the procedure in London, England next Tuesday."

With this, Harvey dropped the Pan-Am envelope on his desk in front of the young lady.

"Provision for reasonable out of pocket expenses. Plus return flights. Club class."

"Club Class? Is that the one with the free Champagne?" She'd perked up now.

"No. That would be First Class. But I'd imagine with over eleven million dollars you could buy a plane when you're done." His attempt at humour wasn't great.

"Tuesday?" she said. "Tuesday's not so good for me. Might need to get some time off work."

"From a Saturday job?" replied the lawyer.

"OK. You're playing hardball. I like it," she reached out for the brown envelope. "I'm in," she announced, like she really had an option.

Harvey pulled it from her grasp.

"You will receive this in London."

"Excuse me?"

"Your itinerary is in there," he pointed at the Pan-Am envelope.

She opened it up, and two plane tickets fell on her lap. She delved inside and removed a Visa credit card and a folded piece of paper. She opened it and read.

"Rendezvous? What is this, some Hitchcock movie shit?"

"It means a place to meet," helped Harvey, grimacing slightly at her vocabulary.

"I know what it freaking means." She looked again at the paper.

"Marie's Cafe, Waterloo… Who am I meeting? Marie? Who's Marie? What's the deal?"

"That's all you need to know. I wish you good luck, sincerely." He actually meant it.

She stood up and attempted to extract the strap on her handbag from his chair. It was painful to watch. How the hell had she got it knotted around the arm in such a short period of time?

"There we go, crisis averted," she muttered as she turned to leave.

"Oh, and one final thing, Miss," remembered Harvey. "Many happy returns of the day."

He meant that too.

THIRTY THREE

"Why the fuck am I the designated driver?" Tash was trying desperately to adjust the driving position of the Mercedes seat.

"This doesn't have a paddle," replied the American perched on the edge of the back seat between Jamie and Tash upfront. Dudley's gun clutched in her hands. "I only drive with a paddle."

"Can you put the gun down?" asked Tash.

Jamie put one hand up. Both ladies glared at him.

"What's he doing?" asked the American.

"I don't know. What are you doing?" Tash asked Jamie.

"I have a question," he answered. "More than one actually."

"Shoot," replied the American.

"No, don't shoot," replied Tash patiently.

"Well, she can't, can she?" reasoned Jamie., "It's Jermaine's gun, look. I recognise the white pearl handle. Just a starter pistol. It didn't break the glass."

Tash turned to examine the gun in the American's grip. She struggled to see in the darkness, so felt around for the overhead light switch by the rearview mirror.

"Quit calling me 'she', my name's Martha. What are you doing?"

"Hang on," muttered Tash pressing a switch. The sunroof started to glide back. She pressed the button again to close it. She flicked another, and light illuminated the interior of the car. Tash turned around to look at Martha's firearm and could see a black metal looking sort of gun with a white handle. She looked back at Jamie.

"What am I looking for? I've never seen a real gun."

"It didn't shoot Raymond, did it?" asked Jamie. "It's Jermaine's gun! I remember the handle. It fires blanks. Probably a starter pistol."

Martha looked momentarily confused, and then a little bit pissed off, to be honest. But she soon found her motivation again.

"They still make a mess of your face this close." Martha leant forward and pressed it into Jamie's open mouth.

"I can see that actually," Jamie tried to say whilst nodding.

"Just drive," said Martha, now distracted by a ream of paper she was struggling to remove from her backpack with her free hand.

Tash crunched the automatic gearbox a few times trying to engage reverse gear. "This really is a massive pain in the fanny, to be honest," she reversed the car towards a shutter door then stopped.

"Jamie – can you get out and leave a note for the Prick?"

"A note?" questioned Jamie.

"He's going to realise we weren't lying about the C5, isn't he? He knows now! And the first thing he's going to do is come right back here! To his life! To this shit hole!"

"Well, what are we going to write?"

Tash struggled to think of a coherent sentence that summed up her frustration at the strangest day anyone ever had. "Something like: 'Told you we weren't liars you knobhead, don't touch anything else, we've been kidnapped again, but will be back in twenty minutes' kind of thing."

"Might be an hour or so," interjected Martha reading some papers.

"Really?" Tash couldn't hide her irritation.

Martha just nodded and forced the gun to Jamie's mouth again.

Tash corrected her dictation. "OK, put: 'We'll be back in an hour. Do. Not. Leave. Kind regards, the weird brother and sister'."

"Can I get out for a sec?" asked Jamie with the gun still hovering on his lips.

"Sooner you get out the sooner you get back in and the sooner we're all done with one another," concluded Martha.

Jamie opened his door and walked into the chain-link fence area one more time. In the dim light, he tried to look through the desk drawers for a pen. Whilst doing so, he raised his spare hand above his head. Martha glanced over and spotted him.

"What's he doing now?" asked Martha.

"What is it?" shouted Tash over her shoulder at her brother.

"I had another question, it's about her," replied Jamie, gesturing at Martha. "It's a good one. I wish I'd asked this one first actually." He carried on fumbling through drawers.

Martha looked at Tash and back at Jamie. "What?"

"Who are you, and what are you doing, and what are we doing and why, please?"

"Four questions, but I like them all," agreed Tash.

"This guy. This heartbreaker. Is this Raymond?" replied Martha, holding up an enlarged grainy black and white photograph of Raymond. He was half blinking from a camera flash but unmistakably their first kidnapper from today.

"Yes," replied Tash. "We don't know him. We've only just met him. We're nothing to do with him. .. Why?"

"Get us out of this shit hole, and maybe I'll tell you."

"Found a pen!" shouted Jamie, then started playing with it. "Excellent, it's got like ten different coloured nibs. What colour shall I use?"

Martha absent-mindedly scratched her chin with the pistol, and there was an almighty crack followed by the sound of glass falling onto concrete, then a smell like Guy Fawkes night.

"Jesus!" remarked Martha, staring at the smoking gun in her hand. An actual real gun.

Tash glared at the smashed glass in the door next to Martha.

"Write the fucking note, Jamie! Or she's going to kill us!"

Martha disagreed with this sentiment wholeheartedly but had the presence of mind to let that threat hang in the air. It suited her purposes for the time being.

"OK! OK!" replied Jamie, his voice faltering with anxiety. "I'm gonna use green," he continued. "No, red."

Tash turned to look at Martha. They sat in silence and waited for Jamie to finish his note.

"No. I'm gonna use green. What am I writing again, Tash? Something about waiting for us?"

THIRTY FOUR

Raymond's porter uniform was a fantastic door opener in St Thomas' Hospital. Even with his anoraked wife in tow. But much as doors opened, it didn't stop constant intervention and interruption from medical staff inside the Casualty reception. It had alarmed Maureen how quickly her respectable husband had fabricated a back story to a triage nurse. Soon Maureen was in a wheelchair cradling the video player and cassette beneath a blanket, as her husband pushed her along the corridors towards the x-ray department. She'd suffered a severe tennis injury apparently. His initiative had now found them secreted in a storage cupboard and she watched as he carefully laid out the damaged VHS cassette on a shelf and straightened the chewed tape that protruded from the snapped front. Half of the protective plastic mechanism that usually opened only inside the video machine had perished under Maureen's size six trainer. Raymond was attempting to create a replica from jointed wooden splints and securing them in place with medical tape. He wasn't convinced they were actually needed, the more critical part of this repair was straightening the scrunched black videotape that spewed out of its housing. This twisted glossy black plastic ribbon held the precious story that Raymond must convey to the reluctant saint outside. He'd even found himself humming 'I Don't Like Mondays' as he went about his work. Maureen was her usual helpful self.

"Faster Raymond. What if someone comes in?"

"Being as quick as I can actually, darling," he replied patiently.

"Well, can you be a bit quicker?"

"What, you mean, be even quicker than I can?" He leant in for his final inspection. His work looked good.

"Don't be facetious, Raymond. How much longer?"

"Erm..." he examined the tape that still hung from the case. "Ten minutes. Maybe less."

He had cleverly chosen a storeroom just off the ward that housed Mr Geldof, and if he was in any doubt about this, his fears were allayed when a deep baritone Irish laugh made the floor vibrate every few minutes.

Excellent, thought Raymond. I'm in the right place, I have the right equipment, I'll soon have a repaired videotape, and Bob seems to be in good spirits. Nothing could fail now.

THIRTY FIVE

Marie's Cafe was about as exotic as it sounded. Function over form, it was a favourite for miles around as the food was delicious and the drinks always hot, but arguably not at all a rendezvous you'd expect for a multi-million-dollar transaction. She'd gone straight to the location from the airport after her flight delay meant a hotel stop-off was out of the question. Her VISA card had enabled a cash withdrawal at Heathrow, but she was unsure what it would stretch to in terms of accommodation. Harvey hadn't mentioned if it was capped, but she was sure that it wouldn't run to the Savoy or The Ritz. She would find out soon enough, but right now, she needed to calm down and find out what the hell was going on in her bizarre little world.

The cafe was warm, and the air was filled with a combination of fried bacon and Benson & Hedges cigarettes. Spandau Ballet's 'I'll Fly For You' played from a Roberts radio that perched dangerously close to the deep fat fryer. A jovial but sweaty looking older lady was simultaneously attending to a frying pan, a grill pan, a coffee percolator and a plate of sausage and chips which she was handing to a suited lady in front of her.

"Are you Marie? I'm here to meet Marie?" demanded the younger woman to the chef, ignoring the queue protocol. She'd never been one for rules.

Marie smiled but dismissed this assumption. "I'm not expecting anyone, my darling. Unless you're from the football pools?"

The suited older lady took her meal and nodded to a spare Formica topped table with two chairs.

"I'm expecting you, Martha. Grab a seat. Can I order you anything?"

Martha shook her head as the handsome woman paid for her meal with a handful of coins.

"Keep the change," she instructed in her unmistakable Queens accent.

THIRTY SIX

Grandma always seemed so proud to tell me that Phillip Oakey lived down the road, thought Jamie as Phil sang about 'Electric Dreams' on the Mercedes radio. He did actually sing with a bit of a Sheffield accent if you listened out for it on this Giorgio Moroder track. How the hell had they met? 1984 was one strange time. Jamie's musings were interrupted by his sister.

"I am trying to show you some fucking respect, but you are the shittest kidnapper we've had today, and that's saying something, believe me!" said Tash as she curled over the steering wheel of the Mercedes.

Jamie agreed. "This is our third kidnapping today. And in fairness, an analyst would probably say they were worsening at an exponential rate."

"Who swallowed a fucking dictionary?" asked Martha.

Jamie squared in his seat to get a better view of Martha as he explained further with the use of his hands. "If you imagine a downward trending curve…"

"I don't give a freaking crap about curves or about your day! You wanna hear about my day! Quit it with the moaning!" Martha turned a map upside down and back again. "This city's built like crap. Why no block system? It's fucked up!"

The car had crossed Tower Bridge and taken the main route along the banks of the Thames. Martha had even allowed herself a "Well, would you look at that" as she passed the floodlit Tower of London. As they continued along Upper Thames Street, Martha lost all her bearings. They were now creating a traffic obstruction just along from The Tower and passing taxis and buses were making their frustration quite clear with relentless beeping and occasional swears from black cab windows.

"Just let me go the way I know! I bloody live here!" said Tash.

They were heading back to St Thomas' Hospital but Martha didn't trust these strangers to take her there so had started the journey in control of the route. Options were limited as her attempts to navigate the way had been well and truly shit. She glanced again at the mug shot of Raymond. Tash clocked her, and a horrific thought dropped into her head. "Oh my God! I just thought! Are you going to kill him?"

Jamie looked utterly shell shocked. "What?… Why did we tell her where he was, Tash? I didn't think she was going to kill him!"

"Of course, she's going to kill him. Why didn't we realise?"

Both were now extremely agitated.

"What?" said Martha. She seemed horrified by the idea. "Kill him?"

"Look. The thing is, he's swamped at the moment actually," said Jamie. "Can we wait a bit and then kill him?"

Tash was horrified. "Jamie!"

"Band Aid, Tash," said Jamie, needlessly. "He's fixing things."

"And THEN kill him?" quoted Tash.

Martha was shocked. "I'm not going to kill him! You two were tied up in a freaking warehouse when we met. You're the bad guys in this scenario. For all I know YOU could be killers."

"I'm an economist from the LSE, and he sells bikes," replied Tash.

"Tash did kill the school's hamster, but other than that we're not killers."

"What, you like walked into class and killed a hamster? That's sick," asked Martha.

"No, she did it at home."

"I was looking after it for the holidays, and it died, I didn't kill it! And why are we talking about this now?" said Tash.

"You did kill it!" There was only ever the actual truth for Jamie.

"The cat killed it, Jamie. The cat."

"You fed it to the neighbours' cat!" Their voices were raised now, this was a full-on sibling battle.

"Sitting a hamster on a cat's back isn't the same as feeding a hamster to a cat!"

"I'm just saying, that's the reason we could never have pets. Because of you!"

"Don't start the bloody dog argument again, Jamie. They didn't buy a dog cos they knew you'd never walk the fucking thing."

"Why do I have to walk it?"

"See? Still trying to get out of walking it! And we don't even have it yet."

"OK! I get it! Totally get it," interrupted Martha. Something on the paperwork had caught her attention. "Time out. Silence!" She read for a moment, looked at her watch and then added, "Right, we got no time to spare. Find this guy now." She tapped the photo of Raymond. "Move it."

"He really is swamped. He's doing something important. Right now," protested Jamie.

With a weary sigh, Martha turned to Jamie and said, "Open wide."

"What?"

Martha gestured at his mouth. "Open wide."

Jamie opened his mouth, and she placed the gun inside once more.

Depeche Mode were now musing, '*people are people so why should it be, you and I should get along so awfully*?' on the radio, and as Jamie tasted the stainless steel of the Smith & Wesson Model 60 on his tongue, he agreed.

"Just drive the way you know," conceded Martha to Tash. "The sooner we get there, the sooner this ends. Let's do this!"

Tash pressed hard on the accelerator, and the Mercedes set off at high speed, accompanied by lots of remonstrating beeps and shouts from surrounding traffic. Thrown back in her seat, Martha seemed pleased. "That's what I'm talking about, girl!"

Jamie was more pleased as the gun was now safely out of his mouth.

The general euphoria didn't last long. Less than a minute later the three of them were queueing at temporary traffic lights just fifty yards or so from the Houses of Parliament. Big Ben was a beacon up ahead indicating their bridge to the South Bank and St Thomas' Hospital. But it was all frustratingly beyond their grasp. Bizarrely a makeshift film-set had been assembled on the broad walkway alongside the Thames, and impossibly bright floodlights lit up some leather-clad actors. Pedestrians waited patiently to be shepherded safely across the road, and the temporary traffic lights seemed to be glued on red.

"Go around," bristled Martha. "Go around!"

"They're traffic lights," said Jamie. "The red means stop."

"I'm from Burlngton USA, not freaking Mars!"

"Write that down, Tash. We're getting a back story. That will help the police."

"Could you take the fucking notes, Judge Fucking Rinder, I'm driving?" replied Tash,

"We don't need any police. I'm gonna be out of your lives before you know it. There's a gap right there. Go!" Martha pointed at an impossibly small space between the film crew and the stationery vehicles. Tash ignored her. The traffic frustration was not solely hers. Some cars ahead started to perform precarious U-turns in the road, and there was a general agreement that the current state of affairs was unacceptable. A strange melodic ping resounded around the car, and a red light illuminated Tash's face.

"The fuck's that?" asked Martha.

Tash stared at the dashboard. "How would I know? It's not my car."

"Gas light, look." Jamie pointed at the needle resting ruthlessly on the red reserve stripe.

"What light?" asked Tash

"Gas. I was speaking American... For her. I was translating."

"Move. Now," said Martha raising the gun one more time. She was growing accustomed to the immediate results a firearm achieved.

Tash steered the car expertly over the kerb and instantly the melee of the film crew and curious onlookers leapt out of her way. She swerved in and out of video equipment boxes, trestle tables and tripods, continuing along the pavement towards Westminster Bridge. Suddenly a sickening thud resonated throughout the interior. Tash slammed on the brakes.

The vehicle had struck one of the actors.

Except he wasn't an actor. And the crew weren't shooting a film. They were filming a pop video. And now, as a backing track continued to sing 'Teardrops will fall...', staring straight back at Tash and Jamie through the windscreen of the Mercedes was a shocked and slightly winded man in his mid-thirties wearing a very warm leather jacket topped with a thick sheepskin collar. But it was his eyeliner that caught both their attention. The horrified man blinked his bewildered eyes as his brain tried to fathom his new position, which was essentially buttered against a cold German windscreen. Tash did her best to avoid eye contact but given that his face was twelve inches from hers, it was impossible. Her most pressing thought was, *Oh my God, we just killed Elvis*, shortly followed by, *didn't Elvis die in the seventies?*

She did a sideways glance at Jamie and whispered, "Is that Elvis?"

"Fuck! You killed Elvis!" shrieked Martha staring at the singer on the other side of the windshield. "He had faked his death after all! But you just killed him! He's double dead!"

Jamie was shaking his head. "No. No. It's not Elvis." He leant over to Tash and whispered "That's Shakin' Stevens."

"What?" Tash did a double-take.

He was right. It was Shakin' Stevens. The '*snow is falling, all around us, children playing, having fun*' Shakin' Stevens that we all let into our homes every December.

Michael Barrett to his friends.

Him.

Shaky had been filming a video for his next single 'Teardrops', loosely based around a man hanging around the Thames pretending to be Elvis but in a shit jacket. The storyboard didn't yet incorporate a road traffic collision with time travellers.

"He's fine. He's blinking. He's fine. And he's not Elvis!" The relief was clear in Tash's voice.

Jamie was becoming more confident in his conclusion. "Yeah. That's Shakin' Stevens." He looked over his shoulder to Martha. "Grandma loves him."

All were still trying extremely hard to avoid eye content as Shaky's face slowly slid down the windscreen in the direction of the bonnet.

Tash suddenly looked even more alarmed. "Was he in er... Was he part of ...?"

"Band Aid?" replied Jamie, still trying to pretend he couldn't see the pop star glaring at them.

"No. I don't think so. Not in Band Aid. Not Shaky."

"Good." Tash took a deep breath and floored the accelerator pedal. She combined this with a sharp twist of the wheel in a successful attempt to shake Shaky onto the ground. They were crossing the bridge within seconds.

"Unless he stood at the back. I never really recognise many standing at the back. Pretty sure it was mostly Spandua Ballet and Boomtown Rats guys," muttered Jamie.

"Is he OK?" asked Martha looking out of the rear window at the chaotic scene they'd left behind. A video director was helping Shaky to his feet as fans supported him with a ripple of applause.

"He's moving, he's fine," replied Tash looking in the rearview mirror to reassure herself and Martha.

"You're one mean bitch!" Martha was ever so slightly in awe. And ever so slightly worried. Who the hell were these ruthless people?

"You've got the fucking gun!" replied Tash. Without further warning, the Mercedes spluttered to a stop on Lambeth Palace Road.

"Stalled it," said Tash, peering down at her feet.

"Automatic, Tash. You can't stall an automatic," replied Jamie.

"What the fuck then?"

"It'll be the fuel. We'll be out of fuel. The gas light came on, didn't it?"

"Can you stop calling it that?"

"What are you doing? Is this a trick? Don't fuck with me!" Martha held the gun up.

They were stranded at the junction by the traffic light filter. Happily, the lights were on red, so they had approximately thirty or forty seconds to find some fuel before the vehicles behind started beeping once more.

"We're out of fuel, we're going to have to walk," said Jamie.

"Walk?" Martha reacted like they'd suggested flying. Then realised they weren't yanking her chain. "Is it far? How many blocks?"

Jamie pointed out of Martha's window. The hospital was right next to them. "It's there."

"Nice." Martha slid straight across to the door and opened it.

"We can't leave the car here!" said Jamie.

"I fucking can." Tash was halfway out of her door too.

The traffic lights changed to green, and immediately the vehicles behind started to beep their horns impatiently. Jamie followed the ladies' lead and climbed out too. They all waited for a gap in oncoming traffic and dashed across the road to the damp grass surrounding the hospital buildings, the sound of cars beeping and protesting drivers ringing in their ears.

"Won't we need the car?" asked Jamie.

"Just do as I say," replied Martha, raising her gun one final time before hiding it in her jacket pocket. "We find my man, we run a quick errand, we all go home." She forced the grainy photo of Raymond back into her bag.

THIRTY SEVEN

The same grainy photograph lay on the cafe table. Martha rubbed her head one more time and accepted a cigarette from the suited lady who she now knew as Bee. *Ms Barbara Fernandez: Attorney At Law* is what her business card said, but Martha was told she could call her Bee. She'd patiently opened the impressive brown envelope that Martha had first seen in Harvey's office last week, and calmly read and further explained the contents. Bee had reassured Martha that the instructions were legally compliant, no international law was being compromised, and there was no suggestion that Martha was compelled to carry out the request. She reiterated that a refusal to attempt though would be taken as confirmation that Martha no longer wanted to receive her monthly income administrated by the office of Eikenberry & Lowe. This would cease in three calendar months.

Martha looked again at the photos inside the envelope and squinted at the crude maps.

"One final thing," explained Bee. "You need to successfully undertake this by four pm GMT tomorrow."

"What?" Martha looked at her watch in disbelief, then realized it was still on EST. "What time is it now?"

Bee checked her gold Casio digital display. "18:47, GMT."

Martha stared back at her, so Bee felt compelled to explain. "It means six, it's the twenty-four-hour clock."

"I'm a musician, not a retard."

"Oh yeah, musician. I forgot."

Was she smirking?

"Why did you say it like that?"

"I didn't say it like anything," said Bee. "You had a dream. I get that."

"Had? Who the fuck are you to judge? Had?"

"I'm just saying. You're not the only one to have a dream. Lady, I was gonna be the first black and the first female President of the United States of America."

Martha absorbed this as she tried to calm down.

"I'm not giving up on my plans, I just need someone to give me a break," said Martha.

"You keep believing, girl. Although you might have different dreams with eleven million dollars burning a hole in your back pocket. Like – which Caribbean island shall I buy?"

Martha stared back at Bee. She wasn't actually as old as she'd thought when she first met her. Her skin was youthful, her make up subtle, and her eyes brighter than Martha could dream of. Maybe she hadn't succumbed to any vices. In fact, if it wasn't for the ketchup on the corner of her mouth, she could pass for an actress or model.

"Why did you say was?" asked Martha.

"Excuse me?" asked the lawyer, forking the last piece of sausage into her mouth like nobody was looking.

"You said you were gonna be President. Why have you given up on that dream?"

Bee chewed in silence for a moment as she pondered her answer. "Sometimes you find better dreams. More achievable ones."

Martha seemed content with this answer. In fact, she found herself saying something nice, which was most unlike her. "Well, I hope you achieve them."

Bee looked over at her client. "I will."

Marie stacked another chair onto a table. "Gonna have to hurry you now, ladies."

The door sign had already been flicked over to read CLOSED to new arrivals, and the kitchen lights were in semi-darkness. Bee started to scoop up some of the paperwork around the greasy tabletop.

"How will they know I've done it?" asked Martha, still a little incredulous about the task ahead.

"Meet me here with the photograph at four pm tomorrow afternoon. That's midday Eastern time. I will send a facsimile to the Vermont office."

"A fucks-what?"

"Facsimile. I've identified a newspaper in Fleet Street that will allow me to rent theirs. New technology. It's essentially like phoning an image to the other side of the world. Takes a matter of minutes. Then, if Mr Eikenberry is satisfied with what you achieved, the funds will be released immediately. You could see them hit your account within twelve hours. Although I'd advise against that. You might want some time to consider loss limitation and also investment potential. You'll be a wealthy woman. Might as well make that money work hard for you."

"What, you mean like stock market shit? I'm out of my depth with that."

Bee delved into her leather portfolio. She extracted some stapled papers with post-it notes strategically placed throughout.

"Your bank account sucks, Martha. We opened that for you on your sixteenth birthday, and it's just a place to keep your money safe. But tomorrow you'll be in a whole new league. The major league. So, I'm offering some free financial advice. Take it or leave it. Your bank is offering a five-year CD yield of eight point eight per cent. And that's if you switch accounts. That sucks even at US standards. But these guys…"

Bee tapped the paperwork that now sat between them.

"… These guys will give you a minimum two points more."

"I have no idea what you just said to me, but you have ketchup on your chin," replied Martha.

As Bee grabbed a napkin from the chrome dispenser on the table. Martha twisted her head to look at the documents. All she could read was the letterhead:

Sint Anna Bay Bank.

Beneath it, the location:

Curacao, Dutch Antilles

"What is this?"

"These people will pay you to bank with them. If you deposit your eleven million with them, they'll give you an extra two hundred and twenty thousand dollars," explained Bee.

"Excuse me?"

"That's on top of the nine hundred and sixty-eight thousand dollars interest from being a CD account. And that's per year."

She let that sink in, which was silly as none of it was sinking in. She tried to explain further.

"So, you need to give notice to get access to your cash, but you don't need to place it all in one account. Maybe just put ten million in this one?" Bee was holding a pen at Martha.

When did she get that out, thought Martha? Why is she saying all these massive numbers? Where do I sign?

"What is this?" asked Martha as she tried to make sense of the papers and the wall of numbers spewing from Bee's mouth.

"It's a new bank account for you. I made preliminary enquiries on your behalf, and this is your confirmation that you'd rather earn an extra two hundred thousand dollars a year for doing nothing but sitting on your ass. You just need to sign here and here, and here."

Bee was very thorough. She had placed post-it notes in all the places that Martha needed to sign.

"My instruction will be deposit the full amount into your new account, if we pay for an expedited service, we might be able to get that wired the same day." Bee was smiling helpfully. Then she added a caveat. "If you succeed in your little task."

"Ladies, can you finish off please?" asked Marie one more time.

Martha was signing her final signature already. She handed the pen and the papers back to Bee and turned to look one more time at the original document Bee had given her when they met. She stood up and swung her bag onto her back.

"One more question. This task. These instructions… Why can't I just knock on the door like a normal person?"

"I don't know. The final Will and Testament state clearly that this was the only way. I guess maybe there are too many locked doors or gates or whatever," replied Bee. "Listen, I have no idea why he would know this. But he was unwavering in his insistence that this will happen…" she pointed to a bold line on the paper beside Martha, "…at that time."

"Was he some kind of clairvoyant? I never knew this. Why did I never know this?"

"All I know is I'm getting paid double time to come here, and I don't come cheap. These are the instructions of our client. I'm treating this as one hundred per cent authentic, and I would urge you to do the same."

Martha looked out onto the street. "It's pretty dark out there."

Bee smiled. "I almost forgot," she replied and delved into a deep overcoat pocket. "I thought you could use this," she handed over a small but expensive-looking torch.

"Can you help me?" Martha pocketed the torch. "If it's legal, why can't you help me do it?" She sounded suddenly vulnerable and childlike.

"I gotta remain completely independent. I'm simply doing my job. I got bills, too."

They walked to the door, and as they stepped outside, Martha took a moment for her eyes to adjust to the darkness of the street. She squinted along to the next block and spotted a red and white plastic 'W' logo projecting from a lit-up shop. The other shops nearby seemed mostly closed.

"Is that it? Is that the store d'ya think?" asked Martha, suddenly buoyed by this vision.

She got no reply so turned to Bee to repeat the question, but the suited lawyer had vanished.

"OK," said Martha to herself. She always spoke to herself when challenged, or lonely, or stressed. "OK. You can do this, Martha. Eleven. Million. Dollars. You can do this. Different city, different country. But people are the same the world over. People are good. You can do this."

As she turned to look back along the street, she watched a man open a car boot, pick the pocket of a limp body inside, then drive away at high speed.

"Jesus Christ, I'm gonna die."

THIRTY EIGHT

Raymond opened the door of his hospital storage cupboard and peered outside. He could see the TV and video stand was still in sight. It had been moved to the entrance of the ward but could easily be intercepted on the way to the curtained bay that contained Bob Geldof.

"Are you wanting to stay here, love?" he asked Maureen, balancing the VCR machine on his good wrist like a silver service waiter with the repaired cassette resting on top.

"I'm wanting to go home and run a bath so I can forget about this horrible day, but it looks like we won't have time for that, doesn't it? I was supposed to be having one when your boss barged into our home earlier and then tried to kill us all, so things aren't really going to plan are they?" She then interrupted herself with a very loud, "Oh my God!"

Raymond quickly closed the door shut to silence her outburst.

"What is it? What?"

"I left the immersion on!" she replied, trying to steady herself onto a chair as the sheer horror of it all sank in.

Raymond looked mortified. Even more than when Dudley had pointed a gun at him. He checked his watch. "That's going to cost a fortune," he whispered. "An absolute fortune." The immersion water heater burned electricity.

"I didn't think. When he turned up at the door, I thought something terrible had happened to you. I wasn't thinking straight, Raymond. What are we going to do?"

"Well first things first, we need to stay calm, Maureen. Stay calm."

"You read about this sort of thing but never think it will happen to you," said Maureen, scrunching a tissue as he tried to remain calm. "Well, there's no way we can play this video to that man now, that's out of the question!" She seemed quite happy that she'd found a reasonable excuse to draw a line under all this silliness.

The images of the children on the news report flashed out in Raymond's mind one more time.

"No. No. We can still do that."

With that Raymond ceremoniously squared up like he was about to go over the top of a trench in the First World War. "We can still do that."

Maureen looked over at her brave husband. He continued in a Churchillian tone.

"Maureen. I'm going to ask you to follow my instructions now. Can you do that for me?"

Maureen nodded.

"Do you stll have our tennis snacks in your handbag?"

Maureen slowly opened her bag and peered in. She nodded.

"Eat yours. And then maybe have a Polo. Wait here for me. I may be some time."

And with that, he stepped outside.

The corridor wasn't particularly busy, and Raymond walked purposefully to his destination. He even made eye contact with hospital staff, that's how confident he was in his new role as porter/Saviour Of The Earth. He plodded on closer and closer to the booming Irish voice, breaking his stride only to grab the TV and video stand. He placed the VHS machine on top of the Betamax one and started to push the trolley as hard as he could, the patchwork cassette tucked under his plaster cast arm.

He was seeing himself in a news report of his own now, or a maybe a Hollywood film. The hero confidently striding forward in the final act, with a crescendo of euphoric music rumbling underneath. As he reached the familiar bay that he'd visited less than an hour ago with Tash and Jamie he was suddenly discombobulated by the Irish voice he'd been listening to.

"You've made great progress, I'm gonna see if Sister can find you somewhere a little bit quieter, Mary, is that OK for you, somewhere you can get your head down for a bit?"

Raymond turned to see a blonde-haired Irish doctor reassuring an elderly lady in the bed behind him. He spun around to Bay 3 and pulled back the curtain. Inside was a horrific sight.

An empty bed.

No bedding, no medical notes, no visitors, no gown, no Paula Yates and definitely no Bob Geldof.

"Doctor, I need some aspirin, how many times do I need to ask for bloody aspirin?"

Raymond turned to see an elderly man lying on the opposite bed glaring at him, red with rage.

"I'm talking to you, man!" he shouted at Raymond.

Raymond spun around a couple more times in the vain hope that Bob would reappear. When he didn't, he sprinted to the reception desk and grabbed the ward's patient list from the nurse in charge.

"Excuse me!" she protested.

"Aspirin!" said Raymond as he turned the sheet around to get a better view.

"I beg your pardon?"

"Rude man in bay four – wants Aspirin."

Raymond's finger slid down the sheet until he reached Bay 3 – R Zenon. He scanned across and there in scrawled biro were the words: Self discharged.

Luckily Raymond's despair lasted only a matter of seconds.

It was interrupted by a familiar voice bellowing.

"Raymond, she was in the boot! She made us drive here to find you! We think she's American! She's got a gun! We think she might want to kill you. We're not sure. Duck!"

Pretty much everyone except Raymond dropped to the floor.

"I'd have led with that, Jamie. I'd have led with Duck. The other stuff really slowed that down," said Tash. She looked at her brother to make sure this registered. "Duck first. Save the life?"

Raymond turned to see a pink-haired lady running towards him, followed by Tash and Jamie.

The pink-haired lady turned around to Jamie.

"I don't have a gun!" Martha turned again to repeat this far louder for the benefit of the rest of the ward. "I don't have a gun! He's kidding!"

She nipped Jamie like they were squabbling siblings, and whispered, "What did you say that for, you freak?" He recoiled from her pinch.

Tash leapt between Martha and Raymond. "Leave him alone! He's a good man. Has a terrible wife, but a good man."

Martha was exasperated now.

"Chrissakes! I do not want to hurt anybody!" She raised both hands in the air. Then lifted the Sony Walkman headphones from around her neck. "No gun! Just a Walkman! She's a joker!"

Staff and visitors started to climb to their feet, and the low rumble of chatter made the ward feel normal once more, even if most of the banter was disparaging and aimed at the strange group of people who'd descended upon them.

Jamie was peering down into the bays.

"Where is he? Where's Bob, Raymond? Bob? Where's Bob? Bob? Raymond? Bob? Bob? Where's Bob? Have you lost Bob, Raymond? Where's Bob? Bob? Raymond? Bob?"

"Seven, eleven, Jamie. Seven, eleven," said Tash.

Jamie started his breathing technique once more.

"Well, that's the thing, actually," replied Raymond. "He's erm. He's checked out."

Raymond held up the ward sheet to show Tash. The head nurse snatched it back off him.

"Checked out?" said Tash. "It's not a fucking hotel!"

"Left, gone whatever they say. I only just found out myself. I was going to show him the film. The video. The news."

At this Raymond lifted the VHS cassette as if to prove his efforts. It looked like it was made from papier-mâché.

"What happened to that?" asked Jamie.

"It's not gone well, to be honest," replied Raymond. "Hasn't gone well at all."

"Right, let's get this freak show on the road," said Martha, tiring of the needless chatter.

"Who are you?" asked Raymond, before turning to Jamie and Tash. "Who is she?"

"We thought you might tell us?" replied Tash.

"You don't know her?" asked Jamie.

"Never seen her before in my life," said Raymond. He gave Jamie and Tash a concerned glance. "Are you both OK? Did she hurt you?"

"Quit it with the talking. I need you to come with me," said Martha as she casually pulled open her jacket to flash the gun at Raymond.

"Oh my God!" he exclaimed.

She took Raymond's elbow and led him and the others towards the lift.

"Where's Maureen?" asked Tash.

"She's having a bit of time to herself, we've had some bad news."

"Really? I'm sorry," whispered Tash.

"She left the immersion on."

Tash nodded. "Nightmare."

"It's been on for hours."

"Can we get his wife?" asked Jamie, appealing to Martha's better nature. "We can't leave her."

"Unless she's between here and the elevator, the answer's no," replied Martha.

"She is," said Raymond. "She's having a rum and raisin Montego in the storage cupboard."

"Great," answered Martha, her sarcasm lost on Raymond.

THIRTY NINE

"This isn't how I thought my evening would pan out, to be honest," said Raymond. "I've never stolen a taxi before." He was handling things well, to be fair.

Outside St Thomas' Hospital, Martha had done an impressive job of securing a taxi. The combination of pink hair and lack of regard for the orderly British queueing system meant Martha was charming a cab driver within nine seconds of leaving the building. She kindly let Tash, Jamie and Maureen climb in the back before asking the driver to help with her old Dad's suitcase. Raymond soon realised he was playing the part of the old Dad in this scenario. Luckily the darkness of the October evening had turned his porter uniform into a mere silhouette. Martha capably mimed dragging a suitcase around the front of the cab towards the front passenger door, and the driver leapt to help.

"Oh my God! Thief," yelled Martha suddenly, just as the driver approached her.

"What?" The driver was baffled. It was dark, traffic was whizzing by, and this pink haired lady was frantically pointing to the car behind.

"Him! Him! Thief!"

Martha pushed the cabbie in the direction of some poor sod legitimately loading his bags into the taxi behind.

The cab driver did the chivalrous thing and set after the thief. "Oi! Wanker!"

Immediately Martha climbed into the back of the cab and shouted instructions to Raymond.

"Drive, old man. Drive!"

"What?" replied Raymond in despair, still standing on the pavement apologising to the irate queue of people at the taxi rank alongside him.

"Do as she says, Raymond. She's a killer!" shouted Maureen.

Raymond climbed into the driver's seat and crunched the cab into first gear. As he skidded into the traffic, he checked his rearview mirror to see the owner chase in protest. It was futile, and the taxi was soon crossing the Thames. The one time he wanted the lights to be against him, they were gifting him green at every junction.

"Put your seat belt on, Raymond," said Maureen. "It's the law."

"Yes, dear," he replied as he fumbled to find the belt with his plaster cast arm and keep the cab moving at the same time.

"I think stealing the car is the most illegal part," said Jamie.

Tash intervened. "Don't stress the guy anymore."

She pondered Jamie's logic for a moment. "I don't think there is a most illegal, is there? Isn't illegal illegal?"

"Well no. There's a scale, isn't there?"

Jamie proceeded to demonstrate his opinions with differing heights of his hand.

"Theft is here," his hand was in front of his face. "The seat belt infringement will be here," his hand lowered.

"What's up there?" asked Tash pointing above both positions.

"Erm, probably stabbing. Stabbing someone."

Maureen winced.

"Murder's gotta go top though, right?" interjected Martha.

Jamie nodded and reset his conclusions, his hand starting high and descending each time.

"Murder, manslaughter, stabbing, stealing, seatbelts."

Martha had another question. "What about knocking someone down?"

"Suppose it depends if they die," answered Jamie.

"She meant Shaky," said Tash.

"Oh, I see."

"Where do you suppose kidnapping is on this scale?" asked Maureen.

The voices fell silent, and the sombre mood took over. The sound of the diesel engine and automatic door locks clicking on and off from time to time became hypnotic.

"I suppose it depends if you start to cut fingers off and stuff like that," said Jamie.

"I think she meant this. What's happening now," explained Tash. "This sort of kidnapping."

Jamie nodded his understanding. All faces turned to Martha, even Raymond in his rearview mirror. Martha was most unimpressed.

"Jesus Christ, this isn't a kidnapping! I'm not a criminal! You two were tied up like a scene from Scarface when I found you! For all I know, it's you guys who are the criminals!"

Maureen didn't take kindly to this. Not one bit.

"We're no criminals, thank you very much. Never had so much a single rent arrear in our whole life, let alone committed any kind of crime."

"That's your video then, is it?" asked Martha, pointing at the VHS recorder that Maureen cradled on her lap.

"No, that's mine, actually. I'm just borrowing it," interrupted Jamie. "And we're not criminals either. Other than Tash killing that hamster."

"Jamie!" shouted Tash, explaining 'accident' to Maureen before turning to Martha as the cab finally pulled up at its first set of red traffic lights.

"If this isn't a kidnapping, we can get out then, can we?" asked Tash, reaching for the door handle.

"No. I'm afraid not. It's complicated, but you gotta stay in the car with me."

"Do we know where I'm supposed to drive to?" asked Raymond.

"I assumed you were driving to a police station, Raymond!" said Maureen.

"Oh, I never thought of that, sorry Maureen."

Maureen didn't try to hide her disappointment and let out her loudest exasperated sigh of the night. Martha started fumbling in her backpack, which now sat on her lap. She switched on her torch and pulled out a crumpled piece of paper, and then mumbled again how crap English roads were and how much clearer a block system was when building a city.

"Is someone wanting to kill my husband?" Maureen couldn't keep it in any longer. If something terrible was about to happen, it was only polite to let her know.

"No. But I need all of you," muttered Martha absentmindedly as she squinted at the paper.

"You need all of us?" asked Tash. "That wasn't the agreement. We're going back to the warehouse. I'm a mother."

Martha leant forward and forced the page through the payment hole in the glass. Raymond took it from her.

"How long to get here?" she asked.

Raymond turned on the interior light and examined the paper. He rubbed his head.

"Well, I'm not an actual cab driver, but I reckon that's at least an hour away."

"Then hit the gas."

"See? I told you they said gas!" Jamie was delighted.

"The lights are red," protested Raymond.

"I meant when they change."

The lights changed, and the cab set off.

Martha looked at the others who were all still staring at her. Finally, she spoke. "You guys will be free to go in one hour."

"Can you please tell us what the hell's happening?" asked Tash.

"No."

"Why not?" asked Jamie.

"Because I got no fucking idea myself."

Maybe it was the darkness, maybe it was the arguing, maybe it was fear, but neither driver nor any of his passengers noticed that they were being followed.

Or that they had been followed since they left Butler's Wharf in the Mercedes.

****

The cab drove slowly down a main road with shops on either side, all of them locked up for the evening. Raymond indicated left, and the headlights lit up two advertising boards; one for the NEW! Cadbury's Twirl, the other announcing U2 at the Academy in Brixton, November 2 and 3.

Sandwiched between them was a street sign:

Clarendon Road, WD6.

Everyone was surprised to hear Raymond mutter, "It's around here I think." He squinted at the piece of paper that he clutched in his hand on the steering wheel. "This looks like quite an old map. There are lots more roads now."

Martha shuffled to the edge of the rear bench seat to get a better look out of the window to the right. She was now clutching a further piece of paper and squinting to read again.

"Wait for the gap in the houses on your right," she read.

Sure enough, a gap appeared between the dwellings. Between a row of 1920s terraced houses and a row of Victorian ones, there was a wide service road.

"Here! Take this turn."

As Raymond turned into the driveway, the taxi headlights lit up an access road only as long as the houses were deep. At the other end was a big open area. Maybe a car park, perhaps private land. A pole barrier was chained in the locked position across the road and brought their journey to a premature stop immediately. Raymond squinted through the windscreen.

"This is the end of the road for us, then."

Martha opened up the document in her hands. It was a copy of an old OS map date stamped 1955. She could see Clarendon Road clearly, and she could also see the small access road that they currently sat on. Ahead of the taxi, beyond the barrier were buildings and trees. The map in her hand showed the outlines of buildings but on a far smaller scale. Urban sprawl was inevitable, but the open land on her map was now taken over by some kind of warehouse.

Martha spun the map around a few times and then took a deep breath.

"Keys please."

"You what?" asked Raymond.

"I'm gonna need the keys."

Martha held out her opened hand to the hole in the glass partition behind Raymond. He reluctantly turned off the ignition and passed the keys to his American kidnapper.

"You can trust us," said Tash. "You just do what you need to do, and we'll wait here."

"We won't go anywhere," appealed Jamie.

"I know, cos you're coming with me."

"We could get mugged," appealed Maureen. "Look at this place."

"Looks alright to me, Maureen," reassured Raymond. "Nicer than our road."

"She doesn't know that, Raymond! She's foreign. Why do you keep getting things wrong?...That was my angle."

"I'm sorry, darling. I'm not used to being kidnapped," he replied, "But that was a smashing angle by the way. I didn't know you had an angle!"

"You're gonna have to tell us what the fuck is happening," insisted Tash, before adding an apology for the profanity that made Maureen visibly recoil. Martha did her best.

"Look. Here's the deal. You've been great. A bit annoying, but mostly great. So, here's what we're gonna do. We are all going to this spot."

With this, Martha held up a map displaying a red cross in the middle of what would have been wasteland. It was a bit like a pirate map other than the absence of sea or a skull and crossbones.

"If you behave, we'll all be back here within ten minutes. OK? Come on."

"Why would we come with you? Why would we believe you?" asked Maureen.

Jamie agreed. "She has a point. You could just take us somewhere dark and then shoot us all in the head to death."

Maureen let out a little "Oh!" at this imagery, whereas Tash was dealing in semantics again.

"You don't need 'to death' after that, Jamie. I think shooting in the head gives an assumed death."

"Yeah, but she might need a few shots. I read about a bloke that got shot in the head, and he lived. He just got a massive headache and lost an eye." He thought for a moment. "Or maybe it was two eyes."

Maureen let out another sound.

"Well, that's a story full of hope," replied Tash.

"Can you just all follow me please? Jesus!" Martha was losing her patience.

Pretty much everyone responded with adamant *'No!'* or *'Well, I'm not'* or *'I'm staying here'* type statements.

"What? Come on! We've come this far!" pleaded Martha. "Don't make me use this!" she added, holding up the gun.

"You don't have the balls. Besides, you've told us nothing, you've dragged us halfway across London, you've made us knock down people and steal cars and stuff, and you still haven't told us what the hell is going on!" said Tash, before turning to Maureen. "And I said hell for your sake, Maureen."

Maureen nodded her appreciation.

"Instead of fuck," explained Jamie.

"Right!" shouted Martha. "New plan. You come with me, and I'll give you each some money."

This silenced them for a bit.

"How much money?" asked Maureen. "Because my husband's lost his job and his livelihood, and unless you're talking about a serious amount of –"

"Ten grand each," interrupted Martha.

Raymond snorted a noise that sounded like: "Beg pardon?"

"Is that dollars or pounds?" asked Maureen.

"Maureen!" said Raymond.

"Dollars," answered Martha.

"Forget it," said Maureen.

"Maureen!"

"Pounds! Whatever the fuck! Is there a difference?" Martha wasn't really up on her exchange rates.

"Maybe twenty to thirty per cent, I'd say," surmised Tash. "More," she added.

"What does that mean? Is that a lot? What's that mean in bucks?"

"Maybe twelve thousand dollars." said Tash, adding for her brother's sake: "Exchange rates in 84 were mental."

"I can do that. Deal." After all, Martha was about to get eleven million dollars and some pretty awesome property. She just wanted to get things done.

"Is it stolen money?" asked Maureen.

"What? No! Of course it's not stolen."

"No amount of money is any use to me," said Tash. "I just want to go home to my son."

"Weird," said Martha. "But what have you got to lose? Give me ten minutes then go find your son. With your cash."

Tash shook her head. "It's not as simple as that."

"Well, we're in." said Maureen. "And as there's two of us, that's two lots of money."

"Cool." Martha was a little surprised but impressed by the shrewd brain of this older lady.

Everyone slowly nodded, and eventually, Tash could see she was beaten. "Okay. This the final ten minutes I'm going to throw at this."

"And then we need to stop that biblical famine, too," said Jamie. "You know. If we have time."

****

They walked around the barrier and were immediately confronted by a massive steel-clad warehouse that blocked the path to the intriguing red cross on Martha's map.

"We need to get here," said Martha, handing the map and torch to Tash and peering around the side of the building to see if an access path would help them on their way. It wouldn't.

Tash glanced at the map and then at the obstacle in their path. She did a quick 360 and seemed to arrive at a conclusion. She turned to Maureen.

"Ever been garden hopping, Maureen?"

"Garden what?"

"You'll get the hang of it. Follow me, everyone."

Passing silently through the garden of thirteen terraced houses might have been easy for a fox or a cat. For a fit adult, it would be quite a test of endurance. And if you had been a resident of any one of the terraced houses between 37 to 61 Clarendon Road, West London in October 1984, you could have done far worse with your time than pulling a chair to a bedroom window and watching these five attempt to reach the pot of gold on their mysterious map. Some wooden fence panels were dilapidated and offered little resistance to the squad.

Occasionally a well-established privet hedge would really slow things down. Still, Jamie soon mastered a technique of corkscrewing himself through them that left a sizeable gap for the others to hurl themselves into. None spotted the ornamental pond in 49, and none had the wherewithal to warn their followers about it either. Maybe the murky water and rotting leaves that squelched from their shoes dampened any remnants of charitable spirit. The fact that any water remained in the pond after the fifth assailant – let alone any fish – was a miracle in itself. Maureen spent most of the time reciting the cost of all her tennis clothes that were slowly being destroyed by their quest. And she didn't take kindly to Raymond's reminders that the volume of her speech was compromising the stealth approach that the group had agreed from the outset. Number 61 at the far end had a substantial plot of land strangely cleared of planting possibly for sale to London's avaricious property developers who were becoming experts at ramming four new-build homes into the space where a single garden once stood. Being the end terrace on an internal corner of dwellings, the residents had been spoiled with a wrap-around back and side garden that stretched fully to the front. Jamie was first into this final garden, soon followed by his sister. As they waited for the others to reach them, Jamie peered around the front of the house and couldn't help but notice something.

"There's a gate, Tash," he whispered badly. He'd never been good at whispering. Whispering and blowing out birthday candles were two of his weaknesses.

"Shhh!" replied Tash, tiptoeing over to him to investigate his discovery. "What about it?"

Jamie opened the wooden gate slowly on its creaky hinges, and the two of them saw a beautifully dry footpath that spanned from the front of this house all the way along the road to the house next to their parked-up cab.

"We could have come this way."

Tash absorbed this information as she removed some privet from her mouth.

"Sake," was all she could manage.

"Psst! What have you seen?" whispered Raymond, helping his wife over the final fence panel. Maureen tumbled clumsily onto the remnants of turf and took Raymond down with her, amazingly he managed to hold the video recorder safely above his head as he hit a pile of leaves. Maureen had insisted he didn't leave it in the taxi in case it got stolen.

"Nothing," lied Tash, as she forced the gate closed and walked over to help the old couple to their feet. "Where's the American?"

"I have a name," came Martha's reply from the other side of the fence.

"She's on the other side of the fence," said Jamie loudly.

"Yes. Yes, I heard Jamie, thanks. And try to whisper." Tash addressed the fence, "Do you need a hand?"

"No. I'm just taking a pee," said Martha, shortly followed by the sound of something comparable to a donkey having its first piss the morning after a night out with the lads.

"Christ!" snorted Tash.

"Realised I hadn't been since I landed at Heathrow."

Everyone waited politely as only the British can under these circumstances.

"And my name is Martha, by the way," added Martha, in raised tones to be heard over her torrent of urine.

"It's making me want to go, that is," added Jamie.

"Don't think about it," said Tash, helpfully.

"It does that sometimes, doesn't it?" said Raymond politely as they all tried their best to pretend there wasn't an almighty gushing sound echoing around the darkened gardens.

One minute later, they were all in different pockets of the garden relieving themselves. Even Maureen. Martha jumped down from the fence and couldn't believe her eyes.

"What the fuck is this?"

"You started it," said Tash, squatting over a vegetable patch.

"Can you see?" asked Martha, flicking her torch on. "Could you use some light?"

"Oi!" protested Tash straight away.

"Sorry!"

Martha pointed the torch elsewhere. Jamie followed its path to see the alabaster white arse of Maureen sliding back into her C&A knickers.

"I've just seen Maureen's arse!" he exclaimed, in a tone you might say, "I've got a splinter!"

"Raymond," protested Maureen, and clipped her husband's head. He was standing alongside her steadying her arm.

"Sorry, Maureen," came his voice from the dark.

Without notice, the garden was suddenly lit up as if it were midday in June.

"There's a light on!" observed Jamie.

"Shhh," replied Tash.

The upstairs bedroom of the corner house was now flooding light into the garden. A distracted teenager danced over to close the curtains in time with John Waits repeating the chorus to 'Missing You'. A radio DJ started to tell us the song had risen one place in the Top 40, but he came to an abrupt end on the teenager's cassette, and the chiming synth intro to Alison Moyet's 'All Cried Out' took over.

"Dad was onto something," said Jamie to Tash, delightedly. "Gobshite DJs!"

He was shushed again, but Tash did nod her understanding as she whispered, "Smart Pause."

All five held their breath and tried to squat as inconspicuously as possible as the teenager finally closed the curtains.

"She can't see out of the window now," reported Jamie.

"Thanks Jamie. Let me know if she jumps out of it," replied his sister.

"Guys," whispered Martha as she slowly stood up straight.

"I wish she wouldn't call us guys, Raymond. Some of us are ladies," muttered Maureen from her dark corner. "Why can't Americans speak properly?"

"Guys!" said Martha, a little louder this time, to squash the revolution. "We just need to get the other side of this fence. And it looks like this is an easy one."

She was right. The final barrier was a well-made timber fence comprising horizontal slats, so it was essentially a very wide ladder. They set about it straight away, in silence.

Naturally, they were all sufficiently wired by their own adrenaline that nobody noticed the solitary figure enter the garden through the gate and follow them on their way.

FORTY

Jamie dropped onto the ground first and immediately skinned his shin on a twisted metal sign.

"Ow!" he shrieked, followed by the inevitable reminder about volume from his sister who was straddling the fence panel above him.

"Climb down this side, don't jump," he offered as he rubbed his shin.

As the others slowly clambered down to join him, Martha lifted her torch to see the damage to Jamie's leg. The steel had cut a hole in his trousers, and the blood made him whine a little, but matriarch Maureen soon established this was nothing, and he should man up.

Martha pointed her torch around the ground to see what had caused the injury and lit up a weathered rusty yellow sign, mostly written in German. The words BECO were prominent and DUSSELDORF but other than that it seemed to contain lots of rules and regulations that no-one could translate. To their side, a skip was overflowing with timber, broken breeze blocks and crates of empty Becks beer bottles.

"Just tread carefully, everyone," said Tash.

Martha was fumbling again with her map. She backed up to the fence until she was leaning fully against it, and then purposefully strode forward, counting yards with each stride.

"What's she doing?" asked Tash.

"She's counting," answered Jamie.

"Anyone else want to answer me?"

"Find out, Raymond, and stop looking at her," instructed Maureen to her husband.

Raymond nodded. "Excuse me, miss? What are you doing?" He was trying his best to avert his eyes from her.

"Don't interrupt someone when they're counting Raymond!"

"Sorry, Maureen."

"Or is that sleepwalking?" she mused. "You've confused me now."

"Best follow, I say," said Jamie and he set off behind the mysterious American. The others followed him.

Martha was only really concentrating on staying in a straight line and reaching a point sixty yards from the perimeter fence. She continued under a railway bridge and at the count of sixty, she stopped and looked to her left. Just thirty more paces and she would be at her destination. As the others caught up with her, she turned ninety degrees and started walking, counting from one again.

"Is this safe, Raymond? It seems deserted. None of the houses have lights on," observed Maureen.

At that moment, Jamie grabbed his sister's shoulder. "Tash! Oh, My Actual God!" He was pointing straight ahead of Martha. "The Queen Victoria!"

Tash squinted to see a pub floodlit by a builder's light resting on the ground. She spun around and realised her brother was doing the same with a giddy smile on his face. He couldn't keep it quiet.

"We're in Albert Square!"

Sure enough, the five of them had broken into the Elstree backlot where the EastEnders set was being constructed from fibreglass panels painted with bricks. The empty houses were just fronts, no interiors and no backs. The square itself was simply grass, with no paths or railings yet. The single floodlight was possibly an attempt to keep the set lit for workers who had clearly recently finished painting the Queen Vic. And right now the pure white glow was illuminating the pink hair of Martha who stood looking squarely at the entrance to the famous pub.

"What's Albert Square?" asked Maureen. "What do you mean?"

"From *EastEnders*!" answered Jamie. "I thought you liked TV?"

"They're still building the set, Jamie," explained Tash. "The show started in '85."

"They're doing that thing again, Raymond. Tell them to stop talking in riddles," muttered Maureen.

"Remember *Auf Wiedersehen, Pet*?" Jamie asked.

"We never watched it," Maureen folded her arms as if this proved her point.

"Shame. They filmed it here. That's what that sign was that ripped my leg!" Jamie was suddenly delighted that he'd end up with a scar from an iconic TV show.

Martha opened the double doors to the pub and walked through.

As the doors slammed behind her, she let out an almighty scream.

The others had recoiled at the ear-splitting noise, and Jamie surprised himself by immediately running to see how he could help. His sister ran behind, not too close, but close enough. "Jamie, don't go in there!"

Jamie ignored his sister, stopping only briefly as he reached out to touch the brass handles of the actual Queen Vic. Dirty Den's Vic! Peggy Mitchell's Vic! The Queen Vic!

And then he walked in.

And then he screamed too.

FORTY ONE

In fairness, Jamie didn't fall far, and his fall was broken by something soft and yet hard at the same time. But he definitely fell. His first thought was, *who puts a hole inside a doorway? There's no hole on the TV show.* His second thought was, *my God, Martha smells amazing.* That was when his third thought dropped into his head. *I've landed on her.* Then he heard her.

"What the fuck?"

"Sorry. Sorry. There's a hole," explained Jamie, slowly finding his feet. He helped Martha up too, and they both took in their surroundings. As Martha rubbed her neck, she saw that they had both fallen into some sort of colossal manhole. Standing up, their heads were back in The Queen Vic, but only just. They were standing between two floors. The pub floor was at their shoulders.

"This is the spot," explained Martha, as she flicked on her torch again. Inside the pub, they could see timber props leaning against the external fibreglass walls that made the facade look so authentic from outside. A massive hinged timber trap door lay flat on the floor to one side, clearly designed to cover the hole they were now filling.

"Are you OK?" asked Tash as the double doors opened, flooding light into the shell of the building. It was mostly empty but for some tins of paint and a trestle table with some brushes and empty cans of Top Deck shandy and Double Diamond beer.

"Don't step inside! There's no floor!" shouted Jamie. "We're fine."

Martha squatted down into the hole. Jamie did the same, and together they could see a derelict storage room underneath the pub. It was pretty huge. At the other end, a ramp indicated there was another entrance to ground level.

They had landed at the head of a staircase, and stone steps descended away to one side.

The three of them suddenly heard voices from outside. Two belonged to Raymond and Maureen, but the third sounded unfamiliar and aggressive. It got louder, and Tash turned to see a grey-haired man dressed in a warm duffle coat, which hung open to show a security officer's uniform with a BBC security badge pinned to his lapel.

"Where are you from, then? *News Of The World* again, is it? Come on, out of there."

He stopped to see Martha and Jamie's heads protruding from the hole in the floor.

"What the bloody hell are you doing in there? Come on, out!"

Martha ignored him and squatted again to look into the vast basement area. She was confused.

"What's the deal here? This is empty."

Jamie was struggling to climb out of the hole and was using the same method he used to climb out of a swimming pool. Zero grace, zero technique, and zero success. His sister leaned over and offered a hand, and together they managed to get him back to ground level.

Martha was fumbling in her pocket. She produced a photograph, which she held over to show the security guard, keeping a secure grip on it.

"See this?"

Maybe it was her confidence or lack of regard for his authority, but he found himself engaging with her and reaching out for the photo. Martha had a skill for making most people feel inferior, and this guy was putty in her hands. The fact that she didn't release her grip on the photo made him fully understand his place in her pecking order. Which was even lower than her, and she was standing in a hole.

He took one step to get closer and then squatted down to examine the photo.

"What about it?" The suspicion in his voice was clear.

"I'm supposed to find it right here. Where is it?"

He looked long and hard again. The photo was pretty dull as photos go. It was a black and white image of a timber crate that was maybe eight feet long by four feet high. The crate, not the photo. Stenciled onto the side of it were the words, *Portland, Maine to London. D.H, Esq.*

"What is it?" asked the security guard.

"No," replied Martha. "Where is it?"

The security man straightened up and looked at the crowd glaring at him, Raymond and Maureen were now standing in the doorway too.

"Are you from TVC?" asked the guard, spotting the video recorder in Raymond's grasp.

"What?" replied Martha.

"They cleared out the shelter a month or so ago," explained the guard.

"Shelter?" asked Martha.

"It's an old air-raid shelter. Part of the backlot during the war. Didn't have much in it, to be fair. I think it just had some old props or scenery in it."

"Where did they take it?" Martha's questioning had a sudden sense of urgency.

"They keep a lot of stuff at Bullens on the A40, I think," he scratched his head. "But now I think about it, I'm pretty sure everything in there went to TVC. Now I'm gonna have to ask you to leave."

"What's TVC?" asked Martha "And how far is it?"

"TV Centre. Shepherds Bush," explained the man offering his hand to Martha to help her out of the hole. Like much of the BBC security in the eighties, he was ex-military and was able to lift her out with little effort.

"Do we know where that is?" asked Martha to others. They all nodded.

"Big place," remarked Raymond.

"Whereabouts at TVC?" asked Martha. "I need specifics."

"Probably somewhere on the outer ring road. I'd go Frithville Gate. Off Frithville Gardens," he answered, convinced that these people were not getting a scoop of the BBC's new soap for the Sunday newspapers. He was closing the massive timber door over the opening like an oversized manhole cover. It made quite a slam.

"Do you know where that is?" Martha asked the others. They shook their heads.

"Are you from Central?" continued the guard. "Cos they tried to contact you countless times about all the leftover crap. The *Auf Wiedersehen, Pet* stuff went in the skip."

Martha finished jotting down Frithville Gardens and turned to the others.

"Guys, I'm going to ask for your support one final time. The deal remains the same, but we gotta go to this place right now. I'm asking you to trust in me. Please? This is kind of important."

Tash, Jamie, Maureen and Raymond all looked at her and then at one another.

Pretty much at the same time, they all spoke.

"No."

Martha absorbed this mini-revolution. But took it in her stride.

"Okay, we're all on time and a half now. Will that work?"

"Is that each again?" asked Maureen. Raymond winced at her sledgehammer approach to negotiations. "Fifteen thousand dollars each?"

Martha did some quick maths in her head and then nodded. She pushed through the group and walked back into Albert Square. They turned to follow her.

"TVC then," concluded Martha.

"I'd make a proper appointment, though. You won't find it as easy to get into there!" said the guard with a derisory snort.

"Good call," replied Martha over her shoulder at him, pocketing his security badge. "Thanks for the advice."

FORTY TWO

Tash tiptoed slowly over to the cot so as not to wake her sleeping son. He was in pretty much the same position as when Tash had left him. He looked even more beautiful than she'd remembered. His tiny cotton gloves kept the chill of Grandma's bedroom at bay. Tash didn't want to wake this precious jewel from his slumber, but she simply couldn't resist gently lifting him and holding him close. She could smell his distinctive baby scent, she could feel his perfect ribcage slowly lift up and down, she could feel his soft, warm skin on her cheek. "Tash," whispered Jamie from his bed. He'd started playing Phil Collins' 'Against All Odds' on his phone which was a song she loved, but surely this would wake the baby and the rest of the house.

"Turn it down, Jamie. You'll wake everyone," she muttered.

Strangely it was the sound of her own voice that made her eyes blink open. Tash let everything come into focus and saw Jamie smiling back at her, he was travelling backwards in one of those taxi seats that fold down. As Tash embraced her son, she felt her hands close in on themselves. He was not there.

Of course not. He was in 2020, thought Tash. As tears started to warm her eyes, Phil was singing *take a look at me now* on the cab stereo, and the volume lowered.

"Is this the scenic route?" asked Martha as she watched the dial on the taxi meter clicked up to £34.50.

"I'm not used to back streets, I'm going the way I know," protested Raymond, a little more assertively than usual. He paused at the Holland Park roundabout and looked both ways whilst scratching his chin.

"Which way now, then?" asked Martha.

Maureen had heard enough. "He's doing his best. It's not his fault we've crossed London twice this evening." She tried to give a stern look to Martha, but the American didn't notice. She was glaring at the road sign up ahead.

"Take the right. It's got to be right. Go up there."

Martha was pointing right.

"You can't go right from here, this is a roundabout," replied Raymond.

"Just take a right. No one's gonna notice!"

"I have to go around a roundabout," explained Raymond as he set off.

"Why do we have to go around so many things in this country? Every route is a rollercoaster. Makes me wanna puke," Martha preferred the vast intersections of Burlington. At least you turned right when you wanted to turn right. Turning left first made zero sense.

As the cab joined the roundabout another sign indicated Shepherds Bush was straight on. "Shepherds Bush, straight ahead!" shouted Martha.

"I'm in the wrong lane now," explained Raymond, looking mightily stressed. He hated driving stolen cars around busy roundabouts in the dark.

"I don't give a fuck what lane you're in!"

Raymond put his foot to the floor to clear the Passat on his left and nipped in front of it, managing to take the Shepherd's Bush exit with just inches to spare before clipping the kerb. The passengers were thrown back into their seats, except Jamie who was in a rear-facing seat. He simply fell full into Martha's lap. As he extracted his face from her groin and muttered apologies, the inside of the cab lit up blue. The unmistakable sound of a police siren was followed by Raymond's first swear.

"Language, Raymond!" snapped Maureen.

"Sorry, Maureen. But I think I might be in a bit of trouble with the police."

Martha was burying her gun deep inside her leg warmers that layered around the top of her Doc Martens boots. "Let me do the talking."

"Why would we do that?" protested Tash. "He just cut up another car. That's all. Let Raymond get his wrists slapped, and we can be on our way."

Raymond slowed the cab down and came to a halt in a bus stop. Across the road, they could see the darkness of some grassland. A sign on the fence read Shepherd's Bush Green. We can't be far now, thought Martha.

A Rover 2400 police car pulled in front of them and two officers climbed out. The siren had stopped but the flickering blue light continued to blind the passengers of the taxi.

"Put your seat belts on. If we all put our seat belts on then, we should be OK," muttered Jamie, nonsensically.

"Should have thought about that before you face-planted my all-day breakfast," remarked Martha.

Maureen's jaw dropped. Tash chuckled.

"That was an accident! I'm so sorry! I didn't mean to do that." The blue lights hid Jamie's red face. One officer stood at the front of the taxi taking down the registration plate, the other was alongside Raymond, who lowered his window.

"Good evening officer," stammered Raymond, covering his NHS badge with one hand.

"I'm sure you know why we stopped you, don't you erm, Niki, erm... Niki.." he was struggling to find the name, so looked over at his colleague for help.

"Lauder," offered his friend.

"That's him! Niki Lauder!" snorted the policeman into Raymond's face. "I'm sure you know why we stopped you, don't you? Niki Lauder!"

Raymond forced a smile at the mention of the new Formula One World Champion. Lauder had secured his victory after coming second in the final race of the season over the weekend. It was enough to give him his third and final World title.

"It was a little bit, shall we say, assertive driving. Wasn't it, sir?"

The other policeman was now back at his squad car holding a CB radio, reporting details of the cab to the station.

"My, erm, my fare changed their mind on the roundabout, and I stupidly thought I could make the exit, and I was clearly wrong, officer. I'm extremely sorry."

"Can I see your taxi driving licence please, sir?"

Raymond's heart sank, but he went through the motions of fumbling around in his porter uniform. A harsh wolf whistle interrupted the awkward moment. The officer looked up and saw his colleague gesturing to join him at the Rover.

"One moment please, sir," said the officer as he wandered away.

"I don't have a licence to drive this thing, what am I going to tell him? This is a terrible state of affairs!"

"Tell him she's got a gun and made you do it, Raymond," replied Maureen nodding at Martha.

"Yes. Yes. That's one way of looking at it," interrupted Tash. "But if you do that, then I won't be heading back to the warehouse within the hour. And understand this…" she leant into Maureen's face and hissed, "I am going back to that warehouse. I need to get home to my son. Do you understand?"

Maureen was taken aback by Tash's sudden descent to brutal intimidator and responded with a silent nod. None of them was expecting what happened next.

"Exit the vehicle on the pavement side with your hands in the air. All of you!"

The voice was loud and echoed off the surrounding buildings.

They looked through the windscreen. The policeman was speaking to them through a loud hailer from the rear of his car. His colleague removed a truncheon and strolled towards them.

"I repeat, exit on the pavement side with your hands in the air."

Moments later, Raymond's face was resting in a puddle of what he hoped was spilt lager and a discarded cigarette end. He couldn't see the others but prayed that his wife had at least found a cleaner bit of pavement to be handcuffed. Raymond could smell the stale coffee on the officer's breath as they exchanged small talk. Well, it was pretty one-sided chat to be fair.

"You are under arrest on suspicion of stealing a taxi cab. You do not have to say anything, but it may harm your defence if you do not mention when questioned something which you later rely on in court. Anything you do say may be given in evidence."

"Thank you," replied Raymond. "Sorry."

FORTY THREE

Raymond had never been inside a police interview room before and his underlying thought was how realistic *The Bill* had been last week. And how disappointed he was that he'd missed last night's episode. Maureen hadn't really been interested, but then she'd never watched *The Gentle Touch* either, so a new police show was pretty low on her must-watch list. Its single window was the same height as the one in his cell, but this one didn't seem to have bars. Unless they were on the outside, of course. It was hard to tell from where he was sitting. Which was on a plastic chair next to a Formica table. Two police officers sat across from him, a woman who introduced herself as Inspector Suttle and a man, Sergeant Beresford. She was easily ten years younger than Raymond, the man younger still. The whirr of a recording cassette deck was the only sound. Raymond had thought this was all a bit heavy-handed for a simple car theft. Not that he condoned crime of any kind, they were all abhorrent. But still, it was only a car theft. It was a bit much to keep them all locked up overnight. What the police hadn't told him was that the Metropolitan Police had suspected the IRA would step up their operations around the capital after the Brighton bombing earlier in the month, hence the increased vigilance. An attempt on the life of Margaret Thatcher and her whole cabinet had rocked the country. And a taxi was considered the kind of transportation that a covert terrorist could make excellent use of, so it was necessary to get a full explanation of last night's theft outside St Thomas' Hospital.

"You are telling us the complete truth, Mr Geldof?" asked the exasperated inspector.

"I am so I am," replied Raymond in his best Irish accent. "The driver took himself ill outside my hospital, and I offered to move his cab for him."

"You moved it to Shepherd's Bush. Wouldn't the hospital car park have been closer?"

"He said he lived at Shepherd's Bush and asked if I could I take it there for him. Kind of thing."

"That's not what he told us," said Beresford.

"Well, that would be cos he was a little bit pissed. Did you breathalyse the fecker?"

Suttle looked at Beresford, who reluctantly shook his head.

"And what happened to you?" asked Suttle, gesturing at Raymond's neck brace and plaster cast.

"I cut myself shaving."

****

On the Formica table sat the Ferguson Videostar. It was a nice machine with a sleek aluminium pull-down flap to cover a lot of the many buttons. Front-loading meant that it could fit neatly into a TV cabinet flush beneath the TV set. And its remote control was amongst the most comprehensive on sale today. Although for all its features, Maureen would probably describe it as heavy.

"So it's not your video recorder?" Beresford was tiring now.

"No," replied Maureen.

"But it's not stolen?"

"No."

"And you intend to return it to your workplace?"

"No."

Beresford looked quizzically at Maureen.

"My husband will. He just needs to find a pop-star."

****

"So you see, it's not a big deal in the US. We car-share for pool lanes, we cab-share whenever we can. We gotta think of the planet, you know? Did you know the smog in LA nearly fucked over the Olympics this summer? We don't want that kinda shit on the East Coast. Gotta stay one step ahead, right? We've only got one world." Martha was so cool, it was unsettling.

Beresford nodded, although he wasn't sure quite what she'd said, but blimey she was pretty, She looked like an American singer who'd had a few hits and disappeared out of the charts at the start of the year. She was called Madonna, and he secretly hoped to marry her one day. Maybe he would now she wasn't famous anymore.

Suttle turned to Martha. "Well, on behalf of the rest of the world, thank you. We can always rely on the Yanks to save the day, can't we Beresford?"

Beresford nodded, despite being confused.

"If you could have a word with Mr Reagan about all those nuclear weapons too, that would be smashing," added Suttle. She was still having nightmares about a BBC drama called *Threads* that she watched last month. A nuclear bomb landed on Sheffield, and it was brutal. Thankfully she'd never been to Sheffield or had any intention of visiting. The South Yorkshire force had their work cut out with the miner's strike right now, so armageddon was the last thing they needed on top of all that.

"So you've never met any of the other passengers in that taxi before yesterday?" asked Suttle.

Martha shook her head.

"And what's in the bag?"

Martha looked uncomfortable for the first time but thought quickly.

"If I'm honest, I don't travel well, and your roundabout things are just too much. I spent the whole ride puking into little plastic bags. Wanna take a look?"

Both police officers declined politely.

****

"He's five months old. He needs me. He needs me with him," said Tash, holding her iPhone at her interrogators. They were both more intrigued by the gadget than the photo on the screen.

"So, just to be clear, you stand by your statement when you were first arrested?" asked Suttle.

"Yes!" Tash leant into the whirring cassette recorder and clearly spoke. "I'm a time traveller from 2020. We're living in a global pandemic, and I accidentally came back to the day of my actual birth. I'm pretty sure I'm not an asymptomatic carrier, but I would wash your hands after talking to me."

She finished with a little cough in their general direction.

****

Jamie's interview was the shortest.

"I saw my actual mum's actual fanny give birth to my actual sister and my Dad had it off with a stranger, and I still need to stop a global famine before I can open my Christmas presents. It's all been a bit much, to be honest."

****

Jamie looked up to the observation window in his holding cell door. It had slid open, and a warmer than usual voice was talking through it. "Looks like we're cutting your holiday short," joked the officer on duty. "Same time next year?"

Some clicks and slams and slides filled Jamie's ears, but sure enough, the heavy prison door swiveled open. It was a very short walk to the main corridor and Jamie was delighted to see all of the others waiting for him. Tash ran over and gave him a hug. Then she toughened up again.

"What a fucking mess, Jamie," she muttered.

Inspector Suttle appeared behind them. "Someone has friends in high places," she said, smiling. She genuinely didn't seem irate that someone had stepped in to vouch for the character of all five of her suspects. She had proper criminals to apprehend, so getting shut of this freak show suited her just fine.

"Well, we certainly don't," replied Maureen, genuinely surprised that someone might think that of her. She was also quite pleased that she might come across as the kind of lady with well-to-do friends.

"Who paid the bail?" asked Martha.

"Paid the bail?" Suttle didn't even try to stifle her laugh. "This isn't Alcatraz! We work on reason and logic, madam. We need addresses for you all as you may be asked to attend the station in the next twenty-eight days, but other than that, you are free to go."

"But who was the friend?" asked Jamie. "No-one knows we're here?"

Suttle examined some papers in her hand and read, "Fernando? Ring any bells?"

Everyone looked baffled.

"Inspector? This isn't reported as stolen. Shall I hand it back?" Beresford stepped out from behind his boss clutching the Ferguson.

Suttle nodded and turned to leave. "Have a good day," she muttered over her shoulder.

Beresford handed the machine to Raymond, who struggled again with his cast but managed to hold it securely whilst Beresford planted the video cassette on top.

"Right, addresses please," added Beresford, reaching out for a pad.

FORTY FOUR

The large timber gates at the rear of Shepherd's Bush police station opened onto just four Victorian semi-detached houses. It was a modest road and looked pretty much like any other part of this vast city that somehow had a relentless grip on Jamie and Tash.

Tash had insisted Raymond call his office the moment she saw a public phone on their way out. She was hanging every inch of hope on the belief that Dudley would have figured out a way to get the C5 back to his warehouse in 1984. Frustratingly, the call had gone unanswered, and now the five of them stood looking tired and hopeless on this damp October morning.

"I know we had an agreement, Martha, but this ends here," said Tash. "I need to get back to that warehouse right now. I'm sorry. This has gone on far enough."

Jamie looked disappointed at his sister's decision.

"We made a deal!" said Martha. "What part of ten grand don't you like?"

"You changed it to fifteen!" Maureen wouldn't let that slip.

"She has a point. Genuine mistake. 15k each. The offer stands."

"Shall we get a nice cup of tea and decide a plan of action?" suggested Raymond. "Shall we? A nice cup of tea?"

Tash shook her head. "No, we can't waste any more time, Jamie."

"Come on, sis. We could all use a drink. Ten minutes more. That's all he's asking,"

A postman was descending the steps of one of the houses behind them.

"Excuse me, sir?" asked Raymond.

The postman did a double-take over his shoulder assuming Raymond was talking to an actual aristocrat behind him. "Me?"

"Is there a decent cafe around here?"

The postman nodded and then gestured with a handful of letters.

"Go that way around the front of the cop shop, cross over to the church, then keep going left down the main road. Hundred yards or so. Jessingers. Does a decent fry up, too."

They followed his instructions, and surprisingly few people bothered to look twice at this unlikely group. A fifty-five-year-old lady wearing an anorak over tennis clothes, a hospital porter in a neck brace and plaster cast carrying a video recorder, a male nurse walking on his tiptoes, a thirty-something fun mum dressed like one of Strawberry Switchblade, and a pink-haired Madonna following up the rear. Jessingers had a slightly more upmarket feel to it than Marie's, thought Martha as she held the door open. A bench table had just come free inside the window, so she claimed it.

"Brunch is on me, guys," she declared as she grabbed a wipe-clean menu.

Maureen leant into her husband. "What's brunch?"

"I've no idea," he replied, so spoke up to Martha. "What's brunch?"

"Don't ask her, you'll look stupid," whispered Maureen.

"Sorry, Maureen."

"It's whatever you want. Like I say – I'm paying!" Martha waved her credit card in the air.

"It's a cross between breakfast and lunch," explained Jamie discreetly to Maureen.

She nodded coldly as if it was the most absurd word she'd ever heard.

"There's always so much choice, isn't there? In a restaurant? I never know what to choose until everyone has ordered!" mused Raymond as he glanced at a menu, clearly excited about the prospect of his first food in fifteen hours.

This sudden euphoria was infectious.

"The full English looks good!" said Jamie.

"What's black pudding?" asked Martha.

"It's delicious. Try it and then we'll tell you what it is," replied Raymond.

"Don't say blood at the table, Raymond," said Maureen.

"Sorry Maureen."

They were behaving like a giddy family on a birthday trip to their favourite restaurant. Maybe it was their empty stomachs or the relief of prison release, but the joy was tangible.

This was too much for Tash. The fact that Paul McCartney's 'No More Lonely Nights' was playing on a badly tuned radio only made things worse. 'I can wait another day, until I call you,' sang Paul. She stood up and clapped her hands to get the attention of the staff behind the counter, then shouted, "Five full fucking English, please!" before sitting down. She stood up again. "Sorry, might have let out a swear there." Then sat down again.

"Any fucking drinks with that?" asked an assertive looking lady in an apron. She was Mrs Jessinger.

"Yes, please. Sorry," replied Tash. Martha asked for a black coffee, and the orders went around the table past Raymond and Maureen (both teas) to Jamie (hot chocolate).

"And I'll have a flat white, please," asked Tash.

Mrs Jessinger stopped writing on her pad and asked, "Flat what?"

"Flat white coffee."

"A flat white coffee? A flat one?" repeated Mrs Jessinger. "What, like on a plate?"

"Latte, then. Latte's fine." Tash realised the rest of the café were staring at her, so she changed tack. "Cappuccino?"

Mrs Jessinger looked at her colleague frying sausages and made no attempt to whisper, "She thinks she's in bleeding Milan."

They laughed.

"Nescaf alright, darling? I'll get it as flat as I can. Might run the iron over it!"

"Actually, I'll just have a hot chocolate too, please."

Jamie tugged at his sister's sleeve. He had a habit of doing this even when he had your attention.

"I've solved things," he whispered very loudly into Tash's ear.

"What things?"

"Getting us home things."

This immediately lifted her spirits.

"You have?"

"Once we get the C5 back…" he started to explain.

But Tash couldn't let that remark go, she started babbling. "You think we will? Cos I think we will. He's going to realise we were telling the truth and then he just needs to follow the prompts on the screen and he'll come back, right? He's probably waiting for us now. Probably didn't hear the phone when we called…?"

Jamie just nodded and continued his train of thought.

"Once we get it back, we need to take it as far as it will go," he explained.

Tash looked confused. "What do you mean?"

"Well, as I see it, the computer is stuck in the twentieth century. So the farthest we can go to is 1999."

"Don't say that, Jamie. I'm a mum. My life is in 2020! How is that solving things?"

"Yes. Yes. Don't panic. Here's the plan. We go to 1999 and meet Grandad."

"But he died in 1999?"

"I know. We need to go to a moment just before he died."

"Bit bleak." Tash lowered her voice as a mug of instant hot chocolate was slopped in front of her. "Why just before? Why can't we go a lot before?"

"Well, we don't know when he nailed the technology to make it time travel, do we? If we arrive too soon, it might stop him actually creating the thing in the first place. Which I think is bad. It was for Marty McFly." Jamie stopped to smile his thanks to the lady handing him his cup of hot chocolate. He carefully placed it on the table in front of him and then knocked it over. Asperger's doesn't respect crucial life moments, it will happily rear its head at a wedding ceremony or funeral. Tash barely flinched, she simply scooped up some cheap napkins, soaked up the spill and topped up her brother's cup with half of hers. She looked up to see the others were staring. "Talk amongst yourselves," she instructed.

Martha placed her Walkman over her ears, and Maureen reached over for a discarded newspaper. The front page of the *Mirror* boldly declared that the NACOD strike was OFF. Unlike the NUM, this union of miners had opted to renege on September's vote to take industrial action. Maureen tutted at the topless lady on page five and flicked a few pages forward to see a full-page ad for the Ferguson Videostar. She looked around the café to check no-one had spotted her sudden guilt and frantically flicked on a few pages more. A headline claimed Maggie was paying millions to store European grain that 'could easily feed an African nation', it was something about EEC protection of prices for their farmers. She tutted again and turned to the TV pages. She tutted one more time when she read that BBC One was repeating *The Good Life* yet again tonight. They can't do that forever, how ridiculous.

Jamie whispered to Tash. "If we arrive on Christmas Eve, say midday, that's well before Grandma sent him out to the shops. We just come clean, we have no choice. We don't mention what we've seen in 1984, but we tell him that the computer has the millennium bug and we need it to be Y2K compliant."

"We could stop him from getting in the car!" Tash was suddenly elated. "We could save his life!"

Jamie interrupted the chat. "I need to pee." He climbed off the pine bench and approached Mrs Jessinger who lifted a serving hatch in the counter and directed him through the kitchen to the only WC the café boasted. He tried the door, but it was locked.

"Being used. Gonna be a long one!" came a gruff cockney voice from the other side of the door.

Jamie headed back to the table, stopping briefly in the kitchen, distracted by an overloaded shelf laden with sauces, condiments and cooking oil.

Tash looked up as Jamie sat down alongside her. He looked very happy.

"That was quick, did you wash your hands?"

"Someone's having a dump," explained Jamie.

They both heard Maureen tut but continued their plan.

"Won't he be spooked to see us in our thirties?" Tash was rethinking the plan already. "What if the sight of us gives him a heart attack?"

Jamie's binary logic kicked in. "You think a man who's invented a buggy that can travel through time would be surprised to meet someone from another era?"

Tash considered this. Jamie always reduced life's dilemmas to A and B scenarios. She nodded and started to feel quite emotional. "Grandad'll know what to do won't he?" she whispered.

"He always knew what to do," replied her brother and gave her a squeeze as he placed something in her jumper pocket.

"What's that?"

"Don't get it out in here, It's for later."

Tash was feeling ten thousand per cent better now. She forgot about the possibility that the C5 might not even be in the warehouse when she eventually arrived back there. She forgot that her son was sleeping soundly in his cot thirty-six years in the future.

She just felt better. And the cheap hot chocolate suddenly tasted better than any she'd ever drunk.

Unlike Martha, who emptied her first mouthful of coffee over Raymond.

"Sorry man, but that tastes like shit," she announced whilst wiping her mouth on her sleeve.

"Wait till you try the black pudding," said Tash.

"Clear yourself up, Raymond," instructed Maureen, as she handed him some napkins.

"Sorry Maureen."

Martha was reading her own handwriting when the food arrived.

"Do you know how to get to Frithville Gardens from here?" she asked Mrs Jessinger.

The cafe owner expertly placed three plates down in front of her guests and leant down to point straight through the window.

"See that road there?"

Martha nodded.

Mrs Jessinger walked off before returning with the other two plates.

Martha was staring at her.

"Where do I go from there?"

"Nowhere. That's Frithville Gardens."

Martha took in the excellent news and smiled at the others before announcing, "Excellent. Raymond doesn't need to steal another cab!"

"I didn't steal the first one."

"Kinda did," reasoned Martha as she prodded the black pudding on her plate.

FORTY FIVE

The Frithville Gate was an underwhelming gate. Certainly in comparison to the Hammersmith Park gate next to it. The Frithville Gate was very much playing Little & Large to the park's Two Ronnies' Gate. The Frithville Gate was plain grey steel with a simple, friendly sign saying '*Keep Out*'. Not that the five of them could see it as they reached the end of Frithville Gardens. Obscuring their view were maybe fifty or sixty teenage girls mulling around, chewing gum, and fixing one another's hair.

"Is this for you?" Tash asked Martha, genuinely wondering if this was part of her secret task.

Martha shrugged a genuinely baffled no. Jamie thought how interesting it was to see teenagers actually talking to one another without holding or staring at a mobile phone. They weren't posturing themselves for a selfie or leaning in to see the latest story from an influencer. Many wore Walkmans like Martha's, although few of them appeared to be Sony. Some stood in couples to lean in to listen from the same headset, others were rubbing AA batteries together to bring them back to life before reinserting them into their compartment. A few of them had weird flip-style cameras with little wrist straps in case they dropped them.

"What's the deal, ladies?" asked Martha.

A few of the girls turned around at the American accent. "Wham! are coming!" said one of them with a giggle before noticing the BBC badge that Martha had pinned to her chest in clear view. "Do you work on *Top Of The Pops*?" she continued, her jaw almost hitting her chest at this apparition.

"Yeah."

Blimey, she was scarily good at lying, thought Jamie.

"Can I have your autograph?" The teenager held out a biro and a *Smash Hits* magazine with "Wham! Make It Bigger!" on the cover underneath a photo of George and Andrew displaying teeth that were whiter than their shirts.

"Sure," replied Martha, taking the magazine and the pen.

"Not on Wham!" protested the teenager flipping the magazine over. "Sign on Depeche Mode."

"Why's she said that, Raymond?" asked Maureen.

"She probably prefers Wham! to Depeche Mode."

"No. Why's she said she works on *Top Of The Pops*?"

Raymond shrugged and moved the heavy video recorder from one arm to the other, forgetting it had a cast on it. He swung it straight back.

"Are you OK?" asked one of the more meek-looking girls, clearly disturbed by Raymond's neck brace, black eye and dried bloody nose.

"Yes. I'm fine," replied Raymond. "Sorry."

"It's make-up," said Martha. "They're both in make-up," she continued, gesturing at her nurse and porter companions.

Jamie nodded to Raymond, this seemed an OK explanation. Raymond nodded back.

"Are you famous?" asked the autograph hunter.

"Well, I wouldn't say famous," muttered Raymond.

"What you in?" asked the girl, taking her pen and magazine back from Martha and handing it to Raymond. He took it from her. "Erm… *Juliet Bravo*," he lied. He waited to see if this was worthy of an autograph. "Do you still want me to…" he mimed signing his name.

"Might as well. Me mum watches that," answered the girl flicking through to an acceptable page to be defaced by this old faded actor. She settled on an ad for *Queen We Will Rock You – Live In Concert*. "Sign there. She likes them an' all."

Raymond signed his name in his best copperplate. His secondary modern education threw about an hour at it, so it looked pretty shit. He handed the pen to Jamie who giddily signed too, opting for the stage name of H. Potter. It made him smile at least.

"Coming through," announced Martha to the girl still blocking their way. The teenage crowd dutifully parted to reveal the boring grey double gates.

Martha wolf-whistled a security guard who slowly walked over before asking what she wanted.

She flashed her BBC badge and said, "Oh man! We're late. Don't tell Eddie, my job is on the line already. Open this please?" Martha pointed to a smaller pedestrian gate to the side that she'd just spotted. She carried on talking to keep up the act, and it worked superbly. "We've got the new Duran video and the paps are all over the front gate."

"That's the 'Wild Boys' video?" interrupted a teenager who couldn't believe what was happening to her day.

"Excuse me?" replied Martha.

"Is that the new Duran Duran video for 'Wild Boys'?" The teenager was nudging her friend, and they were all gazing at it in pure wonder like it was solid gold or like it was the new Duran Duran video for 'Wild Boys'. Their euphoria wasn't lost on Martha who took this in her stride.

"Aha," she nodded in the affirmative and carried on talking to the security guard. "This is the 'Wild Boys' video, and Eddie told us to bring it in the back. It's like the Dallas episode with JR getting shot, remember that? Front page photo of a freaking film reel! Crazy what sells papers, you know?"

The security guy spied the videocassette and recorder weighing down Raymond.

"What's with the recorder?" he asked as he walked over to the small gate and unlocked it.

"A prop. He gets killed by it," explained Martha as she walked through the gates followed by the others. The well-behaved teenagers made no attempt to force their way through the unlocked gate. As she passed through the girls, Tash couldn't help but notice how slim they all were, Not too slim, not at all. But certainly not overweight. Not one of them.

"What time are Wham! coming?" asked a brunette with a bleached blond fringe.

The question alone was enough for the crowd to erupt in chants of "George!" and "Andrew!" which turned into the chorus of 'Freedom' in various different keys. None the same.

"I've told you, love, they're on tape this week," shouted the exasperated guard before turning to Tash. "They don't believe me."

"Tell me about it!" said Martha, and gestured her posse towards the TVC outer ring road.

As they passed the guard, they all offered their typically British thanks.

"Thanks," said Tash.

"Thank you," said Jamie.

"Thank you very much," muttered Maureen.

"Sorry," said Raymond.

Martha tried to walk purposefully like she knew her route whilst simultaneously trying to read every single sign on every single wall as they continued forwards. Straight ahead, she could see a large hangar style door that was wide open. This was their way into TVC. From there, she could figure where the outer ring road was.

"Who is Eddie?" asked Tash, hurrying to keep up with Martha.

"No idea. I figured he can't know every fucker in a place this size. Turns out I was right."

TV Centre on Wood Lane was a pretty impressive structure. It had famously been based on a question mark, a design that allowed all the studios to be connected by a round service road, minimising the cabling required, reducing any technical issues and reducing the distance between any given studio and central services. The common areas were all equidistant from any studio, and the outer ring road allowed equipment to be shifted in and out of studios with ease. Each studio was used for multiple shows, so even if the show was in the middle of a series each night the set would be dismantled, the props removed, and the floor painted for the next show on the next day. This morning was no exception. As they got closer, they saw a hive of activity. Jamie was particularly giddy to see the famous round neon light panels of *Top of The Pops* being moved on a low carrier barrow into the opening up ahead.

"Tash. Tash! *Top Of The Pops*! Look! Look!" He was as giddy as the day they visited the Harry Potter Studio Tour. Tash, despite herself, was a little overawed by this famous glass logo.

"Does she know where we're going?" Maureen asked her husband.

"Er, miss?" asked Raymond.

Martha raised her hand to silence him, she had her eyes set on a suited gentleman looking at some floor plans with a couple of set builders.

"Excuse me, sir. We've just been sent from Elmwood," Martha looked at Tash for help. "Elm Street?"

"Elstree," helped Tash.

"Some storage from their back lot," she continued confidently to the man. "Couple of crates and stuff, this one in particular." Martha showed him the photo of the timber box. "Came down here maybe two or three weeks ago. Where could I find that please?"

The man looked at the photo and then back at this pink haired lady.

"It's a massive place, love. Your guess is as good as mine." He looked at his colleagues who shrugged.

"Could ask Hitch? His lads were squirrelling stuff down there a couple of weeks ago," said one of them from underneath a very full moustache. "Unless we just make another?"

"When do you need it by? If we can get some drawings, we can just make another. Have you got a requisition number?" asked the suited man. "What's the show?"

Martha changed the subject.

"Actually yes, Hitch. That's who they said. Is he around?"

Jamie's ears had tuned in to a very different conversation.

He peered into the vast cavern beneath a sign reading 'Studio 4'. In front of him was the actual *Top Of The Pops* studio. It was fully assembled and mostly lit up just like on TV. The *Top Of The Pops* neon sign he'd spotted on the barrow was one of three, and two men carefully lifted it in into position amongst a wall of other neon lights that flashed. First a circle, then a square, then a smaller circle. When all lit, they illuminated the silver-painted timber frame around them.

It wasn't so different from the set Jamie recognised from his own childhood when East 17, Take That and Pulp would fill his bedroom portable TV. But it was almightily smaller than he imagined. He never imagined in all those years of watching that it was just one hangar door away from the outside. In his head, it was deep in the bowels of the massive TV Centre. Staff were busily pacing around the studio, all of them finding something that needed plugging in our moving or writing down.

"Bill, can we give these a spin please?" asked a man who was clearly in charge. He had a very heavy-looking clipboard laden with pages and pages of notes. His clothes said he was trying to be smart like an authoritarian yet trendy like the show's demographic at the same time. He wore jeans with a shirt and tie. Bill looked like Jamie's physics teacher. All corduroy and facial hair. Not the sort of dude you would expect to be working on the coolest music show on TV. Bill flicked a couple of switches on a massive desk in front of him and a vast light ball started to randomly spin inside a cage above a lady's head. She ignored it, clearly flustered by the chat she was having with another member of the crew.

"We start rehearsals in forty minutes, Vicky. We can't do the run-through with stand-ins," she said as kindly as she could. "It's every time they come on!"

"Gilly, please. Trust me, they'll be here," Vicky didn't look convinced by her own words. She glanced at her watch and pressed it to light up the display. "The office said a car was sent for them an hour ago. It must be traffic."

Gilly raised her eyebrow knowingly. "Please keep them off the sauce when they get here. They trashed a drum kit last time."

She was only partly right, thought Vicky. At the end of miming to 'Margherita Time' last Christmas, Rick had fallen onto the drum kit, taking it all down with him, but everyone laughed. Even Jim Lea from Slade who had stood in to play bass. Quo's bassist at the time hated the song, so they recruited Jim to mime with them. His band had been on the show performing 'My Oh My'. At the time they'd also got a number 20 hit with their first re-issue of Merry Xmas Everybody, marking ten years since its first release.

"He was acting," protested Vicky as kindly as she could.

Billy Ocean's 'Caribbean Queen' suddenly blasted from the studio's massive speakers, shortly followed by the video itself on an enormous screen. The images clicked on and off a couple of times as Bill fiddled with cables behind. The song stopped as soon as it started.

"Vicky! Oi up!" hollered a man behind Jamie.

She spun around to see Francis Rossi standing on the ring road. He was literally inches away from Jamie and was clutching a guitar case with one hand and giving a thumbs up to her with the other. Rick Parfitt leant out from behind Francis, then performed that Eric Morecambe mime with his own hand around his neck, as if a stranger was dragging him out of view.

"Heeelp!" shouted Rick as he disappeared behind his bandmate.

"Status Quo!" shouted a man walking through the studio from the stage to the far door. He waved at them.

"Peter Powell, he fucked an owl!" chanted one of the Quo boys as a reply, and they both pissed themselves.

"See you in a bit, boys!" laughed the Radio One DJ before disappearing into the main building.

Vicky walked over to her 'talent', and as she stood alongside Jamie he glanced at her BBC visitors name badge and a familiar record label. Beneath the BBC logo was her own handwriting:

V. Speight, PHONOGRAM.

Behind Vicky and half of Status Quo, another man had joined Martha and the others. "Hitch, this lady is looking for some stuff from Elstree, can you help her?"

"You brought some stuff down a few weeks ago, we're looking for this crate," replied Martha as she held up the photograph.

Hitch took the photo and looked, stopping only to look up at Raymond. "Are you OK, mate?"

"It's make-up," said Maureen. "He's in *Juliet Bravo*. He just signed some autographs."

Hitch looked again at the photograph. "Let me check my files," he said before handing back the photo and walking away.

Vicky had reminded Francis and Rick that it was a mime performance, but they needed to steer clear of the drum kit. They dutifully nodded and headed into the studio towards the door to the main building. She glanced over at a nurse staring back at her.

"Everything OK?" she asked.

"I thought this show was on a Thursday?" was the first thing Jamie could say. He was a details guy.

"They often record it," explained Vicky.

Jamie was philosophical about this revelation.

"I'm looking for Vicky Speight," he said.

"That would be me. Am I ill?" she joked.

"Excellent. No! It's about Bob!"

"Bob, who?"

"Geldof," said Jamie. He wasn't sure where he was getting this confidence, but he went on with all guns blaring. "He checked out of St Thomas' hospital last night without leaving an address."

"Checked out?"

"Discharged himself. You do know about his accident?"

"Good. Glad he's OK," Vicky nodded. Who was this guy?

"I was treating him before he left, and he didn't leave a home address."

"That's not surprising, is it?" she smiled. "He's famous. He's not in the phone book either."

"No. No. I guess not. It's just he needs to keep taking his medication for forty-eight hours, and he left it at his bedside, and I was in charge of making sure he took it with him when he left, but he left before he should, and now I could lose my job. And he might die."

"Oh my God. That's terrible."

"Well, I'm sure I could find another job. There are a lot of hospitals."

"I meant about his medication. Just call Phonogram?" she suggested.

"I did. I called them, and they said that you would be here today and you could give me the address."

"Me? I don't have the address. I don't handle the Rats. In fact, I don't know who does. I think Bob's been doing stuff himself."

Jamie nodded at the situation as if they now shared the problem.

"And he could die," he repeated almost under his breath.

"Can you give me the medication? I can make some calls."

Behind them, Hitch had returned with some folders overflowing with printed papers covered in handwritten ink notes. He was looking at one page in particular.

"Maybe try the store under the Scenery Block?"

"Where's the Scenery Block, please?" asked Martha, flashing her security badge.

He gestured across the service road to an imposing brick building attached to TVC.

"There's a lift inside the entrance."

"Jamie," shouted Tash. "We're going! Come on!"

Jamie glanced over to see them all set off. He turned back to Vicky.

"I've got to fetch the medicine, how about I meet you back here in half an hour?"

The A&R manager looked confused.

"I parked down the, er…" Jamie muttered as he walked off. She heard him continue talking as he turned back to give a little wave. He said something about thank you and something about his ambulance. Seconds later, Vicky was knocked right off her feet. "Excuse me," came a brief apology from a suited lady rushing past.

FORTY SIX

Inside the cold Design Block, the first thing they saw was the Blue Peter Totaliser. A very tall plywood painted structure in the shape of a glittery lighthouse. Plastic panels with different amounts ascended to the top. The appeal this year would be for Lifeboats. Or that was the current plan. In the original version of 1984, the props department would soon be building a second totaliser as the show launched a Double Appeal – one for Lifeboats, the other for Ethiopia.

Unless Jamie and Tash could get that news report to Bob Geldof maybe the Lifeboat appeal would run solo this year after all.

As they walked past other components of the Blue Peter set, Jamie was enthralled and simultaneously heartbroken to see they were made of glued and screwed bits of plywood with ink markings and general tat hanging from the rear. Martha had already reached the massive lift door and pressed the button. It opened immediately, and they all walked in. All floors were up except one, marked B. As she was closest, Tash pushed that button and down they went.

As the lift doors opened again, the five of them could see ordered chaos inside a vast room much the same shape as the one above. Backdrops hung alongside component pieces of buildings. Doors, door frames, window arches, windows and faux walls all nestled tidily in their allocated space. There seemed to be no logical place where a numbered timber crate could be stored. They set off through the large area to a couple of doors at the far end of the room. They didn't hear the lift doors close behind them as it was summoned up to the ground floor.

The first rear door they arrived at opened to an unlit space, so Martha felt around inside for a light switch. Her fingers found a Bakelite flicker that clicked loudly on. As the others joined her in the room, a fluorescent strip light did its usual 80s trick of flickering on and off for about nineteen years before finally committing to being on or off. Happily today it opted for on, and in doing so, it illuminated a row of cardboard boxes and timber crates. Martha's heart skipped a beat as she started to walk amongst them. Tash interrupted the silence.

"Can you tell us what the deal is now? This silence is a bit weird."

"I have to find this trunk." Martha held the photo over her shoulder as she continued to inspect the cases in the room.

"We kind of got that bit."

Martha had spotted something protruding from under a large oilcloth. "Give me a hand?" she asked Jamie.

He stepped forward, and together they dragged the cloth off the crate.

Yep. That was it.

The actual crate.

The one that had caused Jamie and Tash to be held at gunpoint, the one that had caused Tash to knock down a pop star, the one that had caused Raymond to steal a cab, the one that had caused all of them to spend a night in a police cell.

There was no fanfare or round of applause, in fact, they all stopped for a moment to hear Maureen's tummy rumble very loudly. All eyes looked at her as Raymond did the chivalrous thing.

"Pardon me," he said. Then they all looked back at the crate in front of them. On the sides and on the top were the stenciled words, *Portland, Maine to London. D.H. Esq.*

"Bingo," said Martha. Her smile displayed some pretty perfect teeth, thought Jamie. "Now, how the hell do you get into one of these things?"

"Is it drugs? Are you a dealer? Is it guns?" asked Maureen. This was all becoming a bit much now.

"None of the above. Help me get it open, and I'll do my best to explain. Cos you know what?" she paused for effect. "Even I don't know."

Jamie fumbled in a plastic box by the corner of the room and happily stood up displaying an extremely long slotted screwdriver.

"Take you ages to unscrew it with that," said Martha. She was right. This was a very well made vintage wooden crate. No staples anywhere. This was nailed and screwed together – a real piece of work.

"Not gonna unscrew it," said Jamie, as he set to leveraging the lid off. He inserted the screwdriver between the joints and jammed it into the gap he created, opening it slightly before moving around the full circumference. It reminded Tash of her grandad removing the lid from a tin of paint.

"If it's sex toys I'm having no part of it, either," announced Maureen.

"Wow. Took a turn there, Maureen," said Tash.

"It's moving now!" announced Jamie, a little out of breath already. Martha took the screwdriver from him and started to wedge it into the lid at her side of the crate.

"Moving here too. I think we're in… force it on three, two, one."

Jamie pushed as she said *one*.

"Wait!" said Martha, "You need to wait for *go*. You forced on *one*."

"What?" Jamie examined a splinter that had recently made acquaintance with his thumb.

"Don't," said Tash. "You'll be here all day. I've lost years of my life on this. Counting up doesn't work either. Trust me, you count up to three, and he'll push on three. He has no concept of the word go after a count-up or a countdown."

"I have plenty of concept. But if someone says *on three* they mean on three. Not zero or four."

"Shall I say, 'go'? If you both agree to force it on the actual word 'go'?" suggested Raymond as a peacemaker. He positioned himself in-between them and took the screwdriver to make some progress at the mid-point. Jamie and Martha liked the suggestion.

"That's a plan that works for me," said Martha.

"I was fine with the first plan," argued Jamie. Sometimes life got on his tits when he was constantly reminded how badly he does things.

"Let's go with Raymond's plan. Go on *go*. Over to you, big guy," said Tash.

"Thank you," smiled Raymond. "OK. Here goes. One, two, three, four, five.."

"Where the fuck was *go*?" interrupted Tash "How far are you counting?"

"I was going to go to ten?" said Raymond.

"Ten? Who counts up to ten before a *go*?" asked Tash.

"Let's just get the bloody thing off shall we?" snapped Maureen and she marched over to the timber lid and started to force it open with the others. "Come on. Everyone!"

It's fair to say that everyone liked this new version of Maureen, and sure enough, the concerted energy did force the lid off this massive storage box. As they dragged the cover to the side, they all looked in at the precious cargo. Martha smiled and pulled another photo from her pocket for comparison purposes. She was happy. Extremely happy and very nearly extremely rich.

Jamie couldn't comprehend what he was looking at.

His brain simply wasn't wired to accept this.

Tash burst into tears.

But they were tears of joy. Her cheeks were underwater again in no time.

Raymond scratched his head.

Maureen was simply relieved that it wasn't a tiger or snake or bomb.

Inside the crate was a dusty, cracked, yellowing but very certainly intact pimped-up C5 time machine as created by Mr Ernest Summers.

"How did he get this here?" asked Raymond, scratching his head. "Is this *Game For A Laugh*? Are we being filmed?" He looked around for TV cameras that weren't there.

Tash dropped to the floor to save herself from falling. Jamie looked at Martha with disbelief. "This is ours," he heard himself saying to Martha.

"You're welcome to it. But I just need to take your picture with it."

Jamie was dissembling the front of the crate as he spoke. "Tash, I know you're excited right now. I know you are, trust me, I know. Listen to me, Tash?"

Tash was staring adoringly at the C5 through her happy tears. Jamie continued, "We can't go straight away. I've met somebody that can help. They can help today!"

"What do you mean 'take your picture'?" Tash asked Martha, ignoring her brother's appeals.

Martha offered a large foolscap black and white photo to Tash. "I need to recreate this photo."

Tash took the photo and shook her head.

"What the actual fuck is happening?" Tash had almost made it to her feet again, but this made her drop once more.

She handed the photo to Jamie. It was a printed copy of a Polaroid photo. It was grainy and damaged, but it unmistakably featured Jamie and Tash and Raymond, all squatting by their Grandad's C5. It was easy for Jamie to conclude it was the photo that Dudley had taken earlier yesterday evening before he set off on his wasted journey to the London School of Economics.

"Can anyone tell us what's going on?" asked Maureen. "Isn't there supposed to be our money in there?"

"There is money in there," explained Martha.

"I don't see any," said Raymond.

"I need to recreate that photo right now. With you and these two," Martha pointed to the siblings.

"Why?" asked Tash.

"Altruism. My Grand-Daddy said I didn't understand the word. He was probably right, in a way," she added begrudgingly. "He cut me out of his will."

No-one looked any clearer or indeed sympathetic. Martha felt the need to justify what she'd said.

"I struggled at school when my parents died. Try getting a decent job without going to college."

"I managed," said Jamie.

"I think that's her point, Jamie," said Tash as kindly as she could. She turned to Raymond and Maureen and added, "He fixes bike tyre punctures."

"I solve problems," argued Jamie.

"Maybe it's different in the US," said Martha. "I got a job now! Selling ice cream. Ben & Jerry's. They're gonna be massive by the way."

"They are massive," said Jamie.

"But before that I guess I struggled with being told what to do. I was young. A few bad decisions, and things just got worse. Guess I stole a coupla things."

Maureen tutted to Raymond. "Thought so. Criminal."

"Nice VCR," replied Martha nodding to the Ferguson Videostar that Raymond had placed on the floor.

"We're taking that back," said Maureen.

"Listen. You've all helped me, and I stand by my offer. I'm gonna pay you like I said. But I can only pay you if I get my inheritance, And I can only get my inheritance if I right my Grand–Daddy's wrong."

"Another thug no doubt," muttered Maureen again.

"What was his wrong?" asked Tash.

"No idea," replied Martha. "But his lawyers told me I gotta fly to London to find out. Turns out I have to find the three of you and to replicate this photo. Once they see I've done it, they release my cash."

"Nope. Still clear as dog shit to me," said Tash, she was getting a headache. She stared at the C5 and tried to understand why the fuck it had gone so yellow.

"I'll make it simple for you," replied Martha. "Let me take the photo and then we can all go. I'll take your details and wire you the money I promised. You have my word."

"What the hell happened to this? It looks knackered." Tash was rubbing her fingertips gently across the C5.

"It's intact," said Jamie. "Just looks a bit tired."

"It should do, it's been in this crate since 1955," said Martha.

"Oh my God!" said Tash. "What's your grandad's name?"

"Dudley Hobson," answered Martha.

"Now this is a joke, its bloody nonsense," said Raymond.

"Come on. Gather around," said Martha, extracting the Polaroid camera from her backpack. Maybe she wasn't a details person, but she was taking all this in her stride. Even Raymond wondered why she didn't have more questions. He certainly did.

Tash was laughing and crying now as she climbed into the front seat.

"The Prick wanted us to get home, Jamie. He knew we were telling the truth from the beginning."

"Don't press any buttons, Tash," said Jamie as he stepped in to sit behind her.

"Come on, handsome," said Martha gesturing to Raymond who dutifully stood at the rear of the C5.

"Lean in. Smile," said Martha, and the Polaroid flashed.

The photo wasn't an exact replica of the original. In the first one, Raymond looked bored. In the second, he looked thoroughly baffled. Jamie looked the same – his eyes were closed in both. In fact, they were closed in all his photos. Tash had considerably more tears on the new picture, but they were happy ones. It would take a real twat of a lawyer to dismiss this as a failed task.

"What happens now?" asked Jamie.

"I meet a lawyer in," Martha looked at her wrist, "four and a half hours. She takes this and wires it to her head office in Vermont. They compare it with the original. They release eleven million dollars into my account."

"Eleven fucking million?" Tash was astonished. "What did the Prick do to get that?"

"I'm guessing your mean my grand-daddy? From what Mama told me, he started out with a couple of speakeasies in Burlington."

"What's that?" asked Jamie.

"Prohibition," said Raymond. "The Yanks banned booze in the Twenties. Are we saying he's in 1920?" His brain was popping.

"He's in 1920?" asked Martha. What the fuck did he mean by that? "1920 happened, right? Or am I missing something? He met grandma in 1920. She said he just appeared outside her hospital one Christmas and crashed straight into a tree. She nursed him, they fell in love, he started smuggling booze across the border, she found out, and he switched to radio. They got one of the first transmitters in the East. He made millions. Got into the movies. Rubbed shoulders with singers and actors."

"Douglas Fairbanks Junior," said Raymond.

"What?" asked Martha.

"He owned Elstree studios in the fifties. They were his studios. Mum loved his films!"

"Could have been friends, totally possible."

"That's where Dudley put this, isn't it? He didn't know they were going to build on it," said Raymond.

"Excuse me? How do you know my grand-daddy?"

"Well up until last night, he was my boss," said Raymond. "Who knew he was such a nice guy?"

"He tried to shoot you," said Maureen.

"Oh yes. What a prick," replied Raymond.

"Language, Raymond."

"Sorry."

Martha looked suspiciously at Raymond. Why was everyone saying weird shit?

"I can take that now," came a voice from the doorway.

They all looked over to see a well-dressed lady smiling back at them.

"Bee?" said Martha.

"Hey Martha," replied the lawyer.

"You followed me?"

"Good job I did. Someone needed to get you out of jail."

"That was you?"

Jamie had his hand in the air again.

Martha spotted it. "Question incoming from the handsome guy dressed as a nurse..."

Jamie blushed at the 'handsome' reference but continued with his question to Martha.

"Who is that?"

"Ms Barbara Fernandez: Attorney At Law, Eikenberry & Lowe," offered Bee.

"She's my grand-daddy's lawyer, I met her yesterday. She told me what I'd got to do."

"And you look like you could use a freshen up, honey," said Bee as she walked over to Martha. She reached out and took the new photograph from Martha. "I can get this over to the office before we meet. You might see your payday land even sooner," She looked at the photo. "Congratulations. Good job."

Martha breathed a sigh of relief.

"So, she's definitely rich?" asked Maureen.

"Maureen!" said Raymond.

Maureen explained herself. “I need to know we’ll get our money?”

Bee smiled at them all. “She’s eleven million dollars rich, ma’am.”

With that, Bee turned and walked out, shouting, “See you at four pm Martha. I’ll have all the paperwork you need.”

“Bee!” shouted Martha.

The lawyer turned back in the doorway at her client.

“Thanks. I couldn’t have done this without you.”

Bee nodded and left.

It wasn’t long before Martha noticed the silence in the room. She perused the faces, all glaring back at her. Then the penny dropped.

“Or you. I couldn’t have done it without you either.”

They all muttered like belligerent kids for a while, except Tash. She was walking across the room to some significant racks of cables and wires. In no time she was unrolling an extension cable from its drum to the C5.

“Sis. Slow down. Remember what we need to do.” Jamie took the video cassette from Raymond. He waved it in the air. It looked like it had been through the dishwasher and then dropped from the Post Office Tower before a six-year-old had glued it back together, but Jamie still had high hopes for it.

“Jamie. We have failed at every single thing we have tried to do. Everything. Ever since we got here. Ask Raymond to do it. Ask Maureen. But we’ve got to go home. We can’t risk losing this again.” Tash was wiping the mossy cables that still hung from the rear of the Christmas ride. She stopped from time to time to remove some fluff and dirt before ramming the single master plug firmly into the BBC-branded extension drum.

"What is she doing?" asked Martha.

"She wants to go back to 2020," explained Jamie.

"Excuse me?"

"She has a son, and she left him, we both left him, alone. At Christmas in 2020."

Martha looked at Raymond who surprised himself because he found he was nodding in agreement and also looking baffled at the same time.

"Except we can't go to 2020, cos it's an eighties computer," Jamie tapped the Spectrum, "and their calendar doesn't compute the next century. Which is probably why Dudley went back to 1920." He thought again "Which is good, cos it meant you got born, and you got to inherit his money."

Martha looked baffled as Jamie turned to Raymond. "Although it's bad for you as he was your boss and he paid your bills. Sorry."

His explanation was interrupted by the BEEP of the Spectrum being switched on. Tash was already firmly seated at the front of the extended C5.

"So we're saying twenty-four," she spoke as she typed, "twelve… ninety–nine, right?" Her question was rhetorical as her typing continued. She glanced at the screen:

Destination Date: 24 12 99

Time: 12 00

Location:

"Location… If I type Home," she did, "Yes! He programmed home to his address! Clever Grandad. Oh

My God, we're gonna see Grandad again!" Tash was in a world of her own now.

"Martha, I want you to give all of mine and Jamie's money to Raymond and Maureen please?"

"Okayyyy." Martha nodded slowly "Why. Where the fuck are you going?"

Martha looked around at the solid walls that surrounded them. Tash stopped for a moment and pulled out her father's plans from her pocket. "Raymond, take these. They might be worth a punt," she handed them to a bewildered Raymond. "Get in, Jamie."

Jamie walked over to her and slowly shook his head.

"I can't, Tash. Remember the kids' faces? Remember the news report?"

"Jamie, don't make me a murderer. I'm not a murderer. Ask Raymond to do it, please? Please? Come with me. I can't spend another hour without my baby, Jamie. I can't! Get in!"

Jamie thought.

Tash cried.

Maureen and Raymond looked like they'd crashed the wrong funeral. If shoe-examining were an Olympic sport, they'd be wearing Los Angeles medals right now.

"I can't ask Raymond to do it. I made the problem, and I'm going to fix it," said Jamie.

"It says press ENTER to travel Jamie. Get in!" begged Tash.

Jamie leant forward and whispered.

"Spend some time with Lucan. See him first. Open his Christmas gifts. In fact, yes, that's a great idea. Tell everyone I've gone for a run. Open some gifts. Then swerve the morning walk, let them go without you." Thoughts were flooding into Jamie's brain. "Blame Lucan or something. When they go for a walk, come back for me. I'll meet you at Tower Bridge, 6pm tomorrow. That's the twenty-fifth of October."

"What?" said Tash. "What?"

"Twenty Five, ten, eighty four. Eighteen hundred hours."

"What?"

Jamie leant forward, kissed his sister on the cheek and struck the ENTER button.

The wheels spun to life straight away. Jamie looked over to check the area in the path of the vintage C5.

"Jamie! Get in! Get in!" Tash was shouting now.

Instead of climbing behind his sister, he leapt to the other side of the room to move a pile of cardboard boxes marked "Advent Crown Blue P." that were in her path. He hadn't meant to trip. Who does? All he could see now was inside the cardboard box. His head was stuck. Coat hangers and tinsel scratched at his face as he tried to find his feet.

"Jamie!" shouted Tash.

Sleigh Ride started to play from the rear speaker, and Raymond tried to run over to help Jamie. His foot was caught in the crate lid and dropped like a sack of Cadburys Smash. Maureen leapt to help him. "Raymond!"

"Sorry Maureen," was the last thing Tash heard before her ride set off. Bizarrely she had forgotten all about the fear of striking the timber wall of her Grandma's garage loft. This time she was confronted by her brother wearing an upturned cardboard box and behind him a wall of brick. The last thing she saw was a pink-haired Madonna rugby tackle Jamie out of her path. She closed her eyes very tightly, indeed.

FORTY SEVEN

Jamie had really stepped up since his sister had travelled to 1999. He'd become more confident and more assertive. He and Martha had agreed that Maureen and Raymond should go home. Maureen hadn't handled things well after seeing a grown woman and a motor vehicle disappear in front of her eyes. Raymond had been pretty spooked too but wasn't the type of man to show his feelings. This was 1984, after all. They had given Jamie their address and trusting his good intentions, and those of Martha, had gone back to Gaywood Close to turn off the immersion heater. Martha just had one thing to do: to meet Bee at Marie's Cafe. So it was no big deal to hang out with Jamie until then. He'd done the right thing by her, and besides, she thought he was kind of funny.

Together they waited outside the massive doors to Studio 4. They were closed now as rehearsals were underway, but Vicky clearly knew her way around TVC as she arrived exactly as agreed, half an hour after her chat with the nurse.

"Hi," said Vicky as she approached Jamie and Martha. Jamie was curiously clutching a video recorder with the mangled cassette on top.

"This is Martha, by the way," explained Jamie.

"Hi Martha, I'm Vicky." She turned to Jamie "I never got your name?"

"Jamie. I'm Jamie."

"What's this?" asked Vicky looking at the borrowed electronic equipment in his grasp.

"Did you get Bob's address?" asked Jamie, clearly focusing his full attention on the task in hand.

"I did. Did you get his medicine?"

"Er yes," said Jamie, turning to Martha, who fumbled in her pocket. Vicky put her hand out in anticipation, but Martha didn't produce medicine. She pulled out her gun.

"I thought we were offering her money first!" said Jamie, shocked at the appearance of the gun.

"Crap, we did say that didn't we?" answered Martha. She looked at Vicky. "I have jet lag, sorry."

Vicky looked terrified.

"I think she's seen it now. That's a bit of a game-changer for us," said Jamie before turning to Vicky. "She's absolutely not going to use that, it's not even hers." He looked back at Martha. "Put it away."

She did.

Jamie looked relieved and in a soft voice, tried to appeal to Vicky.

"Vicky. The world seriously needs your help."

FORTY EIGHT

The snow hadn't fallen in Sheffield on Christmas Eve 1999. Not that it didn't feel cold enough. Tash hadn't factored in her landing site. Maybe it was a glitch in the software but she'd completely missed the garage and had landed in Grandad's vegetable patch behind it. She was already planning her next departure, so the first thing she did was climb out of the C5 and wrestle it into a reasonable departure point for the second step of her route home. She felt too vulnerable without her brother. And for good reason, because the place she had moved the C5 to was nowhere near a power source. But all that could wait. Right now, she had to figure out how the fuck she was going to get her Grandad's attention without arising suspicion from her Grandma. She could hear the bath running upstairs and hoped that would be for Grandma ahead of receiving the family for the festivities.

It was just her luck to realise that now at the worse possible moment she needed to wee. Going into the house was out of the question. They only had one toilet, and that was in the bathroom, and that would mean she could risk bumping into Grandma. Tash knew that she mustn't talk to anyone other than her Grandad. Jamie had been adamant about that. She pulled down her leggings and lifted her borrowed skirt before squatting over some weeds. As she emptied her bladder, steam rose in front of her shattered face. She stifled a yawn.

"Excuse me!" came a familiar voice.

Tash spun around to see her beautiful Grandad, alive and well. And annoyed as fuck.

She hadn't quite released how emotional she would be at this moment, and tears added to the public water display that was now on offer. She was a dancing human fountain.

"What the hell do you think you're doing?" he asked, unnerved by her sudden emotional outburst.

"Grandad, I needed to wee!" she managed to whisper through her snot. "I love you so much. I never told you, but I do, and I did. We all did. We all do."

Ernest walked closer to this garden intruder and then looked over at the knackered Christmas ride that rested alongside her. There was clearly no problem with his brain as it pieced things together exceptionally quickly.

"Natasha?" he asked as he leant in. "Natasha?"

All she could do was nod as she slowly pulled back up her leggings.

"You've pissed on my rhubarb!" was all he could manage. Then they both burst out laughing.

Tasha leapt up and into his arms.

****

Ernest walked back into the attic loft and handed his adult granddaughter a sandwich and steaming hot cup of tea.

"Did Grandma see you?" she asked, taking the snack from him.

He shook his head. "She's in the bath with Jimmy Young."

As Tash took a big bite from her cheese and ham sandwich, her Grandad took a long look at her, before looking away.

"We mustn't really talk, I'm afraid Natasha." He looked sad at his own words.

"I've got so much to tell you, Grandad! That's impossible!" is what Tash attempted to say, but Ernest understood little and got covered in cheese from her hungry mouth.

"You're grown into a beautiful woman."

Tash blushed. He spoke again, still gazing elsewhere.

"I need to explain something to you. This wasn't built for messing about with." He pointed to the pure white pimped up C5 that remained in pristine condition by their side.

"I used it for one purpose only. I should have taken it apart after that," he explained.

"What was the purpose?"

"You don't need to know that. Let's just say I was able to put something right. But what I do know is that cause has effect. Saying things and doing things is a bad idea. You need to get back to where you came from. I just need to know why you can't." Then he added, "In as few words as possible."

"Millennium bug," she replied.

"Bugger," he answered. "I knew that would be a problem, but wasn't in a hurry to use this again." He stared at the machine. "The Spectrum is two-digit dates, isn't it?" He was speaking more to himself than her.

"And I travelled from –" Tash was interrupted by her grandfather's index finger gently covering her mouth. He continued thinking out loud.

"So I've got to fetch a computer for you. A small one that will fit onto that…" Ernest pointed to the C5 and then looked at his watch. She had forgotten how he wore it, with the face on the inside of his wrist. It had a gold face with a brown leather strap, and she loved the way he used to patiently wind it up whilst drawing on a cigarette. His pace of life was so serene.

"Right then, love. I'm going to go to Meadowhall. I need you to wait here," he started. But Tash copied her brother and raised her hand to ask a question. He looked at her. "Is this a short and relevant question?"

She nodded and delved into her pocket. She pulled out her iPhone.

"Will this do?"

"What is it?" he asked, taking the plain black piece of glass and metal from her.

"It's kind of like a phone and a camera and a calculator and a music player and remote control. You can pay with it instead of your bank card too. And surf the net."

He was looking for an on-switch. Tash gently took it from him and showed it her face to unlock it. "Facial recognition."

"Don't tell me any more," he said as he took it back from her. He reached over for a slim metal tool and gently started to prise it apart. He pulled over an anglepoise lamp and a magnifying glass on a bracket beneath it.

"I'm guessing you don't have a mains cable for it?"

Tash replied that she hadn't.

He pulled open a drawer full of tiny copper wires and a soldering iron. Tash bit into her sandwich one more time and thought was there nothing this man couldn't do?

She listened happily to the sound of his thinking-breathing. She and Jamie used to laugh at this noise when they were kids. He made a sort of click as he inhaled and after an eternity he would slowly exhale. It was impossible to be stressed in the company of Grandad.

"Can I please just tell you one thing, Grandad?"

"If it's about me, Tash – no," he answered without looking up. "You've already told me you missed me, so I know I'm not in your life anymore." He reached over to plug in his soldering iron. "Now that could mean you've moved away. Or it could mean something else. And my experience with this machine has taught me one thing." He lifted the iPhone up to examine a particular part of the motherboard, then turned to a pile of magazines and extracted one before flicking to an overturned page.

"What has it taught you?"

"It's taught me, Natasha," he turned to look at her briefly, and then at the C5 before continuing, "that with a machine like this, you may change many things. But you cannot change your health."

"But it's not…" Tash was interrupted again.

"Natasha. I don't want to spend every day whittling about something. I do not want to know. And let that be the end of it," said Ernest as he started to strip some plastic from some thin copper wire.

He didn't see the tears start to fall down Tash's cheek.

FORTY NINE

"The next stop is Sloane Square. Please mind the gap." The voice on the intercom sounded unusually chirpy for a man who spends his whole working day driving in and out of underground tunnels on the Circle Line. Jamie had always hated the bustle of the Tube and carrying a video recorder dressed as a nurse whilst sort of kidnapping an innocent record label employee seemed to heighten his angst. He imagined Bonnie & Clyde style tabloid headlines once he and his tooled-up partner were caught. Which they were bound to be. What was Martha thinking of pulling a gun on Vicky? That was never the plan. He'd convinced Martha to give Vicky five hundred quid from her credit card in exchange for Bob Geldof's address. The fact she'd pulled a gun instead had really undermined the charitable aspect of his plan.

As they climbed from their seats Jamie noticed that the fluorescent lighting did nothing for people's appearance. It was a functional and brutal light that only made him yawn a lot and look ill. Yet for some reason, Martha's pink hair looked even more electric in this light. Her complexion was pretty flawless too. And she chewed gum with the indifference of someone delivering junk mail. How was she remaining so calm and so beautiful?

They shuffled through the door onto the platform with Vicky between them. Jamie seemed to have reassured her that being shot was off the agenda for the day, but nonetheless, she was pretty spooked. After all, why did they have a gun if all they wanted to do was show a video to Bob Geldof? And if they were aspiring musicians, why did they want to show it to him? Surely the head of Phonogram would be better than a pop star with a fan base considerably diminished from his heyday? She had never met Bob but heard he was a pleasant, funny but straight-talking man. She would surely lose her job by dragging some randoms to his house. Especially carrying a gun. And what about the Quo boys? She'd just abandoned them. At least the gun was a good excuse for leaving TV Centre with no explanation. If her boss asked. If he found out. Which of course he would.

As they climbed the steps to the station exit, Jamie thought he'd break the stony silence.

"Thanks again for paying for the tickets."

"It's the least I could do. You have a gun," said Vicky.

Jamie cast a glance at Martha. "Told you she'd remember that. Told you."

Martha blew a bubble with her gum. Which was doubly impressive given it was the chewing type, not the bubble type.

At the exit, Jamie tried one more time. "What was the street name again, Vicky? Please?"

"Redburn."

"Let's see if we can find a policeman," said Jamie. "To get directions."

"Really?" replied Martha.

"Why not?"

"Well, I know we're not kidnapping her, and you know we're not kidnapping her but…" Martha gestured at Vicky who picked up the conversation.

"Yeah, this feels like a kidnapping," said Vicky.

They all nodded.

"Yeah, I can see how it might feel that way," replied Jamie. He turned to Vicky and spoke like he'd said this before, but he gave it another shot. "Vicky, on this video is last night's news."

"And you want to show it to Bob cos he missed it."

"Yes. That's all I'm going to do."

"So why the video recorder?"

"Because we found him last night in hospital," started Jamie.

"Found him?" interrupted Vicky. "I thought you said you cared for him?"

"No. No. I borrowed these clothes actually."

"You're not even a nurse?"

"He fixes puncture on bikes," smiled Martha. "In the future. He's not been born yet."

Vicky stared at them both.

"I met the guy last night. He helped me turn my life around. I think he wants to help this Bob guy. He's not lied to me yet. He talks a lot of shit, but he doesn't lie," continued Martha. "If he's right you save a few thousand lives, if he's wrong you call work and say you got mugged."

A police constable crossed the road towards them. Vicky caught sight of him.

"Officer! Police!" she shouted.

"And I'll give you five hundred pounds," appealed Martha as her final shot.

The policeman walked over to the three of them.

"Can I help you?"

"These people," Vicky started to say, "These people…"

Jamie took a deep breath. Oh Christ, to fall at this final hurdle. Maybe I can outrun this guy?

"They want to find Redburn Street, and I'm struggling to help them," said Vicky.

"No problem," said the constable, before giving them directions plus the good news that they were only a few hundred yards or so away.

FIFTY

Tash could hear laughter. It wasn't Jamie, the voice was too old. It wasn't her father, the tone was too deep. Yet is sounded like them both. It was a beautifully familiar noise, and it made her want to smile.

Grandad was laughing.

"Natasha, Natasha. Come on, sleepyhead," said Ernest.

Tash opened her eyes to see her Grandad leaning over her. She had fallen asleep in the garage loft. His hands were cold, and his nose was running.

"Are you OK, Grandad? Why are you so cold?" She rubbed her sleepy eyes.

"I've been fixing your posh computer phone onto you ride home."

She turned to look at the C5. It looked identical.

"It's no different," she said.

"That's mine, love. Yours is in the garden, isn't it? Come on."

He was very sprightly down the stairs into the garage and into the garden. She was struck by how much he reminded her of Dad.

"How are we for time?" she whispered.

"Well, the bathroom light's still on!" He pointed up to the house.

As Tash approached the vintage C5, she was reminded of how knackered it looked compared to the one they had left in the attic. A collection of interconnected power cables trailed into the garage.

"In you get, princess," he said, helping her into the seat. She'd forgotten he used to call her that.

The Spectrum was still there but sitting above it and connected with a myriad of tiny soldered wires was her iPhone.

"I tried to get the front back on, but I think that might be a goner," he apologised.

It did look pretty unusable as a phone. But if it worked as a calendar for the Spectrum, that was all she cared about.

"How does it work?"

"The same as before, but there are four digits for the year."

"No. I mean, how does it work, Grandad? You built a time machine!"

Ernest paused for a moment and then smiled patiently.

"Some of us re-live days in our heads over and over. So that day lasts far longer than twenty-four hours. Isn't that incredible Natasha? Some days last forever?"

"I know that feeling," she replied, thinking about her last eighteen hours.

"Maybe you do, my love." He smiled patiently. He knew she wasn't on the same page as him. Ernest had spent years of his life re-living one day, yet others had come and gone with no redeemable traits. They hadn't stood a chance.

The screen was already illuminated and awaiting Tash's prompts.

"I'll leave you to that, Natasha. I don't want to look," and with that, he turned his back.

She paused before typing and remembered Jamie's kind words. He'd told her to go back to Lucan first. He was adamant. If she went back for him now, it would be even longer without a cuddle with her son, and the despair she felt since abandoning her baby was mighty.

Yes, I'll go to Lucan. Spend some time with him. Jamie will know no difference anyway. We agreed when he would wait for me. It was that quick to decide.

She started to type into the blanks, remembering that it would be better if she arrived home after she and Jamie departed. It would be horrific to bump into herself. No, that wouldn't do.

What time had she got out of bed when she noticed the garage light was on? Was it 1am? 2am? It was two. Or was it one? Put three, Tash. Three.

"I can't hear you typing?" said Ernest.

"I'm doing it, I wanted to make sure I got the time right."

She typed in 0300.

For Location, she started to type HOME, and sure enough, Grandma's address popped up.

ENTER TO TRAVEL appeared on the screen.

"It says ENTER," she whispered.

"Press it then, sweetheart. Take care," whispered her Grandfather, still with his back turned to her.

"Grandad, I really need to tell you …" She was interrupted again.

"You need to tell me nothing, Natasha," said Ernest assertively. "Press it before your Grandma comes downstairs. She'll be in that kitchen in no time."

Tash glanced over at the kitchen window. She could picture the family sitting there without Grandad on Christmas Eve just a matter of hours ago, and Grandma chasing a pickled onion under the table.

"But Grandad, please listen to me…"

"Take care Natasha. No more talking. Just press ENTER."

Tash was strangely uncomfortable in the chair, something was digging in her side. She straightened her jumper and felt a lump in her pocket. She remembered Jamie had slid something in there when they had breakfast. She pulled it out and smiled.

"Can I have a kiss, Grandad? Please?"

Ernest turned and walked slowly over, stopping only when an Airedale Terrier bounded up the garden to greet Tash.

"Pepper! Oh my God! Pepper! And she remembers me!"

Tash sobbed all over again as this much loved and much mourned member of the family licked the sandwich crumbs from her chin.

"Come on Pep, leave her be," said Ernest, and the dog dutifully sat by his legs.

Ernest crouched down to his granddaughter and closed his eyes so as not to read the information on the screen.

Tash kissed him gently on his cheek. At the same time, she placed something in his cardigan pocket.

"For later," she whispered as she struck the ENTER button on the Spectrum.

Her grandad took one step back, and the familiar whizzing sound started.

"I love you, Grandad!" she whispered. "I love you, Pepper!"

But then something didn't happen.

'Sleigh Ride' didn't play.

'Sleigh Ride' always played on this ride, from being a little girl.

'Sleigh Ride' was the tune. And not hearing it was discombobulating. What was she hearing? What was this sound?

The familiar chorus of Band Aid started to play. '*Feed the world, let them know it's Christmas time again*'.

Tash did a double-take at this beautiful noise. Jamie had done it! Jamie had done it!

"Thought I'd change the song! Jamie always loved this!" said Ernest.

The C5 lurched forward and once more, Tash was convinced she was about to die. Between her and her sleeping son were twenty one years and one vast Victorian stone-built house. And the house looked very hard. She was speeding up, faster and faster and faster still. The kitchen window was getting closer and closer. She could see the kitchen door open. Shit! Grandma! Grandma was coming into the kitchen! Pepper was barking too. Christ!

And then everything turned black.

For Tash anyway.

Ernest was a little bit delighted to actually see his machine work as an outsider. He was pretty chuffed with his work, he wouldn't pretend otherwise. It was there, and then it was gone.

He glanced over at the kitchen window and blew a kiss at Dorothy as she turned to look out.

Dorothy blew a kiss back and did a little Christmas shuffle for him.

Ernest patted Pepper's head and reached into his cardigan pocket to extract Natasha's gift.

In his hand, he saw a full packet of Oxo.

FIFTY ONE

Marie's Cafe was just as busy as the night before. Marie was looking hot and tired but just as friendly as when Martha first met Bee. You could tell her day was ending as she was dancing her hips to Strawberry Switchblade and singing along to 'Since Yesterday'. Cigarette smoke gave the place a beautiful filter that even the finest smartphone app would struggle to replicate.

"Want another cuppa, love?" enquired Marie as she took Martha's empty cup away.

Martha didn't see or hear. She was laughing at another fact Jamie had shared with her. The two of them had been giggling so much that Martha's stomach ached and Jamie's eyes were trickling tears down his cheeks.

"But how do you stop your dog from humping another? You can't whisper in an Alsatian's ear 'quit it, you're screwing the Queen's dog' – you're gonna lose your freaking face!"

Jamie laughed.

"What if someone told you to stop halfway through!" she continued.

"Bad question for a virgin!" Jamie laughed, too honestly.

Martha stopped laughing. "You're kidding, right?"

Jamie shook his head with no embarrassment. "No. I want to wait."

"You want to wait until you're married?"

"No, I want to wait until someone wants to sleep with me."

Martha waited a moment. They both burst into hysterics again, then Martha noticed someone was watching her. "You OK?"

"Do you want another drink?" asked Marie.

"No. I'm good, thank you," replied Martha, checking her watch.

Jamie was still slurping the dregs of his chocolate milkshake. Or his second freaking milkshake as Martha has called it. He'd knocked the first over her, but she thought it was hilarious. It was exactly the sort of thing she'd normally do, and it was pure joy to meet someone as clumsy as herself. This was 1984, and clumsy was a word that Martha had heard her whole life. Jamie had too as a child, it was only as he became a young man that he and his parents identified a rainbow of autistic spectrum disorders. The initial reaction from his parents was pure guilt. They'd labelled him as clumsy or slow or lazy. In truth, he had Asperger's and dyspraxia, which instantly explained his difficulty learning to tie shoelaces, to ride a bike, to gauge social signals in others. Martha felt very comfortable in his company. She had almost immediately stepped into the mother figure for Jamie after Tash had departed. She couldn't see that in reality they were two sides of the same coin. They'd both sat on the pavement giggling like school kids whilst Vicky had knocked on Bob's door. Jamie had suggested Vicky do it solo. Not because he was shy, but he genuinely believed in what they were trying to do and felt it could only reflect well on Vicky. The absurdity of listening to a stranger fulfilling

Jamie's corrective plan was not lost on him, or his new American friend.

They had crouched behind a Jaguar parked across the road of Geldof's house and watched as Vicky stammered apologies for disturbing the imposing Irishman during his convalescence. When she reported back, they were spellbound. Apparently he'd dismissed last night's accident as nothing and enquired why his record label was sending A&R around to his home. He was pretty relieved to hear this was more of a personal visit. Vicky was keen to get his take on a news story she'd seen last night as she wondered if the Rats might consider doing a gig to raise some money. She was a massive fan of Geldof's band, so that helped the plausibility. He'd even invited her in for a cup of tea whilst they watched it together. In reality, it was the first time Vicky had seen it too. She didn't feel silly about crying, and neither did Bob. This was an absolutely horrific famine unfolding at the end of the twentieth century. The only time they disagreed was about a plan of action. He said a record would be better than a gig. But the Rats weren't big enough to raise the money to make a change, so he was going to call Paula and discuss other ideas with her. She'd set off to Newcastle for Friday's episode of *The Tube*. When he called her, she told him that Ultravox were going to be on the show so maybe their singer Midge might be able to help. He did.

Considering all of this, Vicky opted not to call the police to report her abductors. In the event, she didn't need that backstory to explain why she abandoned Status Quo at TV Centre as they'd got pissed in the BBC bar with Feargal Sharkey's band who happened to be Madness minus Suggs and hadn't noticed she'd been missing for two hours. Vicky even turned down Martha's five hundred quid. Well, in a way. It actually became the very first cash donated to what would become the Band Aid Trust.

Jamie had been happy to accompany Martha on her second rendezvous with her lawyer. The big one. Together they had managed to find their way back to Woolworths and subsequently Marie's Cafe. They'd even arrived twenty minutes early.

But that was over an hour ago. It was now 4.50pm. That was fifty minutes later than Bee had proposed. Jamie looked up at the cafe clock.

"Can you not call her? It's almost an hour after she said. Maybe she's got the time wrong."

Martha was flicking through the paperwork she'd received from Bee, and none of it seemed to have a contact number for her.

"There's no London number for her," she said, still perusing the papers. They were mostly maps and photos and general instructions. The latter was on Eikenberry & Lowe headed paper, and that did include a phone number, albeit in Vermont.

"She said she was going to send the photo straight away," said Jamie, "So maybe they have it already. There's no harm in speaking to them about it, is there? I'd call them. Call them up."

Martha had used the limit on her credit card when she extracted the cash for Vicky. It had allowed her five hundred and fifty pounds. After handing over five hundred of this, she didn't have a huge amount left for a hotel room. Her return flight was booked for tomorrow. She headed over to Marie at the counter.

"Can I use your phone, please ma'am?"

"Payphone across the road, love," answered Marie.

"I don't have coins. And it's long distance. I can give you this?" She held up a five-pound note.

"Long distance?"

Martha examined the Bank of England notes in her hand, and satisfied she'd found another fiver, she added that to her offer.

"How long distance?"

Martha fumbled with her stash of cash again and added a third fiver to the pile.

'I'll be less than two minutes," said Martha.

Marie considered this, then pocketed the notes into her apron. She gestured for Martha to come around the back of the counter and pointed to a wall-mounted dial phone.

"Two minutes," said Marie holding up an egg timer.

Martha examined the letter headed paper and dialed. She waited an eternity before the familiar single tone ringing sound warmed her ear. It was a little distant, but it was ringing.

"Eikenberry and Lowe, how may I direct your call today?" came a sombre female voice.

"Harvey Eikenberry please, it's an emergency. I'm calling from London."

In fairness to Harvey and his staff, he was speaking to Martha in no time, but his words were doing little to reassure her anxiety. After he'd found some. To start with, he was lost for them.

"You're making no sense, Harvey!" shouted Martha down the phone.

"A facsimile of your photograph was waiting for us when we arrived this morning. Along with your agreement to accept fees for an instant wired transfer. Your full inheritance was deposited into your new account," replied the confused lawyer.

"You keep saying that. But I don't have the details of my new account, and Bee's an hour late. She has all the paperwork. All of it." replied Martha. "Don't you have a copy?'

"The paperwork is with Ms Fernandez. Please try and remain calm. It's highly unusual of Ms Fernandez to miss a meeting. I can only conclude that you misunderstood your scheduled time today."

"I misunderstood shit. Four pm toy town time. She said it."

"I would suggest you sit tight. Good day."

With that, the line went dead.

FIFTY TWO

Tash stood up to catch her breath. She'd not arrived back in the attic, which suited her. The thought of applying the brakes before she went through the back wall for a second time and fell to her actual death had been a concern. Happily, she'd arrived on the driveway, with inches to spare before striking the garage door. The locks on the door must have frozen tight as she had been unable to slide it open as she had earlier. Resigned to the fact that she would be back in an hour or so to fire the bastard up again to fetch Jamie, she'd opted to wheel the machine around the rear of the garage out of sight of the house. It was heavy to move, especially in the snow. Maybe she'd invent a three-wheel drive version for next time. As she stretched her neck and looked up, she could see the gaping hole in the rear of the garage loft left by their departure. She peered around the garage to look at the back of Grandma's house. It was in darkness, which was a good sign.

She scrunched through the still-falling snow and let herself back in through the unlocked back door. Her feet took her silently and effortlessly to the room she'd left her son. As she entered, she was filled with pure euphoria to see him sleeping happily in his cot. She removed her vintage clothes and slid into her non Christmas pj's that she'd packed for Boxing Day. They felt familiar, they fitted properly and they smelt of home. She slumped at the foot of her bed and allowed herself a smile. Glancing over at Jamie's empty bed, she remembered his kind words about Lucan. Tash dragged the pillows off her bed and pulled the candlewick bedspread over her. She sat on the floor, resting her back on her mattress, plumped the pillows behind her head and pulled the bedspread around her.

Her thoughts were clear. Grandad had fixed the glitch that prevented them from getting home. A return trip to Jamie would be relatively simple. She'd need to connect Grandad's extension cables again, and that meant fixing the frozen lock on the garage door, but maybe she could boil the kettle and somehow pour that into the mechanism. Then her frantic thoughts slowed down in line with her breathing. I'll go for Jamie in an hour or so. I've seen Lucan. I can't wait like he said. How could I enjoy Christmas morning knowing I have to sneak back to 1984? Yes, I'll go and fetch him in an hour. That would still leave plenty of time to return, hide the C5, get in bed and sleep a little before Christmas Day.

My God, my son is beautiful.

I'll insist Jamie sits behind me again, cos I totally know how the new calendar works.

In fact, I'm not going to get out of it when I arrive back in 1984.

Maybe I'll take Lucan with me.

What a story to tell him when he's older.

Would I tell him when he's older?

What are the rules with time travel?

Why had Grandad built it in the first place?

When did –

And then she was asleep. Her exhaustion had crept up unannounced.

FIFTY THREE

Raymond looked ready for bed when he opened the glazed door to his house. The tell-tale sign were the striped British Home Stores pyjamas and suede effect slippers.

He heard himself say, "Jamie? Martha?"

So did Maureen, because she repeated both names in a shrill shout from somewhere in the house.

Jamie and Martha entered the living room twice. On their first attempt they'd successfully said the first syllable of "Hello" before being sent back to the hall to remove their footwear. What the hell had Raymond been thinking? He'd obviously apologised, and now the four of them were sitting sipping Horlicks. Well, two were sipping Horlicks. Jamie was clearing up his spillage from the green draylon sofa whereas Martha was wondering why the fuck anyone would let anything like it near their mouth, let alone drink a whole mug of the stuff.

On the G Plan teak coffee table that sat between them, was a small opened letter. Martha had only found it when she upturned her bag on the steps of Marie's Cafe. Marie had locked up behind them, and Martha had decided to undertake one last thorough search of her bag to see if maybe she had slid any details about her new bank account in there yesterday.

All that fell onto the pavement were the original instructions to find the three English people, where to find the camera, where to photograph them, and a copy of the photo they were to replicate. And one further letter addressed to Raymond. Martha had taken Raymond and Maureen's address so that she could send them a cheque for the agreed £30,000 once her inheritance had dropped, and together she and Jamie had navigated the streets of Lambeth and Brixton to find Gaywood Close. Their plan was to flag a taxi, but their non-stop conversation had made the ninety-minute walk feel like ten. Martha had taken some convincing that Boy George would actually agree to sing in the same room as Paul Weller, let alone the Duran boys and George Michael. She was looking forward to seeing if Jamie's story would come true.

Raymond had struggled to comprehend the contents of the correspondence, so decided to read them one more time.

"Why would he give it to me?" he asked again, as his eyes scanned the typed letter, and once again the signature at the bottom – clearly that of his ex-boss.

"I've been thinking about that," said Jamie.

"And?" asked Raymond.

"The Sinclair stock needs to be stored safely for the launch in January. If they're not launched and sold, then Grandad can't buy one and build the Christmas ride," explained Jamie, finally sitting down with the remaining Horlicks in his mug.

"Christmas ride?" enquired Maureen.

"The walls moved. Sounds awesome," explained Martha. It had been just one of many conversation topics as they'd walked through the October drizzle.

"Riddles again, Raymond. What do they mean?"

Jamie carried on "The C5. The time machine. It used to be a Christmas ride for Tash and me. Before that, it was a C5. And before that, it was in storage in Raymond's new warehouse."

Raymond and Maureen considered this, as Raymond examined the letter again.

"But why me?"

"If he just disappears now, the business will grind to a halt. He couldn't let that happen."

"You're a trustworthy, honest, decent man, Raymond" said Maureen, finally coming around to the rationale behind this latest development.

"Absolutely," agreed Jamie. "Plus he didn't have anyone else."

Martha laughed.

"You're an entrepreneur now!" said Martha.

"I'm no good with that computer," replied Raymond.

"I know computers. I can help you with that," said Jamie. "We can go through it all before I meet Tash tomorrow."

The mood in the room lifted considerably.

"Well, I think this calls for a little celebration, don't you, Maureen?" Raymond had chirped up.

"On a Wednesday? No-one celebrates on a Wednesday," replied Maureen.

"No, you're right. Sorry."

Maybe she could feel the eyes in the room boring into her, or perhaps she was genuinely elated, but Maureen reconsidered her remark.

"Go on then. Let's all share that Babycham we had left over from Christmas."

"Lovely!" said Raymond. He was out of his chair before she could change her mind, and he leapt towards their wooden veneered wall unit that housed their posh glasses (free with petrol at the BP garage). As he leant to open the lower cupboard door, his arse revealed itself over the top of his pyjama bottoms. Jamie spotted this and caught Martha's eye. They both stifled giggles. Together they had decided to call Harvey Eikenberry the moment his office opened tomorrow, which was lunchtime in London. Jamie didn't mind waiting around. He quite enjoyed her company. And he would be able to help Raymond with the computer in the warehouse too. He should have plenty of time to get Raymond up to a decent speed before Tash arrived to take him home.

Sadly, Martha's credit card had been maxed, so a hotel was no longer an option for her. It was Jamie's idea to seek out Raymond and Maureen's home. All they needed to do now was pick the perfect time to ask if they could crash there until morning, and an alcoholic tipple should warm Maureen's cockles sufficiently to offer bed and board to these relative strangers.

"Aha!" declared Raymond. He'd found his treasure. He stood to his feet, turned around with some considerable swagger and presented his find.

"Let's get this cracked open!"

In his hand was a tiny bottle of Babycham designed for one.

FIFTY FOUR

"Hark The Herald Angels Sing!" chorused the Kings College Choir very loudly downstairs. Tash broke into a delighted smile before her eyes had the chance to open. She paused for a moment to rub her stiff neck and then saw the bedroom was flooded with the kind of daylight you only see when the world is blanketed with snow. It was like double-daylight. Daylight Plus. Daylight Turbo. She wasn't quite sure why she was on the floor for the first couple of seconds, then memories flooded her brain. She glanced over at the cot. It was empty. She leapt to her feet in disbelief. As she spun around the room in despair, there came a knock on the door. She glanced up at the 60's wall-clock next to the immersion cupboard.

08:11

If Tash had ever harboured any doubt that the brain can compute multiple thought processes in one second, that was instantly resolved.

Where is Lucan?

Why did I fall asleep?

I need to fetch Jamie.

Did I throw the towel in on my marriage too soon?

Why is Tess Daly the primary host on Strictly, when Claudia is so good?

Who is knocking?

"Happy Christmas, Tash," whispered her mum, pushing the door ajar and peering through with a smile.

In her arms was Lucan, dressed beautifully as a reindeer, beaming a big smile at his Mummy.

"Why did you sleep on the floor?" asked Andrea. "I didn't want to wake you, but maybe I should have. You look like Princess Anne."

"Thanks, Mum. Happy Christmas. I was… I was telling a story about the North Pole, to get him back to sleep. Must've dozed off myself."

Andrea peered over at Jamie's empty bed.

"Where's Jamie?"

Well yes. Yes. There's the fucking question, thought Tash. And incidentally, *where the fuck is my sister?* is probably another question currently playing on Jamie's mind. But then she remembered. She could use the C5 to go and fetch her brother anytime she liked – she would still appear at the time they'd agreed. Christ, time travel didn't suit her, Not one bit. It was like re-sitting her physics GCSE while kidnappers held her baby to the school hall window, waving at her manically.

"He's gone for a run," she replied.

Andrea wasn't slightly surprised despite the snowdrifts visible through the window, and it showed on her face. "Come on, brush your hair and let's open some presents," smiled Andrea, beaming back at her grandson in her arms. "Because… He's been! Father Christmas had been!"

Tash hoped her face was smiling back at her mum, but her mind was breaking all speed records.

"I need to do a few things first, actually," protested Tash.

Andrea raised her hand like a police officer halts traffic. "No. It's Christmas Day. No work emails, no messages, no calls to Nathan either. It's this young man's first Christmas, and it starts now. Come on."

Andrea clearly wasn't leaving. Tash stood to her slippered feet and unleashed a moan of disgust when she leant into the mirror to brush her hair. She actually had dried paint in it. Why the hell had no-one mentioned that to her in 1984? Black circles hung below her eyes, and her skin was dehydrated. In fairness she had cried a couple of gallons of water over the past day or so. She took one final glance at Jamie's empty bed and followed her Mum down to the living room.

FIFTY FIVE

The draylon sofa was actually sumptuously comfortable despite Martha's opinion on its aesthetic. The single-glazed windows of the house did less to impress her though. She found her jaws actually chattering together as she turned to squint at the time on the chiming mantle clock that ensured every hour through the night was honoured with as much gusto as their daytime counterparts. It was 2am. The amber streetlights shone beneath the unlined curtains, but they were a poor beacon in the mostly brown room. The pink polyester sheet that covered Martha was working as hard as it could, and she'd even put her coat back on but this was another level cold. Raymond and Maureen had been particularly miserly with their central heating since the immersion heater debacle. Their next fuel bill would be massive, so they needed to claw back savings wherever possible. As Martha rested her head back to the armrest she used the light through the curtains to see if she was indeed able to see her breath. She was. She watched the little vapour clouds evaporate a few times and then grew bored.

"Are you asleep? Jamie? Are you asleep?"

Jamie was sitting under a similar pink sheet, but his was the fitted version, and the elastic edges meant it served terribly as a method of servicing a whole person without the teamwork you achieved with a mattress. He opted to take the armchair next to the freezing windows and had soon regretted it. Since Maureen had turned out the lights, he'd been in and out of anxiety dreams, waking only to establish that he wasn't drowning in a frozen lake or chained to a side of ham in a commercial freezer.

"Don't wake Maureen!" whispered Jamie.

"She's gonna have a shit day if she finds two stiffs in her snug when she gets up."

"She doesn't look the type to have ever had two stiffs in her snug."

Martha laughed. "Now I'm thinking about her snug."

The laughter subsided.

"No. This is fucking ridiculous," said Martha. Then she added with a little less of her usual confidence, "Come over here."

"Pardon?" whispered Jamie. His voice faltering a little.

"We got two fucking sheets. We're not making the best of them."

"Right. Yes."

Jamie slowly stood up from his chair. He'd forgotten that he'd tried to use the elastic sheet to wrap around his feet, so his first step to Martha literally floored him. His head hit the G Plan coffee table on the way down, causing the glass to rattle as it slammed back into the teak frame.

"Shhhh!" said Martha.

"Sorry."

"That's gotta hurt."

"I'm fine. I'm fine," he lied from the darkness. "I landed on my snug."

Martha howled again.

Jamie dragged himself and his sorry sheet across the floor to the sofa.

"How do you want to do this, shall we top and tail, or…" asked Jamie.

"Just get up here before one of us dies," said Martha, shuffling to the back of the sofa. She lifted her sheet for him to lie underneath alongside her. As he rolled into position, he flicked his elasticated sheet over the top of them in an attempt to double their bedding before resting on his side, facing the darkness of the room.

Martha pulled the sheets up around her neck and then flipped onto her side to spoon Jamie, placing her arm tightly around him. Jamie's eyes were wide open, not that Martha could see.

Wow. He wasn't expecting that. This felt warm but also felt nice. He'd never laid alongside a lady that wasn't related to him before. He could get used to this. Martha's eyes were opened too.

"Thanks for your help today."

"Thanks for yours," replied Jamie. "We'll get things sorted for you tomorrow, you know. I'll make sure of that."

"I know you will."

They lay in silence for a while, neither knowing the other had yet to close their eyes.

"Night freak," whispered a very happy Jamie.

"Night weirdo," answered Martha, and nuzzled her nose into his neck.

FIFTY SIX

The hum on an aircraft has a hypnotic effect on many passengers. It's the kind of white noise that experts compare to the sound in a mother's womb. And so it's no surprise that unless you are one of those passengers whose clenched buttocks are keeping the plane in the sky, it's highly likely you'll feel a little sleepy. More so if an alcoholic stiffener has been taken.

"Would you like another glass of champagne, Miss Hobson?"

The voice belonged to an impossibly beautiful air stewardess. She must have taken hours applying the foundation and blusher and eyeliner and mascara. Her pure red gloss lips smiled to reveal the whitest teeth Bee had ever seen.

She put down her book and held up her crystal champagne flute.

"Thank you, honey." She smiled as her glass was replenished.

"Have you visited the Caribbean before, Miss Hobson?" asked the stewardess.

"I have not, no. And please call me Martha, honey. All my friends do."

FIFTY SEVEN

Lucan bounced happily on his mum's knee whilst Andrea directed George on the distribution of the gifts. He was mostly hidden by the tree that he was trying to reach beneath. The presents were many, and all were covered with beautifully coloured paper, spewing ribbons all glittery and gold. These promised a Christmas that little Lucan would never forget. If he hadn't been just five months old. At least Tash would remember it.

"Merry Christmas!" sang Grandma as she shuffled into the room in her festive best. She was carrying a tray overloaded with biscuits and mince pies and scotch eggs. Yes. Scotch eggs.

"Merry Christmas, Grandma!" replied Tash. "Your face looks so much better!"

Grandma ignored this and George tried to look up but he was losing this battle with the Christmas tree. Sometimes you just have to accept that the gifts at the very back of it are going to be something to look forward to in January. After all, the month holds precious little else.

"Merry Christmas, Mum!" came his voice.

"Merry Christmas, Dot," said Andrea, making space on the coffee table for the tray of goodies.

"Wait. Where's Jamie's tree?" asked Tash, looking for the cheap Woolworths tree that he'd shat decorations on the night before.

Her father's arse was protruding from a seven feet tall Fraser Fir that nestled in the alcove alongside the chimney.

"Is this a surprise for him?" Tash nodded at her son and the tree.

"Where is Jamie?" asked Grandma.

"He's having a run, silly boy," explained Andrea.

"Would Lucan like his first gift?" said George finally standing upright clutching a perfectly square and grotesquely massive gift-wrapped parcel.

"OK. Lucan stops from today," said Tash.

Everyone looked over.

"Really? We have a name?" asked Andrea.

"We have a name."

The conversation paused in anticipation.

"Come on then little lady, what's it to be?" asked Dorothy.

"Ladies and Gentlemen, please say Hello and Happy Christmas to… Raymond."

Andrea paused for just a moment before catching her husband's eye.

"Are you sure?" asked Andrea.

"I'm not sure about Raymond. Wasn't he that slow one in *Rainman*?" said Dot.

"Mum," said George.

"Or Ray?" said Tash.

"No," said Dot.

"It's the same name, just shorter. It's Glastonbury all over again," said Andrea.

"I wouldn't rush it," said Dot.

"And who would like cocktails?!" came a giddy voice from the doorway.

Tash's heart leapt in her chest, her stomach flipped, and she could feel her cheeks flush bright red.

She looked up and watched her Grandad enter the room, clutching his traditional tray of cocktails. She hadn't considered that he would look twenty-one years older than when she'd last seen him, and his aged face was a bit of a surprise. But not as surprising as the hair piece he'd opted for that no one else in the room seemed to find fucking bizarre.

Tash glanced across the road at the family oak tree, clearly missing a golden bauble.

Grandad handed a drink to Tash and gave her a gentle kiss on the cheek. She could feel tears pouring from her eyes and pouring down her baking hot cheeks. Her eyes had been really shit recently.

"What have you put in that drink, Ernest? You've poisoned my daughter!" Andrea was laughing.

Tash played along. "My fault! Went down the wrong hole!"

Wham's 'Last Christmas' was playing on Grandad's stereo. George had replaced the carols with the original *Now That's What I Call Christmas* album and the time-warped vinyl was spinning effortlessly beneath the needle that slowly raised up and down.

Tash started to formulate her new plan. She'd say what Jamie had suggested. She'd tell them it was too cold for Lucan to go on the annual Christmas Day walk. After they'd set off, she'd boil the kettle to defrost the garage door lock. She'd seen the snow shovel from her window so could clear a path to make sure it could travel, and if ...

Her thought was rudely interrupted by the doorbell.

The actual doorbell.

On Christmas Day.

In the middle of a global pandemic. The fucking doorbell.

"Make sure you wash whatever it is with Dettol, Ernest," said Dot. She was on top of her Covid game. Ernest was busily pouring a cocktail for Andrea, who had a better idea that would keep the booze flowing. "Tash will get it, you keep pouring, Ernest!"

Tash handed her son to Andrea and stepped out from the warm toasty room into the chilly Victorian hallway. Sure enough, she could see nobody through the etched glass, so maybe this was a parcel delivery made by some poor sod on this sacred day.

As she opened the door, a small snowdrift stood perfectly upright in the opening. Beyond it was a red envelope. She leant over the mound of snow and picked it up. In handwritten green ink she read:

For Tash Summers. Private and Confidential.

Her eyes darted around the street for signs of who had delivered this. Was it Nathan? Did he want to reconcile over Christmas? Like a shit Channel 5 film? Really? Was he that much of a cock?

A thirty-something man was at the bottom of the path, slowly placing his leather boots strategically in the deep snow to avoid falling over. He was well wrapped up in thick black winter coat, tightly knitted multi-coloured scarf and a tweed cap. He turned to look back at Tash and lifted his hat in greeting. Underneath his receding hairline was a very handsome and familiar-looking face. But she couldn't place the man. She couldn't place him at all. But he certainly wasn't her estranged husband, so that was good. As she slid her fingers along the length of the envelope to rip it open the man continued on his way to a black Range Rover that was parked with its engine idling.

Her chilly fingers pulled out a Christmas card. It was a painting of Tower Bridge in a snow scene. She opened the card and started to read more green ink. Simultaneously she began to weep. Her body started to shake. She held onto the door frame to stop herself from falling. She heard herself say, "Seven eleven breathing, Tash. Seven eleven breathing."

She followed her own advice and then reread the card:

Tash.

Don't be sad or mad, but please don't come back for me.

Turns out there IS a hand for every glove.

I love you forever

Jamie x

Tash was strangely calmer now. She wasn't sad, she wasn't distressed, she was just numb. She looked up to see the Range Rover was edging very tentatively down the icy road. It stopped at the bottom of the drive, and the man in the cap smiled one more time from behind the wheel.

Behind him, the tinted window started to lower, revealing the passenger on the back seat.

An elderly man was smiling at her. He raised his gloved hand to wave.

Tash found herself waving back at her brother.

Alongside him was a beautiful woman, maybe ten years younger than him. She leant forward to see out of the window too, displaying the most shocking pink hair. She copied her husband's wave. Tash rubbed the tears from her eyes to look again. In between the pensioners was a little girl in a child seat. Now a lady was waving from the front passenger seat too. As was the driver. Everyone was waving.

And smiling.

They were definitely smiling.

A very happy family, smiling and waving.

"Is it Jamie?" shouted Dorothy from the other room. "Did he not take a key, the silly sod?"

"Yes!" Tash was laughing through her tears.

The car slowly started to edge away.

"Yes. It's Jamie," replied Tash.

"Is he alright?" shouted Andrea.

Tash watched the car pull away onto the main road and waved one final time.

She flipped over the Christmas card and in handwriting at the bottom was a phone number.

"Yes. He's more than alright."

EPILOGUE

"Are you nervous?" asked Maureen.

"He's just a man, Maureen. Just a man like me," proclaimed Raymond as he squared up to his reflection in the wing mirror of the parked transit van.

"Well, no, Raymond. He's an achiever. He runs a bank."

"Yes, you're right. Maybe I should reschedule? And bring Sab with me."

Raymond turned to look at the griffin logo outside his bank and started fumbling in his pockets.

"Nonsense. You've proven you can make that business work. It's just a cash flow problem. Sab said that."

"Yes, yes," said Raymond, looking pained that his pocket search was proving fruitless.

"You haven't got twenty pee for the meter have you, love? Sorry."

Maureen reached into her anorak and removed her purse, as she did something fell on the road.

"We've got luck on our side now, Raymond. Just believe that!" said Maureen, rifling through her coins for a twenty pence piece.

"Absolutely," said Raymond as he bent down and retrieved a crumpled one pound note.

He looked at it for a moment and then squinted at some handwriting.

"This is what Jamie's sister put in your pocket at that bus stop," he remembered. "She's written something on it..." His eyes really were shocking these days. "What does it say?"

Maureen handed over the coin in exchange for the note raising it to her eyes to get a better view. She needed to screw up both eyes for the letters to come into focus.

"Boris. Boris Bocker."

"What does that mean?" asked Raymond.

"No idea."

"Miners Fund. Anything for the Miners?" came a cry.

A young lady shaking a contribution tin appealed to their better nature.

"Abandoned by the brutal regime that calls itself government, Thatcher is a stain on the country, systematically destroying industry and..."

She was stopped by Maureen folding the pound note and sliding it into her collection box and explaining: "Don't need the lecture today thank you very much. We're Yuppies."

The lady thanked her and continued down the road. Raymond knocked on the driver's window of the van. Jermaine wound it down and the radio spilled out to the road. Captain Sensible was 'Glad It's All Over.'

"For the meter, Jermaine. But only use it if you see a warden," said Raymond, handing over the coin. Jermaine nodded.

"And if you don't, I'll have that back," said Maureen.

Raymond turned to the bank door, unfolded George's plans for the SMART PAUSE button and took a deep breath.

"Wish me luck, darling."

"You don't need luck, Raymond."

"No. Yes. Sorry, Maureen."

****

Seven months later an anonymous tennis fan bet £10,000 on a teenage German player to win that year's Wimbledon tournament. The odds were 18/1.

On Sunday 7th July 1985, just six days before the Live Aid gig, Boris Becker won the Wimbledon Men's Singles title. He was 17.

Someone won £180,000.

It wasn't Raymond. Or Maureen.

ACKNOWLEDGEMENTS:

Thanks to everyone who offered help or encouragement along the long road of writing this. Particularly:

Catherine Bailey for her constant support on any project I run by her but this one in particular, thanks to Georgia Pritchett too.

Gareth Edwards for telling me it was a great idea, and that it should be a film. He's always right.

Lucy Armitage for reading an early screen treatment and spending far more time than I might reasonably expect offering expert advice.

David Hitchcock for his encyclopaedic memories of BBC TV Centre in the 1980's, and Sarah Hitchcock for connecting us.

Owen Ryan for doing all the hard research work into publishing then handing it to me on a plate.

Sinéad Fitzgibbon for her encouragement and speedy excellence with editing.

Scott Readman for his patience and awesome graphic skills.

The wonderful people of South Yorkshire for convincing me to get this published.

Special thanks to Sir Bob Geldof for the alternative (and actual) events of October 23rd, 1984. And the aftermath that changed the world forever. These can be enjoyed in full context in the Penguin book "Is That It?" by Bob Geldof

Printed in Great Britain
by Amazon